RAPHAEL SOLOMON

E. ADRIAN DZAHN

For Bill, George, and Sten, and in memory of Anne,
whose friendships nourished this work

PREFACE

ON APRIL 14, 2014, the militant group Boko Haram kidnapped 276 high school girls gathered to take physics exams in Chibok, Borno State, Nigeria. The public outcry was extensive, with heads of state, religious figures, and celebrities condemning the abductions. Yet Boko Haram's violence was not new; over the previous decade, the group had murdered tens of thousands of civilians in West Africa, Muslims as well as Christians. And since as early as 2010, the group has specifically targeted students. Less than two months before the Chibok kidnappings, in the town of Buni Yadi in adjacent Yobe State, Boko Haram militants hurled explosives into school dormitories and stabbed and shot those trying to escape, killing fifty-nine boys.

My recent book *Communities under Siege* examines a number of Nigerian villages enduring Boko Haram's reign of terror prior to 2014. After the book's publication in May of 2014, I began working on a small supplemental volume about the world reaction to the Chibok kidnappings. In the course of my research, I learned that two Americans, Raphael Joshua Solomon and Joseph Michael Tanner; a German citizen, Werner Lukas Ulrich; and a Dutch citizen,

Ismail Tuhami, had lived in Borno State in 2013 and returned there in the wake of the kidnappings. According to a Nigerian Army report, on April 25, 2014, the truck the men were riding in hit an improvised explosive device planted by Boko Haram. Solomon, Tanner, and Tuhami were instantly killed. Ulrich survived with serious burns when the vehicle went up in flames.

Media accounts either hailed the men as heroes or branded them as naïfs. I was not interested in the four as individuals, for as an ethnographer, I study communities. Nevertheless, the men's response to the kidnappings aroused my curiosity and prompted me to consider whether their response might merit some discussion in the supplemental volume I was preparing or even lead to a broader inquiry.

To that end, over the course of several months in early 2015, I conducted a series of interviews of people who knew Mr. Solomon. However, Mr. Ulrich and his family and friends, Mr. Tanner's family and friends, and Mr. Tuhami's family and friends declined all contact, recent events remaining too painful. Additional obstacles, including my grant not being renewed, forced me to abandon all work on the supplemental volume.

Left with materials about a single individual not significant enough to warrant publication, I would have shelved my research, yet I recognized that the people interviewed had agreed to the sessions only because they believed they were contributing to a work touching on Mr. Solomon's life. Consequently, I decided to make my work available through this limited publishing. Transcripts of the interviews follow, along with certain related papers.

For ease of reading by a lay audience, I have divided the transcripts and organized them into chapters arranged in a rough chronological order, from Mr. Solomon's childhood to his death. However, several interviews were conducted well after the compilation was in progress, so the added material may be out of chronological order. Moreover, neither the transcripts nor other materials have been edited for relevant content. In some instances, I have included entire journal paragraphs and email threads where only one or two sentences bore on Mr. Solomon's moral development or other subjects I wanted to examine.

Because of the limited nature of this publication, my transcribers were asked merely to use their best judgment in adding emphasis to words, supplying punctuation, eliminating extraneous utterances, and ignoring hesitation sounds like "uh" and "um." The transcribers also were instructed to forgo certain formalities required of a professional publication in terms of formatting and to omit statements recording the date, time, and place of each interview; this information is available upon request. I have done a cursory review of the transcripts to insert paragraph breaks and change or add punctuation and emphasis to better reflect the speaker's intent.

The typists copying documents such as emails, journal entries, and school essays were similarly instructed to forgo certain formalities required of a professional publication.

The villages near Chibok where the men lived are referred to as Iskoki and Lambu, not their real names. The residents of Iskoki and Lambu have been provided with fictitious names as well, to lessen the chance of retaliation by Boko Haram. I have used the spelling Kibaku for the people and language while retaining the spelling Chibok for the town, in conformity with general media practice.

Bernice Xenia Williams, PhD, April 2015, Chicago, IL, USA

Raphael Joshua Solomon

Interviews and assorted papers

Chapter 1

Patricia Mary Eriksen (Pat)

YOU'LL HAVE TO BE PATIENT if you want to hear the whole story. It should have been his to tell, not that he would've done it. And I want to get it right; I want to be fair to everyone. The reporters were looking for something titillating or scandalous, not the *real* story. Raphael hated that—when people didn't see the forest for the trees. And didn't want to be in the picture himself. In that way, he was like his father. So that's the only reason I'm doing this: to honor his wish, which would be to give attention to what really matters and tell it as truthfully as I can.

I assume that you're not interviewing the whole block, that you singled me out, someone told you the Solomons and Eriksens have never been just ordinary next-door neighbors. The people on *this* side—well, let's just say I speak to them only to point out the raccoons knocked over their garbage can. *Again.* And remind them how to secure the lid. It's not rocket science, you know.

It says here in your email—you'll have to excuse me for rereading it, but the old gray memory ain't what she used to be—you're interested in what he was like growing up? And you're recording what I say in that gizmo? Tiny compared to the tape recorders of *my* day. You've probably never laid eyes on a reel-to-reel. My grandson Todd might have used something like yours, the little spy! I'll tell you about him later.

When Raphael first mentioned Boko Haram, I thought he meant a band we listened to back in the sixties. I can't remember the songs. How we ramble on, and I'm only seventy-three. You're thinking *only*? I just mean: imagine how boring I'll be if God lets me live till ninety. Not that I want to. No, I don't want to.

You haven't spoken to Daniel, his father? Reading between the lines: he refused, like Joseph's parents. So unless you get his permission, I'm going to stay away from the personal and private.

Since you said I should go chronologically, I'll start with pictures from when Raphael was a child. I don't have many. Here he must've been six or seven, around the time a grocery clerk asked if I was his grandmother. Me with these round Irish cheeks, blue eyes, and long hair straight as dry spaghetti, and he with his dark mop of curls and trim build! Yes, he had Susan's coloring, what my mother used to call "Mediterranean." Daniel's much fairer—not blond, but not dark.

And here he's four or five, so cute in that rugby shirt, the blue and white stripes and little blue sneakers to match. He liked to run in a loop across our lawns, and Susan would intercept him and raise him high in the air, and his stern little face would erupt in giggles.

Before I forget, tell your readers he never went by a nickname—everyone always used his full name, the first name. It's a bit of a mouthful, three syllables. Okay, on the soccer field, someone might shout "Over here, Raph," but that was all. Susan called him a hundred things—sweet-ums, cupcake, sugar pie. Before kindergarten, he put an end to that. "My name is Raphael." She never called him cute names again. Oh, to me, she might say, "Guess what little devil ate all the carrots I planned to pack with my lunch!"

And the last name—there's a story that goes with that. Daniel's grandfather's name was some long unpronounceable Russian tangle, and people told him to shorten it. Lopping off the *evsky* or *ovitch* or whatever it was, it sounded a little like Solomon, so that's what his grandfather chose. Daniel's endured *decades* of jokes about being a "wise guy." He isn't at all. The opposite, if you ask me. I don't mean stupid—I mean he doesn't go in for cleverness.

The basics, Pat, the basics. Raphael was born here in Seattle, in 1990, his parents living next door, where his father still is. So I knew him since he arrived home wrapped in a hospital blanket. You don't want to hear baby stories—so what if Susan asked how to get rid of diaper rash and when I started my kids on solid foods . . . who wants to read that? I did teach her you don't need Tylenol for a temperature; just dab the forehead and arms with a moist washcloth, and the fever drops in minutes. You can tell I'm not a big-pharma fan.

Growing up . . . growing up, Raphael was like other boys. Yet he wasn't. Oh, he played the usual games—especially soccer. He was a good teammate, *liked* being a teammate. When they scored a goal, he was always in the mix, the playful hitting and hugging, no different from my son and *his* teammates. Though Ryan was a towhead as a child, and half his friends were too, so you couldn't see who was who on the soccer field.

I'm sure you noticed this part of town is pretty White. Now Ryan's hair's a light brown, lost even the trace of carrot top that showed up in his teens. And he's put on a paunch—not as much as yours truly, and he's taller, so it doesn't show like mine. That Norwegian bulk: bone and muscle mixed with the fat. Arnie's side of the family. To hear Beth, his wife, tell it, Ryan's a bump on a log, but he remembers his soccer days fondly. Some things are universal in childhood. No, I guess they're not. That's why you wrote that book. But you don't want a philosophical speech from me.

Yes, Raphael played like the other boys, but he played harder. His teammates' parents—they'd gossip on the sidelines like there was no game to watch—they thought he'd turn into a soccer star. But that wasn't it. It wasn't to win. Or get his teammates' approval. Or his coach's. He always had his father's approval—no secret there. Raphael wasn't the best player, though he was good; he could run fast and had coordination. Arnie and I went to most of the games, and we agreed it was Raphael's *concentration* that made him different. All the boys played hard, tried hard to win, but with Raphael you got the feeling that trying his best was more important than winning.

That's just how he was. You didn't know where that intensity would lead—would he be a Nobel Prize winner? Musician? Poet? Not politician with a capital *P*—he wasn't capable of false friendship any more than I'm capable of sticking to a diet. Or a stockbroker—riches weren't the pot at the end of *his* rainbow.

Daniel and Susan weren't concerned about money either—*overly* concerned, I mean. We all need to make ends meet. Let me put on the kettle and steep fresh tea, and then I'll tell you about her. The bathroom is around that corner.

Your reply to my nosy email about your middle name, you wrote Xenia was your great-grandmother's name? I mentioned it to Clara, my younger daughter, the "classics professor." She said it's Greek for something, I forget—oh, "guest or stranger." Well, consider yourself a guest, Bernice, not a stranger.

Back to business. Susan and Daniel introduced themselves the day they moved in. I was fumbling with an old rocker, hauling it to the garage. It used to be there by the fireplace. I haven't laid a fire for years—at this time of life, the fireplace is just for show. So there they were, busy carrying all their *own* furniture, and see me struggling with the rocker and put everything down on the lawn and rush over to help. I was only in my late forties. I can't believe you're over thirty, but you must be, to take this on, and you said you've been a journalist—no, I'm sorry, an *ethnographer*—for twelve years.

Okay, I'm struggling with the rocker, and they must've figured me a prime candidate for cardiac arrest. My husband used to croon I'm broad where a broad should be broad. I can't repeat that around my daughters—I'll get the full feminist manifesto. *I* marched for the ERA in the seventies! They pretend not to remember that little fact.

Arnie loved musicals, God rest his soul. I think I wrote you he died in 2011. The rocker, by the way, was a hideous eyesore. Not that I'm Martha Stewart—take a look. I might be able to dust in under an hour if I packed up all the little art projects the grandchildren sent and my own three's doings and the knickknacks. That collage loses an elbow macaroni every month, I find it on the rug. And the contraption at the end, Braden's shop project, he said it's supposed to store paper clips and thumbtacks. I keep those in a desk drawer. By the way, *that* rocker, if you want to try it out, is God's gift to the overstressed. A book-club friend crocheted the cushion.

Anyhoo, Susan and Daniel rushed over to help me and graciously introduced themselves. "New marrieds," Susan said they were, so I should expect newlywed arguments, dishes shattering. She was joking. A lively thing, and Daniel—I used to call him Genial Daniel, not to his face, of course—Daniel couldn't summon a decent rage if he tried. Even now. It's his temperament. Such a contrast with Raphael, Mr. Intensity. Susan called Raphael "my little engine," so the intensity was obvious before. Still, his grin could melt an iceberg. Such a cutie—and he *stayed* a cutie. But I'm getting ahead of myself.

As you know, Daniel's a high school history teacher. Back then he was a newly minted PhD. Not many PhDs want to teach high school. "Teenagers don't care about the past," he says, "but they care deeply about injustice, so to teach history, you use injustice as a hook." He's very popular, wins teacher awards. No amount of hijinks get under his skin. I wish *I* was like that. Ask my kids—they sure wished I was.

Which isn't to say Daniel wasn't sorely tested when Susan died. Some idiot reading a magazine, only one hand on the steering wheel, the other flipping pages, probably *Playboy*. She at the curb with a bag of groceries, waiting for the light to change. He plows right up on the sidewalk! That corner had flowers for a full year. Arnie would mention when he got home, "More flowers." He was still at Boeing then.

I couldn't go to the funeral—twisted my ankle and wasn't about to climb in and out of the car. Arnie said Susan's parents looked as miserable as you'd expect. And the idiot driver didn't have insurance! Daniel got *some* money from some policy, but how does that mend a broken heart? He confided in Arnie he used the money to pay off the mortgage. If the worst happened to him, he said, and Raphael had to go live with one of Daniel's sisters, he hoped she would stay at the house for a while first so the boy could adjust to the grief and a new parent before being whisked off to Dallas or Boca Roca.

Susan's death was rough on all of us. I know this isn't true, but I used to think it hit Arnie harder than it hit Raphael, because the boy was only five. Raphael was . . . let me find the right word . . . subdued? Yes, for a time after, very subdued. He might've been sobbing himself to sleep every night, for all I knew—Daniel never let on—and I was more aware of Arnie's distress. Maybe she was one of those last crushes men have before their you-know-whats dry up. Susan *was* a darling—I couldn't blame him. And it's not like I didn't shed plenty of tears too. Just five years older than Mia, my eldest.

Before I forget: Was that enough information I sent you about me, date of birth and all that? Just describe me as an aging beatnik-hippie. Got my bachelor's in art and, for a full thirty seconds, considered getting a master's in teaching. Instead moved to a commune in Iowa and took up painting I called feminist abstract with some Georgia O'Keeffe thrown in. Most people called it junk. Then swept off my feet by an engineer headed to Seattle, so did the wife-and-mother gig for umpteen years. Now the widow who makes pottery. Oh, my daughters accuse me of humble-bragging, parading my hippie credentials, but that's a ploy to get me to cut my hair. I understand: nobody wants their parents to look strange. It's okay if the children plaster themselves in tattoos and pierced this and that, but Mommy and Daddy are supposed to be the Cleavers.

Raphael wasn't that way. People weren't fashion contestants to him, and being different was just one more thing to tickle his curiosity. Daniel's fine with the eccentric too, though he comes across as straitlaced. Wears button-down shirts, necktie—yes, at a public school, he wears a jacket and tie. Only the children's math teacher ever did that. Of course in *my* day—ancient history, you know—all the male teachers wore ties, and all the females wore skirts and dresses. A woman in pants would've been like Jean Harlow sashaying through a nunnery.

Focus, Pat, focus. Raphael's childhood. Okay, when he turned one, Susan went back to working part-time for the lung association. Raphael went to a day care nearby. But we saw plenty of him. He loved playing outside, chasing bubbles Susan would blow or just running in big circles through our yards. Sometimes *both* of them would run, him giggling up a storm. Our lawns have always been connected—we aren't hedge families. And ours being so much larger, we encouraged him to run here.

Oh, don't think I'm rich—we bought long before the housing market went berserk. Seattle used to be a sleepy little watering hole, everybody worked for Boeing or the vendors. Nowadays—well, Arnie said you have to be a hedge-*fund* family to afford to live here. Except for Daniel and the kitty-corner—in their nineties and still gardening!—our end of the block is all new. Ryan says I could be a millionaire if I sold this place, even *without* fixing it up. If I told you what we paid in '65! But I'm staying put. I have all I need: my friends, my book club, my tai chi. Don't be afraid to laugh, imagining me doing slow motions. But I have an excellent sense of balance. I'm not agile—ha ha ha—but I can hold a position longer than my kids can.

And my pottery. Later I'll take you down to the studio so you can see the wheel. When all else fails, when you're afraid the world is going to hell in a handbasket, try putting your hands around clay. If you can't shape the world, you can shape a vase. This is the point where Clara would say, "Mom, you're off on a tangent. *Again.*"

Yes, he was a happy little boy until the accident. After that, Arnie and I began to have them over for dinner a few nights a week. Nothing formal—I'd knock on the door and tell Daniel we were sitting down to a simple stew or chili and they might as well join us. He always brought beverages and fresh bread from one of the bakeries. And paid us back in his own way. Not just mowing the lawns: he pruned our shrubs, did the edging, and fixed every darn contraption that went tits up. Which Arnie appreciated, with his shoulder, and later his knee, problems.

Their house must have felt so empty. Ours had been empty for a few years—all three through college and married. Or was Clara only engaged? She held out until twenty-six; my other two graduated and bingo: marriage *and* babies. Ryan didn't even *wait* to graduate before he and Beth tied the knot and had Nick.

The statistics might say differently, that their generation postponed settling down, but my three sure didn't wait. And not for ignorance about birth control, I'll have you know—we weren't laggards in that department! Yet I'm glad they popped them out quickly—Arnie got to see the grandkids grow up. He missed a little of the dirty laundry later on, but that was for the best. Nothing *too* awful, thank God.

What else? Raphael liked to play with our cats. Susan was allergic to dander, so they had goldfish and turtles and parakeets. Those animals don't last long. After she died, I mentioned to Arnie that Daniel should get the boy a kitten or puppy, but when he suggested it, Daniel said he was worried how Raphael might react if it died. Tragedy heaped on tragedy. We let him play with our cats whenever he liked.

CHAPTER 2

[Grade school essays by Raphael Joshua Solomon (Raphael)]

Are Spiders Good Or Bad? [fifth grade essay]

There are lots of kinds of spiders. Some do good things, and some do bad things. People should not hate or scared of all spiders. Some are poisonous but some aren't poisonous. And the poisonous kind need poison for self defense and to kill for food. They don't eat human beings so when they bite human beings its self defense. How can you blame them when we are humongous compared to them?

Some spiders eat dead insects that helps the environment. Some also eat there own exoskeleton that's the outside shell.

A tarantula can live to be 30 years old. Its bite isn't as bad as you think. The brown recluse is worse. You can tell it because its back looks like it has a violin drawing though you might not want to get that close. Even poisonous spiders are helpful because they eat other insects that can harm people, pets and crops.

Chores [sixth grade essay]

In our house we divide chores 50-50. I go to the grocery store and cook. My father cleans and buys things that are heavy or hard to carry like milk, gatorade, potatos and meat. It's a good plan because his cooking is pretty bad. The lady next door teaches me a lot and gave me recipe books. We do our own laundry.

The outdoor chores aren't 50-50. He says when I weigh more than the lawn mower he'll show me how to pour the gas and push it. He's fussy about how the edging looks so I can't do that either. We have an apple tree and I take them down from the top branches. I could use the ladder but I like climbing instead.

We had a wasp nest under the garage roof. It looked like a gray foot-ball. We didn't spray it because cats and other animals could step in the stuff and its poison. If they licked their paws they would die. After it got dark the man next door came over with a big flashlight. My father climbed the ladder. He wore a hat, gloves and extra jacket with tight sleeves. He put a large plastic bag around the nest and tied it shut really really tight. I brought the metal garbage can over before that and he put the bag in it and the cover on really really tight too. We didn't take the cover off for a week and then stomped all over the bag but they were already dead. I found out later the man next door's wife wanted to pay for an exterminator and do it for us but my father is pretty stubborn. He was very careful and nobody got stung.

CHAPTER 3

Pat

THE MACHINE'S ON? I saw you looking at the photos on the mantel, probably trying to figure out who's who. I won't bother with the grandchildren. You'd think I have a hundred, not eight, but with all the ridiculous graduations they have these days, from *elementary* school and *middle* school and *high* school, my goodness—why don't they graduate them from learning to tie their shoes?

The photos at the far end are my three. Mia, the one with Ryan's coloring, the reddish highlights, which they got from Arnie's father, not my Irish roots. I mean it: her freckles are pure Norwegian; my side has no freckles. She got the extra *pounds* from me. Oh, she watches her weight much better than I do. I just mean she does have to watch what she eats, not like her sister, who can gobble everything in sight and wear a size four.

That's from drama club, eighth grade, Mia had a bit part in *Oklahoma.* I sewed *three* farm-girl outfits for the cast, poplin skirts and gingham tops. Plus kerchiefs to match. She had the drama bug all the way through high school, could belt out "It's the Hard-Knock Life" as if she'd lived it. The hardest knock she ever had was when her toy ukulele broke during the luau we did for Clara's ninth birthday.

Clara liked drama too: the other kind—"Tiffany did this" and "Amber said that," and "Jeremy broke up with Sally and wants to date Kimberly." Here's a picture of her with the Raggedy Ann she lugged everywhere till it was truly raggedy. Clara's the mongrel, but if you saw a photo of Arnie's great-aunt, they could be twins. Their hair, *très chic brunette*, is supposed to date back to a French soldier in the Napoleonic Wars. My side can only trace back to the early 1900s, when they landed in New York. The potato famine dislocated everybody before that, so who knows where earlier generations lived. I tell people I'm from malarkey.

Where were we? Raphael's childhood.

My daughters throw around the phrase "quality time." I don't know what that means, but after Susan died, Daniel gave Raphael plenty of *quantity* time. Brought him on errands: shopping, the car mechanic, the dentist, wherever he had to go. Raphael would come over and tell me everything he learned. How the men came out of the ground into the car—you know, the Jiffy Lube fellows? That impressed him. And hardware stores; he loved watching the key machine. Daniel taught him to handle a two-wheeler—by six or seven, Raphael was tearing all over the neighborhood by himself.

It's a nice area, isn't it? Some people let their yards go a little wild—mine's no Kew Gardens—but most keep the sidewalks swept, weed as best we can, and you rarely see litter. Rhodies are very popular—soft pink, bright pink, white—and bamboo for privacy, and in the cul-de-sac there's a yard full of wildflowers—daisies and asters and bluebells and bunchberries—just lovely. You should come in April, May. Across the street is the only real show-off: purple irises and hydrangeas. My primroses and petunias aren't sorry sights. You say you're from Cleveland Heights. I hear it's very nice. One of the women in my book club used to live in Shaker Heights.

What else? We would have the boy over a few hours on the weekend so

Daniel could grade papers. Arnie taught him checkers, and I taught him to bake cookies, cake, even an apple pie from the ones on his tree. And plum tortes, we have plenty of plums. We used activities to *cushion* him, not make him frail and timid—and you can tell he didn't grow up timid.

And all three of us were firm believers in giving Raphael space: to be in his own thoughts, do his own thing. My daughters seem to think children need activities every second of every day. Though *they* weren't raised that way. When my grandchildren visit, I say, "You're expected to clean up after yourselves and be on time for meals, but what you do for fun is your business." Clara says that's pushing them away, but I don't want them hanging around me because they *have* to. Usually I see them only at meals. We have a treehouse out back. They climb up there to play on their iPhones.

Yes, our bond with Raphael grew after Susan's death. I always brought him with me when I walked to the store. He carried the empty bags and a full bag on the way back. He was so interested in different fruits and vegetables, their names, where they came from. Each time, I let him pick out something. And popsicles in summer.

With my own kids, the times I look back on as the best were elementary school, the years parents walk on water. Before that, your children need you and want you, but by six or seven, they *worship* you. You cook the best, sing the best, know everything there is to know—you overhear them bragging to their friends, "My mom did this," "My mom did that."

God's just setting us up for the teens, when you're the stupidest animal to ever roam the planet. You know nothing, can't do anything right, and Katie's mom cooks *so* much better.

Susan being gone and Gillian not yet on the scene, I guess I became Mrs. Walk-on-Water to Raphael. Of course I spoiled him more than my own kids, but this block was different then—no one his own age to play with. My own had a gang, kids in every other house. I'm sure Raphael played with others at after-school care, but in the late afternoon, when Daniel was cooking dinner or cleaning or something, Raphael might run over here. And in the summer, when he wasn't at day camp, he would climb our trees or toss the ball up and catch it in his mitt or tear around on his bike. I always gave him money for the ice cream truck.

My grandchildren were coming along at that time, but they were scattered: Ashland—that's down in Oregon—Boston, Sacramento. Todd was born the year before Raphael, and Ryan's Nick just a month before, and Braden, Mia's second, came the following year. So the *few* times Mia would drive up, Raphael had playmates nearby, had Todd and Braden.

If you're in your twenties or early thirties, seven hours by car is nothing. By my mid-forties, it was climbing Everest—I couldn't spend *three* hours in one seat without wanting to open the door and roll out, hoping to get run over. But Mia was always "too busy" to make the trip. Her children could've bonded with Old Grandma back then. "I *work*," she said. Not like *me*, was her point. Cooking and cleaning for a family of five wasn't work? She wouldn't know: she fed the kids prepared meals from her *organic* grocery store and had a woman come in to clean. Okay, I know the generations do it different. And she *is* a clinical psychologist, does have to go to an office.

I see them all at Thanksgiving—that's our do-or-die family holiday, not Christmas. Clara likes to go somewhere warm in December, and you can't blame her, living in Boston. Mia and Fred, down in Ashland, put on a *huge* shindig. I don't mean just tree and presents: Fred strings lights like a Las Vegas casino. Throws a bash for the whole neighborhood and another when his brothers and sisters bring their families. Ryan likes to stay put too—he's the one in Sacramento.

"Be glad you raised such independent children," my friends say. "They're not unemployed and living in your basement." Yes, I'm glad for that, and I once used that line on Daniel. But you don't want to feel forgotten—no one wants to feel forgotten. Oh, my daughters call regularly. Checking up, wondering if I'm ready to be put out to pasture—you know: assisted living. And Ryan is always pushing some new gadget on me. For heaven's sake, civilization lasted two thousand years without cell phones. Plus, half the nonsense they do, a sane person wouldn't *think* of doing. Who wants to see *Lawrence of Arabia* on a tiny screen? Oh, Peter O'Toole, he was a dream come true. Why am I talking about this? You want to know about Raphael. I get distracted so easily; you must learn to interrupt me.

I was telling you about elementary school, the walk-on-water years. I have to say, besides the intensity, Raphael seemed like my own children and their friends. A little different from some boys because he liked to cook. We spent many an afternoon in the kitchen, flour and measuring cups all over the place. He wanted to make things his father liked, but Daniel's so easy to please, he'd eat whatever you put in front of him. Yes, Raphael and I ruined a couple of good chunks of meat experimenting. But we had fun, and Arnie, he was like Daniel, didn't complain. As long as it wasn't okra. Okra's popular in Nigeria, Raphael said.

Mia says that "according to psychologists"—whoop-di-doo—childhood is the *formative* period, and the rest of our lives is spent trying to adapt our formed selves to the world around us. Do you think that's true? I don't. I think there's a lot of luck in this world, and that shapes us more than anything. Who your teachers are, your friends, who you fall in love with.

What else? Arnie taught the boy songs: show tunes, folk ballads, hits from the fifties like "Smoke Gets in Your Eyes" and "Blue Suede Shoes"—my husband liked every type of popular music until it became mean and angry. I left my brand-new Rolling Stones albums at the commune!

When Gillian came on the scene, she taught Raphael madrigals. Her voice is so-so, not at all robust. Nothing about Gillian is robust. I told my book club, way back when, she reminded me of a little church mouse. You said she agreed to be interviewed; well, she won't drown you in nonsense. And maybe can persuade Daniel to talk to you.

She's not just his roommate—I assume you figured that out. Girlfriend, partner—whatever word they use these days. A good ten years younger, but don't get the idea she's some trophy bimbo. The opposite: a Holocaust scholar. Though Presbyterian through and through. As quiet as Susan was vivacious.

Gillian moved in on September eleventh—yes, *that* September eleventh. Raphael had just started sixth grade. The year before, Daniel had let him come home alone after school—he'd been pushing for more independence. Of course I was always here that time of day.

She was on a fellowship or some such thing. We knew about the towers in the morning, but there was a lot of confusion, still sorting things out. And that fourth plane, the Pennsylvania one, hadn't crashed. It still gives me shivers.

Around two, I saw her car in the driveway. I would've gone over if I'd thought Raphael was coming home to an empty house. And I would've handled it differently, you can be sure of that. The two of them watched the news coverage till Daniel arrived. Can you imagine: an eleven-year-old glued to those pictures!

I baked a huckleberry pie—that's how I calmed my nerves before taking up pottery, and huckleberries are plentiful here the end of summer. Arnie and I went over around seven. Everyone sat at the table, the TV was off, and Raphael explained what he'd learned about Osama bin Laden and the Pentagon plane and the Pennsylvania and the Trade Center collapsing. Then he started in with: Would more planes crash, how many people were in the towers, how would they get the bodies out, was there going to be a war?

Gillian did most of the answering and, thank God, without all the drama—I'll say that for her: she was no hyperventilating newscaster. Daniel kept interrupting to tell Raphael he shouldn't worry—the government was on alert. The boy didn't look too frightened. *I* was, but Raphael was mostly curious.

Arnie was fit to be tied. I'd never seen him so angry. It was the pictures of the young people jumping. But we didn't talk about that in front of the boy. He knew, though.

The next few days, Gillian carried in dozens of boxes plus armloads of clothes. Which surprises me, now that I think about it, because she seems to wear the same two or three outfits over and over. Not that I'm one to talk, you're thinking, in these baggy old-lady pants.

Yes, from then on, Gillian's car was parked in the driveway when I turned off the porch light at night and when Arnie took in the paper in the morning. She'd moved in. A very busy lady. Not just with her Holocaust studies: she arranges conferences and book talks and ferries elderly survivors to sessions where they speak about their ghastly experiences. I've never gone, thank you very much. I admire all she and those groups do, I really do, but dwelling on certain things is too upsetting.

Was she a good choice for Daniel, being so serious? That's for him to say. She provided stability when Raphael was young—you didn't worry she'd run off with someone her own age. And Raphael grew attached to her. Though I think his mother's death made him shrink from investing too much in any woman who might step into that role. Listen to me—Dr. Freud, here! I hope you're not swallowing everything I say. Mia, a certified psychologist, would have me locked up for even *pretending* to know something about human nature. Seven decades on Planet Earth, and I'm supposed to be a complete idiot. Sometimes I think I am.

Yes, Gillian was a comfort to Raphael, to both of them. A *solid* presence—made you feel the world wasn't ending. Arnie and I saw a little less of them after she moved in, didn't have them to dinner so often. But we didn't become hedge families.

Oh my, it's that late? I'll have to show you my studio next time.

CHAPTER 4

Gillian Paige Burke (Gillian)

AS I WROTE, I'M SORRY we have so few emails and school reports, things like that, to show you—Daniel and I haven't been in the habit of saving much. You did get the photos I forwarded, the ones Raphael took in Nigeria with his friend's phone? His generation does a lot of its communicating via text messages, and Raphael's phone was lost in Nigeria. And the ones he had before that I think Daniel erased and gave away.

In high school and college, Raphael and his friends used different social media—I don't know what—Messenger? I sent you copies of the handful of emails we came across, some from high school and some from college, and copies of his high school journal pages. I have to confess, I just skimmed everything quickly and tagged the email strings and journal entries that mentioned anything political or philosophical, without bothering to edit out the personal or trivial—I assume you'll do that during the editing process. The elementary school stuff is just for, I don't know, a lighter touch? I did send your request out to his college friends, those I had addresses for, the ones who wrote Daniel after the alumni magazine printed the obituary. The editors wanted to publish a longer piece, but Daniel asked them to keep it to a paragraph like with the other students. And I sent you the little information we have for tracking down Aleecia.

And you have the emails Raphael sent his grandparents? Daniel found them sorting through papers after they passed away. After their being so resistant to getting a computer and learning email, Daniel went to New York and installed it and explained everything, and Raphael sent a few test messages, and Mr. Feingold was delighted. Mrs. Feingold was already having vision problems, but she was glad her husband could carry on a correspondence.

Pat said she told you I moved in on 9/11. That's not entirely true—I kept my own place a few more months. And I slept in Daniel's guest room. We didn't want to add another upheaval. In November, I think, Raphael asked—in the middle of dinner!—were we "sleeping together." Those were his words. I tried not to laugh, it was embarrassing. Daniel answered truthfully that no, we weren't, but that we had been at my place for a while and would again at some point. Raphael shrugged and said he didn't care, we could go ahead. I think it gave him some street cred at school to say his father had a live-in girlfriend.

Yes, that happened just before I went to my first Thanksgiving at Pat and Arnie's. Daniel and Raphael had a standing invitation, I imagine dating back to when Susan died, but I hadn't realized their three children and their spouses and all the grandchildren would be there. There were over twenty of us. Quite a lot of effort went into the dinner and preparations.

Pat's daughters have always been a huge help in the kitchen. When he was younger, Raphael apparently wanted to help too, and Daniel had to explain the kitchen would be crowded with Pat *and* Mia *and* Clara. We always brought something, a side dish and fresh bread, so Raphael would help me with the side dish or else ride his bike to Daniel's favorite bakery for the bread. I'm sorry: you can't want all these mundane details for your book.

Let me just say I never felt like I filled the role of stepmother. I fixed Raphael's breakfast on the weekends, sometimes did his laundry, took him to the doctor and dentist when Daniel couldn't. But he was already eleven when I moved in, and I think what happened is we became *friends* quickly. I know that sounds funny, given the age difference. But Raphael was . . . I don't like the word "precocious"—I'm not sure what to say. Serious? The only other children I know are my nephews and nieces, and I don't know them well—I only see them when we all go to my parents' in Minnesota in late spring, after school gets out for everyone.

What I'm trying to say is that Raphael and I had adult conversations right from the start. He wanted to learn more about the Holocaust, knowing it was my field. Not the Holocaust itself, not the concentration camps and tortures and murders—no, I study the moral systems survivors put into place. Much of what I examine is too arcane for an eleven-year-old, but I was amazed at what he was able to understand.

Let me back up. After Daniel and I had been dating awhile—I guess when he realized we both were serious—he had me come to dinner. Before then, Raphael and I had seen each other only half a dozen times, when I would drop off books for Daniel. The university library has far more than the public.

Around March of 2001, I think—yes, that's right; we had just had a big earthquake. Not damage-wise, but things fell from shelves, you could really feel it. Everyone had a story. I was in the library stacks. I won't go into that, visions of being *literally* buried under thousands of books, but I was fine. Daniel teases me that that's probably my idea of the perfect death.

I came to dinner, and it was a natural topic of conversation: where were you during the earthquake. When I said I was doing research, Raphael wanted to know about what, so I told him. He knew things already—every Jewish child does, even if the parents aren't religious. And he was the son of a historian.

Daniel and I used to quibble about the term "historian" and to what extent it means a student of history, a teacher of history, or a researcher. It was the first debate I won, getting him to accept the term for all three. Was there a specific time you felt you crossed over from being a student of ethnography to a researcher? I think all scholars remain students. At some point we stop paying tuition and begin drawing a stipend or salary; that's the main difference.

All right, over the next few months and years, really, Raphael asked many, many questions about the Holocaust. I described things most people don't learn until college, like the punitive terms of the Treaty of Versailles ruining the German economy. The soaring inflation and widespread poverty, the rise of extremism—both communism and Nazism. But as I said, I never went into detail about the camps. I'm sure he read a lot as he got older.

What always impressed me were the connections he drew. After hearing how poverty during the Weimar Republic made scapegoating attractive, he compared it to the bullies at school. They weren't actually angry at the particular kids they picked on but used them because they were easy targets. He did want to know why the non-Jewish Germans singled out *Jewish* people, as opposed to, say, rich people or people from other countries. "Did the Nazis just go 'Eenie, meenie, minie, moe'?" he asked.

The Nazis *did* go after other groups, I explained: Roma, homosexuals, even to some extent Catholics. And later, Slavic people, especially Poles and Russians. But anti-Semitism had been prevalent in Europe for centuries and was absorbed into Christian teachings. It puzzled him, the "Jesus was Jewish" contradiction in anti-Semitism. I couldn't explain it—I've never understood it myself.

As I mentioned, my research focuses on the *victims* of cruelty. I examine the different moral systems their suffering gives rise to. Because you *do* find differences in particular times and places when you compare the moral systems of early Christianity to those during the horrible violence in the Middle Ages and later the Holocaust. And I'm sure there were different moral systems during slavery, although it's not a period I've studied in any depth.

Is this something ethnographers or other sociologists look into, comparing moral systems among cultures in the present day? We historians play it safe and stick to the past, which is why we're much less useful to public-policy groups and lawmakers. My insights, assuming I have any, would only be useful to academics.

I'm smiling because I remember a conversation with Raphael in college while he was home on break. He argued against my point that the purpose of my research is simple understanding. "In your own academic way," he said, "you're as much an activist as anyone." Was he right, that I have some hidden ulterior motive? It's never been part of my conscious thinking. The book you published on the Nigerian communities and this one you're working on, they're forward-looking: you're hoping to promote constructive change. I'm afraid I'm just a self-indulgent scholar. Daniel sees great virtue in knowledge for knowledge's sake. I'm not sure.

Now I'm remembering . . . Raphael pressing me for stories about the martyrs of early Christianity. I think something in the teen psychology is drawn to the ghoulish. My brothers went through a phase of poring over books about medieval torture chambers, how the racks worked—made me shudder back then too. Arnie, Pat's husband, he once joked that Christianity itself is ghoulish, dwelling on the torture and death of a man nailed to planks.

I certainly was exposed to plenty of that growing up. My father's a Presbyterian minister, a conservative one. Or conservative about his *own* dogma, not always the dogma the synod wants to promote. He admires Thomas Aquinas greatly, includes many of his writings in sermons. Like the idea that God wants us to make use of our ability to reason and our senses to better understand the natural world. After all, the natural world is God's creation that He bestowed on us. But some members of the synod view Aquinas warily for having been part of the Catholic Church. Though he lived pre-Reformation.

I think all churches except the most fundamentalist have tensions between those clinging to the orthodoxy of earlier generations and those eager to incorporate science and reason into a modern creed. Don't you think it mirrors human nature? Daniel points to the irony in current politics: how some people who hold up George Washington as an icon of traditionalism forget he led a rebel army. "Context is everything," Daniel likes to say.

How did I get on this subject? Oh, I was talking about Raphael's interest in persecution. As he got older, he was bothered by our own nation's persecutions, slavery and what was done to Native Americans. Also more recent events, like the Khmer Rouge and Maoist purges, and even in his own lifetime—Srebenica and Rwanda, yet he was too young to know about them when they occurred. He was very critical of the Israeli government's treatment of Palestinians.

Some of that broad empathy came from Daniel. I'm thinking of our first date—we went to a nice Indian restaurant near the university. I'm embarrassed to say they asked us to leave. We were too engrossed in conversation to notice the staff had put the chairs up on all the other tables and were mopping the floor.

During dinner, Daniel complained that some Jewish people who use the phrase "Never again" ignore holocausts going on all the time. North Korea has its entire population in a concentration camp, in his view. In parts of Asia, Africa, Central America, people are routinely brutalized by government forces or their proxies. So how can we assert that holocausts are a thing of the past?

I understood what he was saying. But to adopt the slogan "Never again" isn't a bad thing, is it? The age-old problem: Who is my brother when I'm charged with being my brother's keeper? Who is the neighbor I'm supposed to love like myself? Raphael had a lot of opinions on this subject when he was older—but you thought it would be easier if I proceeded chronologically, so I'll wait.

I think Raphael always felt a special bond with the victims of the Holocaust. In high school, he came with me to a number of survivor talks, and if I chauffeured the speaker, Raphael would sit quietly in the back seat during our chitchat. You know, about the weather, that kind of thing. It wasn't like him to not join in. Maybe I'm reading too much into it, but I had a sense he felt a reverence for those who survived the camps. Many of us do, but I think his Jewish identity may have enhanced it.

Daniel would be annoyed to hear me say that—about the Jewish identity—at least in relation to *him*, Daniel. "What Jewish identity? That I like rye bread?" He was raised without faith and feels that the label "Jewish" is applied to him by people with an agenda. The agenda might be anti-Semitism or might be Jewish people feeling very much a minority and therefore wanting to swell their ranks. Whatever the reason, he doesn't like it. Oh, don't get the impression he resists being seen as *ethnically* Jewish; the assumptions that follow are what annoy him. I feel silly giving *you* a lecture on this kind of thing.

Raphael, though, I think *did* have a Jewish identity, which he may have kept hidden from his father. He never attended services after his bar mitzvah, not that I know of, but he took his Bible to college. His mother hadn't been religious, so it wasn't for a connection to her.

I doubt he would've told me—told me he had a Jewish identity. How can I explain it . . . Raphael was very protective of Daniel's and my relationship. So confiding in me something as intimate as faith or a heritage-based identity would've seemed a betrayal of his father. I don't mean the faith or identity part, only that it would have felt a betrayal to interpose a secret between the two of us, between me and Daniel, by asking me to keep something from Daniel. Does that make sense? I don't know how to explain it better.

I suppose Raphael could have viewed Jewishness as a connection to his grandparents. They were religious but not strict—didn't observe any of the dietary laws or Sabbath. I never had much of a glimpse into their interactions— the only time I met the Feingolds was at Raphael's bar mitzvah, and I tried to allow them as much time alone with him and Daniel that weekend as possible. Health issues prevented their flying out again, and, as I wrote you, they passed away a few years ago, within months of each other. Daniel's parents, as you know, died before Raphael was born.

Maybe Raphael's friends could tell you about his sense of Jewishness. I hope the names I gave you are helpful. I'm sorry I don't remember the girls'—I didn't meet any of them more than a few times. The boys from school and soccer I saw more often. And after he went to college—I sent you the only names I remember, Joseph and Aleecia. There was a Rachel, but Daniel doesn't remember her last name either, and we both had the impression they didn't date very long. And the fellow Lance, whom we never met but sent Daniel a card.

Maybe Raphael took the Bible to practice his Hebrew.

But this is jumping ahead.

In September 2001, his attention, like everyone else's, was on Osama bin Laden. The question that nagged him was: No matter what bin Laden's grievances were, why did he target the people on the planes and in the buildings? "Some were just kids," he kept saying.

I explained the little I knew of bin Laden's ideology at the time. What Raphael was keen to understand, and what most of us want to understand, is how an ideology allows people to inflict unnecessary cruelty on the *innocent*. We understand bombing munitions factories but not Dresden.

There are rationales—there are *always* rationales. But the fact that people feel the need to justify certain actions shows right away—I'm sorry: I'm going off on one of my academic obsessions. By the way, Raphael understood that the hijackers weren't representative of Muslims in general. In fact, he said, "They hijacked Islam." I don't know if he heard that at school. Seattle is a quite liberal area.

I don't want to leave you with the impression that all we talked about was human suffering. Like everyone else, at dinner we recapped our day: who we ran into, trivial mishaps like a copy machine breaking down in the middle of a huge project, misplacing the car keys. Daniel might relate a funny story he heard at lunch or how his pickleball game went, things like that. Raphael told us about his classes and soccer and antics at school. Yes, there was a lot of playfulness in Raphael. A rascally sense of humor.

But to get back to religion for a moment. I think 9/11 started his phase of curiosity about different faiths. He accompanied a friend to a reform synagogue, the one he later chose for his bar mitzvah, and had me bring him to church services in the neighborhood. We went to a Presbyterian, Lutheran, and Catholic. And special services: a Christmas mass and several Good Friday and Easter services. We didn't know anyone who attended the mosque nearby. I doubt he would have gone anyway, would've felt he wasn't welcome, because of all the Middle East problems. I wonder if when he took Arabic in college, he found someone to escort him to a local mosque.

"If I ever convert to Christianity," he once said, "I'd pick a denomination into good works. That's what I believe in, and I don't have a spiritual side." I had to laugh—not in front of him, but to myself. He was only fourteen or fifteen, a little young to know he would never develop a spiritual side.

So I can't say for sure what his religious beliefs were—either as a child or adult—or whether he identified as Jewish, whatever that might have meant to him. We all approach issues of faith and identity differently. My brothers and I have gone in different directions. The oldest still attends services regularly. The second takes his kids only at Christmas and Easter—I don't think he believes anymore. The youngest goes to an Episcopalian, his wife's denomination.

What am I? Daniel says I'm a Deist. I don't know. You don't need it for your book. Except for the times I took Raphael, I rarely attended church, not since my first year in college. Though lately I've been going to the local Presbyterian. I like the music.

CHAPTER 5

Daniel Ira Solomon (Daniel)

YOU HAVE TO UNDERSTAND this isn't easy for me—nine, ten months isn't a long time. I get that you want to interview us while our memories are fresh, but most of what I can tell you goes back six years or more. Raphael and I didn't talk much after he went to college, not regularly. He was closer to Gillian. But she thinks doing this interview will be good for me. She might be right—she does seem to know me better than I know myself.

Let's be sure I've got the ground rules straight. I skimmed the email attachment—I assume it's the same you sent her, a boilerplate kind of thing. You reserve the right to print everything we say unless we preface it with "This is off the record." We can't slip that in afterwards—it's got to be upfront. I guess if you're looking for honesty—what we *actually* remember as opposed to what we prefer the past looked like—your rules make sense.

And we can contact you before it's gone to press if we want to add or clarify something. We're consenting ahead of time to being recorded on the phone when we talk. I don't mind if you edit out the "ums" and extraneous words—if you make me sound more articulate than I am.

Out of curiosity, did Gillian mention why I relented and agreed to do this? She showed me the article where you were interviewed about your book *Communities under Siege*, and you posed the Chibok kidnappings question—I should say the *world reaction* to the kidnappings question. You asked: *Why now?* The barbarities in that region had been ongoing for five or ten years, longer if you spread your gaze farther. Why did this particular incident prompt the first big international outcry?

As historians, Gillian and I are always asking why did such-and-such happen at a particular time, when all the ingredients seemed to exist beforehand. Was there a special charismatic leader who seized the moment? Was it a fortuitous combination of symbiotic events? Was society as a whole now *ready* for a change in a way it hadn't been previously?

The steam engine was conceived in the first century CE—yes, way back then. Hero of Alexandria devised a prototype. But it took until the *seventeenth* century for people to want to improve on Hero's prototype and make it practical, and it wasn't until the *eighteenth* century James Watt and cohorts completed the tinkering. So they are the ones credited with inventing the steam engine.

Of course, they were among the first to see the widespread utility, recognized that manufacturers could make use of it. Hardly the first time the lure of profits spurred a scientific or engineering feat. On the other hand, the lure of profits has led many a person to ruin as well, so Watt's mental acumen counts for something. And I'm sure he made refinements to Hero's design—I don't mean to begrudge him his fame. Some would argue that's how it *should* be: providing benefit to humankind is more important than scientific genius. To me, it's obvious you need both.

In any case, my point is that the issue you raised in the interview—why now—is an important one for historians. Though let me confess: I didn't read the whole interview—it triggered a lot of pain. I did read enough to—I hope this doesn't sound presumptuous—to get a sense of you. Maybe I'm wrong, but the person reflected wasn't looking for a soapbox, didn't have an agenda, or seem to. You were "thinking out loud," which in my view is the best of academia. Trying to sift through information in order to *understand.*

I apologize if your research goes in a different direction entirely. But it should please you to know that my impression, or misimpression, got me to agree to talk. We had some big-name journalists and public yappers calling we rebuffed. Maybe your being closer in age to Raphael is helping me open up. Though Gillian says you're thirty-seven. Allow me to say you don't look it. I mean you look younger.

I appreciate your indulging me and walking while we talk. Makes it doable, moving, taking in the fresh air and scenery. You see, it doesn't always rain in Seattle, and some late-February days feel spring-like. Look at those bulbs—crocuses, I think. Purple and white are a nice combination. And the forsythia brightens up everything. Our trees aren't all conifers. Maples, maybe—I'm not the expert. Raphael was pretty good at identifying trees and plants—I think that was Pat's doing. After Susan, my wife, died, Pat took him on walks—parks, the arboretum. In the fall, he'd bring leaves of different colors home, all bright colors: red, yellow, orange. In second or third grade, he told me, quite solemnly, you should only collect fallen leaves, not remove them from living trees. I think his views on not messing with nature moderated once our apple tree began producing fruit.

Keep to the side; as you see, this path is popular with runners. I like how the view includes a span: water, lawns, shrubs, trees. The lake's usually calm, and there, see the ripples where the duck came up. Those are mallards, easy to tell by the emerald head and neck. Gillian and I saw a heron in those reeds.

When we get around to those lawns—I wonder if that's new grass, it looks so deep green—from that spot, if it's not too cloudy you can see the Olympic Mountains. They're our sharper, more defined range. The Cascades are rolling and lose their snow sooner. The jagged slopes of the Olympics are great at sunset. I forgot—you've been out here before, visiting your aunt. Sorry for playing the tour guide.

By the way, the list of questions you emailed was helpful—I'll try to cover all the bases. It must get a little tiring, the interview process—it's not like a conversation. You're smart to spread it out over several sessions, though don't count on the nice weather holding. Gillian said she gave you dates, places, people involved?

Proceeding chronologically—but you can't want to hear what he was like as a baby? Actually, that might help me get started. Those early years are far enough away, and I've already found a safe zone, mentally speaking, to talk about Susan, about my wife. Does time heal all wounds? No, but it puts down scar tissue.

I guess Raphael was a normal baby. Not colicky. Which, according to Pat, made him "wonderfully abnormal." He was docile—if there was a terrible twos or tantrum phase, I didn't notice. Susan stayed home his first year, and when she went back to work part-time, he was in day care. The staff told us they saw dozens of great qualities in him, but I'm sure they buttered up all the parents. He had the usual childhood illnesses, the usual childhood ups and downs. He liked kindergarten and was on track with his classmates—learning the alphabet and numbers. To us—Susan and me—he was a budding genius on a thousand fronts, a Leonardo da Vinci and Shakespeare and Isaac Newton rolled into one, but you can chalk that up to typical parental delusions.

Look—aren't they beautiful, the trumpeter swans? See the graceful S shape of the arching neck? They're almost prettier from a distance, such a sleek, white sheen, and gliding so effortlessly, as though resting, not paddling, and the water smooth as a mirror. Up close the feathers can look fuzzy, like a thick towel. You don't want to get too close—they'll savagely attack. Someone told me swans mate for life—they're monogamous. And male swans help build nests. Very smart animals.

I've taken an interest in birds, bird-watching—maybe it's therapy. I never paid much attention to animals before. Susan took Raphael to the zoo a few times. I did too, later.

If a person can be perfectly suited to motherhood, she was. Usually children tire their parents, but she seemed to *gain* energy. Together, they amazed me. If there's any silver lining to her death, it's that she didn't have to know—her heartbreak would've been unbearable. Maybe I'm wrong. Maybe she would've said his goals will live on in others. I wish I were generous enough to care about that.

Yes, even as a baby, Raphael found the world fascinating. He wanted to take in everything. Neither Susan nor I made a big fuss about things like first steps or first words, though probably at times we were as ridiculous as the best of them, marveling at a drooly smile. Her parents—Susan's mother in particular—got annoyed at our lackadaisicalness. "Why didn't you tell me he started crawling" or "got his first tooth" or whatever milestone loomed large in her mind. I'm sure my parents would've done the same had they been alive, although my sisters had already produced several grandchildren for them to dote on.

Raphael was very expressive—you knew when he was happy or frustrated. Most of the time he was just curious: what was Susan doing with the coffeepot, why did some shoes have laces and some not, which animals came out at night? She used to joke he'd grow up to be a detective. He was watchful, observant. Maybe all kids are—I don't know. I guess *I'm* not very observant.

Naturally, he took her death hard, didn't understand why she wasn't coming home. Her parents explained heaven to him, which surprised me; I wasn't aware that Jews believed in heaven.

I had no religious education. My parents grew up during the Depression, and either that or the Holocaust left them thinking that being American was the best identity to have. America conquered poverty and Hitler. I suppose their outlook, like everyone's, was to some degree provincial. *They* were able to escape poverty and assumed, therefore, everyone could. I know that's not the case, but as I say, they were thinking of their own subgroup.

I went along with my in-laws' heaven business because I didn't know how to explain death to a five-year-old. The hardest thing for me, I think, besides my own grief, was watching how it played out in Raphael. You could no longer read his mood from his face—he buried the grief somewhere inside. It's what we all do, I know, but up to that point, like I said, his emotions were there for all to see. Hiding his feelings was new. Or it was the first I became aware of it. Maybe Susan noticed him concealing reactions and never said anything, though she never held much back either. Or I have gone through life oblivious to how much people are holding back. I feel that way about myself: what you see is all there is.

Gillian's different—I've always known she holds things in. I can't see *what* she's holding in, but I know there's more, far more, than meets the eye. "Still waters run deep," Pat says.

It took Raphael a year, more or less, to begin bouncing back. Children change as they grow older, which makes it hard to parse which changes in his personality came from ordinary maturing and which from residual sorrow. School had let out only the week before, before the accident—he'd just finished kindergarten. I had the summer off, so I was with him a lot. We rode bikes, swam in the lake, went to library readings—they had an afternoon slot for his age group. I took him to the zoo, on ferries, flew kites. He tried T-ball.

It wasn't that he didn't enjoy the activities, but he showed none of the spark, the exuberance, of before. Arnie, Pat's husband—he passed away a few years ago—Arnie taught Raphael to dribble a soccer ball, and he was intrigued, so I took him to a U7 team practice right before school started, and to my amazement, he tore around the field with the other boys. To my *delighted* amazement. He wasn't all smiles, but he was attentive, focused.

An important milestone had been reached, it seemed to me, in his recovery, if that's the right word. And first grade, learning to read, was a big, big help. In retrospect, I'd say that by the end of that first year, it wasn't at all unusual to see him laugh and joke with friends and be excited about activities with me and also with Pat and Arnie—they were a godsend. Yes, he was willing to have episodes of happiness. For me it took a bit longer.

Be careful, the rollerbladers come through pretty quick. The weeping willow—the branches remind me of Susan after a shower, bending her head to wrap her hair in a towel. The draping. Yes, we lucked out today: blue skies, decent temps. So much forsythia, that bright yellow. And look how green the grass is. Whatever species grows here doesn't turn brown. We're lucky to have so many conifers—keeps the city green in all seasons.

Nothing stands out about the next few years—elementary school. He was a good student—As and Bs—and had friends, and we had our routines. Made a yearly pilgrimage to Susan's parents in New York—with their health issues, travel was difficult.

You really want to hear mundane details like that? I can't imagine anyone other than family and close friends caring. Gillian says I'm as much a private person as she is, but I don't think of it as privacy—I don't want to *bore* people. I've never kept a diary or journal—never imagined my day-to-day activities would hold much interest. Although as a historian, I value diaries and journals greatly. They provide some of the best records, not just of events but customs, perspectives.

Do you mind if we stop a moment so I can use the restroom? Should I unclip the microphone? I guess I don't need to; it's wireless. I'll trust you won't be recording me.

CHAPTER 6

Raphael [seventh grade essay]

THE SCHOOL RULE SAYING WE CAN'T chew gum isn't fair. There reasons keep changing. "We stick it under our desks". "We make noise chewing". "It's gross". "It takes our attention away".

People stick it under their desks only so they don't get caught. If we are allowed to chew, we will put the gum in the wrapper when we are done chewing it and toss it in the trash.

We can have our right to chew it taken away if we are noisy. Teachers shouldn't punish all kids who chew just because a couple kids are noisy. They don't say adults can't drink alcohol just because some people get drunk.

Chewing gum is not gross to most people. Why should just a few people get to say what's gross and what's not for everybody? That's dictatorship.

For some of us, chewing helps us concentrate better on what the teacher is saying. Doesn't that help our education?

Rules should have an important purpose and not be random.

[Raphael was twenty-three when he sent the email below, but I have included it here because of its discussion of childhood events. Sarah J., a physician and former Peace Corps volunteer, declined to be interviewed but said she had met Raphael several times in Maiduguri, Nigeria, in 2013. BXW]

[November 19, 2013, email from Raphael to Sarah J.]

If you're wondering how I found time and opportunity to email, it's because I'm stuck in a Maiduguri infirmary with at worst a "simple, minor" fibula fracture, maybe only hairline or not even, waiting for the x-rays. I wouldn't be here at all if Joseph hadn't dragged me. He has hypochondria-by-proxy, and if that's not a recognized syndrome, it should be. I'd split except the doc thinks I should use crutches, and they can't find any. With luck I'll get out before dark. In any case I'll be walking "perfectly" in no time or so they say. Is that optimistic? I asked if they were putting me on antibiotics and he said no, otherwise I would've demanded dawadawa as a substitute and referred him to you if he had questions. (I do know there are different kinds of antibiotics and it might not have been the right one—I was just testing his knowledge of indigenous plants since he's British.) Anyway a resident loaned me his laptop while he tries for some shut-eye.

Glad you've adjusted to life in the middle of middle America. Loved your father's reaction to putting peanut sauce and red pepper on prime Nebraska steak. Was it considered mere cultural rebellion or actual heresy?

You might've heard that things are getting dicey here, but in 7 weeks I'll be stateside and can actually talk on a phone, assuming your rotation isn't 24/7. Did you take Joseph's survey yet? He found a statistically significant difference between folks returning from pc/ngos in Africa versus E. Eur/C. Asia. The Africa volunteers resume daily showers at twice the rate. But I think his n is 9.

Re your ps question: the only time I remember thinking about being a doctor was way back in middle school. My dad and I rode our bikes on a lake trail, probably in Oct, and stopped to rehydrate. It was sunny and the lake calm and blue like you see in pictures. The sky was even bluer and you could see Rainier, a heaping white mass dwarfing everything. Can't remember if other mountains had snow, what I remember is trees around us and in the foothills blazing red, orange, yellow but like on fire. And details like trees and shadows crystal clear, nothing like those fuzzy harmattan sunsets.

The thing was, I'd seen that view dozens of times before but always looking through a car window. Which got me thinking: did biking in fresh air start some physiological process that made senses sharper? The idea that the senses can be altered (not by chemical means :)) made a big impression on me. A roundabout way of answering that that's the only time I thought of becoming a scientist or doctor. It would be cool to understand things like that. Besides, I sucked so badly in high school chem, premed had to be crossed off the list. No regrets, though I would've aced anatomy and all the medical terminology. Speaking of which, how could a child in Omaha have kwashiorkor, beef capital USA? You must've knocked the attending off her stool when you pulled that out of a hat. (Kind of an aside here: my dad always lectured me not to worry about a career, that I'd figure it out in college. I *wanted* to figure it out before then.)

Now during my forced idleness (which you're reaping the benefits of unless this is boring) botany actually shows up as a possibility. Chie taught me and Joseph how to distinguish some edible and poisonous plants. Did you know pawpaw is native to the western hemisphere? It tastes different from any papaya I had in the states. Also inside doesn't look as pink. I wonder if the species differentiation occurred before it was brought to Africa? And if came from north or south America.

Can you get a degree in botany and avoid chemistry? Maybe you could tutor me in the anes and enes and ines and ides. (I couldn't pay you doc's wages.) The only math/science course I totally aced was statistics, and mostly what I remember is when it comes to betting, the house always wins.

This has got me reminiscing about bike rides with my dad. If I didn't have a soccer game on the weekend or much homework and he didn't have a ton of class prep, we'd pack sandwiches, nuts, raisins, whatever and head out to the trails. There's a bunch to choose from that go around Lake Washington north and south and then east. Lots of neat stuff, like old Burlington Northern railroad tracks, long abandoned mining camps, ranches (other side of Cascades). North we went through abandoned pulp mills (smell like sweaty socks), pastures, wetlands, dairy farms, all with a mountain backdrop. Back in elementary school we hit beaches, did the clamming bit, looking for geoducks or whatever. Even in an infirmary bed with rubbing alcohol everywhere, I can conjure up the smell of the ocean. Laugh all you want, midwesterner, but it's a delicacy. The smells here in Maiduguri or Iskoki or Lambu are different.

I'll make you a deal. When I get back I'll send you a salmon (frozen fresh) and you can send me the top of the line steak and we'll see who's got it better.

Recuperatingly yours,

R

CHAPTER 7

Daniel

ARE WE GOING on the record again?

Gillian gave a rundown of some of the differences between your discipline, ethnography, and ethnology. Plus anthropology, sociology—I won't pretend to understand all the fine distinctions. I do get that you look at groups and cultures in a *qualitative* way, not quantitative or data-driven. You conduct interviews instead of pore over statistics, make observations instead of crunch numbers. Write a narrative instead of comparing graphs.

Historians are less data-driven too and more interested in telling a story than analyzing pie charts. Which doesn't mean we aren't concerned with facts—I'd take the position we are *more* interested in them than many data crunchers. But is the study of history properly a social science anyway? Some universities house their history departments within the humanities.

Which isn't to say all books claiming to be history are entirely right about the facts. Even contemporaneous records should be approached with a healthy skepticism. Churchill's history of the Second World War is my favorite example. While it's a font of information—no question about it—Churchill spins such a flattering self-portrait in places, you almost have to laugh. Oh, I think he was a great man, I really do. I should qualify that: he did some very great things. Yes, now I'm more careful about praising the man—or woman. I should zero in on the deeds.

You don't want to hear about this. You should cut me off when I go on one of my tangents. I think it's old age, the mind wandering. My students noticed it. Brought me up short, actually, the last round of evaluations.

Back to Raphael, what he did as a child. Let's see. We played catch, with a baseball and gloves, and he liked to fly kites. Went through a phase of beach-combing—looking for shells and snails, that kind of thing, at different spots along the sound.

But the more he played soccer, the more other pastimes fell by the wayside. Maybe twice a year we'd take the kites out. I guess that's true for most of us, the changes. I played ice hockey in junior high; I doubt I've put on a skate since. Don't get the wrong impression: I was second string, the kid they subbed in when the good players fouled too much or got injured. No regrets—I kept all my teeth. But with Raphael, he was so good, so *talented* at so *many* activities, you just wish . . .

Gillian said she gave you copies of pages from his journal, things he wrote in high school. I didn't want to copy the whole thing—a lot's repetitive and, frankly, not very interesting, or wouldn't be interesting to anyone who didn't know him. It began as an assignment in tenth grade Language Arts, but he continued writing in it occasionally his junior and senior years. I had no idea—when we came across it sifting through his things, you can imagine quite a few tears were shed.

I guess I should describe Gillian's arrival on the scene, so to speak. We met at a bookstore talk. The author had written on the short-lived League of Nations, and we lingered afterwards to ask him questions. After a three-way conversation, I offered to walk her to her car. Not as part of any grand dating strategy but for courtesy, safety.

You must have figured out I'm not a go-getter kind of person. And my life was proceeding—I want to say "comfortably." But Gillian and I, even just walking the short distance to the parking lot, had a rather in-depth conversation about the principles of national self-determination. So we made plans to go to dinner, and one thing led to another. I don't suspect Wilson's Fourteen Points have ignited many other romances.

She's afraid she talked your ear off about the Holocaust. Raphael's fascination with it wasn't anything I took too seriously. Everyone who's Jewish goes through a phase of what you might call "deep immersion." Maybe you're familiar with a parallel having to do with slavery. So did the Holocaust affect him to an unusual degree? I don't think so.

Now I'm reminded of something a little embarrassing. I don't think I've ever mentioned it to anyone. When he was in third or fourth grade, still pretty young—and this was before he met Gillian—Raphael and his friends were playing a cops-and-robbers game in our backyard. I didn't pay much attention until I heard them shouting words like "gestapo" and "Jew." I went out on the patio and realized they had made the game a Warsaw-ghetto-fighters versus the Nazis.

Maybe that sounds awful, but when I was young, we played cowboys and Indians, which isn't really any different. Did you or siblings play games like that? Children relish the excitement of pretend battles. I'm not convinced that affects who they grow up to be. I think Gillian used to play soldiers with her brothers, and you can't find a more pacifist personality. I mean pacifist *temperamentally*, not ideologically. Just like there are no atheists in foxholes, there are no pacifist Holocaust scholars.

Understandably, Raphael's interest in the Holocaust grew once Gillian moved in. I do remember him finding the *sequence* of events interesting, Hitler's rise to power, the laws that were passed. I suspect children want to be on the lookout for a repeat, the thought being that if you can identify the chain of events leading up to a cataclysm, you can nip it in the bud if it should start again. Of course, history doesn't repeat itself in such a pat fashion—the acts that should constitute red flags take different forms.

By the way, Gillian was *very* vague about what went on in the camps. Leaving it to Raphael's imagination was a good thing, I told her, because no decent human being could dream up what was actually done.

If you don't mind, I think this might be enough for one day. There's not much farther around the lake—let's enjoy the sunshine and scenery. So much is still green—the lawns, pine trees. Aren't the geese beautiful, flying in precise formation? People hate them for leaving such a mess, but it's a small price to pay for a sight like that.

Look at the kids, the ones playing soccer, practically taking a mud bath, from their hair down to their ankles. A real bath and hot meal when they get home. Yes, let's continue another day.

CHAPTER 8

Pat

I THINK I ALREADY TOLD YOU that after Gillian moved in, I spaced out the dinner invites. Daniel was trying to patch together a new family, and I wanted to give him elbow room. Raphael still dropped by if he wanted company to the store, and I was his soccer-practice driver and snack supplier. When Arnie retired, he joined us for the games on the weekend. Daniel did too, but Gillian stayed home. Doesn't like sports, she said. You don't have to like sports to be supportive. Arnie said she had little time to herself, keeping a busy schedule at the U. Daniel was plenty busy too, but he found time.

I don't remember when I told Raphael to call me Pat, not Mrs. E. I didn't need to be *Aunt* Pat, which would've annoyed Susan's parents. Susan was their only child. Should we be thankful they passed away before all this? Anyhoo, it was for them that Daniel had Raphael bar mitzvahed. Did he tell you about that?

A lot goes on before the actual ceremony, I had no idea. There's Sunday school, Hebrew lessons, writing your speech, learning the songs. "The clap-trap," was Daniel's word for it—outside the boy's hearing. Daniel can be pretty irreverent. He's less religious than *I* am, and I'm a Unitarian. I hope I'm not offending you.

Arnie and I didn't know what to expect—we'd never been to a bar mitzvah before. I'd gone to a seder in college. I'm skeptical it was authentic. Bread was banned—I remember that. People read from a book before we ate, explaining that this food and that on the platter symbolized something or other, but they were substitutes. I'm sure they were; I have a *very* hard time imagining rose hips and winter savory growing in Egypt.

The synagogue isn't a large building. From the outside, you'd think it was insurance offices or some warehouse. And the entryway is bland. I was expecting more pomp.

But the sanctuary or whatever they call it is *beautiful*. The pews looked spanking new then and modern and a much lighter wood than you usually see in churches—maybe teak? The windows let in *oceans* of sunlight. And the stained-glass windows had none of those morbid cathedral colors. You can tell from looking around here I'm a fan of natural pastels. The synagogue wasn't pastels, no, but everything that wasn't a light wood or glass was a bright blue or gold or ivory. Only the drapes—I think they were drapes—were a deep royal blue.

You're talking to a painter here. Okay, a long-*time*-ago painter. What I'm trying to say is that the décor was *cheerful*. They had the sense to bring in someone with taste—an interior designer, maybe—instead of throwing together a mishmash from discount church furniture stores and old, drab moth-eaten tapestries.

Arnie and I sat in the back. There were enough people so we didn't stick out and everybody wondering who the party crashers were. It turns out I didn't need to bring a scarf, and they gave Arnie one of those little beanie things, *yarm*ulkes. Susan's parents sat up front and behind them, Daniel's sisters and their families. His parents had died long before. I didn't get a good look at anybody until the reception. Gillian sat towards the middle.

The rabbi stood on some sort of stage—do they call it an altar? He did the usual preachy stuff: sermonizing and reading from the Bible, I guess, and the whatchamacallit, that scroll-y thing. He didn't drone on as much as our priest at Saint Joseph's did when I was a girl, but I wouldn't call it a hootenanny either.

Then came Raphael's turn. He stood up there in his dark suit and a lovely white shawl—looked like satin—his curls neatly combed and the yarmulke probably held on with bobby pins, he had such a head of hair. He rattled away in Hebrew, which was Greek to me, but he could speak it like he'd learned it in the womb. Then he said things in English, something about Jewish law or a Bible story—I don't remember, wasn't really paying attention. You see, the sun coming through the side windows distracted me, the way it reflected off the polished pew backs, spreading light everywhere; and the blue drapes, elegant, regal; and the congregation's faces so attentive and happy; and that peaceful sense you can get in a house of worship. The sense of *Sabbath*, Bernice, *Sabbath*.

What brought me out of my trance was Raphael's tender voice—a mix of song and chant. It had that Vienna choir boy sweetness, just in a lower register. Imagine: a tenor with a child's innocence.

A book-club friend sets us howling; she can imitate boys' voices when they go squawky in adolescence, up and down the octaves like a frantic chicken. Raphael spared us that. He looked a little self-conscious in the limelight, but he had nothing to be embarrassed about.

The congregation sang too. It was in Hebrew, so who understood a word, but there was beat, pulse, "vibrancy," Arnie said later when we filed out. I thought he said "vibrator" and shushed him. What I'm trying to explain is: I was so used to hymns sounding like they're reaching for the heavens, but this music was of the earth. Like folk music. Such a welcome change. Maybe your church is different. Yes, when the congregation sang, you heard tenors like Raphael, but the baritones dominated—strong, manly baritones. Arnie was just itching to join in—I could tell. He had a lovely bass.

The reception? Just some tables set out with little sandwiches, raw vegetables, hummus, baba ghanoush, that kind of thing—healthy tidbits that make you crave a real meal. I remember thinking Gillian must have been in charge. Daniel looked happy, maybe that it was over, but happy just the same.

He introduced us to Susan's parents. They seemed *very* frail. I don't think they smiled the entire time. Just watched Raphael mingling with the guests. Completely ignored my chatter, so they weren't stupid. I'm sure they felt proud, but all I saw was watchfulness.

When I mentioned it to Mia on the phone, she said they might have been tired from the time-zone change. I told Arnie if that was the kind of brilliant insight she offered her clients, they'd want their money back.

Daniel's sisters—all I'll say is they bought new outfits for the shebang. You could tell from across the room. I was surprised they didn't leave the price tags dangling.

So that rite of passage went smoothly, and Daniel survived it better than he expected.

I'm drawing a blank here on anything else from Raphael's early teens. He did drop by now and then while I was preparing dinner and talked about his classes and classmates. Which teachers were good and which were goof-offs. Anything out of the ordinary his friends were up to. What he was studying.

Something always interested him, even in math class, which wasn't his favorite subject, though I'm sure he did fine—he was in honors this and that. Which I only found out because he showed me the sign he'd drawn for a protest at the middle school. Against tracking. I had to ask was he being tracked, and he said he was being encouraged by his teachers to take certain classes, and his friends were being *dis*couraged. It was wrong and unfair, and a group of them were going to march for half an hour before the bell.

I felt so gypped—born too early to be part of the college protests, the big ones, against the Vietnam War. I spent that decade chasing after my toddlers, picking up toys scattered across the living room while the TV showed crowds of students in denim and tie-dyes and bandannas singing "Give Peace a Chance." But I was a commune hippie *before* that became fashionable. We thought of ourselves as beatniks, and our commune we called a co-op, but it's the same thing.

Math class . . . something I wanted to mention. What was it? I remember: Raphael liked to say, "Everything's a sine wave." This must've been when he was taking algebra or something. He meant going from one extreme to another. The boys on his soccer team who loved winning the most hated losing the most. The kids who were thrilled at an A on an exam fell into the dumps with just a B. *Just,* you're thinking! But he was right: that was Clara. Getting anything less than an A mortified her the way the rest of us would feel if our skirts fell off in the middle of the cafeteria.

Raphael was so proud of the examples he thought up. His friend who was super excited about asking a certain girl out, and when she said no, he sulked for weeks. The one who loved her dog was inconsolable when it had to be put to sleep. "It's the sine wave," he'd say.

Don't you think he was right? If you never hit rock bottom, you never felt thrilled. I wonder if that's why Clara wrote her dissertation on the Stoics. All I could think when she described them was: Why bother being alive? The nuns weren't fond of me.

What else in middle school . . . Did Daniel or Gillian mention Erin? Slight young thing, lovely blond hair almost to the shoulder. The only time I saw her she was wearing a pale-pink sweatshirt three sizes too big and dozens of sparkly bracelets on both wrists—such thin wrists. I really don't know if I should be the one telling you about Erin. Ask Gillian. She knows more anyway. I'll just say the wrong thing.

CHAPTER 9

Clara Eriksen Wolfe (Clara) [telephone interview]

HAPPY TO HELP, BUT I DOUBT I can add anything to what my mother must have told you. I usually saw Raphael only at Thanksgiving, and there was such a crowd, I was lucky to get a word with Daniel or Gillian, who were my peers. Raphael was my daughters' generation.

They had terrible crushes on him. Brooke is four or five years younger, and Jody, six or seven. Jody had it worse. But what twenty-year-old boy notices a thirteen-year-old girl?

It was always a madhouse, Mia and Fred and their three kids, Ryan and Beth and their three, and the four of us. Four boy and four girl cousins. My two are no wallflowers—they can assert themselves—but they were never rambunctious the way the boys were.

You add one more boy to the mix, and what do you expect? I will admit Raphael wasn't rambunctious, but I'm going to be candid, Dr. Williams: I resented his presence. We could take the trip from Boston and spend seven days in Seattle only once the entire year. We took the girls out of school all

Thanksgiving week so they could spend quality time with their maternal grand-parents, aunts, uncles, and cousins, who *all* live on the West Coast. Raphael was able to see my parents the other 350-plus days of the year. He didn't have to come over during *our* time.

I don't mean he was there constantly. Still, he'd show up in the afternoon to join games like he was one of the family.

Family bonds are special. My mother says you're staying with an aunt near Seward Park? So you know what I mean. Luckily, I can visit more often—if I can't manage a conference in Seattle, then San Francisco, and I still work Mom into my itinerary. She won't travel—hates being confined in a car or airplane seat. Which is why the Thanksgiving visit was important, the only time Brooke and Jody saw the Eriksen side. They're so much closer to their Wolfe cousins—Derek's family—who live in Boston, Newton, the North Shore.

Thanksgiving wasn't *sheer* pandemonium. My dad set up the basement with a boys' bedroom and a girls' and a main room where they could play games. And there was another *bathroom*, thank God. My hoarder parents never threw out the games and puppets and toys from my childhood, plus they'd bought a foosball table. And Ryan always brought games, like Twister and Dance Dance Revolution. They made a racket, the horde of them.

It was a miracle some of those toys survived. Dad built an elaborate doll-house when Mia and I got chicken pox, two floors and nine rooms, stood about three feet tall so our Barbies would fit. My mother helped us furnish it using odds and ends. The dining room table was a small cardboard box with the sides cut off, just the corners kept for legs. We used soda bottle caps for platters serving the food, which consisted of grains of rice and Cheerios, that sort of thing. What were the dishes . . . dimes, that's right! We made beds out of little matchboxes and used toothpicks for curtain rods and cut up remnants for spreads and carpets. The sink was a thimble, and empty spools were the end tables. Every time my mother couldn't find something in her sewing basket, she knew where to look. Very creative: She made a wheelbarrow from bobbins and a plastic spoon. A hair clip became a piano bench.

For our birthdays and Christmas, we got a piece of *real* doll furniture, new, from a store. A dresser or wardrobe or desk. My absolute favorite was the baby stroller. The wheels were shiny silver chrome, and the handlebar, a tiny chrome pole, was covered in *real leather*, powder-blue with tiny stitches. So elegant, I just loved that powder-blue stroller. I don't remember what Mia got that year, maybe the hairbrush and hair dryer set, but I just loved my stroller. With its matching blue-and-white checkered blanket.

Brooke and Jody played with the house for ten minutes before getting bored. Amy might've gotten some use out of it—you'll have to ask Beth. The boys had games too. The basement was a great rec hall not just for me and Mia and Ryan but our kids too.

Unfortunately, I always had to be the meanie at Thanksgiving, the one who went downstairs and insisted on lights-out. Nobody wants to spend the next day surrounded by cranky children who didn't get enough sleep. But it was a wonderful bonding experience for the cousins, something we *all* cherished.

One year I went down and found Raphael—he was probably seven or eight—in a sleeping bag on the floor of the boys' room. He swore his father knew he was there. Daniel did know. Still, I wonder if he was telling the truth that my parents had invited him. I suspect he'd invited himself. My parents weren't the kind to say no. And Daniel probably leapt at the chance to have an evening to himself.

Do I sound petty? Cliquish? I just felt Raphael crossed certain boundaries. It's not easy juggling marriage, career, and raising two daughters. I'm not *complaining*—I'm just saying it's difficult when you want the best for them.

And they're doing well. Brooke is in Barcelona for her junior year. Thank heavens for Skype! Jody's at Columbia and gets home now and then. I'm just sorry my daughters saw so little of the Eriksen side growing up. Mom got all excited when Jody was accepted at the U—the University of Washington—but then she got accepted at Columbia, which made it a no-brainer.

Anyway, about Raphael, I'll say what I said before: He wasn't unruly. Or bullying or even sarcastic, the way teenagers get. I could write a book about the *eye*-roll, the swear words showing up sooner than you'd hoped, the tantrums because no one's giving them a ride to the slumber party until *all* the dishes are done. Mia says children are better behaved in other people's homes than in their own. I'd like to think so. Maybe Raphael was a terror around Daniel and Gillian.

You must know I feel awful about what happened—we all do. A horrible tragedy. But the point here is for me to be honest about my recollections, you said. According to my mother, that's what Raphael would have wanted too—the unvarnished truth, not glib praise. And my frustrations, as I said, came only from concerns for my daughters. It's only natural to prioritize one's own children.

You know my field is classics. I teach the *Iliad*, *Odyssey*, *Aeneid*; the plays of Aeschylus, Sophocles, Euripides, others. A few of the philosophers, the Stoics and Epicureans. Of course Greek and Roman mythology get incorporated in every syllabus. If I had to summarize this whole terrible tragedy, Dr. Williams, I would point to the tale of Icarus, the young man who flew too close to the sun. He had what the Greeks called hubris. There's no perfect translation in English. Hubris combines elements of pride and arrogance and a sense of immortality.

My students dismiss the classics as out of date. What possible relevance could they have in today's world? But once they begin reading, they see how human nature is human nature. I just graded an essay where the student likened Odysseus's hearing the sirens to someone experimenting with drugs. He isn't far off. Or they get into heated debates over whether Antigone was an extremist or a brave idealist compelled to fight both injustice and sexism. Sound irrelevant? Two millennia ago people faced the very same problems we face today.

Speaking of which, I have a class to prepare for. I wish I had more to offer you, but my memory of Raphael is limited to tidbits. My mother has probably told you enough to fill ten volumes.

CHAPTER 10

Gillian

SO THIS WILL BE A SHORT SESSION—you're talking with Ryan in a bit? That's convenient, his visiting his mother now. We can resume tomorrow, when my schedule is freer.

I think where we left off was middle school. You asked about Erin, and that was when Raphael was in eighth grade. She was only in sixth. So delicate, almost waifish. Came to dinner once or twice—it wasn't unusual for Raphael to bring friends from school or soccer. Though sometimes we had to scramble to put something on the table besides leftovers.

I suppose we were a little concerned that he'd brought a girl and that she was younger. Two years is a big age gap, a teenager and a preteen. And she was quiet, hard for us to get a sense of her. Usually Daniel was able to draw Raphael's friends into the dinner conversation but from her got only monosyllables.

One night—it must have been a Friday, yes, a Friday—Raphael told us Erin was in his room but didn't want to come out to dinner. We asked if she was sick, and he hemmed and hawed, which was unlike him. I'm a little embarrassed to admit my first concern was whether they were getting too intimate.

Then he said she'd been beaten by her father. Daniel beelined for the bedroom, worried she needed to go to the ER. Raphael ran after and stopped him, saying she was okay, and we had to understand why it happened. "Erin's trans," he said, "and her father's been freaking out."

This was back in 2002, 2003—being trans was much more hidden. It still is hidden, probably even in Seattle, although less than in other places.

Raphael insisted she wasn't badly hurt, just bruised, but Daniel convinced him to have her join us at the table. I think it was a way we could gauge the extent of her injuries. Though her eating and gaining a little weight would've been a good thing too.

She had the beginnings of a black eye, which she said was her only injury—her nose had stopped bleeding and didn't hurt. The issue then became what to do next. She did not want us to call the police or DSHS—the social services agency. And she didn't want to go home, although she didn't want her mother to worry where she was. Daniel and I were a bit bewildered. As her teacher, he would've had guidelines to follow, but he wasn't. We were over our heads, not knowing the law, our options, if we could be charged with kidnapping or something. Raphael pleaded with us not to send her home, and we certainly hoped we wouldn't have to.

I tried reaching a colleague whose husband is a lawyer. He doesn't practice criminal law or family law, it turned out, but he promised to get me the names of lawyers who did. While we were waiting for him to call back, Erin phoned someone and was able to get a message relayed to her mother that she was all right and would be in touch by Sunday.

What a flurry of phone calls that evening and Saturday. This was back before most of us had cell phones. Daniel and I had long debates: Should Erin file a criminal complaint against her father? Pursue a claim through DSHS? Although we did agree it was something for a lawyer to advise her on—we were just wondering. Her mother wasn't entirely to be trusted—I had the impression there may have been some domestic abuse there, or at least intimidation. And Erin had two younger sisters she was very concerned about. Not their physical safety—she just didn't want them to feel in the middle and witness their father's rage. They were about nine or ten, identical twins.

I better finish the Erin story tomorrow—you have to meet Ryan soon. By the way, thank you for sending the draft of your preface; I appreciate your letting me review it. It's not that I expected to find something offensive, just that phrasing here or there could—I don't know—sting a little *extra*? Most of it's going to sting. Though I doubt Daniel will read a word, not for a few years.

You mention media accounts accusing Raphael and Joseph of being naïfs. I read several of those accounts, and the accusations are unfair. The boys—the young men—knew the dangers; they had lived near Chibok the year before, for a full twelve months. They just wanted to do their part.

Daniel would be angry to hear me say that. He has always maintained that Raphael's "part" was back here in the States. *Raphael's* position was that he was no different from a soldier who ships overseas to help an ally.

I don't have the answers, Bernice. Do parents of soldiers feel the same, that they should've chosen safer ways to serve? Some families have long and proud military traditions and consider service an honor. Many fathers, especially, want their children to follow in their footsteps.

My father would've liked at least one of my brothers to have heard the call of ministry. That hasn't been expected of us girls, has it? Married and having babies was my parents' wish for me, I'm pretty certain. They never actually *said* so, and the fact that all three of my brothers married and provided grandchildren probably takes some of the heat off me. I wonder if, as second best—if I don't marry and have children—my father wants *me* to hear the call of ministry? Our church has become more open to the idea of women clergy—some of our sister churches ordain women. But the ministry has never sparked my interest. As I mentioned before, I'm just a self-indulgent academic.

Yes, my brothers' supplying grandchildren takes some of the heat off me. If I'd been an only child, certainly the pressure would've been greater. Or felt that way. My editor says my metaphors confuse more than explain, but I'm going to try this one on you: I think of children like spurts of new growth on a tree. There can be a delight in seeing them branch out in different directions and create new possibilities. But if you have only a single shoot, you concentrate on shielding it from deviating too far from the trunk.

Oh, I don't think Daniel was looking ahead to grandchildren. Certainly he would've loved them, but he wasn't anticipating—he has never spoken about that as an expectation from Raphael.

One minute I'm trying not to cry; now I'm trying not to laugh. Raphael was quite the Don Juan in high school, and I remember Daniel lecturing him about *not* extending the family line. You know, taking precautions.

Here I've been delaying you! I'm so sorry—let me get your coat. Don't worry about cutting this short—it gives me extra time to straighten up before Daniel gets home. He knows you were coming, but he doesn't need a reminder the moment he walks in the door. It's not personal—in fact he admitted he found you easy to talk to and said he'd try at least one more session.

Here's your coat. Pat's daughter Mia says nine-tenths of therapy is "in the articulation." I think that could be said of prayer—not rote prayers but speaking to God. What's important, what's restorative, is speaking from the heart, regardless to whom one is speaking. Oh my goodness, your machine is still running. So sorry to ramble on.

CHAPTER 11

Ryan Bruce Eriksen (Ryan)

NOT SURE WHAT YOU WANT ME TO SAY. To be honest, I'm doing this to please my mom. She said you were coming to interview Gillian, and since I'm here, I should give you a shot at me. But I never got to know Raphael other than, you know, a neighbor's kid. I already had a kid of my own, just barely, when Raphael was born, and I was still finishing college, WSU. That's in Pullman.

I must've been visiting not long before because Mom made me haul over a bunch of stuff like an old high chair, playpen, crap that had been collecting dust in the garage for twenty years. I couldn't believe the neighbors would want it, but she cleaned it up nice—I almost didn't recognize it. I guess the Solomons hadn't been here long enough to make close friends, the kind that will throw baby showers and chip in for the expensive stuff.

Whenever I came home, my parents would go on about them, my mom especially. She should've gotten a job when I went to college instead of becoming the block busybody. Don't get me wrong: she means well. But she practically *adopted* the Solomons, especially after the wife got killed. Maybe it's our fault, me and Mia and Clara, for moving out of state, but I got a job offer in Sacramento I "couldn't refuse"—was able to pay off my student loans in three years. Beth—we got married right before senior year—she nixed Seattle because she hates cold and clouds. And she knew LA was close to a deal-breaker for me. Sacramento is pretty much midway.

Daniel's wife was nice, the couple of times we met. Kind of peppy but not in a way that grates—I've got Beth's sister for that. Might've been the contrast with Daniel, who's pretty laid-back, that made her seem peppy.

After she died, it might've been a little weird, Raphael dropping in out of the blue and Mom fussing over him. Like when we visited without our own families—just the three of us coming in for my dad's birthday, say, or something like that. Raphael'd bop over, and Mom'd give him cookies. I figured she was trying to deal with the empty nest, and hell, the kid lost his mother. It kind of made sense they'd latch on to each other. There are worse kinds of neighbors. The guy next door to us, he mows the lawn at seven a.m. *Sundays*. Not a big deal if you get up early, but a lot of us don't, at least until he starts the motor.

Raphael's dad didn't come over, except maybe to fix something, like a leaky faucet. *My* dad was the engineer but totally useless for anything nonelectrical. He rewired the basement and couldn't caulk a hole in the shower, if you know what I mean. So you might be hanging out at breakfast, and Daniel would show up with his tools and climb under the kitchen sink. Raphael would watch or else play checkers with my dad. Mom would ask them to stay for lunch, and sometimes they did.

I didn't see the big deal, but Clara did. She never complained in front of the folks—I'll give her that—but she'd whine to me and Mia, "Mom cares more about Raphael than her own grandchildren." Her kids were three thousand miles away and visited once a year! "Blood should be thicker than water," she once said, which goes over *real* big with me. Our daughter's adopted.

Mia-the-great-psychologist said Mom and Raphael were "mutually overcompensating," whatever that means. She also told me that Clara has "middle-child syndrome." People pay good money to hear Mia's theories. Sums up Oregon, for you—and they complain about California!

You want a soda or something?

At Thanksgiving, when all our kids came along, sure, Raphael'd hang out with them, but he was just a year younger than Todd, Mia's oldest, and the same age as Nick, my oldest, and Jake and Kirsten are close behind. If anything struck me as weird about Raphael, it was he didn't get into fights. I don't mean fistfights, just the obnoxious teasing that always goes on. Maybe because he didn't have any brothers or sisters, he didn't know it was part of the package.

They liked to kick the soccer ball around with him, even Jody.

I don't know what else to say.

When Raphael was older, sure, I might talk to him like I might to anybody. He followed the Mariners, I think, which is as crazy as following the Cubs. You watch baseball? I can't remember if he was a Seahawks fan. He used to talk to Fred—that's Mia's husband—who's bilingual, and they'd go on a bit in Spanish. I guess Raphael liked learning different languages—he might've known five or six by the time he finished college.

You're interested in his politics, Mom said? There were a couple of blow-ups he was at, but I barely remember them. People argue politics all the time. Beth's brother is so far gone, he thinks Nader's a capitalist tool—*Ralph Nader*.

The only argument that sticks in my brain was when my dad was alive, and it had to do with Hiroshima and Nagasaki, dropping the bombs. I don't even remember if Raphael was there, though he could've been—it was definitely one of those group discussions. My dad was arguing we had to drop the bombs to avoid invading Japan, which would've cost a ton of American lives and probably just as many Japanese as the two bombs did. Daniel knew all sorts of stuff my dad didn't know, and I didn't either. He's a history teacher, so no surprise there.

He said Truman knew the Japanese were going to surrender—it was behind-the-scenes stuff having to do with the Soviets and I forget who else—and knew we wouldn't need to invade. A bunch of ulterior motives, that's why the bombs got dropped. It's pretty amazing we'd been duped for so long. I get the *government* wanting to lie to us, but I figured the reporters would've come up with the truth. Just like they did with the WMDs, right? Ha!

And while we're on the subject, let me point out that I changed my mind about dropping the bombs, which proves my mom's wrong when she says I argue things I don't believe just to win a point. I say what I think—she just doesn't like what I think. That's okay—she's off in kumbaya land half the time. "Takes all kinds to make a world" was my grandmother's line. Dad used to say, "Not all kinds make it better." Amen to that.

I also think a person can do good stuff without putting out a press release. I'm talking about one of my sisters. Who shall remain nameless, right? Now they'll both be mad at me. Half the clothes my wife buys, she wears them once and suddenly they don't fit right or are the wrong color and she donates them to Goodwill. And most of their customers aren't White. It's not like we don't do charity stuff.

About Raphael, he didn't get under my skin, I'll cop to that. Look, I don't see why I need to be part of your project. I'm sure it'll be a good book—I'm just not crazy about interviews. Especially when I don't have much to say. You want to talk about the Forty-Niners, I'll keep you here all night.

Okay, I do have another memory—it also has to do with my dad, before he got cancer. He liked to hammer out folk songs and show tunes on the piano and sing along—real corny stuff. If the Solomons were here, Gillian sang too. She knew multiple versions of some folk songs, and they had a good time comparing the words. I remember one had an Irish version and a Northern Irish and a Scottish, and she knew them all. Something-something "blooming heather"; that I really liked. Wasn't crazy about "Foggy Foggy Dew." Mom had a book of Irish lyrics they used, but she had a rule: no "Danny Boy." It made her imagine, and I quote, "useless old geezers crying in their beers."

Anyway, the rest of us stayed at the table finishing dessert or whatever, except Raphael. He joined in sometimes, *singing*. When he was a *teenager*. None of the other kids did—not even the girls. I wouldn't have been caught dead doing something so hokey at that age.

Gillian came over on Christmas or Christmas Eve—I think Daniel and Raphael went to New York then—and she'd sing carols with my folks. I liked the idea of them not being alone on the holiday. We go down to Beth's parents in December, do the Hanukkah routine. Some years we lucked out, and Hannukah was already over while the kids were still in school, so we hit Disneyland instead. We raised them sort of mixed. Maybe I should say "pure commercial"—whatever religion was celebrating something: Christmas, Hannukah, Easter. Presents, food, and candy—that's what they think religion is.

Beth does go to temple on the High Holy Days—you know what they are? She didn't take the boys when they were younger, because—she admitted it—she wanted a few hours away from them. Don't get me wrong: she was a great mom. That was the problem; she wasn't big on taking time for herself, so she needed to grab what little came down the pike. And by the time we got Amy, we'd both given up on getting any religion into anybody.

What do I believe . . . I guess I'm still a Christian in a vague sort of way. Not Unitarian like my mom, and not Lutheran like Mia—she's the only one who stuck with my dad's. He wouldn't be caught dead at a Unitarian service; they're practically political. Maybe that's just Seattle. Anyway, I kind of figure that God isn't obsessed over Ryan Eriksen's soul. God's got bigger fish to fry. If, when the time comes, He decides I wasn't religious enough, that just trying to live each day like a decent person—a mensch, Beth would say—if that doesn't get me a hall pass into heaven, I'll see how the lower half lives.

How'd I get on *this* subject? That's right, Gillian coming over at Christmas. When my dad got sick, she brought him a bunch of folk song CDs and sometimes stayed and listened with him. I taught them both how to download iTunes, which is way easier. Like I said, my parents were lucky to have them as neighbors.

Anyway, that's all I remember about Raphael. If I think of anything else, I'll let my mom know, and she can pass it on.

CHAPTER 12

Gillian

WHERE DID WE STOP LAST TIME? I was telling you about
Erin, that's right. Oh, I forgot—you take sugar, let me get it . . . here you are.

What are you reading—the cathedrals book! Daniel bought me that. Aren't
the photographs beautiful? For years we talked about a trip to Europe. He's
never been. His parents tried to get him to go—not Europe in particular, just
take a nice vacation. They were generous when he got his degree, but he used the
money for graduate school and, later, towards the down payment on the house.

The money they left him when they died wasn't much because he didn't
have a child, so most went to his sisters' children. He could've asked his sisters
for some when Susan got pregnant, but that wasn't like him. And *her* parents
were very generous with what they had. Yes, Daniel would enjoy a trip to
Europe. He would love all the history. We couldn't go inside the British
Museum, because he'd never leave. To see the actual Magna Carta . . .

Erin. Raphael was pushing for us to take her in permanently—to go
through whatever legal steps were needed, including adoption. We weren't

ready to promise something like that, even if it was legally feasible. You can't agree to such upheaval on short notice.

Erin herself wasn't certain what she wanted. She seemed lost—remember, she was only eleven or twelve. Yet showed remarkable courage in insisting on her identity. It would've been much easier for her to just put boys' clothes back on. Easier in terms of family harmony.

In the midst of our debates that weekend and the phone calls and the lawyer's input, Pat and Arnie brought over a pie. It turned out Raphael had gone over and explained everything to them and asked if they'd hide Erin. He was worried her father would figure out where she was, maybe from talking to kids at school. I could tell Daniel was annoyed Raphael entangled Pat and Arnie, but I was glad to see Erin finally *eating* something. She was awfully thin.

Arnie asked, as we were sitting at the table discussing her home situation, he asked if her father owned guns. That raised the specter of even worse violence, and I breathed a big sigh of relief when Erin said no. And to her knowledge he didn't know how to use one—had never been in the military. That was very astute of Arnie—to ask those things.

And Pat had the presence of mind to ask Erin if she had a therapist. I'm afraid Daniel and I were a bit over our heads. She didn't have one, she said, and Arnie or Pat gave her an index card with some phone numbers. I remember Raphael leaning over to read it and asking what a crisis line was and Pat being evasive, saying something about a place to call when you needed help. I'm sure she'd been on the phone with Mia, her daughter who's a clinical psychologist.

Erin got up and went to the bathroom, and Pat quickly explained to Raphael it might be good to get Erin to talk to a professional who could evaluate her for suicidal thoughts. That hit him hard—you could read it in his face. He looked very relieved when Erin came back from the bathroom.

The upshot of our frantic, anxious weekend was an aunt coming over—I don't know if it was the father's or mother's sister. But Erin called her, and they hugged when she arrived, so we felt Erin was safe, felt safe. Her aunt brought her some of her own clothes, so she changed out of Raphael's old sweats before leaving.

The next week, Raphael reported she'd returned to school, and he saw her a few times in the cafeteria. She had a group of friends—not just other sixth graders but older kids—who were very supportive. There was an LGBT club, at least an informal one. Raphael didn't sit with them at lunch—he ate with his own friends—but said Erin was working things out at home.

You feel torn in those situations, Bernice, between wanting to help and wondering if you're intrusive and will only exacerbate tensions. I hardly knew her. And she seemed to have a good relationship with her aunt.

Eventually Raphael got around to telling us how he'd come to befriend her. After school one day he saw her sitting behind a dumpster crying and asked what was wrong. She said she was locked out of her house until her parents got home from work—she'd forgotten her key. That's why he brought her to our place the first time. Evidently something similar happened a few times after that, but in the course of their conversations, Erin finally told him it was really about being trans and her father's reaction. The day her father hit her, she didn't go to school, just hid somewhere until she saw Raphael walking home.

Weeks went by, maybe a month or more. Raphael's soccer practice started back up, and I think that was the year I was saddled with a slew of grant renewals—you know what that's like. And I was doing more outreach for Holocaust survivor talks—visiting nearby assisted-living facilities and trying to encourage people to come to the local schools. We were all busy with our own lives. To be honest, I sort of forgot about Erin, the whole incident.

One day I came home and found Raphael slumped in a chair—that corner chair. He looked so forlorn. I wondered if he'd gotten a bad grade on a test. He said Erin had hanged herself.

If he knew much more, he didn't share it. I asked about a funeral service, and he said there wasn't one. Some of her friends organized a memorial gathering at a park that weekend, and he asked if I'd drive him. Daniel was going to a two-day conference . . . up in Bellingham, I think.

I remember the sky being overcast and gray. Not raining right then, but it had been—the streets were wet, and the grass looked damp. There must have been forty, fifty people—mostly students. I wondered if the adults were teachers. Some of the younger people wore rainbow-themed clothing or carried something with a rainbow—maybe an umbrella or small banner.

Raphael joined a few friends; I just waited nearer the parking lot. The speakers were hard to hear, with the street traffic and planes passing low overhead. A young woman with a guitar sang a song I didn't recognize and then led everyone in "Amazing Grace."

Afterward, while people mingled, I waited in the car because it had begun to drizzle. Every drop on the windshield seemed like another tear wending its way down. When Raphael got in, we sat a few minutes to let the parking lot clear out. It was so grim, these young people with hurt in their faces. Two girls, obviously twins, walked past, and I did a double take—they looked so much like Erin.

From then on, he never missed a pride parade. Maybe he would've gone anyway, as a general statement of support. Did it affect him on a deeper level? I would guess so, but he never spoke about it.

CHAPTER 13

Pat

I CAN HEAR THE KETTLE EASILY from this spot. It was always my chair in the old days, when we ate in the dining room, because I can even hear the toaster pop. The wall must be paper-thin. Clara says I should knock it out, since it feels like one room anyway. But I need all the counter space I can get.

Gillian told you about Erin? Terrible tragedy, just terrible. Mia saw it coming. No, she didn't see it coming—she saw it as a *possibility*, a distinct possibility. I don't know if the child had a therapist of his, of her own. If she did, you have to wonder.

Arnie was so furious at the girl's father, he wanted to march right over and throttle him. He had a long list of things to yell.

"You don't even know where he lives," I said. "Plus, maybe he's changed and is on board with, you know . . ." Arnie wasn't hearing any of it. He was convinced the child did it to escape her father.

Raphael came to me with loads of questions about being transsexual. And sexuality in general. Why me, I have no idea. He talked with his friends at school, but I think there were things he was embarrassed to ask. I knew almost nothing until the Erin business but gave Mia the third degree, so I wasn't a *complete* ignoramus. She recited half a dozen psychobabble words. The only one I remember is "gender dysphoria." I could ask Clara the Greek roots but don't want to know.

The strangest question Raphael asked was: How do you know if you're trans? "You feel you're in the wrong body," I said, starting to wonder if he was wondering about himself.

"But you only know the body you have," he said. "Wouldn't it be like getting this idea that you should have six fingers on each hand? Or a tail? How can you feel like your own body isn't the right one?"

I repeated Mia's line that nobody knows *why* certain people feel that way, but they do. "It's a deep and sustained feeling," she said.

Was it because of gender roles, Raphael asked, but immediately shook his head, answering his own question. "It has to be a huge deal," he said, "if you're going through changing your body."

To be honest, I think it threw him for a loop. Because he was so happy with his *own* body. Don't get me wrong: he wasn't a preener—far from it. Or vain. But people who are … let's say "athletic people," people who like sports—they get *pleasure* from their body. Even two-ton me enjoys tai chi. Isn't that a kind of enjoying your body? I'll stay away from other subjects—I don't want your book to get banned.

Raphael was trying to understand how enjoying their body works with "trans" people. Renee Richards was one of the first—you're too young to remember her. Used to be a man, a professional tennis player, so she certainly enjoyed her body. And back in those days, to buck convention like that … Arnie and I had a good laugh. He said, to buck convention in those days "took balls, and I don't mean tennis balls." There's a double entendre in there, so you don't have to print it if you don't want to. I just mean that I don't think the whole gay movement had started when Renee Richards went trans.

Back to Raphael and Erin. She attached a long pink scarf to an iron hook in the garage and stood on a pile of tires.

Let's move on to high school, can we? Teenage boys—oh my: lions and tigers and bears. I can't pretend to be the total authority, but I did raise Ryan and got to know *plenty* of his friends. I didn't get to know Raphael's friends—who wants to be introduced to the old lady next door?

But *he* wanted to hang out with the old lady next door. Would even be seen walking to the store with me. I think he used it as an opportunity to ask things he didn't feel comfortable asking his father or Gillian. Not only about trans but basic birds-and-bees stuff. I've never been a Mrs. Grundy—oh, I can tell that's from before your time; mine too, but I heard it enough. It was *me* Raphael asked what girls liked. If he wanted to give someone a gift, say. I'd quiz him about her personality. Rarely were they the roses-and-chocolates sorts. I might suggest a small plant or blank journal.

Yes, the girls, the girls. Raphael was no saint and, my goodness, no celibate. Sins—the smaller sins—meant nothing to him. But what should you expect from a handsome young man? Not especially tall—five eleven-ish. Ryan is six two. But Raphael was very good-looking, a nice slender, muscular build. I don't mean skinny, like my grandson Jake—trust me, that's my daughter-in-law's genes. Raphael had real muscle—all his volunteering at the food bank, the size of the crates he hauled.

He gave me a tour of the storerooms and walk-in freezers when I brought zucchini from my garden. I watched him heave packed crates onto high shelves and haul out ones on the bottom. Another year, I would give you an armful of zucchini to bring your aunt—this long, as big as a baseball bat—but I didn't do anything to keep out the rabbits, raccoons this year—rats, for all I know. It slipped my mind, the whole vegetable garden. The flowers in the front, they got all the attention.

Raphael had the look girls went crazy for. Sal Mineo more than Farley Granger. You have no idea who I'm talking about. My first crushes as a teenager. One or two of Raphael's girls might have lasted a full month. I remember an exchange student with an Irish brogue, Eileen, in the summer. She asked what county my ancestors came from—dumbo here had mentioned the old sod—and I stood there dumb as a doorpost, since I have no idea. I didn't use my malarkey line, she seemed too sincere. And a gal who'd recently moved from Georgia, y'all, with a blond ponytail. Arnie watched from the upstairs window the two of them kicking the soccer ball around. Arnie was impressed she could dribble past Raphael—I suspect Romeo let her.

They weren't all "lookers"—that was my *grandfather's* term, which is *really* going back. You couldn't pin down Raphael's taste. Fat, thin, tall, short, gussied up like Zsa Zsa Gabor or plain-Jane like Goodall with her chimps. One had bright turquoise hair. Another wore army fatigues and combat boots.

Still, no matter how many girls wore their hearts on their sleeves, he wasn't conceited. My husband put it crudely: "He's in it for sex, not conquest." Arnie meant Raphael didn't care about bragging rights or notches in his belt.

I don't think it's fair to hold young men to the same standards as older men. If you ever have a son, you'll understand. Young men's you-know-whats take over their brains. A ten-year flu is what it is. I always told my daughters: don't get serious about a boy until he turns thirty. Like they listened to me!

They didn't just marry young but popped out the kids, one, two, three. I'm not complaining, mind you—I'm just saying that all my lecturing and Arnie giving Ryan the birds, bees, and rubbers talk, they got down to business fast. During Ryan's teenage years, I looked the other way when I picked the magazines off the floor to vacuum under the bed. What you don't know can't hurt you.

One of Raphael's soccer games Arnie and I went to we called "the libido game." Honestly, I remember it like it was yesterday. Early autumn, a lovely time of year here. Hot as blazes in the sun but heavenly in the shade. A gentle breeze, leaves starting to turn. The grass had stopped growing but still green as limes. Who could stay indoors? The air begged you outside.

At halftime, the boys came to the sidelines for snacks and juice. The amounts they could consume, and the lucky stiffs burned it all off! So they're sitting in the grass talking and laughing, and Daniel's chatting with the other dads, and all the sisters or girlfriends are sitting along the bottom rows of bleachers. Arnie and I are in our chairs under a big old oak, just delighting in the beautiful weather. It was one of those times you think *All's right with the world*. Raphael is joking with his teammates but not sitting down—he's standing a few yards away and bouncing the ball from one knee to the other. Not to show off—it was absent-minded, like he didn't even know he was doing it.

I say to Arnie, "Look at the girls." The sisters or girlfriends. Every last one of them had her eyes *glued* to Raphael. "They're in puppy love," I said.

And Arnie says to me, "Look at the moms." I did. It was the same.

It wasn't *only* his disheveled kind of handsome. It was his smiles and friendliness. Most gorgeous people think they're God's gift to the world, and if they're nice to you, there's enough patronizing laced in to make you puke, pardon my French. But Raphael wanted everybody to have as much fun as he was having. If the other team won, he had no problem congratulating them. He probably would've congratulated a rival running off with his girlfriend. Until Aleecia, I mean. We'll get to her.

No, nature didn't plant a selfish bone in his body. If people accuse me of exaggerating, all I can say is *I* never saw unkindness in him. He *disagreed* with people—he wasn't milquetoast. There were some doozies—I'll get to those too. Sparks flew. But not in middle school or high school, not that *I* saw.

What else? He worked at a bike shop, I think, in the summer and winter break. The stock room, inventory—though if they'd been smart and put him on the floor doing sales, they'd be millionaires today. They probably *are* millionaires today—management, I'm talking about, not the clerks.

I already mentioned the food bank, his volunteering? All the high school students have to do community service. His prom picture—Gillian gave me a copy—did she show you? It's in this chaotic carton—come look.

Filled to the brim with photos of the grandkids. I'm so glad they now send pictures on the computer so I don't have *stacks* of cartons. I put all the prom pictures in a manila envelope so they'd keep. Todd, and *Nick—in a tuxedo*, Mr. Torn Jeans. Kirsten—I guess she didn't want to leave much to the imagination. Yes, here's Raphael. Wasn't he a dashing young man? I thought of Vronsky in his uniform. All I remember from my own prom is how it ended, praying to the porcelain goddess. Oh, I wasn't the only one!

I guess that sums up what I remember about high school. Wait—how could I forget! His senior year he volunteered at Children's Hospital. Not a good fit, not at all. I'm not sure what his job was—bringing toys to the children's rooms or samples to the labs? When he finished his shift, he came over here to unload. And unload he did.

He was ashamed. The supervisor told the volunteers, "Don't get emotional around the kids; you have a job to do." She wasn't being coldhearted, just practical. Who wants the surgeon weeping into your open incision? Raphael understood that. But the sight of little tykes with bolts sticking out of their skulls and hooked up to IVs and losing their hair . . . it bothered him. And it bothered him how *much* it bothered him.

"I suck at sucking it up," he said. "I'm useless."

Mia and Clara, who can fight like cats, the one thing they agree on is that men are always wanting to *fix* problems—if they can't, they go bonkers. Don't ask a man to sit quietly and listen to your whining. Either take his advice or shut up.

I'm not saying I agree or disagree with them. But according to *one* of my brilliant daughters, Raphael was even worse because anything short of *curing* the children was beneath him. He didn't think that doing the routine chores he was assigned to do were worth his time—he had to be some kind of *hero*. I can hear Clara pronouncing "hero" like the first syllable went on forever.

I don't buy that. At the food bank, he was happy as a clam just being one of the group. Like I said, he hauled crates, repacked fruit, sorted through cans—none of it glamorous or heroic.

"So you're not cut out for hospitals," I told him. "Do you have to be perfect at *everything*?"

"Everything?" he says and goes into a long list of things he was no good at. None important, in my opinion. "Am I a ballerina?" I asked. "A concert pianist?"

I kept a comfortable home for my husband, Bernice, and raised three kids into responsible adulthood, and yes, I can bake a perfect pie, but those are my only claims to fame. I'm fine with that.

Still, I understood where Raphael was coming from, as a young man. Even as someone older. Feeling helpless at the hospital.

I did what I could to ease Arnie's pain, but those hospice nurses, they deserve the Nobel Prize.

CHAPTER 14

Daniel

I'M NOT SURE WHAT GILLIAN and Pat told you—you can't want to hear the same thing over and over. By the way, before I forget, I did finish reading the interview article, about *Communities under Siege*, and a point you made resonated with me: the debate among sociologists over which events should be singled out as important. Historians debate this on end. Should we focus on the large-scale, on nations engaging in exploration, war, colonialization? Economic changes like the Industrial Revolution? Apologies if we already touched on this . . . I repeat myself a lot.

Gillian can give you an earful. She feels strongly that historians should pay more attention to the day-to-day lives of ordinary people. I would probably agree with her if I didn't think the lower grades did such a poor job of teaching the basics. Students *do* need to know about the European monarchies and theories like the divine right of kings, if for no other reason than to understand the schools of thought that arose in opposition. You can't understand American history if you assume the US Constitution sprang out of thin air.

Sorry, off on a tangent again. You wanted to hear about Raphael as a teenager. You must know that interviewing a teacher is setting yourself up for long digressions.

He had his bar mitzvah, didn't seem to mind the assignments leading up to it, made friends at the synagogue, liked learning Hebrew. Gillian's pretty knowledgeable about biblical history—that was a subject they certainly enjoyed bandying about. Yes, he made friends at the synagogue, like he did at school and on the soccer team—he was never short of companions. *And* he started dating.

In high school, my God, the dating made your head spin. A different girl every other week. Nice girls, but they couldn't have had much claim on his time, considering school and soccer and tutoring and the food bank. I don't know how he found time to sleep. Understandably, bike rides and the other things he and I used to do together fell by the wayside.

He attended another high school, not the one where I teach. We agreed that was a good idea. But I'll tell you, Bernice, having a child the same age as one's students is an interesting experience. You can't help but make comparisons, wonder how certain ideas will be received.

Usually we ate dinner together but rarely at a set time—I'm afraid we were a haphazard household. Gillian might pick something up on her way home—Chinese or Thai takeout, that kind of thing—or Raphael might concoct a dish if he didn't have practice or work—he was actually quite a good cook. Didn't get that from me, I assure you. It was from Pat. He had so many talents, so many concentrated in one human being.

By the way, did Gillian mention the digging she did into *your* background? Oh, don't worry—nothing truly private, just your education, before Spelman and Chicago. It showed up on the university site that you went to parochial schools, and it prompted in her something of a counterpoint to your inquiry of what made Raphael tick: What makes *you* tick? I don't expect you to answer, nor does she—we'd have to get our own grant money for that. But she couldn't help musing on your path to the discipline you're in now. Religious education is just the kind of thing to pique her curiosity.

Okay, high school. Like the rest of us, Raphael became more complex. We had our differences—most fathers and sons do. Daughters as well, no doubt. I argued with my own father, especially about my choice of profession. He complained I could find something more remunerative than public-school teaching, and he was right. I probably could make more as a plumber.

Raphael and I argued about his decision to go to Nigeria, but that wasn't until after college. Before that, our arguments were pretty academic. Which doesn't mean we couldn't get our hackles up. Still, despite disagreements here and there, up through high school, certainly, we tended to be on the same page. Our politics and personal philosophies, our moralities, were aligned.

Naturally, we were both happy at Obama's election and for pretty much the same reasons, although we may have weighted them a little differently. For me, the principal delight was that we'd elected such a clear-thinking man. Coupled with decent values, it should go without saying. Raphael may have been more thrilled at the breaking of the color barrier, though for him, too, it was cause for celebration that our president would be someone of such impressive raw intelligence, wide-ranging knowledge, good values, and what I'd call a judicious temperament. Do you have any idea how rare that combination is in a politician, especially one seeking *national* office? I can't think of another in my lifetime.

I sound like his campaign manager, don't I? In my defense, if you've studied the Constitution's framers and their idealizing of certain virtues, some hearkening back to the Roman Republic and some to the Enlightenment, you'd realize that Obama, to a great extent, embodies them. But here I go again, praising the person and not the deeds.

Raphael and I got into more debates after he started college, but it wasn't personal. There's a pleasure in testing one's ideas against a worthy opponent—I'm sure you've experienced that. Gillian *sometimes* was able to get a word in edgewise.

I'm trying to remember the "long-term versus short-term fixes" argument. I might have the chronology wrong, because we had several arguments about that. Just in casual conversation, the kind you might have at lunch that spontaneously veers into philosophy and the question of how should we—ourselves and people in general—contribute to the greater good. This one was not just in terms of long-term/short-term but small-scale/large-scale.

You must be familiar with the old saw: you can give a man a fish, and he's fed for a day, or you can teach him how to fish and feed him for a lifetime? Raphael argued that in a crisis, there's no time to teach. World War II was one of his examples. Although Germany's poverty helped fuel Hitler's rise to power, you had to first defeat Hitler before you could institute any sort of Marshall Plan. But now I'm thinking this discussion was much later.

I guess I can finish the train of thought. Before his first trip to Nigeria, we argued about him *personally*. I said he was right—there are crises, situations where you don't have the luxury of teaching a person how to fish—but that didn't mean he was the right person to be doling out the fish, to carry on with the metaphor. Other organizations, other people, are, were, better equipped for that. Where *he* could do the most good was by making a long-term investment in teaching—getting his degree, for starters.

Give me a minute—this isn't an argument I wanted to be right about . . .

Okay. I didn't say all that because of my own partiality to teaching. It's because I'd seen him in action. When he was in high school, he tutored French and Spanish, being already pretty fluent in both. On the days I drove over to the middle school, where he was tutoring, to give him a ride home and waited in the hallway for him to finish up, I could hear what was going on in the classroom if the door was open.

He had a knack, an empathy, I envied. I'm probably more devoted to my subject than to my students. I have them for a year, and they move on. It's not like college and graduate school, where you form lasting relationships. Raphael could make a personal connection, and what that does is *motivate* students. Makes them *eager* to succeed. I tend to rely on the subject matter as the enticement.

Here's an example: He was tutoring a boy in Spanish, and I picked up from their back-and-forth that the boy hadn't bothered doing the homework. Later, in the car, Raphael explained why: kids had made fun of him because he was new to the neighborhood and his parents didn't speak Spanish, whereas they were all bilingual. Not only was the boy getting ribbed, but the other kids were misleading him on vocabulary, teaching him the words wrong. I don't know if that meant they were substituting obscenities or just teaching "large" for "small," "dry" for "wet," that kind of thing. Getting chastised by the teacher and ridiculed by his classmates, the boy had become withdrawn. And Raphael had taken the time to get to know him and learn all this.

The lesson I overheard was about colors and nouns, everyday objects. The examples in the book were words like "sky" and "water" and "flowers"—typical vocabulary. Raphael modified the examples to make them about some girl the boy knew or could imagine.

"Her eyes are green. Are they green the color of grass or green the color of old cheese?" The boy would have to answer in a full sentence. "Was her hair the color of corn or a stale french fry?" "Were her lips red like a rose or a dead bug you swatted on your arm?" You get the idea.

This sounds very silly in the telling, but the boy laughed at the examples and worked hard to come up with the right answers. Look, I'm not claiming Raphael was the first person to use pedagogical gimmicks—hardly. What impressed me was his knowing how to tailor the gimmick to the particular student. It was a gift.

And *he* knew he had it. He was teaching a Nigerian girl, Mary, English, but she wasn't a serious student like her older sister, Esther—maybe you'll want to hear about Esther later. With Mary, Raphael was using the 1884 Berlin Conference for vocabulary so he could do double-duty and help out his colleague teaching history. Mary was having a hard time keeping the different European powers and their proposed colonies straight.

It's a little astonishing to us today: a conference with the explicit goal of divvying up another continent like a birthday cake. Some of my students argue that the multinational assemblies like the WTO and G7 have just as much power over the developing world, and I try explaining that the control these organizations exert, while real, is not at all on a par with outright colonization by invading armies.

As I said, Mary was having trouble keeping the nations and colonies straight, even with mnemonic devices and other tricks of the trade. Esther accused her of being too distracted by gossip, and Raphael seized on that tidbit. He pumped Mary on her classmates and friends—what they were like. She might've said one was bossy and one two-faced and maybe some other greedy or distrustful—that kind of thing. Raphael pointed out things about Great Britain, France, Belgium, Portugal, and asked Mary if she could compare them to her friends, and she was quite happy to draw parallels. Viewing the conference participants as subject to the same insecurities and having the same kinds of goals as her friends enabled Mary to begin to understand the power jockeying that went on and learn who colonized what. Raphael sounded so excited telling us over the phone.

I certainly can relate to that—most teachers can—the excitement in that moment when you *observe* a student putting two and two together. The recognition shows in their eyes; their facial expression actually changes as they *get it*. And their pride and sense of accomplishment. They realize that learning can be thrilling, as thrilling as a ball game—and for *them*, not just for some straight-A student. I can't think of anything more satisfying for a teacher.

Go ahead and write off what I'm saying as the delusional ravings of a doting father—write what you want. But I wasn't the *only* one who saw Raphael's ability to reach people, to teach them as individuals. Which is why—never mind.

Where was I? The high school years. We stopped taking bike trips but did still go for occasional runs together. And this was nice: in the summer, at dawn on a Sunday morning, we'd drive down to the park by the lake. No one was around, not a soul. We'd run an hour on the trail, looping back to the park. It was still early, the sun barely up, and hot and sweaty, we'd yank off our shoes and race into the water. Our own biathlon.

Imagine it: the sun rising over the rolling blue-green Cascades as our backdrop. We could see north to Mount Baker and south to Rainier, two majestic, monumental snow-topped beauties. Between them, the silhouetted smaller mountains in a dozen shades of blue and green. The park was still deserted, except maybe for a dog-walker and the napping ducks on the lawn. Preternaturally quiet; you could actually hear the waves lapping softly against the stone wall near the beach. Farther out, the water looked completely calm.

Diving in was a refreshing and exhilarating sensation, the coolness washing over our overheated bodies. Coming up to the surface, we're greeted by lake, mountains, sky, sunshine. Raphael said the combination of scenery and physical sensations was nirvana. I guess it was.

CHAPTER 15

Mia Eriksen Mendes (Mia) [telephone interview]

I'M SORRY I CAN'T GIVE YOU more time—I wasn't expecting back-to-back sessions this afternoon, but I need to squeeze in a client having a bit of a crisis.

Am I the last of the Eriksen family? Clara and Ryan said they didn't feel very helpful. I doubt I'll be—I never really got to know Raphael. And I'm a clinical psychologist, so I have a higher bar than the rest of my family for forming opinions about people. Snap judgments are . . . never mind—you don't need to hear my peeves.

The longest I ever spoke to Raphael at one time was probably five minutes, and they were the kinds of conversations you have with your parents' neighbors—light, superficial. I wasn't his friend, confidante, colleague, much less his therapist.

I formed *impressions*—that's hard to avoid. As long as you understand these are not professional opinions. I'll try to stick to my own observations and not include my mother's, but I can't promise they didn't influence me. I also need to warn you that I wasn't taking notes when I interacted with him, so my memory could be faulty. I'm sure it *is* faulty.

To answer the first few questions in your email, I remember almost nothing from when he was young. Usually we only saw him when we drove up for Thanksgiving, and I was busy with my parents, sister, brother, in-laws, nieces, and nephews. Complete mayhem. He didn't stand out, not when he was younger. Except for his dark curly hair, until my own children's hair turned dark.

We did come in the summer for a week, but the kids were usually outside. The only trip that stands out is after 9/11. I wanted to see how my parents were handling it and drove up by myself a few days later.

That must have been when I first met Gillian. I don't know how long Daniel had been dating her—I do remember my mother saying they let Raphael get to know her at a comfortable pace. That could have just been my mother doing her usual pedestal thing with Daniel.

The Solomons came over briefly during my visit, and needless to say the Trade Center came up. I may have paid extra attention to Gillian because I hadn't met her before, and I did notice she talked to Raphael as an equal. It *is* appropriate to behave toward preteens as adults *if* you don't cede your authority to them—that's where the trouble starts. I was impressed, thought she handled it well. Later my mother told me Raphael wanted glasses like Gillian's. In other words, Gillian was remaining an authority figure. "Poor thing," my mother said, "his eyesight's twenty-twenty."

Dr. Williams, if I had to use a single word to describe Raphael—to give my *impression* of him—it would be "simple." I don't mean simpleminded, not at all. Let me elaborate.

A toddler can go from the heights of exhilaration to the depths of utter misery in seconds. Give him an ice cream cone, he's on cloud nine. It falls on the sidewalk, he's utterly devastated. At that age, each mood is—I like to use the term "all-embracing." There's little retention of previous moods, of memory, and very little of perspective, the long view. Say the ice cream cone was on the way to an amusement park ride. For the moment of misery, the child doesn't remember what lies ahead. And doesn't remember the past beyond the fallen cone—that moment is the center of his universe. But as he gets older, he starts to carry more emotional baggage from the past, and he anticipates the future. These cognitive abilities will moderate his reactions.

I always felt Raphael retained something of that childlike attention on the moment. It didn't rise to the level of a disorder or a pattern of behavior needing intervention—nothing like that. It wasn't on the autism spectrum. It didn't even rise to the level of an eccentricity, which you know isn't a DSM term. I'm trying to avoid jargon here.

An example: My mother was carrying a pie to the table, and she tripped. With the children running everywhere—mine and Clara's and Ryan's—the rug had gotten bunched up. Raphael was maybe twelve, thirteen at the time. She didn't fall or hurt herself, but the pie slipped out of her hands and landed on the floor. Several of us helped clean it up, and everyone said the usual: it didn't matter, there was plenty to eat. She always cooked for about ten extra people, and if there was one pie, there were seven.

So we all dug into dessert and stuffed ourselves silly. My father at one point clutched a fork and spoon in each hand and pounded lightly on the table and whined like a spoiled child, "Where's that last pie?" And everyone laughed because there was plenty of pie left.

What had to be at least *half an hour later*, we're storing leftovers, and Raphael murmurs to my mother that he hopes she's not mad at herself about the pie. *She'd* forgotten about it—*he* was the one dwelling. Still locked in that moment, the fallen ice cream cone. And it wasn't even his fault—Ryan's boys had bunched up the rug.

If you include this incident in your book, let me add, I'm not *criticizing* Raphael—I'm *describing* him. He was an unusual and brave young man, had many, many admirable qualities. Such a shame it all is. Excuse me one moment—there's a text I have to answer . . .

Now you have my full attention. What else? My mother said you heard about Erin. So sad. I was sorry I couldn't have been more helpful, but it's hard long-distance, especially when she's not your own client.

You can never know who is going to take such a drastic step, especially among teens and preteens, which makes prevention hard in the individual case. You want counseling services available, especially for at-risk children, but controlling a child's environment is close to impossible unless you lock them up. The final straw can come from family, friends, a school bully, or just an offhand comment. It's often only *after* the tragedy that people can begin to identify the lead-up. And despite what the media likes to say, it's never one thing. The blame game is *not* helpful, no, not helpful.

Which doesn't mean I excuse her father's behavior. If he had been support-ive, the odds of her taking her life would've been far less. But as I say, you can't identify the tipping point or blame anyone in particular, not even him.

What else… When Raphael was in high school, we had a *hilarious* conver-sation. *He* didn't think it was hilarious, and I acted serious, but internally—I'm borrowing my mother's language—I was busting a gut. He was such a *teenager* and missed the whole point.

It must have been after Thanksgiving dinner, people had moved into different rooms, and either I'd finished in the kitchen or gotten shooed out of it. I was walking past Raphael and Brooke—she's Clara's older—and overheard them talking about the movie *Casablanca*. Brooke said it was a beautiful love story, and Raphael disagreed, which is what grabbed my attention. How can you think *Casablanca* is *not* a beautiful love story?

He described the airport scene at the end, where Bogart says to Bergman— I'm probably getting the line wrong—something like "The problems of three little people don't matter in this world." According to Raphael, the movie's message, then, was that romantic love is unimportant, and saving the world from tyranny is all that matters. Romantic love is narcissistic, he said, not realizing that "narcissistic" has a specific meaning in psychology.

But ignoring that, I had to come to Brooke's defense. I said that the Bogart character only made the comment about personal problems not being important because he wanted to come out of his victimhood. He'd been feeling sorry for himself as a jilted lover, and then he realized the way to step out of his victimhood was to refuse to be a home-wrecker and to allow Ingrid's husband to carry on his important work with her at his side. Though it was the right thing to do, it was breaking Bogart's heart and Ingrid's too, which is why it was a love story.

I didn't linger to hear Raphael and Brooke's reactions—I doubt I was welcome. Years later, when he was older and had fallen in love, I should have asked if he'd changed his mind. But I better get ready for my one o'clock.

CHAPTER 16

Gillian

THE HIGH SCHOOL YEARS were a lot of fun: Raphael learning to think for himself, posing intriguing questions. Even the less-sophisticated ones challenged us. "Why aren't dress codes the same for men and women—why can't women go shirtless in summer? In some African societies, women do." Another was "Why is equality so important when it comes to rights like voting but not important when it comes to money?" He had that idealism young people bring to issues.

I think, though, that living with two historians frustrated him. In political discussions, we were always pointing out the historical record. For example, he thought communism in its ideal form made a lot of sense, was more egalitarian, which I guess it is. But we said that communist governments haven't shown good results. The old Soviet Union, Cuba, and China before it opened up its economic system, they were way behind capitalist societies in standards of living. Plus, communist governments have had a poor track record in terms of freedom and democracy. Raphael didn't understand why that had to be, and even if Daniel and I didn't have an answer, we're attuned to history's lessons. As we understand them.

Our answer to the women-going-shirtless point was that whatever their origins, customs endure because they give people a sense of security and tradition, which we all want. Daniel suspected it wasn't the double standard that bothered Raphael but the "visual deprivation."

Sometimes Raphael did get the better of us in an argument, and, to tell you the truth, I think it made Daniel secretly proud. It made both of them proud. Yes, Raphael's ideas, realistic or not, were interesting and provocative, and we had many dinner conversations last well into the evening. "Do you turn in a friend for breaking the law if no one was hurt?" That was one. Another was "How far back in time do you go to right a wrong?" I think it came up in the context of Native Americans—Raphael understood the impossibility of returning all the land to the tribes. Or maybe reparations. Daniel thought he should consider becoming a lawyer because he never shied away from thorny issues.

As far as his social life went, Raphael's girlfriends, the ones in high school, seemed quiet, at least around us. I'm not sure how to put this, but to me they looked *vulnerable*. Growing up with three brothers, I harbored no illusions about teenage boys' reliability. Raphael wasn't what I would call uncaring, but he was definitely care*free*. The girls gave the impression of being a bit more—I don't know—*devoted*? But they weren't around long enough to become overly entangled, emotionally, was my impression.

Yes, he seemed to take everything in stride: school, college prep, work, volunteering, chores. *My* high school years were one long stretch of anxiety. Not from anything truly earth-shattering—just the worries typical of that age. Like school work and fitting in, or at least not sticking out.

Actually, now I'm starting to remember arguments in high school that were a little . . . tense? Uncomfortable? This might be more relevant to your research than what I've said so far. I guess I shouldn't be surprised they happened when Raphael was taking American History.

One had to do with the Constitution. I should give you background. Daniel's doctoral dissertation was on the push to ratify it. Is this something you studied—the Federalist Papers and all the pamphlets, articles, speeches pro and con? Everyone's education is different, and mine's spotty for that period. I did read his dissertation when we started dating. I'm a little embarrassed to say I've forgotten many details. I hope I don't get them wrong here.

In this argument I'm remembering, Raphael took the position that somehow the Constitution wasn't much of an improvement over the Articles of Confederation. I'm smiling because, looking back, I can see he was taking direct aim at Daniel's citadel! Whether this was his history teacher's view or his classmates' or something he'd read—I don't know.

I'm sure Daniel said many things in response. The one that sticks out for me was about giving up power. The states did that, to the federal government, but what impressed Daniel most were the actions of certain of the Constitution's framers: Madison, Jefferson, Hamilton—he puts them on a pedestal. And Washington too. He says that throughout history, almost no one has given up power voluntarily. When that occurs, it astonishes us. I think of Gorbachev and de Klerk in our own time. Daniel says it's hard to appreciate how rare that is.

The way he sees it is the Framers were part of an aristocracy, although not a formal one based on heritage, like in Europe. They were highly educated at a time most people weren't, and they were politically powerful. Most were professionals or landowners and significantly more advantaged than merchants, tradespeople, the small farmer, and certainly the poor.

To Daniel, that these aristocrats advocated for a constitution that would dilute their own power was . . . I want to say "awe-inspiring." The federal government came out of the Constitutional Convention a big winner, yes, but so did the ordinary citizen, especially with the Bill of Rights. You didn't see anything like our system of government elsewhere.

Of course, "ordinary citizen" didn't include everyone—enslaved people and women were left out. Still, the Constitution was an enormous step forward in expanding democracy, given its period in history. In Daniel's mind, for the Framers to knowingly set in motion their own loss of influence and power was *principled.*

Though he doesn't believe all of them acted out of principle—many were political animals in the worst sense of the word. But that's why he has respect for those who *did* put the public interest ahead of their own. He calls the Constitution a "miracle of idealism." And esteems Washington for refusing to run for a third term, which most historians agree he would have won handily. Washington gave up personal power for the good of the country.

You and I, Bernice, and our generations may have trouble appreciating this. Our own experiences are so different. During our own lifetime, *many* nations have been democracies. The statement "all men are created equal" says nothing startling. So we are more likely to notice the shortcomings in the Constitution, like the people who were not included in "all men are created equal."

Daniel understands the shortcomings, he does.

Which *finally* brings me back to Raphael. I apologize for the long explanation. Would you like something to drink—coffee or tea? Let me get us more water. This has been a long day for you.

When you drive here, do you go through the arboretum? Oh good. I love the winding road, the canopy of arching branches. Every season has its loveliness. The deciduous in winter make me think of Minnesota, a lattice of brown and pale-gray branches against a snowy background . . . though we don't get much snow here. There's a special beauty in winter's bleakness, don't you think?

Have you stopped at the Japanese Garden? Beautiful, especially in spring.

Raphael was quite angry learning about the Japanese American citizens rounded up during the war, the detention camps. He asked how we could be so indifferent after seeing what happened in Europe. But people here didn't know all that was going on in the concentration camps.

This conversation must have been when Raphael was in middle school, yes, because I remember his mouth open in shock when Daniel explained that we went to war with Germany over the invasion of Poland, not over what was being done to Jewish people. Raphael'd had the impression the major reason was to liberate the camps.

I was surprised, Raphael not knowing that. For the families of the Holocaust survivors I work with, it's a special source of pain they pass on to their children: no one wanted to help Jews. It's something of a credo: Jews can rely only on themselves; they can never trust another nation to protect them. Daniel, I guess, stressed other things when he spoke about the war.

And when Raphael wanted to know why no one cared about the camps, Daniel gave what he calls his "I'll scratch your back if you'll scratch mine" speech. It's a staple of his history class. If Nation A wants its borders respected and no interference in its internal policies, it agrees not to interfere with Nation B's borders and internal policies.

It's not how we would like governments to behave, is it? Human rights should matter. I don't think any of that sat well with Raphael. But I think not long after, he began his bar mitzvah preparation, and that may have helped.

I'm sorry my memories are so scattershot.

And Raphael and Daniel's relationship wasn't all debates about politics and history. Daniel went to Raphael's soccer games. They went for runs and bike rides. Sometimes they'd watch a Mariners game on TV. And old comedies, like Charlie Chaplin and Harold Lloyd.

My father, who's authoritarian in many ways, *loves* the Keystone Kops. He took all of us into the city to see a Buster Keaton series at the university, and the antics and chase scenes made us laugh ourselves silly. I don't remember other times we laughed together like that, as a family.

I think this might be a good place to stop. I have more time Thursday.

CHAPTER 17

[Emails between Raphael and Tony P., eleventh grade]

[October 17, 2006, email from Raphael to Tony]

Take the offer, youll make a great goalie, like Joel said youre an octopus. Half glad Max got injured and you subbed. He should be stopper instead which Greg doesn't want anyway. His mothers a lunatic, you can hear her 60 yards down field embarrasses the hell out of him and fucks up his concentration. Someone needs to buy her a dildo if his dad isnt doing the trick.

[October 19, 2006, email from Tony to Raphael]

Ask Lisa out. Worst she can do is say no.

[October 19, 2006, email from Raphael to Tony]

Got B- on math test and half hoping they kick me back to regular. My dad hed get over it eventually. Keeps saying its not about the grade but applying myself. Only half true. He doesnt care about the grade but he really means dont get somebody pregnant. How likely when all I hear is not yet, not ready, etc etc etc. Been carrying the same pack of condoms for six fucking months. Six NON fucking months! Whats their shelf life anyway?

[October 20, 2006, email from Tony to Raphael]

Save your precious rubbers Debbie would go down hell shes done keith and his brothers even the stinker. And trence got chrissie to. your too picky is your problem.

We creamed you in debate. Not every time something goes wrong is on purpose. People fuck up. And the reason brownie got the job was politics pure and simple, didn't know fema from his ass. Money means power.

[October 20, 2006, email from Raphael to Tony]

Im not picky, just dont want to catch what Trence got. Besides I actually have to like her or else porn works better.

Indifference is racism. We laid it all out, sorry if too many steps for you. Seriously you should read Communist Manifesto, its potent. Made me understand why was big in Europe back then, saying abolish child labor and give free public education.

Going to Bens tomorrow? I hate drinking right before a game, hope someone brings weed.

[October 20, 2006, email from Tony to Raphael]

Yeah probably go to Bens. You bring weed for a change. Or is mooching just part of your "each according to his needs."

[October 20, 2006, email from Raphael to Tony]

I always pay for weed but cant keep it here. If we got busted my dad might lose his job. I guess we could all move in with you.

[Excerpts from Raphael's handwritten journal, eleventh through twelfth grade]
2/18/07

Lost game against Orcas big time 4-1. Their midfield had distance and aim, made it easy on their forwards. Told Tony he kept us from losing 10-1. I fucked up one kick, could have gotten it, totally my fault, assist was perfect. Only consolation is we would've lost anyway. Went for chili after at P and As and got into argument whether Obama will screw up the field and it's Hillary's turn. That was Clara's position P said. P herself liked Obama because "he's not some old fart dying to start a war." A said you have to project power to prevent war. I said it can start an arms race. Dad and G just listened, but P and A really went at it, bet they had a hot make up session later. Not a bad trade off.

7/8/07

Watched Live Earth. Great music and speeches, especially Gore. He should've been president. I was supposed to help my dad finish chopping up old prunings but used concert as excuse to go to Lori's, figuring we could manage some stuff while her parents weren't in the room but her stupid little brother there the whole time. At least he didn't sit on the couch but even when he left it was only for a pit stop or grab something to eat. Rachel Weisz might be my first older woman crush. Trence swears by them.

8/19/07

Dad and Arnie got into it again about the war. Arnie admits it was stupid and the whole wmd was fraud but said countries have to be held accountable when they violate UN resolutions, otherwise resolutions are just a piece of paper. Dad says resolutions are just a piece of paper. Or the penalties are worse than the violation. For the heck of it I took Arnie's side and then we went down the appeasement rabbit hole again. Everything in foreign policy is speculative. No one knows shit. Dad says that's why people become historians. After the dust settles they argue the significance of facts but not the facts themselves. If all you want to do is win an argument, sure, but if you want to change things?

11/09/07

So fucking sick of these essays. What makes you a good fit for our school? What can you bring to the student body? How have you been disadvantaged? Max says I should do a dead mother essay, he's doing a dead father one, claims the applications people always go for a sob story if you can't do race, homeless, immigrant. Losing a parent isn't the same as disadvantaged, I told him, just means you've been hurt. Gillian's proofreading everything anyway, she'd know it was total bs, she keeps me honest.

12/11/07

Promised Madeline I'd go to eco rally Saturday, she said if we get a big turnout and make the news the government will take notice. If she asked a billion other guys and she doesn't mean it as a date I'll split and tell her later got lost in the crowd. Saturday's my only day for homework because Sunday's game is up in Shoreline and we'll probably end up going for pizza after.

12/13/07

Ms. Walters gave me a hard time for my intonation in She walks in beauty. I sounded too "swooning". It's a fucking love poem! She liked the repeat better, when I did it like a sports announcer.

Ms. Damont exact opposite, made us read news reports like they were serenades. She butchered Il a mit le café dans la tasse. But Adele read my facial expression and smiled. Chère Adele, Adele of the coal dark eyes. She walks in beauty. I chose Rappelle-toi Barbara for my final and she told me she almost cried. I didn't tell her I cried practicing.

12/18/07

Actually glad we got knocked out at semis, more time to study for finals and crank out last essays for damn applications, don't want them hanging over my head in NY. With Grandma and Grandpa in assisted living Dad and I are free to hit wherever we want in the evening. He's cool about the stuff I suggest but won't let me use fake ID to get into clubs. Grandma and Grandpa are generous springing for tickets for shows, I always give Grandma the program after. She writes the date in the corner. Grandpa complains it'll be a pain when they croak to get rid of them and the apartment doesn't have much room but you can tell he's joking.

CHAPTER 18

Daniel

LOOK AT THE RAIN COMING DOWN—you got inside in the nick of time. Wow, it's really pouring. The sky got dark just like that. A good thing I cleaned the gutters, it's really gushing, even under the larch. Already a puddle in Pat's driveway. Susan said when she was a little girl and it rained hard enough to splatter, like it's doing now, she believed the drops must be fairies dancing. They do seem to defy gravity when they hit the pavement and shoot back up.

I better put on another light. Too bad we can't go for a walk, but we have the house to ourselves—Gillian's at the library. She might come back soon or might get bit by one of her sleuthing bugs and rummage through volumes better left dusty. Your generation might be surprised at the number of resources you can't get through Google, things you need to see in print. One of Raphael's girlfriends never heard of microfiche.

I don't remember where we left off. I do remember rereading some articles after we were done last time. A journalist used the phrase "extreme altruism" in reference to Raphael and Joseph and the others, which annoyed me. Was it extreme or just risky? How would you define "extreme"? He—the journalist—didn't discuss what else would fall within his definition. The volunteer ambulance drivers of World War I? I only mention that in particular because the other day when I was waiting for Gillian at the bookstore—yes, some of us still go to bookstores and browse among the hardcovers and paperbacks—I perused the blurb of a Hemingway biography. I hadn't known that about him—the ambulance driving—thought he was just a safari hunter. I never read any of his books, unless maybe I was required to in high school.

Anyway, public service was certainly a value we inculcated in Raphael, Gillian as much as I. Not necessarily by instruction, by lecturing him, but in the way most of us learn values: through observing what those around us praise and do. He saw that helping others was something we value.

I don't want to come across as saintly—Mother Teresas we're not, or anyone of that caliber. And I certainly don't believe public service should be on a person's to-do list continuously. Some years you're taken up with getting a degree, or raising children, or work. In fact, you could say that finding the time to engage in public service is a *luxury* of sorts. Working, running a household, tending to children or sick relatives, fixing a leaky roof—a million demands keep the species busy. Some people are stretched to the limit just getting food on the table and the rent paid.

But Raphael had the basics—food, security, close bonds with friends and family—so it was natural he'd look for fulfillment in a moral sphere. Maslow's hierarchy, which I'm sure you know about.

Ryan, Pat's son, we got into a friendly tiff about this. On their back patio, I remember. Ryan was grilling up hamburgers—could've been the Fourth of July. Kids running in the yard. I seem to recall his wife, Beth, setting out scented candles that are supposed to keep the yellowjackets away and Pat telling her they never do.

The argument Ryan made was that public service isn't altruistic but a form of self-aggrandizement, of ego massaging. Fine—I'll concede the point, for what it's worth. I went into public-school teaching instead of private because I want to reach children who might otherwise fall through the cracks, scholastically. If that's a salve to my own ego and not from a generous impulse, so be it. Contributing to the welfare of people other than kith and kin, to the wider community or society, is something that gives me pleasure. No, "pleasure" isn't the right word. "Satisfaction"? Yes, that's a better word.

I'm hardly alone—giving to the wider community is important to many people. People do it through their churches, houses of worship. Arnie used to make recordings for the blind, way back when, before audiobooks became a hot commodity. Mystery novels, for some reason. Totally voluntary—he did it for no pay. While working full-time and raising three kids.

And like I said, some do charity through the church, and not just by fattening the coffers. Raphael said many local ones routinely send volunteers to distribute the food at the food bank. Despite what I said before about your being an academic, I bet you researched and wrote *Communities under Siege* in part to do good, by prodding consciences.

Yes, altruism takes many different forms. I couldn't even *begin* to itemize all the kindnesses Pat has showered on us. Even before Susan died. Whether we ultimately do it for ourselves or others is just splitting hairs.

Somehow I got sidetracked. Didn't you want to know about Raphael going away to college?

Nowadays, it takes more effort to submit an application than write a dissertation. He handled most of it himself, occasionally coming to me or Gillian for advice. I don't think he had his hopes pinned on any particular place, which made it not so bad when he got some rejections. He did get to apply online, and that's a huge labor savings. I still send letters of recommendation for my students through the US mail. Thankfully, those are one-page affairs. The unofficial word from college admissions people is they don't read past the third sentence.

Raphael was stunned by the full-tuition scholarship—we all were. It wasn't like he was valedictorian. I suppose it might've been that he was fluent in three or four languages. *Something* obviously impressed them. I said if he had his heart set on another school which wasn't offering a scholarship, we could make it work; I'd been saving for that eventuality, and we would take out a loan. He made an offhand comment that the only school he might have preferred had rejected him, so it was a nonissue. I have no idea which it was, as they all seemed pretty comparable. Maybe a girl he had a crush on was going where he got rejected.

I recall Gillian thinking I'd have warm-and-fuzzy feelings that he was going to my home state. But people in western and eastern Pennsylvania don't necessarily carry a sense of commonality. Who knows why. Perhaps because we root for different football and baseball teams. Those are our deeper, our tribal loyalties.

In any case, the three of us pored over the brochure that came in the mail and did our own googling—I was curious if I recognized any names in the history department. Raphael seemed excited and expressed no regrets at leaving Seattle. Gillian once told me she had had mixed feelings about going out of state to college—she got scholarship aid as well. On the one hand, she was eager to get out from under her father's rigid thumb. Yet was sorry to be separated from her friends.

I commuted to college, and many of my classmates were in the same boat, the same financial straits. It wasn't until after my senior year that the family business really took off, and going away could've been an option. I'm sure I would have leapt at it.

By the way, did you have any luck tracking down Aleecia? The snippet in Raphael's alumni magazine said she was in the DC area, I think the University of Maryland. Her parents are in Silver Spring—Gillian might be able to dig up an address. I'm not sure how she spells her name now. Originally it was *A-L-I-C-I-A,* but somewhere along the line she changed it to *A-L-E-E-C-I-A,* which was the spelling I last saw. I should get in touch with her—she may be hurting too.

That's Gillian's car, the headlights. I think this would be a good place to stop anyway. I appreciate your willingness to space this out. I feel guilty I can't be more concise and help you finish, but my stamina isn't what it used to be. When I was your age. Maybe she'll be up for a session, but I don't want to speak for her.

CHAPTER 19

Gillian

DO YOU WANT ME TO START WHERE HE LEFT OFF? Hold on a moment. Daniel, if you're going out for milk, pick up some romaine and a cucumber, will you? And the cheese you said you liked . . . I'll be right back, Bernice.

Sorry. Okay, you asked about leadership positions in high school, and I can't think of any. He was never the captain of the soccer team or president or treasurer of a student club. I'm not sure he *joined* any clubs, wouldn't have had time. A friend of his was a National Merit finalist and ended up going to Oxford—I seem to recall Raphael and others taking him out to celebrate. England seemed so much further away than Pennsylvania, which seemed *plenty* far away. Daniel liked that Raphael was just a few hours from Susan's parents. During winter break, Daniel would fly to New York, and the four of them would spend a week together.

Plus, Daniel got a vicarious kick out of Raphael being so close to Philadelphia. When he teases me about being a Deist, I tell him he's a

Republic-ist. I know I've already gone into his admiration for the Framers and their sacrificing power for principle. Which doesn't mean he sees them as perfect—not at all. But since you wanted to proceed chronologically, I'll put off talking about some of the later arguments, the ones I still remember.

I guess I'm a little defensive on his behalf. I have heroes and heroines too. I put on a pedestal the resisters in the concentration camps and the women imprisoned in Nazi munitions factories who sabotaged their own work, knowing they'd get caught and hanged with piano wire. It's a slow and painful death. Like a crucifixion.

In high school I had a photo of Dietrich Bonhoeffer on my wall. As a young man with wire-rimmed glasses and a kind smile. Only thirty-nine when they killed him—think how much he could have accomplished. Martin Luther King too, thirty-nine.

Why do we latch on to one hero or another? Maybe I was influenced by the martyr-and-saint stories in childhood. All I'm certain of is, I wouldn't have had the courage of those who resisted the Nazis. I told Raphael that once, and he said the people who know they're going to be martyred are a separate category from the rest of us. He and I, we'd be like the common criminal who doesn't think he'll get caught.

When he returned after their year in Nigeria—the 2013 year, before the kidnappings—he boasted how he and Joseph and their cohorts Ismail and Werner "stayed under the radar." Meaning Boko Haram never found out about them. Joseph quoted a line Daniel later told me was famous: "He who fights and runs away, may live to fight another day." Raphael and Joseph felt like they'd—how did Daniel phrase it—"pulled a Houdini."

What else, what other philosophical phases did he go through? Nothing you haven't heard before, maybe experienced yourself. He had T-shirts with slogans like "Power Corrupts," things like that. Aleecia was a big fan of getting unusual sayings printed on T-shirts. I think she gave him some of the ones he wore.

I'm smiling because every time the three of us—Daniel, Raphael, and I—had a discussion and I felt a consensus had been reached, even on a small point, someone always threw in a wrinkle. Like with corruption. Who could say it was good? But Daniel did. He said only the corrupt Nazis were willing to sell Hitler out, to give away his plans to Allied spies in exchange for money. True believers would never do that.

I guess those are all the discussions that come to mind from Raphael's high school years, things you might see as stepping stones to his decision to go to Nigeria. His college years we only had glimpses of his trains of thought, what he chose to tell us. His visits home on break always seemed so brief.

Daniel accompanied him east the week before freshman orientation, first to New York to see Susan's parents, and then they took a few days touring Philadelphia, the historic sites like Independence Hall, the Liberty Bell, places Daniel had seen before but Raphael hadn't. I teased Daniel by calling it a pilgrimage.

They also enjoyed modern Philadelphia—cheesesteak, wandering along the river, different neighborhoods. Raphael didn't know how often he'd get away from campus but was happy to look around, and I think he did end up going to the city a number of times. And New York. I remember him asking Daniel not to mention certain trips to his grandparents because he wouldn't have time to stop in and see them. He did visit every December and occasionally during the school year.

Daniel and I are clumsy texters, so usually we communicated with him by email or phone. He'd tell us a little about his classes, extracurricular lectures, a few things he did for fun, but nothing stands out. He didn't mention parties. We assumed he was living a typical student life.

Oh, he did go to hear live music. I don't remember what kind . . . jazz? In high school, he dated a girl who was in a jazz ensemble, and I think that shaped his tastes. Daniel said Raphael had tried violin lessons in third grade but only for a few "excruciating" months. He also took lessons on Pat's piano, but that didn't stick either. We sang together, just for fun—folk music usually— while cooking or doing dishes. He was curious about Gregorian chants and madrigals, but I had the impression most of the time he listened to the music popular among his generation: hip-hop, indie this and that. I don't know the different genres.

Back on the subject of classes: my inbox was filled with interesting questions when he took a course on the biblical eras and the dawn of Christianity and then the Reformation. Did mass conversions occur because conquering groups forced their own religions on the conquered, he wondered, or did the priests decide that they could maintain their upper-tier status by falling in with the new rulers? Was Christianity the first grassroots movement in the area, at least among religious conversions? Why were there so many doctrinal splits after Luther? Did they spring from different theologies, or did the different theologies spring from ethnic antagonisms? Or did a charismatic leader appear?

As if I had the answers! Not that he was coming to me for answers—he knew these subjects had been debated for centuries, and that will continue. Perhaps in your own field? Is this where ethnography overlaps history? I'm sorry; we're doing an interview.

Yes, revisiting periods I studied as an undergraduate and graduate student was fun for me. Raphael didn't write as often to Daniel, but that seemed part of growing up: separating from your parents. As I said, I never really filled the parent role.

Certainly Daniel could relate to the distancing, having gone through something similar himself. His parents never got used to his refusal to join the family business. They and an uncle ran a few small jewelry stores during Daniel's childhood, and it was a bit touch and go, until they eventually managed to secure a spot in a mall, and then another, and then the business really took off. It might still be doing well—Daniel hasn't been in contact with his cousins in Pittsburgh. But in high school he helped his parents and uncle with bookkeeping, which made him realize he had no interest in a career in business. He stuck to his goal of teaching US history in the public schools. They couldn't understand that. Not the teaching part, but that he'd struggle to support a family.

I don't want to portray them as crassly materialistic. They grew up in poverty, so being blasé about money—which is how they viewed public-school teaching, especially in a city, on a city payroll—to them that was being blasé about providing for one's wife and children.

Susan getting a job only confirmed for his father that Daniel wasn't capable of supporting a wife. He couldn't understand a woman *wanting* to work. Both of Daniel's sisters married successful businessmen and are happy as homemakers. Mr. Solomon went to live with the one in Boca Raton, not the Dallas. Mrs. Solomon had passed away by then. He had a heart attack when Susan was eleven weeks pregnant with Raphael, before they'd told anyone, so he never knew.

I apologize for this strange digression. I was circling around to making a point: Raphael didn't pick a college in Pennsylvania to get away from Daniel. The deciding factor was being offered a very generous scholarship. The two of them kept the rapport they'd always had, which wouldn't have happened if . . . what am I trying to say? . . . if Raphael had wanted to be *free* of Daniel. And it would've been evident in his tone of voice, his manner—Raphael was terrible at masking emotions. I'm the opposite. A minister's daughter: repress, repress, repress. Yes, he always seemed happy to see us, goad Daniel into a run or bike ride. Not that Daniel needed goading.

All right, there *was* a small bump in the road. Freshman year, Daniel complained about not getting an answer to an email, and Raphael said, "Dad, I'm eighteen, swamped with school, making friends, and doing stuff. I don't have time to write every day."

After we got off the phone, Daniel said he'd emailed him exactly twice in the previous weeks and about forms Daniel was required to fill out so Raphael could leave student housing, which Raphael had *asked him* to fill out. I think what happened is Susan's parents kept emailing Raphael and expected long emails back. And may have been pressing him to visit, so Raphael lumped all the pressures together and took it out on Daniel. In any case, Daniel backed off.

I wonder if being an only child made it a little harder for Raphael to break away, feel more guilt. You said you have sisters and brothers, and I have three brothers. Don't you think it would be a heavier burden to be the *sole* focus, to feel as if your parents hang on your every move?

I won't repeat my metaphor of the tree with the single branch. But it's funny how when we're little, we *eat up* our parents' attention. I remember my youngest brother pulling pranks just to be noticed—at nine or ten, I don't know how, he got hold of an inflated balloon in the shape of a naked woman and tied it to my father's car antenna. Parked right in the driveway.

When we become teenagers, we want to forge our own paths and not feel held back by our parents' expectations. As I've mentioned, I'm not on the path my parents wished for me. I always avoided explaining my plans—I don't like confrontation, even with my mother, who's a quiet person too. It's never been about rebellion, just veering in a different direction. I try not to feel like a disappointment.

I wonder if that's why I visit only once a year. In late spring, when my brothers usually can bring their children because school's out. My parents travel to see them too, but my siblings are nearby: two in Minnesota and one in La Crosse. They've never been out here; my parents have never met Daniel, never met Raphael. I think they view my relationship with Daniel as just "dating," not a committed or serious relationship. We've been living together almost fifteen years! Yet after Chibok and everything, they call more often, which is nice. I used to be the one to call.

Daniel doesn't like confrontation either, but he isn't intimidated by it. The reason he avoids jumping into large discussions, he says, is because his mindset is, and these are his words, "mired back in the Enlightenment." What he means is, well, the big philosophical ideas at the time were about championing reason and science over church teachings, which at least up until the Renaissance dominated Europe. I know that seems old-fashioned—he wouldn't claim church teachings dominate society today . . . How can I explain? So many Enlightenment ideas are now part of our culture and not controversial. The belief in reason and science, the belief in social good, the idea—the *expec-tation*—that governments will be responsive to the needs of the people . . .

Daniel thinks people lose sight of these overarching principles when they get too wrapped up in one or another side of a debate and forget the importance of the debate itself.

I already mentioned this tension between the idealists and the realists, didn't I? The Framers? Some thought people were inherently good, with the capacity and willingness to cooperate as citizens, and others thought we're inherently selfish and need laws to rein in our worser impulses? Raphael felt he was among the realists, while Daniel was clearly drawn to the idealists.

Personally, I think both camps oversimplify human nature. We're generous *and* selfish, have good impulses *and* bad. In the monotheistic religions, at least, that's the burden of the human soul: using our free will to follow the good.

My father's catechism must have shaped me; I'm never surprised by evil. It can *shock* me—the form it takes, the scope, the context. Who isn't bewildered at how people raised in the culture producing Bach and Beethoven constructed and operated gas chambers? Still, even if evil is innate, it can be overcome. Isn't that one of the goals, not just of religion but also of education, to nurture the aspects of humanity that civilize us?

Hearing myself talk, I guess I have to admit I haven't closed the door on a spiritual dimension. Daniel has: he's an atheist, not an agnostic. But I think in his own way, he worships. His altar is Reason. Science. Progress. I'm not *against* those things. I just wonder if they have their limits.

Where was I going with this? Oh, I think all these different notions of mine and Daniel's made their way into Raphael's thinking, which is what you're trying to pin down. I wish I could give a timeline. Yet who arrives at personal morality without twists and turns and blind alleys along the way?

Let me try to refocus on college.

With Susan's parents' help and the full scholarship, Raphael didn't have to get a part-time job, which was nice. And we splurged every year for an extra trip home at Thanksgiving. He liked seeing Pat and her family. Her grandchildren were like cousins to him.

His actual cousins—Daniel's sisters' children—Raphael only saw them five or six times his entire life. They were eight or nine years older. He went to their bar and bat mitzvahs, and they came out for his. And he and Daniel went to two weddings, both in Dallas, I think. I didn't go. Not because Daniel didn't want me to but because of a schedule conflict. He's not close to either sister and said he'd actually welcome the "dilution" my company would offer—having other people around. I guess they have few interests in common.

Yes, early on we fell into a pattern of dealing with our families separately. It began with Susan's parents—I sensed they weren't thrilled when he first mentioned we were dating. Both eventually developed health problems that made travel hard, and Mrs. Feingold lost most of her hearing. The bar mitzvah took a special effort: Daniel put them up in a nearby motel that had ground-floor units and special fixtures in the bathrooms. I sent you the dates of their deaths? Within eight weeks of each other, the summer of Raphael's graduation. I'm glad Daniel was able to drive them to commencement. She was already doing poorly but appreciated it. And then he had a stroke.

It's funny, looking back. They may have been a little frosty toward me because they were afraid Daniel and I would marry, and my father was a little frosty because we *weren't* married. One set trying to push us apart, and another wanting us closer together.

Do you think it's odd we never discussed marriage? We're private people, Daniel and I, and marriage—you know, as an ethnographer—is a very public act. The wedding, but also announcing a personal bond to the outside world. A couple can express love, devotion, and loyalty to one another privately; they don't need a ceremony. There are benefits to the community acknowledging the bond, especially once children are involved, but all I'm saying is the bond itself doesn't need to be formalized and announced in order to be strong and permanent.

I suppose my reluctance to get married is because a lot of attention makes me shy. Daniel—both of us lean toward the path of least resistance in many things. Which could be why we've always dealt with our families separately.

Raphael would have married. He didn't mind the public eye. Unless his fiancée would have felt differently—he was very much a feminist in terms of relationship equality. I suppose in that way Daniel's and my relationship provided a role model for him.

As I said, he always came home for Thanksgiving and a week at Christmas, the winter holidays, after a visit to Susan's parents. We don't celebrate anything, really. During Advent, I put a few white candles on the mantel and over there on the hutch, where the tiny flames look so pretty reflecting in the cabinet panes. Even the dark wood emits a shine just from the candlelight. And I put green candles on the top of that little bookcase, and here on the sideboard I place my small manger scene, a gift from my parents when I was seven. I loved the tiny wood barn and cloth figures. The wise men are in white cloaks and carry their gifts, and Mary is seated on a bale of hay, holding the infant Jesus swathed in a dark-red blanket. Joseph leans on his staff. Three little white sheep. I think the set was made in Hungary. I so much wanted to play with them year-round, but my mother insisted we store them away with the angel ornament and star that always went on the top of the tree.

I like candles. I light the menorah from Susan's parents, a small bronze candelabra. And place pine branches in vases around the rooms, for the scent. There's something very soothing about traditions, don't you think?

CHAPTER 20

*[Emails from Raphael to Lillian and
Samuel Feingold, freshman year]*

[October 20, 2008]

Dear Grandma and Grandpa,

Thank you for the gift, which I already put toward what I said, a decent
bike. Classes are okay but have a ton of reading. Freshman year they
make you take required courses in different departments like humanities, physical sciences, social sciences. Depending on your major and
if you took any AP courses in high school, you might have to also take
math or computer science or languages. Luckily my AP exam scores
got me out of math and the foreign language requirement, but I'm
taking Russian anyway. And by pleading with my advisor on bended
knee I finagled my way into a philosophy seminar next semester. In

social sciences, we're reading Aristotle's Politics. The syllabus includes Machiavelli, so maybe I'll learn some sneaky tricks.

Sorry to have to tell you, Grandpa, what you already know, that Phillies fans hate the Mets more than anyone, even teams that trounce them worse. So I'm going to spend 4 years in the closet hiding my Mets allegiance. At least it's safe for me to root openly for the Mariners. Nobody hates them. Some think they're Triple-A.

I went to hear Senator Obama's speech in Philly and thought of what you said, Grandma, when Adlai Stevenson was running, that he was too smart for the job. (Yes, Grandpa, I know you think she meant "too smart to get the job," but she told me she meant it as she said it.) Obama is definitely smart and his heart's in the right place.

I'll let you know if I can make it up to NYC the weekend of November 8.

Love, Raphael

[November 18, 2008]

Dear Grandma and Grandpa,

Sorry I wasn't able to visit. Like I said on the phone, the faculty seem to think a 3 day weekend is their chance to kick back and relax, not ours, and pile on assignments to keep us too busy to bother them. I've got 2 papers due next Wednesday.

The photo was taken in front of my dorm. Sorry it's so blurry, but you can see the ivy, just like colleges are supposed to have.

Did you watch Obama's election night speech? We were in the dorm lounge, everybody cheering.

Since I'll be going home for Thanksgiving and exams will be waiting for me when I get back here, I can't visit until winter break, but Dad and I will be up in December for sure.

Love, Raphael

[December 4, 2008]

Dear Grandma and Grandpa,

The picture arrived in perfect shape. That must've been incredible, just falling out of the book. I'm glad you decided to cheat, and it is cheating to look up crossword clues, according to my dad that is. I think it's weird to leave blanks instead.

She was cute even with her mouth full of braces. I definitely inherited her hair and eye color, but guess I inherited my dad's jaw and teeth, either that or he was too cheap to take me to the orthodontist. Only kidding. The lady next door once said I had a movie star smile and her husband said "Yeah, the guy who plays Frankenstein."

See you in a few weeks!

Love, Raphael

CHAPTER 21

Pat

IS THE TEA HOT ENOUGH? I'm glad I remembered to pick up a lemon. Living alone, you forget to stock the basics for guests—I don't have many. The book club when it's my turn, and friends, people who raise my spirits. The one who crochets and the one who dishes out sarcasm. She's the icing on the cake.

Widowhood with your children living in other states isn't so horrible as people make out. I do miss Arnie every darn day, but when your husband is eaten up by cancer and the radiation and chemo, and *he* wants to die, it's different. You grieve during the illness.

Mia says I miss caring for him, it gave me a sense of purpose. Even emptying the "puke pail"—that's what he called it—didn't bother me. Watching him retch was harder. Raphael said taking away purpose is a form of murder. I'm trying to remember what brought that up. He was in college. Something to do with prisons? This noggin's useless.

He was good with words, not just languages. I once told him to be a writer, and he said someday he'd write about the places he traveled and people he met. I meant a novelist, and he said he didn't have the imagination, was too stuck in the "outside world." I scolded him for sounding so wistful. We are who we are. But he was right: the outside world had a hold on his attention. *I* don't have the imagination either, which is why I make pottery. "Let your fingers do the walking." You're too young to remember that.

Yes, we "outside world" types, I don't know if it's good or bad. I'm a newshound, or used to be.

So where were we? College.

I didn't get emails the way Daniel and Gillian did—why would I? Besides, my computer always crashes. Many of my friends *live* on the darn thing. Except for checking email every few days, I don't use the monster at all. Arnie was so annoyed with me. "You act like it's a puzzle. It's just a typewriter."

My children are worse, if I don't answer the same day. What's wrong with the telephone? I like to hear a voice. One book-club lady brags her ninety-eight-year-old mother is in five chat rooms and three thises-and-thats and Facebook and who knows what else and sends photographs of her grandchildren to all her friends. Who wants to see photographs of other people's grandchildren? I *spare* my friends that!

Ryan tried to show me how to make the print larger, but I always mess it up. You can tell I don't have a lot of patience. I relied on Arnie—I could whine just a little, and he'd fix it. You should congratulate me on printing out your emails. I can do some things if it's worth it. But just to gab with family and friends?

No, I didn't exchange much more than a birthday email with Raphael when he was in college. He did send me one when Obama got elected. It may surprise you to know how many of us wept—White people—wept tears of joy. That our country could, you know, "overcome." And such a smart young man, to boot. Arnie voted for McCain—to him, Obama was a pip-squeak with no business running against a war hero. But he came to admire him, especially after they got bin Laden. He wasn't in hospice yet, and the way he was glued to the TV—you know, Obama's announcement—honestly, I thought it accomplished more than all the chemo.

But back then, when he was elected, Raphael waited a few days before sending Arnie an email. It said he hoped Arnie wasn't too disappointed and that he, Raphael, wished McCain had gotten the Republican nomination in 2000. Arnie recognized the thought behind the message. And my husband was no fan of the Bush crowd, let me tell you—"self-important prigs," he called them. That's with a *G*, though if your machine thinks I said something else, that's even better.

Anyhoo, Raphael's going away to college meant we only saw him at Thanksgiving and the second week of winter break and, if we were lucky, spring break and a little in the summer—the beginning and end. That's how it was with my kids too.

The first Thanksgiving, he brought a Jewish girl from New York. Oh, quite the guest! Angry at the whole world. Americans were "consumption wolves." She growled the way she said it.

Mind you: I agree we go overboard on possessions. And I was the commune hippie, or beatnik, depending on where you draw the line, and anti-materialism was practically our motto. But I didn't bite people's heads off.

It was the Black Friday advertising that set her going. For me, Thanksgiving should be fun, sharing, family, and friends. A hearty debate—that's okay. If she'd been Native American, I might've been sympathetic—they're entitled to complain about the holiday. What I *didn't* want was a lovely meal with our families—mine and Daniel's, and with all the grandchildren—I didn't want it to be a time of anger. I wanted joy and laughter.

Fortunately, Raphael was able to thaw her—he just had a way. An art *I've* never had. I'm too blunt, as you've noticed.

Rachel—that was her name—Miss Angry—she was reading aloud all the new gadgets advertised in the newspaper. This was before we sat down to eat. The grandkids' ears perk up, and they're praying Mommy and Daddy are listening and will get them fancy-schmancy contraptions for Christmas. And Ryan *was* listening, it turned out, because he left the house at five a.m. to buy an electronic something or other.

My, that Rachel—did you ever know somebody who was *determined* to be miserable? Didn't want to be talked out of it? I'm off subject again.

I think the next summer Raphael came for just a few weeks—someone in Philadelphia was teaching an African language he wanted to learn. Maybe I've mixed up the years. That could've been the summer he dated the little Chinese gal—from China, not Chinese American. She gave me tai chi pointers. Arnie said Raphael was treating the female sex like an international buffet. If that's how you want to look at it.

Our granddaughter Amy's from China. Ryan and Beth adopted her when she was a tiny thing. Beth couldn't have more kids and really wanted a girl. And lucked out: Amy *loves* girly stuff—jewelry and dainty tops and frilly this and that. Usually if you plan for that, you get a daughter who lives in sweats and hiking boots.

His sophomore year, it must have been, when Raphael brought Aleecia. His first *real* girlfriend, and I'll get to why I know that. From the start we saw a difference. He wasn't just his usual affectionate self, which is not to say he was big on—what was Jody's phrase? PDAs. Public displays of affection? I can't keep up with the abbreviations. TMI—I used to get that one *all* the time.

Focus, Pat!

Raphael's tone of voice, facial expressions, that's where you saw it. Did Daniel or Gillian tell you about Aleecia? Okay, I'll be the first.

She was African American, and I hope I'm not offending you when I say she was far more American than African. Raised in Silver Spring, Maryland, her father an ophthalmologist or something like that and mother a librarian. Aleecia took *French* lessons, *music* lessons, *tennis* lessons—she had more lessons than Mia's and Clara's kids combined. But she bragged to Raphael how connected she was to her African roots! Connected, my foot—I'm more connected to Saint Patrick.

"She's young, in college," Arnie used to scold me. "Trying out new ideas. Remember Mia was vegan for a year." I did remember—now *that* made for a fun Thanksgiving.

Aleecia's quite stunning. Right away I caught Clara sizing her up, noticing the clothes, hair. "College hip," I would've said. Didn't seem starstruck with Raphael, very self-confident. And yet here she was, the only Black person in a group of how many were we—over twenty, if you count the grandkids. Nobody wants to feel *that* outnumbered—whether it's race, sex, or what have you.

And the rest of us had known each other forever—she was the newcomer. A college sophomore—how old—eighteen? Nineteen? Yet had the poise of—I was going to say someone in their fifties or sixties, but I still don't have that kind of poise. Maybe it was an act, but it convinced me.

"The Thanksgiving with Aleecia," Arnie called it. There was another, just not as exciting. You know: I think I'll save that story for next time. I've gotten too distracted, thinking about John McCain and what he went through, a prisoner of war. Arnie was awfully affected by it. Who wasn't?

CHAPTER 22

Ryan

MOM GOT ON MY CASE for not telling you about the Thanksgiving arguments, says you want perspectives on Raphael's political views. To be honest, I don't remember much. One argument had to do with slavery, believe it or not. Don't worry: nobody was saying slavery was good. We're not that—what's the word she used, Raphael's girlfriend? "Reactionary." We were all "reactionary." Whatever the hell that means. She was from some New York Jewish commune or something. My wife's Jewish, but she's LA Jewish, which is a whole different ball game.

Raphael and his dad were always pretty normal. You could tell they were Jewish, but they acted like anybody else. Anyway, one of the big arguments, his father was saying something about Thomas Jefferson, something positive, and this girl gets all bent out of shape because Jefferson owned slaves. And Daniel is saying, yes, it was wrong and a fault, but people are a product of their times.

Clara says something about Shakespeare and *The Merchant of Venice*, and for once I knew as much as she did, or almost, because we had to read it out loud freshman year, the Intro Hume course, and I got stuck reading Antonio. If you don't know the plot, Shylock, the Jew, is a total bastard and wants to take a chunk of flesh out of Antonio's body, literally carve into him. And from spite, not because it gets him anything. Just because Antonio couldn't pay back a loan, which wasn't his fault to begin with.

Clara was saying Shakespeare didn't have to make Shylock a Jew or so evil or something, and I'm wondering what Daniel's thinking, is he going to chime in and agree, but he says something like "Shakespeare was a product of his time too." Like: no big deal. And Clara probably used the word "nuanced," Shylock wasn't nuanced—it's got to be her favorite word.

Raphael's girlfriend—like I said, she was Jewish—she wasn't buying it. Human tornado. Cute, though. Not someone you'd ever want to marry—make your life a living hell. But definitely cute.

The girl he brought home after that was cute too. And argued, just not like we were all Satan. Which is funny, because she was Black, so had way more reason to be mad at Jefferson. I'm pretty sure we also talked about him that year—yeah, we did, because she got pissed at me. It's kind of weird, Jefferson coming up at Thanksgiving dinner all the time, given the Pilgrims came like a hundred years before he was even born. He had nothing at all to do with the holiday. I don't think it *was* a holiday when he was around. Probably invented by the turkey-farm people.

Not sure I met any other girlfriends. My mom did; she can give you the rundown. Maybe they all liked to argue. Opposites attract? Raphael was pretty laid-back. I'm not saying he didn't take a stand on things—he wasn't a wimp. No, he wasn't a wimp—look what he did. Not that it was the smartest idea. And it was kind of selfish. I'm talking about towards his family and friends. His father can't be doing too great. Even my mother's a basket case—no matter what she tells you.

Don't get me wrong: those crazy Islamic butchers need to be wiped off the face of the earth. But leave it to the professionals. And like my wife always says: we have plenty of children *here* who could use help. Parents stoned out of their minds, on heroin, meth. You don't have to go packing off to Africa if you want to help the poor.

Look, the last thing I want is to criticize him. He paid the price for his mistakes or whatever. Which is why I'm not crazy about talking about him. I'm supposed to be honest, but you're going to print this stuff, and I don't want to be disrespectful of the dead, and I sure as hell don't want to be rubbing salt in the wounds. The world's messed up, and he tried to make it better and got caught in the wrong place at the wrong time.

Maybe you can chuck what I just said and keep this: He was always in a good mood. Even as a kid showing up and not sure if he'd get included in the games my kids and Mia's and Clara's were playing. I'm no good at analyzing people—talk to Mia if you want that. I'll stick with this: His glass was half full. Maybe three-quarters. I'm that way myself—drives my wife nuts—but Raphael was even more. It's a shame his life was so short, but he probably got more out of it than most people. Let's leave it at that.

CHAPTER 23

Gillian

PAT REFERS TO THE THANKSGIVING dinner when Raphael brought Aleecia home as some kind of fiasco, but I don't think anyone viewed it that way. Yes, there was arguing, spirited at times, but we respected each other's opinions.

Her Thanksgiving dinners were a lot of fun. Chaotic, but that was part of the merriment. Always some child underfoot or small disaster, a spilled drink or bloody nose, that wasn't really a disaster. Unless it rained, Raphael and the other children would kick the soccer ball around in the backyard while the adults were finishing the preparations.

My mother would've gotten upset that they came in to dinner a little muddy, but Pat didn't care, and her daughters were too busy cooking to pay attention. I do remember Pat taking one child into the upstairs bathroom to give him a quick scrubbing and clean clothes. Ten minutes later she was working on the stuffing like nothing had happened. That's not me! And if I tried to help, she shooed me away. As I say, her daughters are very competent in the kitchen. I *did* help once the meal started. I would go back and forth to the kitchen if anyone needed something—I didn't want Pat or her daughters getting up.

I thought everyone talking at once was fun, not at *all* like when I was growing up, when you waited for my father to ask a question or introduce a topic. Even serving the food had lightheartedness, kind of an assembly line, different people dishing out the turkey and stuffing and mashed potatoes and yams and salads and passing plates around. Arnie always did the carving in the kitchen, and Pat would come in with separate platters of dark meat and white, and a vegetarian stuffing for whoever was vegetarian—it seemed to vary among the grandchildren, especially during their teen years—and one of them has a gluten allergy, so he had a separate stuffing altogether.

After Pat and Arnie sat, Ryan proposed a toast, usually to his parents and then to everyone. In my family we always said grace. I suppose each custom has its pluses and minuses. In their own way, both are an acknowledgment of good fortune: breaking bread with family and friends.

When the politics started, I sometimes felt a little bad for him, for Ryan. He seemed more conservative. Arnie might have been too, but he never joined in and seemed to have a twinkle in his eye, as if they were all angels-on-the-head-of-a-pin arguments. But Ryan did get involved, and I used to think he would have felt more at home at *my* parents'. Very traditional in their views.

The one with Aleecia . . . I do remember they arrived a few days before the holiday, and that first evening, she and Daniel were already debating. I'm not sure how it started, but Aleecia said that the Constitution was an immoral compromise that sold out Black people. And Daniel, well, I'm afraid he fell into his "professorial" tone.

I don't remember exactly what he said, but I've heard him often enough to give you an approximation. It was, basically, "The Framers did *not* sell out the enslaved people, because there was never any question—*any* question—about whether slavery would continue in the Southern states. It *would* continue. It would continue regardless of what the Northern states wanted. If the Northerners had insisted on abolishing slavery, the Southern states would have walked out of the Constitutional Convention. There would have been no changes to the Articles of Confederation—which permitted slavery."

I believe Raphael made the point that the states wouldn't necessarily have reverted to the Articles and might've worked out a different compromise. Yes, and Daniel stood up and paced around the living room, which was unlike him. He didn't yell—I've never heard him yell except over a stubbed toe. And I wouldn't say he raised his voice, just that he became . . . emphatic.

He said that the only other possible outcome if the North had insisted on putting abolition into the Constitution—instead of falling back on the Articles—was a split into two separate nations. The South would have kept slavery, and the North would have gone alone on the road to abolition. And if we had split into two nations, he asked, I think rhetorically, would slavery *ever* have been abolished in the South?

No one answered, so Daniel himself said, "Not for many decades or even centuries." The North didn't have the capacity to wage another war, after all the revolution debts. Plus, the citizenry wouldn't be up for a second war, particularly against the South, which had fought alongside them against the British. As for later generations: How likely was it that the Northern nation would invade a sovereign Southern nation to put an end to an *internal* Southern policy? "The odds were zero," Daniel said, "if you look at history."

I think it was a bitter pill for Raphael and Aleecia to swallow. I hoped their frustration wouldn't linger, and Raphael's didn't seem to. I couldn't tell about Aleecia.

By the way, I'm glad you were able to track her down. She wasn't upset we suggested contacting her parents in Silver Spring? Perhaps her memory of these arguments is better than mine—I only remember the topics and certain moments. I do remember clearly that she and Raphael were very keen on each other and very—I want to say "embroiled" in the controversial issues of the day. That's an exciting time, the college years. My campus had all sorts of demonstrations, protests, boycotts. I never took part, not because I disagreed with the causes but I had too much schoolwork. I never knew how my classmates found the time.

And they went out in all sorts of weather. *You* know what the cold and winds are like in the Midwest. My housemates used to bring the protesters hot cocoa when they marched back and forth holding up signs. And here I was feeling sorry for myself just rushing to the library. I can still remember a gust shaking a large branch, snow falling down under my scarf and trickling down my neck. The backpack bouncing against my spine made it even worse, but I couldn't stop and take off my scarf and coat in the middle of the quads, in the freezing cold. *Brrr.*

But those can be exciting years, college, especially for students who throw themselves into causes. The energy and passion they bring to what they believe in. It has never surprised me that revolutions around the world—Europe, South America, the Middle East—often started among students, among the young.

CHAPTER 24

Aleecia Lynn James (Aleecia)

SURE YOU DON'T WANT THE FUTON? A cushion for your back? You see I don't have space for much furniture. What studios go for—I don't know if Chicago's as bad, but I could have a townhouse some places for what I'm paying here.

When I first heard what happened, last year, I couldn't process it, couldn't think about it for too long. I knew he'd gone to West Africa but thought with an NGO or Peace Corps. And not *Boko Haram* territory. That was serious shit. In a way, it's still not registering.

And I couldn't help thinking—and this wasn't nice—why would a White boy think he could get away with being there, doing what he was doing? I *know* why—they think they're immortal. Raphael could be like that. Still, he didn't always think he was the smartest in the room, like some I've dated. I've dated plenty of White boys—maybe you have too—and I'm done.

I guess I cut him some slack because he was Jewish, and there was the Holocaust, and they've experienced some serious discrimination and shit throughout history, even if now they have it okay. Plus, a lot of them showed up for civil rights, even got killed for it.

In a weird way, Raphael was—I can't believe I'm saying this word—at the same time he thought he could get away with anything, he was *humble*. Which maybe is why we lasted almost two years. And why none of this makes sense.

We hadn't been in touch, or I would've talked him out of it, going to that part of Nigeria. I'm not saying he couldn't be stubborn. We had some blowups, for sure. His dad didn't like me, and Raphael couldn't see it was racism—kept saying it was that I didn't like *him*. I'm not saying I did—his dad was just another White liberal—but I wasn't living with his dad, so what did it matter?

My parents liked *him*, Raphael. Still, they thought sooner or later he'd dump me. They were shocked when it was the other way around. Then they were: "But if he truly loves you." No more of the "He'll never completely understand you" shit my sister used to get. Joanne ended up marrying a Trinidadian. An aunt on my father's side is afraid their kids will be too dark. My parents aren't that way, thank God. But you know how it is. Hypocrisy has no color.

Damn, this isn't fun. You know I googled you? Because my first reaction to your email was: Why write about *him* and not the schoolgirls? Who needs another book on a privileged White male? But you did write about the girls and their families. And I read the article where you were interviewed. So, okay, I wouldn't get tied in a knot that you were writing about a White guy, especially him. Can you hand me those tissues? He *was* one of the good ones. We even talked—

You know, I need to take a short break, hit the restroom. My mother's amazed I can live in a place with such a tiny kitchen. Like I have a choice?

Okay, how did we meet. Second semester freshman year.

By the way, I would've gone to Howard, but my parents are in Silver Spring, and that was too close, back then. Being older now, I'm okay with them nearby. They know not to get in my business. Besides, I'd had two boyfriends at Howard, one my junior year and one my senior. The first didn't know I was still in high school, though I was old enough he couldn't get hit with statutory. I spent a bunch of time hanging around the Yard, going through the experience.

You must've had something like that at Spelman—stepping into what feels like paradise for the very first time and also feeling like you're returning home? I'm not knocking it, believe me. I wouldn't be who I am today without the Yard. Still, by the time I was applying to colleges, people were starting to piss me off, assuming I'd go to an HBC. I did apply to some. Maybe I was feeling a little rebellious.

And started enjoying how much it pissed Carl off when I got accepted, because it ranked higher than Cornell in some departments, where he went. He's my older brother. Thinks he's so great because he works on Wall Street *and*, according to *him*, knows where to hear the best hip-hop, blues, jazz. I told him he just goes to those places for street cred—can't admit he's *totally* preppy. "I'm forced to act preppy," he complains, but he's been like that his whole life.

Anyway, my reasons for picking the college sound kind of immature and probably were. But I went there and met Raphael.

By accident, really. He was waiting for the bus and saw me running as it pulled up, so he stood with one foot on the first step till I got there. Those drivers don't give a damn—even if you're only three feet away, they close the door. You know.

I wanted to thank him, but he'd gone to the back. He got off at the same stop, by the campus, so then I was able to, and we walked to my dorm.

I'd just been to a book talk about Prévert—Jacques Prévert, the French poet? I was still pretty hyped, probably talked a mile a minute, especially because Raphael knew his poetry! We decided to meet later that week so I could loan him a collection, and we ended up sitting on a bench talking for hours, *literally*. About—I can't remember specifically—but things like the morality of art for art's sake. That was definitely one of our early discussions. Baudelaire was big on *internal* growth, becoming a saint within yourself—it was all an individual thing. I was already starting to reject that. Raphael and I kept agreeing with each other, it was uncanny. We believed art and scholarship should contribute to social progress. He wanted to switch majors from poly sci because they were reading Aristotle and old Romans, and the world was so different then. And that was how *I* was feeling—my French Lit assignments seemed irrelevant to the twenty-first century.

You have to understand, we were eighteen. The change in perspective from eighteen to twenty-four is kind of like the difference between being eight and fourteen. You're two different people.

I wasn't thinking serious dating at the time. I'd broken up with a boyfriend a few months before and just wanted my space. I figured Raphael would be a friend, platonically. I felt such a strong *mental* connection. But then the physical spark, you know, ignited. Wasn't expecting it, sure wasn't looking for it, just snuck up on me. He had this smile . . .

Second semester, I was still in the dorms, and he was supposed to be too, but there'd been a mix-up, somebody's room got assigned to a transfer student, and he was able to be the one to move. He knew some guys renting a house, which turned out really lucky for us. They gave him the whole top floor—kind of an attic but with wide windows, three side-by-side, overlooking a quiet street and cherry trees. You could look out the window and see like an arbor of pink blossoms down below, and the scent came inside—you smelled cherry blossoms waking up. Talk about aphrodisiacs!

That first spring we'd stay in bed for *hours*. I might read him Prévert or Romantics like Lamartine, and he'd read really old stuff, like Villon. *"Mais priez Dieu que tous nous veuille absoudre."* Damn, he could recite.

I was stuck taking courses in the classical period, Corneille and Racine—not my thing. Did you know that even though Lamartine was a Christian, he super admired Muhammed? For spreading a *spiritual* empire. Not at all the same as colonialism. And his spirituality wasn't caught up in mysticism; it dealt with the real world. I'm not religious—different strokes—but I can't stand people who use religion as a druggy experience. My sister lives in Southern California and meets a lot of White women "finding their essence." Just do the damn drugs and don't pretend it's religious.

Feel free to take off your shoes. Raphael used to tease me this was the "clutching-sheaves pose," like it was yoga. I had this dark-yellow bathrobe, kind of a mustard color, and when I sat with my legs up and arms around my knees, it reminded him of someone harvesting wheat. Sorry if I sound flip. I need to skate on the surface some, if you know what I mean.

He knew so many languages: French, German, Spanish, Hebrew, was taking Russian. Hadn't tried African languages then. Nobody taught those—we were lucky to have an African *history* course. A single course for all of Africa! You know I mean sub-Saharan. Egypt gets its own *department*, some schools.

When I complained about that once, his father brushed it off, saying they had only one required history course when he was in college, and it was Western European history. Which didn't include the Balkan countries or Poland, Estonia, et cetera. Raphael pointed out it was really just history of the *colonial powers*, but his father still didn't get it. Went off on some long thing about history departments not getting enough funding from their institutions, so the European history professors also had it rough. Kind of a White-lives-matter-too argument. I sort of blew up at him a couple of times, his dad. It's nothing I'm proud of.

Nobody else in my family has a "short fuse," my brother David calls it. Once I told a date's parents—he'd gone to the bathroom—we were in a *really* nice restaurant—this was in high school—I said loud so a bunch of tables could hear, "You're racist pigs," and just stood up and walked out. They'd been going on about how great *Gone with the Wind* was. I never heard from him again, LOL.

Okay, the Africa thing. One reason Raphael wanted to study African languages was because the histories coming out of Africa were "stamped with a colonial perspective"—that was his phrase. Histories are written in English, French, whatever, and from *sources* in those languages, like diaries and newspapers. So the colonial perspective infiltrates the mindset of the writers just from the language. I had a T-shirt printed, a yellow one with black letters, saying, "Colonialism infects the mindset of historians." I don't know what happened to it . . . probably got lost in a move. I had lots of T-shirts with shit on them. I took it as gospel that you should never ignore racism or colonialism or shut up about them. Part of me still believes that, and part of me thinks you have to pick your battles, the time and place. But at eighteen, nineteen . . . Sometimes it's hard to look back at yourself.

Oh, I knew Raphael's idea wasn't original—the idea that words are loaded. But I liked that he knew a lot about African issues and wanted to study their languages.

And was so earnest. Other guys always did this jaded, cynical act. It became a joke between us: the importance of being earnest. Which is why we went to see the play, not knowing it was just a drawing-room comedy. Kind of silly but not terrible. And two of the actors were Black.

I wonder if he would've stayed earnest or if it was just a younger thing, like perspective. I wonder about age and how it changes us, don't you? My sister just turned thirty-two—we have an eight-year gap—and she whines her ovaries are drying up. Our mother was *forty-one* when she had David. Joanne's husband wants to wait. She's a licensed physical therapist and co-owns her business with plenty to keep her busy—like I said, she lives in LA—yet she's obsessed with making babies. I don't think I'll ever be like that.

Sorry, back to our relationship.

Usually, when Raphael and I finally did get up in the morning, if it was still morning, we'd go to our favorite coffee shop, a little hole-in-the-wall. The owner was Moroccan and made the *best* coffee. Most of our classes were afternoon, and we studied till nine or ten at night and would meet somewhere for pizza or sushi or whatever. On the weekends, if we wanted to have fun, we might go to a bar with live music or dancing. He wasn't a great dancer but knew not to move too much, so I didn't get embarrassed. I saw him do this line dance at a wedding once, it was just men—an orthodox Jewish thing, not gay—and he was really sexy—they kind of shimmy with their arms up and chests out. Better than this Chippendale clip I once saw. By the way, I cut the wedding ceremony, the orthodox thing, and he was cool with that. They made the women sit separate. He also was cool about my skipping out in New York when he went to see his grandparents. I guess we weren't ready to deal with families. I had Carl take me to lunch at this swanky place near Wall Street.

What else did we do? Sometimes went to a talk by a visiting scholar, if it had to do with political stuff. We were trying to figure out how to contribute to positive change. Is it better to volunteer at the local shelter or work on *systemic* poverty? Do Black communities need jobs more than decent schools? Which should come first, institutional changes or White people's attitudes? I know it sounds random, but we were just freshmen or sophomores. Carl would say "sophomoric."

Then Raphael got interested in international issues. He had this idea he took from NIMBY but flipped it. I don't mean flipped it to "yes in my backyard"; he wanted people to think of "backyard" differently. We should see it as *large*. Say a whole town—we should feel an ownership that grand. If that's how people felt, they might be okay with putting a prison, say, somewhere that made sense for everybody, because it was *all* their neighborhood.

We do that when the country gets attacked, like Pearl Harbor or 9/11. Nobody says "Who cares—that was off in Hawaii" or "That's an East Coast problem." It's *our* country. So why can't you stretch people's minds past the boundaries they usually see? Like national borders? It *is* all our backyard. Climate-change scientists keep trying to get that through people's skulls.

We might've been a little naïve, but we never believed you needed to change *everybody's* attitude. "There are always going to be Nazis," Raphael used to say, "and let them be absurd; just keep them away from the levers of power." And there will always be racists. Obviously here they have all the levers of power, but that can change. *Some* White people are starting to get it. Anyway, I guess Raphael had me optimistic for a while that people could expand their idea of what they're part of.

He had an okay sense of humor, could make me laugh. Not by acting clownish. And never made jokes *at* people—I don't like that either. Has anyone shown you pictures? Sorry, I don't have any here—stored a lot at my parents'. Wait, I have one, with my younger brother—it's here on the shelf. Raphael was teaching him how to dribble a soccer ball around a cone. It was hopeless—David's a total klutz. Plays three instruments—piano, sax, and oboe—but a *total* klutz with his feet.

Isn't—wasn't Raphael cute? His hair all messed in the wind—it was December. That's David. He was the only one who thought we should keep dating. Like I asked their opinion?

But you know what? All those things: his politics, sense of humor, how cute he was, the smile—now I think that wasn't what made me fall for him. It was the poetry, how he recited it. I told him if he'd lived in the Middle Ages, he could've been a troubadour.

Okay, the Shakespeares weren't that big a deal. "Shall I compare thee to a summer's day?" Et cetera. But Langston's, and Prévert, and especially Maya. Lots of couples have a song—we had "our poem." He taped it to the corner of the closet-door mirror. "Where We Belong, A Duet."

In crowded places
I searched the faces
Hoping to find
Someone to care.

Other guys just *bought* me things. Sure, I liked the jewelry, clothes, but that was what they thought they were *supposed* to do. So did I—I admit it. But haven't you ever felt gifts were bribes? Or else guilt trips, a way of saying *Now you should sleep with me*? I know what you're thinking: some of the brothers say they have to prove themselves, show they can take care of a woman; I get it—I'm not stupid. Okay, I might've been hanging around the wrong kind of guys, might've needed to prove to myself guys *would* give me those things. All I'm saying is: you can understand why poetry and the sweet way Raphael recited it made me fall and fall hard. And he didn't have a lot of money—spending money. I might've been past that anyway.

Sure you don't want a soda? Want more water?

I should tell you about this specific incident. We hadn't been dating long, and it must have been the first really beautiful spring day. I mean *everybody* cut class. You didn't even need a sweater; folks were roller-blading, tossing the Frisbee, jogging, walking their dogs—anything outdoors. We found a lawn full of buttercups—thousands, for sure—but ended up in a spot we nicknamed the "tree convention." A bunch of trees in kind of a circle around a large lawn. In the summer, folks set out blankets for picnics.

We lay on our backs right on the grass and looked at the sky and talked and talked. Pretended like we'd decided to get married, which we hadn't—it was a game. Where we'd live, what jobs we'd have, if we'd have kids. He wanted four—I didn't want any. I felt like bringing children into the world wasn't fair, with global warming and all.

"You know how much time I'd be pregnant for four kids?" I asked him. "The equivalent of three years!"

"The first few months don't count," he said.

"If I have morning sickness they do!"

"I'll make myself throw up to keep you company."

"How's that going to help?" I tried to sound angry, but he just made me laugh.

Honestly, I remember like it was yesterday: lying in the sunshine, flowers all perfume-y, the breeze tickling your arms. You didn't want to *do* anything. That's what hit me: I'd never before luxuriated in doing *nothing*. In high school, at football games or the beach, the weather was just background, like scenery in a play. When we were little and visited my great-aunts in their little Podunk town in North Carolina—this was before cell phones, and they didn't even have a TV—we'd get bored and ask what there was to do, and they'd say, "What's wrong with just sitting on the porch?" My brothers and sister and I thought they were loony. But on the grass with Raphael that beautiful spring day, I understood.

The point of the story, though, is what happened *after*. Walking back to his house, we passed two White guys, *big* guys. Dressed kind of redneck. Loud enough so we could hear—it was pretty obvious—one said, "Bet that brown sugar is sweet, yum yum." I stiffened and stopped holding hands. Raphael grabbed my hand back and kept walking. I looked to see if he was afraid, but he smiled the way he always did. And kept the same pace.

Back at his place, I didn't bring it up—I wasn't as clear in my thinking as I got to be. Some little voice inside was saying I'd brought it on myself, dating a White. How this country messes with our minds!

We smoked a joint and then talked. He wasn't angry at them, which at first hurt my feelings. "They're assholes," he said, "and who wants to waste time on them. I don't know how many years I'll have on this planet. Imagine on your deathbed looking at a list of all the minutes you'd wasted arguing with assholes. Wouldn't you wish you'd put the time to better use? Like making love?"

And he leaned over, and one thing led to another. I guess I pretended, because my mind was churning about his privilege. Later I said I was still bothered by those guys, and the only reason he could shrug off racist shit was it didn't happen to him every day.

He got quiet, which got me worrying I'd been the capital-*B* bitch. Society's mind games again. Then he started some story about his neighbor's cat. I'm thinking: *Your neighbor's cat*? Like: *this* is how you respond? I swear, I almost got dressed and walked out on him. But he tells this story.

He was in the neighbor's rec room playing chess or something with one of the neighbor's grandkids—a whole bunch were visiting and hanging out. The cat was sleeping in a chair off in a corner. Every few minutes, a kid would notice the cat and rush over to pet it. So it kept getting woken up. When one of the littlest of the bunch joined them, he got all excited seeing the cat, but the second he touched her, she hissed, jumped up, and ran away.

Raphael's done with the story, and it's not registering—I must've still been high. He says, *"Tu es comme le chat."* He was saying that I was like the cat. He meant: I get lulled, but it's a false sense of security because I keep getting jerked out of it, again and again and again and again. I have no place to hide, no place to escape "the continuing disturbance of racism."

It impressed me—I have to admit. He described it in a way I'd never heard before, and I've talked about it my *whole life*. And so has everybody I know or read—from Du Bois to Maya, we've all said the same thing different ways. So it wasn't like he was the first to figure it out. But the image blew me away, even without his having lived it. Like with the colonial history bit. I don't know why, but I've always been wowed by people who know how to use words and images. In awe, really.

And he wasn't trivializing, either—wasn't saying racism is no more than waking a cat. He was saying—and this is very French—that we each have a deep reservoir our souls need to visit to be replenished and restored, an emotional grotto as important as sleep. You can call it spiritual or religion or what people get from meditation or yoga or going out in nature, even music—I'm not trying to put a spin on it. All I'm saying is that we do need replenishment in a kind of mental grotto, and White society doesn't let us dwell there, not for long.

Look, I'm not claiming he was brilliant, and he definitely wasn't perfect. And sometimes his White guy invulnerability—nothing rattled his ego, not badly—that sometimes got to me. But it was also a goal to strive for, how *I* wanted to be, to become. To not care about the thousand little cuts. I'm not sure a Black person in this country can ever achieve that, but can't we get closer?

You sure you're not thirsty? Let me get more water . . .

In retrospect, I'd have to say that first year was pretty smooth. We both grew, as people. I had a lot to learn about my own prejudices, against Black people as much as White. I know I taught *him* a lot. This was before Ferguson and even Trayvon, when most White people were *completely* clueless. And Raphael was seeing firsthand, because there were other incidents like the one in the park, not as blatant but not subtle either.

Wow, it's almost five. I can meet tomorrow, like I said—I have a few hours between classes. Maybe we can find an empty room in one of the buildings or the library.

I owe you a big thank-you, you know, because before you contacted me, a lot of the good memories had disappeared. All that stayed were the things that got on my nerves. My other exes, it's the same—I only remember the bad.

Chapter 25

*[Emails from Raphael to various recipients,
freshman and sophomore years]*

[February 27, 2009, email to Samuel and Lillian]

Dear Grandma and Grandpa,

Thanks for the gourmet cookies. I made the mistake of offering a few
to my housemates and then had to fight them off. I especially liked
the almonds.

I've been drowning in schoolwork. Classes are still pretty interesting.
We're past the Greek and Roman philosophers and reading Thomas
Aquinas and some very strange medieval dudes. Half the time it seems
like instead of following a logic to see where it leads, they've already

picked the end point and concoct strange twists and turns to get you there. I guess it was safer than being burned at the stake for heresy.

Speaking of burning, my lab partner almost blew up the place last week. Luckily the TA saw what was about to happen and turned off the Bunsen burner in the nick of time. By the way, he's Israeli, so I'm getting Hebrew practice (it was getting rusty). He loaned me a book about irrigation projects in the desert written for teenagers, which is my reading level at this point.

I'll let you know when I can get up to NYC again.

Love, Raphael

[March 14, 2009, email to Gillian]

You're right, the flagellant movement really took off during the Black Death, which we got to in this week's readings. And like you said, once they started doing mass marches, the authorities got worried (civil and ecclesiastical both). The part that puzzles me is that some places the flagellants were brutally murdered and other places they were the ones brutally murdering supposed heretics. And reading about all their craziness and the hair shirts guys and parading in chains, I wonder how they found time for such a waste of time. Wouldn't a trade or hunting or fishing or growing food give greater rewards? A friend of mine keeps pointing out that people don't know to think about options, that all of us just see the options those around us see. I guess that's true. Maybe I'd be happier crabbing in Bali or herding reindeer in Finland, but no one I know does those things. Next week we'll be reading about the popes, I think in prep for hitting the Reformation.

[March 23, 2009, email to Daniel]

Any chance I can soak you for an extra hundred bucks? A friend wants to go to NYC for a weekend, and with the train and other stuff it won't be cheap. She'll pay her own way and we'll stay at her brother's and he's got museum passes and we'll also hit the cloisters, so you can see the trip has educational value :) I'll stop by (solo) to see Grandma and Grandpa for an hour or two, but don't tell them I'll be staying in the city overnight.

[April 27, 2009, email to Daniel and Gillian]

Dad, you won't believe it, but prof made a big deal about both your nemeses, Beard and Becker. It was a lecture, so I didn't have a chance to show off my deep knowledge (ha) of their theories. His pov is that Beard nailed it on the framers fighting for their own economic self-interests and Becker got it right about not letting go of the divine, just clothing it in "inalienable" and "natural" "rights." I'm pretty cynical about this stuff. (Gillian, back me up on this, I was the one telling Arnie that Cheney was gung ho about Iraq only because of financial ties to Halliburton). Still it drives me crazy when Beard, Marx, the prof are dismissive of everybody else's purported motives but take their own at face value. Of course they have no self-interest and only seek the truth! LMFAO. Academics' self-interest is ego tripping by coming up with something different and iconoclast. I guess if you crave praise for being brilliant and want to get famous off some book, you need to knock a few statues off pedestals. I'd write my own book about it if I had nothing better to do.

Luckily I do. Already told you about the French philosophers seminar they're letting me use for some humanities credits and my statistics course, it's really good, I actually understand it. No comment on freshman sci.

[May 27, 2009, email to Daniel and Gillian]

Went to a wedding that was borderline orthodox and don't think I discredited the family honor with too many blunders. And didn't try integrating the women into the men's section or stage a sit-in protest. I thought about it! Anyway, the food was great. Maybe I'll surprise Pat with a Jewish cuisine cookbook if I can find a decent one.

[October 28, 2009, email to Daniel and Gillian]

Got in a long bike ride with one of my housemates. There are some decent hills here but he thinks the Appalachians are real mountains.

Btw tell Pat I'll probably bring a guest again at Thanksgiving. Guess I may as well tell you too. Her name's Aleecia, and she's auditing the French philosophers seminar.

CHAPTER 26

Aleecia

I PICKED THIS LIBRARY BECAUSE I knew the guard would let you in without a student ID—I helped his cousin write his résumé. No one's ever in this corner, and it's my favorite study table. I don't know what all these books are—look pretty old. If someone does show up and complains we're talking, I know another table we can try.

You really had me going down memory lane yesterday. I'll try to be more informative, though I'm still not sure exactly what you want to hear. My parents totally freaked I'm telling you *anything*, but they'll live—I'm not giving away family secrets. Should I just continue saying what I remember about him?

I guess we settled in as a couple pretty quick. Both serious about school. I hadn't yet decided on graduate school and French literature and actually switched to anthro and took all sorts of courses—your field, right? I told you about Raphael's "colonial perspective" idea but didn't realize how *much* bias infects history and also sociology, anthro, and psych.

After the general requirements and this one French poetry, all I took was courses like poly sci and anthro. Not sure why I held on to the poetry—should've been a sign that it spoke to something in me. French as a language, as a culture, has *soul.* So many moved to France: Baldwin, Wright—wait, did you see the Baker photo? That's from *Zouzou.* Raphael gave it to me.

Even the older French poets—the Middle Ages and before—plumb deeper than Keats, Shelley, Byron. Wordsworth writes a lot about nature, how we should experience more delight in it, but he never actually *brings* you there.

Carl makes fun of me for liking French impressionist painters—they're too popular for him—but they do bring you *into* nature, so you can breathe it, smell it, inhabit it, not feel you're looking through a window. There are exceptions, sure, some poets writing in English—especially poets of color. But the French language, it's like comparing a high-end Canon and taking a picture with your phone.

Okay, maybe that's unfair, because people grow up with different sounds. German people probably think German poetry can be caressing, and I know I can't appreciate the sounds that might be beautiful to Cantonese or Mandarin speakers. But I grew up with English, so I think I'm in a position to criticize English-speaking poets.

Plus, the White poets are into individualism. The famous—Emerson, Whitman, Dickinson, Frost—are into relationships with nature that are *solitary,* not *communal.* And they treat nature like a vacation or pastime, not something deep. Allen Ginsberg, he might be one of the exceptions, and there's probably others. But French poetry, even when it seems on the surface about an individual, it's reaching wider or plumbing deeper. If I'm feeling really shitty, that's what I read.

You're probably wondering why didn't I study Black poets, but try finding a Black professor teaching them! I'd understand more than any White professor. Besides, certain poets you hold *so* close, you don't want just anyone handling them, *man*handling them. I'm thinking of Maya.

Poetry was intuitive with Raphael. He got it. And he could read Baudelaire in French and Neruda in Spanish and Pushkin in Russian. Damn, life gave him so many gifts other people never get, especially our people, even those like me with a plenty privileged background. He took it for granted, and that's why he could throw it all away. Can our people do that? Okay, the other guy, Joseph, threw his life away too, but he had that church connection. Damn him! I'm talking about Raphael.

I'm not actually mad. Or if I am, isn't it a stage of grief—you know the five stages? I had a roommate who was into that stuff.

Do you want a soda or something? They have vending machines. Let me get one real quick.

Sorry I got distracted and on a poetry jag. I wanted to tell about this one night Raphael and I went into Philly. We liked this area with fun bars—the streets all lively with people, a lot high but nothing crazy, and neon lights flashing different colors, music blaring. We were looking to drink, dance; it was warm, so just being out was fun.

This one bar had the door propped open, and you could hear Aretha all the way on the sidewalk. "Chain of Fools," I'm pretty sure. We were moving to the music and debating: Would a straight place play something that old, or was it gay? I had on kind of a skimpy dress—purple with fringe here, real cute. He wore this black shirt and white tie I gave him—kind of a gangster look. I don't know if you used to do that when you were young, the lipstick on thick and super-high heels—maybe that wasn't your thing. Like I said, we just wanted to have a good time.

So while we're trying to decide whether to go in this bar, a squad car pulls up, and a cop gets out. White cop. He says to Raphael—not mean or threatening, but we didn't know how to take it—he says that soliciting prostitution is a class-something misdemeanor.

The cop didn't realize how pissed Raphael got, never having seen him normally. In this really sarcastic voice, Raphael says, "My *girlfriend* and I are deciding whether to enter this establishment."

I figured the cop figured Raphael was just standing up for me—being chivalrous—and not that we were actually a couple. But then Raphael launches into a long speech about us being students at the university and it being a warm summer night and who wouldn't want to go out unless he had to work, and why would the *officer* get the impression that a crime was being committed? Would the officer like *his* wife or girlfriend to be mistaken for a sex worker? "Don't you think you owe her an apology?" he asks the cop. Which totally freaks me out.

But back up: the whole time he's talking, I'm thinking two things simultaneously, like I'm watching this double screen. First is that Raphael's going to get himself and maybe me killed. That's my biggest fear.

And then I'm hit with how *confident* he is: He can argue with a cop and *not* worry about getting killed. I was like a five-year-old watching a Disney movie and wondering if the world is really that way other places—enchanted isles or Neverlands—where the *cops* are the scared ones. Where a person doesn't have to be afraid to remind them they're public servants? I wished I could've waved a magic wand and made Martin appear so I could say to him, "Did you ever even *think* to dream that our country could be *that* free?" It was like seeing a unicorn, I swear.

Meanwhile, another squad car shows up, this one with *two* cops—both White. Now I'm just plain scared. They ask our cop what's going on, and Raphael didn't stop staring in his face, and our cop said "Nothing." He heads to his car, and Raphael takes my arm and escorts me into the bar. I'm shaking like a fucking leaf.

Turns out the bar's *totally* gay—not a single woman except a drag doing karaoke to that old . . . what was it, the Diana Ross? "Touch Me in the Morning." And Raphael and I look at each other and try not to burst out laughing—we didn't want to offend anybody. So we go back to the open door and see the cops have left, and we split and hit a bar down the block that we knew was straight. And then we let it out. *God*, how we laughed. 'Cause we realized the cop thought I was in drag and Raphael didn't know it or that the bar was gay.

"He was just being a pal and trying to protect me from a rude surprise," Raphael says. Seeing the whole scene through that lens made it funny. We laughed about it all night.

Later I got mad—you know, racist cops. And probably a little resentful of Raphael too: all that White-privilege confidence. Like I said, I'm not mad at him anymore. How can I be? I'm just trying to be honest about who I was, which is what you asked for. That's not always easy.

You know, months later we went to a panel discussion on legalizing prostitution. Some were arguing it's exploitive of women, and others, that it's their choice. On the way home, Raphael says, "I don't think I could do that—bribe somebody to have sex with me who doesn't want to. For one thing, it takes away half the fun." He really was like that. Then he says, "But I think outlawing prostitution just drives sex workers underground and makes them more exploited. People have to realize they don't think they have other options. Legalizing it lets the government at least force the businesses to provide health protections."

I said, "Is that the speech you're going to make the *next* time a cop stops us?"

Luckily, we never got stopped again.

Okay, so things were pretty smooth for a while. We both might stay up all night cramming for an exam or writing a paper, but we could cut classes the next day and go to movies at midnight.

We followed the health-care debates. Checked out groups pushing for same-sex marriage. Climate activism. Civilian oversight of the police. A fundraiser for Haiti after the quake. Our college was pretty progressive, the speakers we got. Couldn't get Michelle Alexander but got *someone* about prisons. You remember how exciting it was those first years Obama was president, feeling almost anything was possible? Wherever you looked, people were awesome. Carl got to meet Eric Holder, and my mother met a super close friend of Susan Rice's.

We wanted to join it all and find a way to contribute. Not just make a lot of money and say the hell with other people. His father suggested becoming a lawyer, and Raphael thought about it, especially after a bunch of us rented a van to go hear Bryan Stevenson. Raphael nixed it, law, said he didn't have the "killer instinct." I said Bryan wasn't the killer-instinct type of lawyer. It just didn't click for him, though. I didn't care—I was searching too.

It's not easy, finding the best way to help. I thought of helping people in *really* bad circumstances, like you do. After graduation, I worked for an organization trying to restore ex-felons' rights. That didn't click for me. I wanted it to. Still, it taught me about myself. I'm not an administrative person. And not as much of a team player personality as I wish.

I hated myself for that. Who wants to fall into a privilege mindset that work's supposed to be fulfilling? I did a *lot* of stressing, always asking: Where are the greatest needs? What's *my* role? It wasn't a simple journey. Maybe for other people, but not for me.

Nowadays doesn't feel as exciting, but that's *good*, because it means Black people holding positions of prestige and power and influence is becoming normalized. We can address poverty and the fucked-up criminal justice system without always having to explain why. I'm starting to sound like Raphael—all optimistic.

I shouldn't be surprised where he went. He could be ... not exactly naïve, not per se—but he didn't always take situations seriously. I was afraid to go along to score cheap weed because he'd trust some corner boy. Okay, that's not fair—he wasn't stupid. But he acted like knowing jujitsu made him invincible. Doesn't do a damn thing against a bullet. Excuse me for laughing—I used to tease him that he thought it made him invincible because he thought it was spelled *J-E-W* jitsu.

Meeting each other's families, *that* was a challenge. First I met his, at Thanksgiving. Like I said, his dad and I didn't hit it off. He picked us up at the airport, and on the way to their house, he pointed things out, historical kinds of things, the Native tribe names, different White immigrant groups that settled in the area. I asked why they named the state after a slaveholder, and he seemed surprised and said something about Washington being the first president, a great general in the revolution, and it was to honor that. And I said if Hitler had done good things besides imprisoning and torturing and killing people, still, nobody'd want their state named Hitler.

That probably got us off on the wrong foot.

CHAPTER 27

Pat

THERE WERE *two* world wars here, two dinners that turned into battles.
I didn't mind—by my age, you learn that wedding and dinner-party disasters
provide amusing stories for years. We got more mileage from the drunken
brawl at my cousin's second wedding—she was dumb enough to invite her
ex!—than we got out of the ceremony. Turn lemons into lemonade. Arnie said
we should consider arguments part of the holiday tradition, a serving right
along with the candied yams and mashed potatoes. I miss that man!

The first world war was the first Thanksgiving Raphael brought Aleecia
home. The year before with angry-Rachel didn't rise to the level of a war—just
a skirmish.

"Set the stage," Mia would say. She's got the mind of a theater director and
might've enjoyed the fight the most, but, like my husband, watches from the
sidelines. There were I don't know how many of us: Mia and Clara and Ryan and
their spouses and children. No, Beth—Ryan's wife—couldn't come that year.
Her mother had fallen and broken her hip. But their three children—Nick, Jake,

and Amy—came. And Mia's three—Todd, Kirsten, and Braden—and Brooke and Jody with their East Coast accents. Not Hah-vahd Yahd, thank goodness. Most of the children weren't children anymore—teens and preteens. Just little Amy, six or seven. A tiny thing, all dolled up in a frilly pink dress and patent-leather Mary Janes. Clara must've helped her put them on.

And there was Daniel, Raphael, and Gillian. And Aleecia. Dressed in a beautiful, and I mean *beautiful*, jade-colored tunic. With matching slacks and silver earrings. I still remember! My daughters are as different as night and day on clothes. Clara's the power-suit professor—nothing worn and tweedy in *her* closet. Mia takes after me—a little artsy folk style, Joan Baez and Mama Cass rolled into one. Clara says I'm "aging hippie." I probably already told you that.

Raphael and Daniel always wore sweaters over button-down shirts and looked nice and trim. I'm sure Arnie wore his usual: flannel shirt and corduroy pants that he'd had since the gold rush. I kept mending them so he wouldn't be mistaken for a hobo. He was always clean—that Norwegian scrubbiness.

Why am I telling you how everybody dressed? I doubt I even remember. I'm just trying to give you the *impression* we might have made.

And you can't expect me to remember the argument word for word—I can only tell you the basics of what each person said. Later I'll explain why I remember so *much*, and it's not because the old gray noggin is sharp. It's because a certain grandson taped it, that's right, like you're doing. But he did it *secretly*.

What was the spark that ignited everyone? Maybe the kids asking about the presidents. Arnie used to give them each a few dollars before we sat down to eat—fresh clean bills he got at the bank—said it helped quiet them. They liked to imagine how they'd spend it. And I think he gave the older kids some two-dollar bills. They'd help string the Christmas lights, which we always turned on the following week. And so people were talking about Washington and Jefferson.

Aleecia says something like "Honoring them is like honoring Adolf Hitler." She didn't say it loud—maybe only to Raphael—but I happened to hear it and so did Ryan. Who *could* have let it slip by. But *had* to ask her why.

She says because they enslaved people, and he says that having slaves wasn't the same as gassing six million people, especially if the slaves weren't treated badly. Oh boy—light a stick of dynamite, why don't you?

Clara joined the fray by saying slaves *were* treated badly and besides, just owning a slave is a criminal act. Derek, her husband, is a lawyer—that's where she gets her ammunition. Raphael said people back then knew slavery was wrong: abolitionists had been screaming about it for years. And that Washington and Jefferson loved to wax eloquent about freedom. *Patrick Henry* was a slaveholder. "Give me liberty or give me death" said by a slaveholder. In old hippie language, it boggles the mind.

Arnie was mum, as he reminded me after—probably helping himself to seconds while the rest of us were getting roiled. Mia was likely keeping an eye on the kids. There's always one who fills up the plate and then doesn't eat a bite. And one who eats only potatoes. I don't fuss about those things at Thanksgiving. I already raised my brood, thank you.

So the rest of us were throwing in our two cents. Daniel said that throughout history, certain groups were treated as less than human, and while it's inexcusable, people who have done truly great things should be honored for *those* things, even if they're criticized for others, rightly criticized. I'll be the first to admit I don't like praising the English—what they did to the Irish was murder, pure and simple—so to get me to say yay even to Churchill is like pulling teeth. But we *are* a mixed bag.

Ryan wasn't having any of it. He said comparing Washington and Jefferson to Hitler was crazy. I don't know if he used the word "crazy." He repeated the numbers—six million versus how many slaves did Washington and Jefferson own? "Even assuming for the sake of argument they gassed them all to death," he said. You have to remember his wife's Jewish and technically his boys too.

Aleecia came right back at Ryan with numbers, statistics, how many people died on the voyage across the Atlantic and in South America and the islands—the Caribbean and whatnot—and how many hundreds of years slavery went on. You probably know all that. There was a momentary lull, and Gillian said, in her quiet way, that comparing atrocities didn't make much sense—they're all bad. But Washington and Jefferson were distinguishable from the Nazis in various ways—I forget her points. Oh, one was that they never possessed the *hatred* that characterized the Nazis.

That's when I threw in *my* two cents. I said that other slave owners *did* hate Black people. I'm not sure what my larger point was or if I even had a larger point.

I remember all this, I started to tell you, because my grandson Todd recorded it. He talked his way into a graduate course in sound engineering and told me that as part of a class project, he had to do something with a monitor on his belt and putting gizmos here and there on the table and on that lamp and the chandelier—don't look, I haven't dusted up high in ages. Todd was very insistent I wasn't supposed to tell anyone, because they'd bug him with questions. He was very methodical, I'll say that, gizmos under the table and all. If I had known they were microphones and he was recording us!

I don't know how many he hooked up: eight, ten? That was the easy part, he said. His lab partner had to filter out all the silverware noises and pass-the-potatoes and children whining—no they were past the whining by then. First Todd had to go through and separate out the voices and identify them and have someone type it all up. I hoped they got an A on the project—it was an awful lot of work. I think it helped that people yelled over the dishes clattering.

After he handed the project in, he sent a copy of the transcript to me and Arnie as a gift. Did we ever laugh. I never showed it to Daniel—some people are quite uncomfortable about secret recordings. And I made Mia promise to give Todd a scolding and erase the tape because secret taping is illegal in our state. Not a harsh scolding—he didn't mean any harm.

I hope you don't expect me to go look for the transcript. I wouldn't know where to start—the basement is *crammed* with papers. From my *children* and the *grand*children, plus *my* old college textbooks and Arnie's. It's a firetrap. I'm sorry. You'll have to rely on my memory for who said what.

I do remember Derek kept repeating Clara's point about Washington and Jefferson participating in a system that let *other* slave owners be brutal. And Fred argued the opposite. If everybody who participates in a "system" is guilty, then as Americans, we're all guilty for the Iraq War.

Oh my goodness, did *he* go on a tangent. How the clothes we were wearing that "very minute" probably came from a country treating its workers like slaves. How was anybody supposed to know that, I asked. I mean it: How are we supposed to know what goes on thousands of miles away?

I forget who kept repeating there's "not knowing" and "not wanting to know," maybe Derek, who also said that throwing a grenade into a mall without intending to kill any specific individual is just as bad as meaning to kill somebody specific. And I'm thinking: *Oh,* great—*the day before Black Friday, you're going to make everybody afraid to go to the mall.*

The argument went on and on, and then came the kicker: Ryan said the Jews in Germany had been equals—you know, doctors, lawyers, government stooges—and then they were turned into subhumans, but the Founding Fathers had had no experience with Blacks as equals. So what the Founding Fathers did was out of ignorance.

That's when Aleecia shouted. And I mean *shouted.* You'll have to excuse my French, Bernice, but you wanted the truth. She shouted, "Fucking bullshit." I'm sure all of Todd's microphones picked it up.

We're no strangers to bad language here. I learned some Navy words when Arnie dropped the car jack on his foot. But it felt very out of place at the dinner table. And with the grandkids. It got quiet, and I remember Daniel looking uncomfortable. I'm sure he felt responsible—he'd brought her over—but it wasn't his fault.

Bless him, Raphael jumped in. What a soothing, patient voice he had. Told us things I hadn't known, and I bet no one else did, except Aleecia. This must be old hat to you, White people knowing so little. It's a disgrace, I'll be the first to admit.

He told us Martha Washington owned a young slave woman who ran away, escaped to the North. What was her name? Ona Judge, that's right. When he first said it, I was confused and thought he said "Own. A. Judge." Which I'm sure must go on—how else do you explain what half of them do?

Anyhoo, Raphael described how this Ona Judge escaped to New England and married a sailor and went about her life just fine, living as a free woman, starting a family. Then on the street one day, some Virginia tourist recognized her. He sent word to Washington, who hatched a plot to kidnap her back to Mount Vernon. Can you imagine? Luckily, Northerners helped foil the plot and hid her, and when all was said and done, Washington never got her back.

Raphael's story took us by surprise, like I said. We had to mull it over, which was a good thing—people getting more food in their bellies, which is calming.

It bothered me that Washington was so *persistent*. Why not just accept Ona was gone? Buy Martha a nice bracelet or shawl or something.

I also mulled over how the discussion got so angry. I don't mind debates, but keep it pleasant. Though I wasn't exactly *blaming* Aleecia, I was less than thrilled with the language. Still, she wasn't the only one participating. *All* of them—Clara, Derek, Fred, Ryan—could've used a mellow toke before dinner. My goodness, I hope my descendants don't read this—Great-Grandma the stoner. I haven't touched the stuff for half a century. It was a figure of speech, children!

I wish I could say the argument ended there, but my pit-bull son just had to add, "If Washington hadn't pursued the girl, his other slaves would've tried to escape. Washington *had* to make an example of her."

So another stick of dynamite tossed on the fire. Gillian, she told how the Nazis slaughtered whole villages—men, women, and children—to "set an example." She didn't say it directly to Ryan, but she was letting him know that you can't use that as an excuse for barbarity.

I really thought the topic would never be dropped. Washington this, slavery that, everyone repeating themselves. Then, for a second, there was a pause. Complete silence, complete silence. Little Amy, smart as a whip, pipes up, "Maybe Washington was so mean because his wooden teeth hurt."

That brought the house down. And, thank God, got us onto stories about dentists and root canals. What a crazy evening. Here, let me get us more tea.

You know what else I remember, Bernice? It wasn't on the transcript. Later in the evening, after the pies had been eaten and the table cleared, after the leftovers had been stored in plastic containers in the refrigerator, after the Solomons and Aleecia had left and the children had taken their racket downstairs . . . Mia and Clara must have been finishing the dishes. The men had disappeared, probably to watch football in the den.

I came into the empty living room to turn on more lamps and went over to that window to look out on the street. And suddenly had a déjà vu. It took me back to a dinner *decades* ago, when Mia and Clara and Ryan were young. Arnie's cousins up in Bellingham and the ones who used to live in Ballard came every holiday. It must've been one of those times.

A retired nurse owned the Solomons' place then. Eleanor lived alone. A pleasant soul, mostly kept to herself. Had a few friends come and go, and I think she volunteered at the garden club.

Come look. Yes, by this pane, right by the Chinese Garnet Coltrane is where I was standing. It's a new plant. I don't remember what was here before. Look at the beautiful, elegant leaves. The way the deep-green shine sets off the red veins—almost rose. And the delicate, smaller curving veins, gentle streams bringing nourishment to the tips. I don't usually picture garnet as pinkish; I think of it in the rust family. Aren't rose and deep green lovely together? You can rub the leaves through your fingers, they're so smooth. And this beside it is a Lemon Lime Dracaena—you can see how *it* got its name, those long lime-green leaves and the darker down the middle. The one in the kitchen looks more yellow. I like having plants around, as you can see. They keep me company.

So, right before the déjà vu . . . I was standing among my plants, looking out at the night. The street was silent, dark. The Solomons' curtains were drawn, and their lamps made nice little halos, one at each window. And remembering standing in the same spot decades ago, when my children were young, and saying to myself back then: *How nice Eleanor has it*. Quiet and peaceful among her plants and furnishings . . . the soft lamplight . . . stillness . . . able to hear herself think. Breathing in the sweet solitude like she's in an empty church.

Just to not be interrupted every two seconds to bandage a skinned knee! Clean up a spilled milk, a chair knocked over in a game of tag, a child crying for her lost Polly Pocket. *Some*body wanting *some*thing. Eleanor was sitting in quiet serenity. How I yearned for that.

Now I have it every night. Be careful what you wish for.

No, it was *Jody* who kept losing her Polly Pocket. Mia and Clara kept losing Barbies.

When Todd's transcript of Thanksgiving dinner came in the mail, Arnie and I read it from start to finish. For a long time after, we repeated lines and laughed. Yes, we did. Or we'd see something in the paper and say, "That was Clara's point," or "Just what Fred said." If a cashier wouldn't take a little boy's boatload of pennies, Arnie'd whisper in my ear, "She must have wooden teeth."

Then he got diagnosed, and for a while we didn't laugh about anything. But he went ahead and had the surgery, and afterwards the doctors were ecstatic. "The margins are clean," they told us, which Mia translated into English. He would still need radiation and chemo, but then he'd be cured. He got the radiation and chemo, and you know what happened.

I'll say this: When Aleecia came the next year, she was sweet as honey. Not a peep of politics. She knew about Arnie's cancer and brought him a DVD about Amundsen, the one who got to the South Pole first. Why that's so important, I'd like to know, but the Norwegians are very proud of it, and Arnie loved the movie. He said the English got "royally smeared." Still, I've never watched it.

CHAPTER 28

Daniel

NATURALLY, IN COLLEGE RAPHAEL'S LIFE changed in ways both big and small. He gave up soccer but learned jujitsu. Only went biking occasionally—I mean long trips. All the habit changes most of us go through.

The first girl he brought home, Rachel, was from New York and reminded me—in rather trivial ways—of Susan. A little bohemian in style, I guess—nothing radical or attention-grabbing. Though temperamentally, the two were quite different.

In any case, as far as politics was concerned, Raphael didn't seem to care about presenting a united front, although he was...I want to say "protective"—he didn't want Rachel to feel completely outnumbered. A few of her ideas were, for lack of a better word, "extreme." She might like the term "radical."

With Aleecia, the girl, young woman, he brought home the following year, it was different. For starters, there was no question Aleecia could hold her own. At times I had the impression she was perhaps *too* influential, and by that I mean Raphael was losing the natural skepticism he used to bring to new ideas. Is this the father in me talking? You know the line: "*My* son couldn't have been the ringleader." Parents are eager to absolve their own children of all blame. I suppose the blame, if that's the right word—the *cause* of Raphael's lessened skepticism should be placed squarely on him.

I believe I already told you a little about our running debate between helping people in the short term versus long term. While Aleecia was visiting we were on the subject, and I remember her saying, "Unless there's an unavoidable, overwhelming crisis—New Orleans during Katrina, for example—there's no point in trying to rank important needs. A person should still complain about microaggressions and sexist comments, even though there are hundreds of women and children being raped daily in the Congo." Her examples often went for the jugular. But I guess it's a way to clarify issues.

You'll learn more about the evolution of Raphael's thinking in college by talking to her and his friends. Aleecia was—probably still is—an energetic arguer, very attuned to current politics. I don't want to give the impression she's a starry-eyed idealist—her feet are firmly planted on the ground. But she believes, or at least she did, that, number one, the human race can radically change its behavior, and two, it can do so in a short period of time, in a single generation.

Except for the conversions to Christianity and Islam, history doesn't teem with examples of rapid and widespread deep cultural change. And those conversions took centuries. Even political revolutions are rare—*successful* revolutions. Look at the Arab Spring. The French Revolution succeeded in bringing down the monarchy, but democracy didn't take root, really, until well over a hundred years later. The Russian Revolution was just a coup, one dictatorship ousting another.

Progress is generally incremental. I know it bothers people that the right to vote initially was granted only to White men, but the reality is that often it takes getting a right *established*—even if established only for White men, say—before it can be expanded to other groups.

Yet Aleecia was a very sophisticated thinker for her age—for any age. We had a number of discussions; I can't keep them all straight. She posed difficult questions. For instance: How would I feel if Hitler had authored the Declaration of Independence—would I erect a monument to him in the nation's capital?

It's difficult to transpose the twentieth century dictator who set up a massive system of annihilation—its *purpose* was annihilation—on the 1780s Founding Fathers of the world's first modern democracy. Maybe she was right: I was ducking the issue.

I remember a different argument about Jefferson better. Not the where-and-when but the views expressed. Aleecia again brought up the slave-owning, and, I confess, I gave it short shrift, an attitude I'm a little ashamed of now. At the time, I saw debits and credits columns. In Jefferson's debits: owning slaves, owning human beings. In the credits: drafting the Declaration of Independence and *crafting* the Constitution and Bill of Rights.

The Constitution and first ten amendments were not a simple thing. It wasn't a matter of sitting down and setting out a fairly straightforward position. I don't mean to suggest the Declaration of Independence wasn't carefully thought out and various wordings debated, but the Constitution is enormously more complex—balancing powers, authority, rights, freedoms. Of course Jefferson didn't do it alone; other great minds were brought to bear—Madison, Hamilton, to name just two—to reconcile the various provisions thrashed out by the delegates. But Jefferson's contribution in wisdom, in intellect and knowledge—hard to quantify, hard to overestimate.

I probably gave a long speech on the subject, like I'm doing here—I'm a history teacher, after all, so this is my element. No doubt I pointed out that Martin Luther King Jr. was not perfect. Yes, I did, because Raphael came back at me about "context" and "proportion" and other concepts I'd drilled into him. Cheating on one's wife—if, in fact, Martin Luther King did—was a far cry from owning human beings. Raphael was right. Hoisted by my own petard. Deservedly.

Why was I so indifferent to Jefferson's owning slaves? One reason is that it happened long ago. I don't get upset thinking about the persecution of Jews in the Middle Ages or their expulsion from Spain or even the Russian pogroms in the 1800s—not the way I can get upset about the Holocaust. I won't rule out some degree of racism—slavery might have loomed larger for me if its victims had been Jewish or if I identified with them for some other reason.

But to give kind of a counterexample: I identify with President Obama—more so than I do with many, perhaps most, White people. He and I share a lot of the same attitudes, and when he's under attack for sounding like an academic, I certainly get my dukes up, figuratively. I feel he's "my" people, even though you may feel more strongly or in different ways that he's "your" people. This topic isn't really up my alley, Bernice. I suspect you have studied the tendency of people to group themselves, form identifications with family, friends, and others.

Overall, though, I think my historian's focus on context lessened my condemnation of Washington and Jefferson. They weren't the first in their families to own slaves—they inherited them. All the neighboring estates had slaves. One could say it was *customary*. I realize how hollow that sounds. I don't excuse my obtuseness, my indifference, my racism. You want a personal history here—some humiliation on my part is inevitable. Yes, I did place them on a pedestal and to some extent still do.

Gillian and I tussle over the *fact* of placing people on pedestals. She rarely elevates someone to hero or heroine status. Maybe her father's original-sin sermons took root. But I feel I have a low-expectations view of the human race, so the pedestal itself isn't far off the ground. To put it another way: I *expect* dirty laundry in the closet. Maybe that's why when I encounter greatness, I want it in floodlights.

I do remember stressing to Aleecia that despite Jefferson's faults, his *grave* faults, he accomplished truly astounding things. The Bill of Rights has become part of our DNA and will be for all subsequent generations of Americans. Can you imagine *not* cherishing the rights of speech and press and religion, the right to complain to and about the government? We take rights for granted, but trust me, the Chinese and Russian people do not. Or those in smaller authoritarian countries.

I'm not sure I made any headway. Gillian says Aleecia and I just have different focuses.

By the way, to return for a second to the issue in your interview, where you gave short shrift to the Great Man theories of history? You said you favor focusing on culture and communities, on the village baker and blacksmith instead of Louis XIV, and I don't necessarily disagree. But how can we dismiss individuals like Gandhi, Martin Luther King, Mandela—how can we argue they, as individuals, weren't pivotal in large-scale events, events that ultimately affected communities? But perhaps they're the exception.

I'm a relic. Too indoctrinated in the Enlightenment canon that the individual is important. Society is *equally* important—that's what our concept of freedom is about: allowing the individual some elbow room not only for his, or her, own benefit but for society's too.

Famous people can also be a heuristic tool, a way to hook students' interest in the past. In the hormone-fueled years, attention is usually on the present. On the attractive student two desks over.

In the final analysis, though, whether Jefferson was a good man is an ethical, moral, or religious question. For me as a history teacher, what's important is whether certain of his ideas were significant. And laudable. I believe they were. As President Obama has often said, more eloquently than I can, we are a nation still trying to deliver on the promises in our Constitution, but the key thing is that we *are* trying to do so. To form a more perfect union.

What were Raphael's views in these debates? I don't want to use the word "moderator"—perhaps "kibitzer." Occasionally he'd throw his two cents in. To the extent he agreed with Aleecia that Washington's and Jefferson's great deeds were overshadowed by their role as slave owners, I chalked that up to his acting the solicitous boyfriend. For me, as I said, the issue was never about a moral judgment on Washington or Jefferson as private citizens but on their roles as public figures.

We didn't talk only about history during Aleecia's visit, but that's mainly what I remember. The two of them kept very different hours—sometimes sleeping until noon. Raphael did join me on some morning runs. Aleecia had an aerobics program on her computer—we could hear the music through the walls. Not that it was loud—just had a beat. And she'd brought schoolwork and stayed in his room to do it. He'd brought work too, but I think let it slide. He and I lingered over coffee or lunch, trading stories about the neighborhood, high school friends, things like that. He tried out my new bike, found it too heavy. Traction versus speed—we have our own preferences. I'm sure age plays a role.

CHAPTER 29

Aleecia

HE MET MY PARENTS AT CHRISTMAS. We only went for a few days—like I said, I never could put up with my family for long, not back then. I told them beforehand he was cool with how we celebrated, that he didn't do the "I'm Jewish, so don't wish me Merry Christmas" bit. I'm not putting people down for that, but seriously: we endure—year in, year out—White folks being "the norm," so when people act like Christianity is the norm, Jewish people can just get over it.

This has me remembering something from early on. He knew who Frederick Douglass was but hadn't actually read him, so I loaned him the narrative, and he reads the whole thing and comes back with, "All the stuff my grandparents and other Jewish people told me about Jews valuing education more than anybody else isn't true. It was just a lot of self-serving bullshit."

He didn't know either about us becoming teachers and starting the public-school systems and the HBCUs. Actually, he didn't say "bullshit," called it *mishegoss*—the Jews as being more for education than anybody else. He taught me some Yiddish, and if you want to learn a *really* colorful language . . . Not Hebrew, Yiddish. If you didn't have the machine on, I'd teach you some.

Back to visiting my parents. I gave him a couple of instructions beforehand of things to say and not say. My mom likes people to compliment the food when she's gone to a lot of trouble—even breakfast. He was easy with that. My dad doesn't have a great sense of humor. Jokes go right over his head, so you have to be careful making a joking comment because he'll take it seriously. Which cracks us up—me and my sister and brothers.

And Raphael was okay with pork—didn't do kosher. We used to go to a place in Philly that made great collard greens and ham hocks, but I told him my folks avoid a lot of that—they weren't raised in the South, for one thing. He says he only learned Jewish cooking from a friend, not his dad.

Okay, so *our* Christmas tradition starts with singing the night before, after dinner, which is—this might sound weird—apple and blueberry pancakes. Sausage too—my dad won't eat a meal unless there's meat. My mom made a big deal when we were young that we create our own traditions—she looks down on people who stick to the way things have always been done. The hat business at church drives her batshit crazy. A whole side of her family drives her crazy.

Raphael knew some carols and joined in, and that went fine. My dad is the only bass, and David's a countertenor, so it was nice having a tenor balancing all us sopranos, especially since Carl doesn't really get into it, though he'll play the piano. Maybe he was jealous of Raphael's voice. To be honest, Carl never liked him. Behind his back called him a goody two-shoes. If that's what Raphael was, he was the *horniest* goody two-shoes I ever met.

Maybe you can edit that out? Whatever.

Christmas morning, whoever doesn't go to church finishes straightening the house and any food prep my mom puts on the list. My sister stopped going to church in high school, and my brothers and I mostly followed her example, though sometimes I'll go on a holiday just to see everybody. It really depends how sociable I'm feeling.

In the afternoon, my two great-aunts come up from Richmond for

Christmas dinner. Doria is pretty deaf and never says much. Betty makes up for it, but it's always "Jesus this" and "Jesus that." My dad tunes her out, but my mom climbs the walls. They're *her* aunts, her mother's sisters.

I groused about Betty's nonstop Jesus afterwards, and Raphael said he thought it was because a lot of the dinner conversation was about colleges. They wanted to know what ours was like, and Carl spouted off about Cornell, and my parents talked about Howard and Morehouse and what my sister'd said about UCLA. And David listed the reasons he wanted to go to Oberlin. Betty had only graduated high school, so Raphael thought she was just trying to claim some dignity. But she was always like that, even if all we were comparing was McDonald's and Burger King.

There was one awkward moment—even now it cracks me up. Doria also can't *see* too well. She was next to Raphael, and he helped her load her plate— holding the bowls and serving platters and dishing stuff out, asking if she wanted more, that kind of thing. She *loved* the attention, plus being old and half blind, she gets nervous about spilling.

He excuses himself, probably to go to the bathroom, and after he leaves, she asks whether he went to church with us in the morning or was—and she lowers her voice—was he *Catholic*. That's the worst thing you can call someone in her mind. I said he was Jewish, and David pops up with, "Not Sammy Davis Jewish—Raphael's White."

You'd think he was cheering the Klan, the way she bites his head off! Curses David, practically, calling him an evil sinner and a whole string of words you never could imagine her uttering. Half of me wanted to laugh—I didn't know she had it in her. But mostly we're stunned.

Betty or somebody says Doria was mad at David for teasing her, for pulling her leg about Raphael being White. He *looks* White—you saw the photo. I guess if someone said one of his parents was Black, you might believe it. The dark wavy hair and all, though it's not kinky. *Wasn't* kinky—shit, I'm talking present tense.

David insisted he wasn't lying, and everybody else backs him up. This makes Doria even madder because she feels ganged up on. And I'm thinking:

Raphael is going to come back any second, and she'll ask him directly, and he'll be awkward, and who knows how my parents are going to take it. Will he come across like he's offended? Or sound patronizing?

Doria puts it to Betty, knowing she won't lie: "Is he White or Black?" Raphael comes in a *split* second later, and seeing him, Betty pauses. He's surprised we're all silent—I'm sure he figured we were talking about him. Carl is smirking, and David is still looking like *Why is everybody mad at* me? My mom, I can't tell what she's thinking, and my dad's probably thinking *Raphael better not act insulted that Doria thinks he's Black.* And everybody keeps staring at Betty, waiting.

And Betty says, "Jesus sees the heart, not the skin."

Raphael sensed he was kind of on the spot and just punts, saying, "He set an example for all people."

Carl has to make gagging noises. David grins like Raphael just pulled a rabbit out of a hat, which I guess he did. My parents look down at their plates hoping the conversation goes elsewhere *fast*. Usually my mom can change the subject on a dime, but I guess it threw her. Doria smiles at Raphael and pats his chair as a signal he should sit and says, "You wouldn't believe what they were trying to tell me."

To this *day*, I thank God he knew not to ask, just offered her more pie and told my mother the crust was incredibly flaky and got everyone talking about pies. I've dated boys who would've put *both* feet in. My parents—though they'd never admit it—I think they respected him after that. Not for the Jesus comment—they knew it was total bull. But because he didn't want to hear what everybody had been talking about. Could just sit down, change the subject, and shut up, which no one in my family knows how to do.

Let me hit the can for a sec.

The visit wasn't *all* tense. We had fun at the park. Raphael had seen an old soccer ball in the garage—Carl played in high school—and asked if anybody wanted to kick it around, and it wasn't too cold, and I was *dying* to get out. My mom can be like she's scrutinizing every move. David said yes, even though he didn't do any sports—like I told you, he's a klutz. Carl came along probably to get out of the house too.

You can't have a game when it's just four people, so Raphael practiced taking shots at the goal. David would run after the ball if it missed. Carl did a few kicks but lost interest and got on my case for not bringing any weed. Raphael remembered he'd hid a joint in his wallet like months ago, so we shared it—not David, because he won't smoke on account of his oboe and everything.

It was good stuff, amazingly, and we had some laughs. David started asking Raphael to say words in French, Spanish, German, Russian—kept trying to stump him, though none of us knew Russian. David wasn't being mean—he was blown away. I think he crushed on Raphael. David's gay. My aunts don't know, but you can print it—they won't read your book.

When we got back to school, Raphael sent David a translation of Pushkin's poetry, thinking it might spark an interest in Russian. I'll always associate Raphael with poetry. And most of all, Maya. If you decide to include my memories in your book, promise me you'll end my section with "Where We Belong," at least part? He always recited it. I guess I grew past it, but he didn't, so in my mind it became his. Which doesn't mean it isn't a beautiful, brilliant poem.

CHAPTER 30

Pat

ARNIE WAS DOING POORLY, throwing up from the chemo. Only time he was comfortable was fast asleep. Ryan flew here with "the absolute best" new iPhone—whatever kind it was—making it easy for Arnie to listen to any music he wanted. Daniel and Gillian were a help with groceries, and my book-club girls brought cooked food, which I ate and Arnie couldn't keep down. Soups were all he managed—broths, not hearty things. He was a big man, and watching him lose that strength was hard.

It must have been spring break that Raphael was here because that's when I make plum pies and don't use fresh fruit. You can't see it from the windows, but we have a tree in the back that gives enough plums to cram the freezer. Would your aunt want some? You're sure? I have half a billion.

Look at that tree across the street, the walnut, branches bouncing up and down in the wind. I hope we don't lose power. In the fall, when the branches bob like that while the leaves are turning a bright canary yellow, I think of children bouncing happily on a trampoline. My kids loved ours, but we had to give it away when the insurance raised our premiums. Thank heavens the company never knew about the tree house.

Focus, Pat: Raphael, spring break. As I remember it, he dropped by while I was rolling out the dough and volunteered to help, just like in high school. I went to check on Arnie, who was fast asleep, and when I got back to the kitchen, Raphael had put on Arnie's old apron, the one with the silly "Rib Bib" on the front Clara'd given him *centuries* ago. A minute into the rolling, he said he'd broken up with Aleecia. I kept mum; I know when to listen.

Right away he corrected himself and said she'd broken up with him. I asked why. Just between you and me, Bernice, I'm old enough to know that *whatever* she said wasn't the real reason. I don't mean she had a new boyfriend in the wings, not necessarily. But if you give a reason, *any* reason, then they try to argue you out of it. I've been on both sides of that equation. Ryan's first girlfriend said, "It's not you—it's me," and he asked, "What the hell does that mean?" I told him it was just a quick way to end the discussion.

Aleecia said they had no future—they wanted different things. She wasn't sure she wanted kids, and there was too much racism in the country for an interracial couple to raise a family anyway. I was surprised she thought that, in this day and age. Raphael tried to convince her that a strong love could "transcend social garbage." That phrase stuck with me, because that's all racism is: social garbage.

The whole thing caught him by surprise, he thought things were fine. Oh, he knew she felt conflicted about wanting to teach French Lit but feeling it was selling out. He didn't think she felt conflicted about their relationship. In my opinion, the "conflict" meant she had a sexy French professor—a Jean-Paul Belmondo look-alike? Ooh-la-la. No one could dangle a cigarette from the mouth like him. That's before your time.

Yes, she felt teaching French Lit was "bourgeois." Mind you, I was the *queen* of scorn in my beatnik-hippie days. Materialism, consumerism—I condemned the whole kit and caboodle before everyone *else* did. And quite noisily too. Our commune shared chores, baked our own bread, wore simple clothes, snubbed the military-industrial complex. Those peasant dresses could hide the flab, I'll say that.

Arnie liked to give me a hard time when we started dating, calling the commune a "commie cell." He was finishing up his engineering degree. "You love turning your backs on the industrialized world, as long as you can keep your fancy stereos and record collections, all of which are made from petroleum." That really galled my housemates. It was reel-to-reels we loaded up on—we just borrowed records to make tapes. Are they made from petroleum too?

Back to Raphael. Yes, he was puzzled by Aleecia's—what's the word the nuns loved? "Self-abnegation." That's my word—I forget what he used. Lessons about the Carmelites and fasting and self-flagellation and the hair shirts. Sister Margaret *loved* giving us the full coroner's report on how the saints died. I thought I was done with all that, until I took art history in college. Saint Sebastian with arrows poking all over his body, and Saint Agatha—I won't go into Saint Agatha. Where was I? Self-abnegation.

No, Raphael didn't understand the concept of self-denial—as foreign to him as wanting to change his body. Fasting, Lent, keeping the Sabbath, all those rituals were head-scratchers. He didn't *ridicule* them, goodness, no; he respected them the way he did transgenders. He just didn't understand them. He didn't understand why we'd deprive ourselves of pleasures, the ones that don't hurt anybody.

Yet here he goes and lives in a Third World village for a year, giving up all the comforts of home. But it wasn't really giving up anything, not for him. Nigeria was an *exploration*, an *adventure*. Didn't young aristocratic men in Victorian England scurry off on safaris and such?

Anyhoo, he tells me Aleecia said she felt guilty for her life of privilege. I can still remember his sleeves bunched over the elbows and flour all over his arms. Such nice arms. His eyes looked sad.

So I gave my speech how everyone suffers heartbreak and is sure it will last forever, but it doesn't. I told him after crying my eyes out over my first two boyfriends, every day I thank the Lord, because if they hadn't dumped me, I'd be keeping house in a yurt in Mongolia or else living on a shoestring supporting Mr. Next Picasso. Thank you very much, but no thank you.

Luckily, Aleecia had moved off campus—he wasn't sure where—so he probably wouldn't always be running into her. She wanted a "clean break." I think that's okay. I'm no fan of long goodbyes. I healed faster from Mr. Picasso than Mr. Yurt, who wouldn't give a firm "get lost." Let me beat my head against the wall for *months*.

I reminded Raphael of his many girlfriends before Aleecia and how he got over them, and he confessed, a little shamefully, he might've *thought* he was in love before but wasn't—Aleecia was really his first. And he didn't *want* to stop loving her.

Ain't that the truth of it! So I gave *another* speech, the one I gave Clara when Mr. Med School ran off with a kindergarten teacher. "Of course you don't *want* to stop loving her. Love is a river of happiness flowing through your mind and body. If you dam up the river, you have to mourn not just that person but the drying up in *yourself*."

I won't pretend I wrote that. Our commune had a scrapbook of sayings, Omar Khayyam, Kahlil Gibran, our own brilliant thoughts. Arnie called it "Poor Pat's Almanac." That was one of my favorites.

I don't remember if we talked about Aleecia again. Yes, I gave him some parting words. I reminded him of his own sine-wave business. He felt so bad about breaking up with her because he'd felt so good when they were together. I'm not sure that was a consolation. More like a consolation prize, if you know what I mean.

What else from that visit? He used the iPhone Ryan gave Arnie to play for him the songs they used to sing with Gillian. My favorite was sailors at sea singing fond thoughts of home, their native Ireland. I think it was called "The Holy Ground." The stanzas were about stormy seas and whatnot, and the chorus . . . how did it go? "And still I live in hopes to see . . . the Holy Ground once more." And then came a flourish, "Fine girl you are!" Which made you think the sailors were homesick not only for fair Ireland but some innocent lassie pining over their miniature portrait.

When Raphael was in high school, he and Arnie sang it soulfully, quite harmonious and moving. Until the day Gillian springs on us—she's quite the researcher—that according to some sources, the "Holy Ground" was a well-known Dublin brothel. From then on, Arnie and Raphael belted out the chorus like hearty sailors, not mournful monks.

But that spring break, Arnie got a kick out of listening, but he couldn't sing, didn't have the energy. In July we moved him to hospice. He passed September 23.

I should be talking about Raphael. Thanksgiving, the first without Arnie, Raphael brought Joseph, a classmate. The two of them hung around the grand-kids—they're all the same generation even with a ten-year age span. What I mean is: they understand the same jokes, which fly right by me. Brooke brought a boyfriend, *thank goodness*—she'd been gaga over Raphael for years. Though she and Joseph seemed to get along *more* than fine. Her boyfriend didn't seem to notice; I think he was downstairs playing foosball.

Yes, the circle of life keeps on. Ryan's Nick is the first to get engaged. The wedding's set for the weekend before Labor Day. And I lucked out: the bride's family is from Chehalis, just a two-hour drive. I can return to sleep in my own bed.

I could be a *great*-grandmother before you know it. A milestone Arnie would've loved.

CHAPTER 31

[Emails between Raphael and Lance C., junior year]

[May 4, 2011, email from Lance to Raphael]

Whoa dude you're not out there protesting the seals killing bin laden? Thought you're against capital punishment. I should've had you over for a beer. No I forgot you've given up beer or so you say. Had to celebrate alone ginny was out proofreading the article she's coauthor on.

[May 4, 2011, email from Raphael to Lance]

If you're in a declared war you've got every right to target the enemy because you owe it to your country you've sworn to defend. Bin Laden declared war on us. And I don't think leaders are entitled to special deference and we're supposed to target just those on the battlefield, who anyway probably didn't have much choice about being soldiers. With capital punishment, the convicted person is already in prison and not a threat. Pretty different situations.

[May 5, 2011, email from Lance to Raphael]

Whatever happened to your "one man's terrorist is another's freedom fighter" or was that just when you were a punk freshman. Did I ever mention that we could all hear you and your girlfriend thumping away upstairs. Tom thought you'd injure yourselves and we'd have to take you to the er. I was worried you'd bust the floorboards and plaster and the landlord would keep the security deposit.

[May 6, 2011, email from Raphael to Lance]

I still believe some people we label terrorists are freedom fighters but anyone targeting civilians can't complain about becoming a target himself/herself. You punching me in the nose doesn't give me the right to kick your dog. You still have her, what's her name, Betsy?

[May 6, 2011, email from Lance to Raphael]

Betsy went to the canine happy hunting ground in April. Ginny thinks the vet screwed up saying it was a virus. Who the fuck knows. You still up for a beer tomorrow night? Ginny says lets go to the yardbird its less noisy.

[May 10, 2011, email from Lance to Raphael]

Thanks for walking me dude. Had a little extra, hate to let the bottom of a pitcher go to waste. Usually Ginny's there to put on the brakes. Can't wait till her damn article is sent off and life gets normal again. Still don't see how you can bitch about starving kids in Africa when there's starving kids in Asia and everywhere else. And sex slaves in Asia when you know full well they're in Africa and South America and probably under our noses. Don't you ever get tired of the world's misery? Why don't you just own up to the basic fact that misery is out there always has been always will be. Rape murder starvation disease none of it ever ends. And hell we all wind up dead anyway. You always act like you just found out about some atrocity and are shocked shocked. Deal with it and live your own fucking life like everybody else. Grow up.

[May 11, 2011, email from Raphael to Lance]

Not sure I get your point about misery always out there. Next time you go to the doctor what if she says quit your bitching, we're all going to die anyway? I'll bet you still want treatment for the time you're alive.

[May 11, 2011, email from Lance to Raphael]

I pay my doctor so have every right to expect medical competence in return. You know ginny calls you saint raphael

[May 13, 2011, email from Raphael to Lance]

Ginny calls me a saint though she let me score all her weed last winter? You two are worse, bending over backward at the altar of Saint Ayn. If you're so happy with your "Darwinian philosophy" then explain why you need a philosophy in the first place. Just say "I'm selfish and so what," why cushion it in some "survival of the fittest" bullshit. Admit it, morals do matter to you. And before you start some distortionist lecture on Darwin, he never said selfishness is best for the species. Tell it to the army ants.

[May 13, 2011, email from Lance to Raphael]

Jeez dude you're full of it. Rand never said every kind of self interest is terrific and I was the one who said would've gone to nam. We aren't the draft dodgers, that's your cohort. Btw ginny said she used to let you buy her weed because you got the best price. She's a capitalist to the bone.

[May 16, 2011, email from Raphael to Lance]

You seriously arguing "I can't help all starving children so why help any"? Obviously the need for help (food, medicine, freedom from tyranny) will always be greater than resources available to meet it. And I never said I have the formula for what anybody else should do to help or in what way. That's got to be a personal decision. The sum total of my "catechism" you called it is that people pitching in where and when they can leaves the planet in better shape for *all* of us than if we sit on our hands.

[May 16, 2011, email from Lance to Raphael]

Sorry dude but I don't think a stoner or former stoner should be handing out morality lessons and talking about sitting on one's hands.

[May 16, 2011, email from Raphael to Lance]

First you complain I act too saintly, then too sinful. I told you a dozen times I don't hold myself up as some kind of example others are supposed to follow. If you remember, this whole argument began with you getting on my case about giving up weed and limiting my beer drinking to the weekend. I told you it's for personal reasons, not a Carrie Nation gig. I went back to long-distance biking and am not in shape and don't like getting winded easily. You going to be around over the summer? I landed a job with a linguistics prof and am renting a room not too far from your place. Like I said, still available for beer on the weekends.

[May 23, 2011, email from Lance to Raphael]

Isn't linguistics one of those touchy feely subjects like psych? You'll fit right in. No I won't be around for the summer. Out of here for good bright and early TOMORROW. Bitch gave me the shaft. To be accurate her econ ta was giving her his shaft. She was giving him t and a. She lied to me for six weeks. "Proofreading this and that and need a recommendation from him and could make or break my grad school applications." Total cunt.

My uncle in Schenectady offered me a job selling little old ladies money market funds. Don't worry, they're safe, all rated. Sayonara Spinoza.

CHAPTER 32

Daniel

HE AND ALEECIA BROKE UP LATE WINTER of his junior year. I never heard the details except that she was the one calling it off. It was obvious he was upset, but I didn't worry—he was what, twenty, twenty-one? True, some people find a deep abiding love in their teens or very early twenties, maybe marry high school sweethearts. But most of us battle through years of unsuccessful dating, and rejection goes with the territory.

I did notice he didn't bring girls home from college after Aleecia. But that actually seemed *healthy*, in a psychological sense . . . for him to take a rest. He'd been dating pretty much nonstop since ninth grade, maybe before.

And had his friendship with Joseph. A fun fellow—he reminded me of some of Raphael's high school friends: sarcastic banter, put-downs that were more a game than serious. And Joseph had the same talent for languages. Once I dared ask what they were saying back and forth—it sounded like a mix of German, Spanish, maybe Russian—and that sent them into howls of laughter.

Raphael said they were seeing who knew the most slang in the most languages for certain body parts. I didn't ask him to elaborate.

Joseph was knowledgeable about wild animals—how different species form groups, hunt, divide up prey. Maybe that's what triggered his interest in Africa. Or maybe his church tours—the ones to Nigeria—triggered his interest in animals. I don't recall exactly when I heard about the sister-church connection; I might've assumed he had gone on some kind of safari. With Raphael's knowledge of plants and trees, they made kind of a Lewis and Clark exploration duo. I could imagine them taking all sorts of camping trips. I didn't imagine them going to Nigeria.

Yes, they liked to joke. I remember Joseph pleading with Raphael to date his—Joseph's—ex. "Do it as a favor to *me*," he said, "so she'll stop texting ten times a day."

It was well after that, maybe spring break his senior year, that Raphael and I revisited the Washington and Jefferson argument. You know, whether owning slaves, owning people, disqualifies the presidents from being revered icons? To my mind, you can't eradicate the fact that Washington inaugurated the tradition of the peaceful transition of power. No small thing—you pretty much have to go back to Cincinnatus to see something similar, all the way back to the four hundreds BCE.

But obviously we start the icon business earlier, in what … kindergarten, first grade? The cherry tree story. My view is that we tell the story not because it teaches about Washington but because it teaches the importance of honesty, of telling the truth. As a value to hold dear. What I'm saying—what I said to Raphael was: Washington-the-man is only a conduit for instilling the importance of truth.

You know what he answered? I have to chuckle—really, I do. He said there have to be better ways to teach the value of the truth than by telling a lie. What a zinger. He said why not tell a *true* story of someone refusing to lie. I suppose there's an economy in making it Washington—at the same time, you're teaching he was our first president.

Are myths so dangerous? One man's—or woman's—myth is another's religion. And how many people are truly devastated, over the long term, by learning Santa isn't real? Or the tooth fairy?

Well, enough of my soapbox orating. I'm not sure what else to say about Raphael's college years. The bonds between parent and child weaken, *continue* to weaken. I don't mean our caring for one another changed, just that we were less a part of the other's daily life. And if the caring does decrease at all, it's the child who changes, and that's in the natural order of things.

CHAPTER 33

Gillian

YOU COULD TELL DURING SPRING BREAK Raphael was still quite upset about Aleecia. He acted mopey, and the night we went to a movie, he didn't pay any attention to the young women there.

Over that summer he was hired to do research for a linguistics professor. We were excited; it seemed a great fit for his interests. His emails said he'd become friends with someone named Joseph who was studying Nigerian languages, which turned out to be Hausa and Kibaku. You said you learned some Kibaku? It made sense to us, a friendship forming from a shared interest in languages.

Daniel was teaching that summer at one of the community colleges, and I had my adjunct position and was working on several articles. Eventually I was able to get two published! It was also the summer Arnie declined. We'd been so hopeful, but the cancer came back aggressively, and Pat had to move him to hospice. Ryan and Mia came up many weekends, and Clara flew cross-country *several* times. Raphael came back before starting senior year and got to visit

Arnie briefly. It was nice to see Pat supported and surrounded by children and grandchildren at the funeral.

Raphael didn't change his major, but we assumed that switching to linguistics so late would've been complicated. What I'm trying to say is: looking back, I can see warning signs, if you want to call them that, of his interest in going to Nigeria. But we weren't picking up on them. Not that it would've made a difference, that I can see.

He brought Joseph with him at Thanksgiving, and what fun conversations we had! Such interesting topics: his grandfather's time as a sharecropper, his aunt starting her own business from scratch, designing children's clothes that are now sold throughout the South—I forget what else. And some difficult subjects—a branch of the family had lived in the Greenwood District. Grandparents, three sons and their families, seventeen in all, died, were killed.

He may have mentioned his church's program in Borno, and if he did, I think I assumed it involved sending supplies and instructional materials, not on-site teaching. No, we never put two and two together to see they were hatching a plan.

I also remember, during that Thanksgiving visit, Raphael asking me many penetrating questions about the articles I was writing. One had to do with women imprisoned in Sobibor and one with Jews and Roma from Kyiv. Astonishing courage the young women in the camp showed. And I was intrigued by the spirituality, almost with Russian mysticism overtones, of those who managed to escape the massacre at Babi Yar. These were not large groups. I've told you a few times that as a historian and not a sociologist, I don't have to draw *useful* conclusions.

What else that year, Raphael's senior year . . . I made my yearly pilgrimage to Minnesota in late spring while Daniel flew east and drove Susan's parents down for graduation. They both died that summer. Daniel took care of all the arrangements and estate matters.

I didn't see Raphael again until September, when he returned for the memorial dinner Pat hosted, on the one-year anniversary of Arnie's passing.

Her children were coming in for it, and Raphael wanted to be there. Up until then, his phone calls and emails only hinted he was making plans for the future but never specified anything. I assumed graduate school—I'm not sure why. Perhaps with a little break or sort of gap year first.

I picked him up at the airport, and, in retrospect, I bet he was glad it was just the two of us on the ride home. It allowed him to test the waters about going to Nigeria.

He elaborated on what Joseph had told us the year before: that his family's congregation in Tulsa had a sister-church relationship with a Nigerian congregation in the village of Iskoki. The population wasn't even five thousand, and most were Christian, Protestant. But split among a few separate denominations. Tulsa's sister church had taken its students out of school because of Boko Haram activity elsewhere in Borno. He mentioned Maiduguri in particular. Did you go there? He described it to me as a large, modern city with universities, hospitals, an international airport. I realize now that when he said Maiduguri was a target of "activity," he meant violence.

The words he used to play down the dangers! Like, the militants didn't have a "presence" in the immediate area around Iskoki. I suppose that was true. He said it was eighty or so miles southwest of Maiduguri, in a remote spot where the roads are washed out much of the rainy season. The militants didn't want to deal with getting stuck in the mud, being partial to motorbikes. The only other good-sized town was some distance to the east. He might have been referring to Chibok, but the name wouldn't have meant anything to us then. Joseph's church also had connections with some other villages nearby, and they, too, had not encountered Boko Haram activity. Joseph had actually visited Iskoki the year before.

I don't know if the younger children were removed from school or not; Raphael said elementary-level education is compulsory. And free, like here. But the secondary schools are all private, is that your understanding? And many families can't afford to send their children to high school? I suppose some might be needed at home for farming. I was surprised—I don't know why—when Raphael said that over 70 percent of the country still farms. With all their oil, I thought the economy would be more diversified. But the cost of secondary education certainly explains how important the Tulsa church program is, the support it provides.

So for the teenagers pulled from school, the congregation set up an "underground" school, with teachers meeting in homes and courtyards instead of publicly. The curriculum was the same in that it prepared the students for the exams they would need to take to be admitted to the university. Raphael, Joseph, and the other volunteers' role would be to provide support for the teachers.

One way was by procuring supplies. Raphael wasn't sure about specifics—maybe arranging to buy pens and paper, textbooks, lesson plans. But he kept insisting the program had been up and running for at least a year, that he would *not* be, in his words, "reinventing the wheel."

I did ask: Of all the places in the world needing help, why pick one so far from home? He pooh-poohed the distance. For young people—maybe for you too, Bernice—flying eight thousand miles is nothing. He also said he'd be able to email and call—there were cell-phone towers and Wi-Fi. If he couldn't contact us directly from the village, he could email and phone from Maiduguri.

As you yourself must have discovered, the electricity situation in rural areas can be a little touch and go. Raphael told us later that it's because it's generated from a hodgepodge of small grids. Maiduguri may be on a large grid, but that has its own problems.

I just want to mention that after he arrived in Borno, Raphael became enthusiastic about local efforts to harness solar and wind power, which would expand the smaller grids. That's a wonderful thing both for the Nigerians and the planet. But as Daniel says, sadly ironic for an OPEC nation. That it can't satisfy its own citizens' energy needs, he means.

One thing we didn't find out until much later was how frequent the outages were. Iskoki had *some* electricity, *sometimes*, but not often. We assumed it was due to administrative incompetence, which, from what others have told us—friends who've traveled in certain parts of Africa—is not unusual. But also it was Boko Haram sabotaging facilities and cell-phone towers. I don't know if Raphael intentionally misled us, or the church misled him, or the sister church in Borno had misled the Tulsa congregants.

Or if Raphael told the truth, that it *was* administrative incompetence. During 2013, the year he was there, Boko Haram made significant inroads throughout Borno and the neighboring states, so many problems then were due to the insurgency. In Maiduguri too. But before he went over, based on what had happened up through 2012, I'm not sure anyone could have predicted how much more deadly 2013 would turn out to be.

By the way, Raphael never hid the fact that smaller towns in Borno also suffered terrorist acts. But he likened it to visiting Israel. There, out of the blue—it seems to us, at least—a bomb goes off in a restaurant or bus. But that doesn't deter people here or in Europe or elsewhere from going to Israel to vacation, work, study. Daniel was the one who said that although 9/11 surprised Americans with the unpredictability of terrorism, it's a lesson the rest of the world has known forever.

Back to my conversation with Raphael, the first one that September, the drive from the airport: I'm sure I continued to express concerns. At one point he said, "Haven't you ever encountered a situation where you felt you just *had* to do something? You just couldn't let it be?" I shook my head, and he came back with, "You have, yes, you have! That's what your Holocaust studies are all about."

But I didn't *do* anything, I protested—I was merely a historian. I'll never forget his roguish smile. "You mean you don't do anything *dangerous*. But that's only because the Holocaust is over and done." I wouldn't have known *how* to help stop the Nazis even if I'd been alive then, I said. He countered with something like "You would have hidden Jews."

I emphatically disagreed. I said I didn't know *what* I would have done; I may have been an utter coward. No one can say for sure how he or she would behave in circumstances so different from what they've experienced. Besides, there are always good reasons to not take chances. Putting your own family at risk is one.

His comments stuck with me, Bernice, haunted me. I wrestled with the question of whether my interest in the Holocaust might have stemmed from guilt. From a suspicion I would not have had the courage to help my friends. I didn't share those thoughts with him. At some level I was ashamed.

I *did* say that putting oneself in danger wasn't to be taken lightly. But I didn't press the point, because I knew Daniel would. Instead, I asked whether his plans were likely to be effective because the group was so small. Weren't there other organizations better equipped to help?

He listed problems with the others. The Peace Corps doesn't go near war zones because even one death among their volunteers could hurt recruitment. Doctors Without Borders takes risks, but their role is medical. He also pointed out that there were actually a number of other churches involved in the program besides Joseph's—in the Netherlands, the UK, and Germany—and they ran these underground schools in other villages.

We both knew the conversation with Daniel was going to be hard. I saw both sides. Or, if I was on Daniel's side, I didn't see what difference it would make—Raphael would go anyway. All we could do was make his path as smooth as possible, the parting as smooth as possible. I didn't want Raphael to leave with bitterness between them.

We continued the conversation at home but quit talking when we heard Daniel's car in the driveway. His grin was a mile wide when he came in, and they hugged like always.

Would this be a good time for me to show you Raphael's room? See if there's anything there you might want to ask about?

CHAPTER 34

Gillian

THOSE ARE THE SOCCER TROPHIES from high school. Their team did pretty well. He wasn't in one of the very competitive leagues where they travel to out-of-state tournaments, like Pat's son, Ryan, did. That drawing—I'm not sure if it's a tree or a flower—is from a girl he dated briefly. And all those quotes—well, you can see who impressed him in high school: Neruda, Camus, Walt Whitman, Ida B. Wells. Is that Trotsky? I think the photos on this wall are musicians, contemporary.

I suppose someday we'll repurpose the room. Though neither of us has had any urge to do so. We don't need the space. Daniel has his study, and I use the guest room, which has a small desk and enough shelves.

We can start up again. Though I see your tape has already been running.

We had a nice dinner that first night back. I remember Raphael describing the linguistics research he'd helped with over the summer. And told us about a bike ride along the South Jersey coast. After the brief service for his grandfather—it was only him and Daniel and a few of his grandparents' friends—he stayed with a friend in New York and ate at a West African restaurant, where he ordered in Hausa. They understood him! The chef even came out and gave him some recipes. Raphael said the staff was very tolerant of his mistakes, corrected him politely. Honestly, Bernice, he seemed to absorb languages like osmosis. My only foreign language is German, and I'm far from fluent.

At *our* dinner, Daniel had prepared chili, I'm pretty sure—it was a favorite of Raphael's growing up and the most complicated dish Daniel knows how to make. It was a special thing between them, especially when Raphael was younger. If they saw a movie they both loved—sad or happy—or when Raphael had the cast come off his arm after falling from the jungle gym, and when he got accepted into college, Daniel made chili. I always need a large dollop of cheese.

We kept the conversation light. Daniel may have told amusing stories from school—a kind of "what the next generation is up to." I do remember thinking how it wasn't so long ago that Raphael was in high school.

When Daniel went to his study to grade homework, Raphael helped me with the dishes, and I asked when he'd tell Daniel his plans. I didn't want the subject to come up during the memorial dinner at Pat's the next night. He said they were going for a run in the morning, and he might then. He went to bed early, being on Eastern Time.

We sat in the living room, Daniel and I, sipping wine and listening to something pensive—Monteverdi, Purcell? Or Fauré; Daniel likes Fauré. We had only the one lamp on. We like to do that, listen to music with the lights low. The room looks cozy with the warm earth tones, the soft greens and golds and amber; I've always appreciated Susan's taste. Daniel was so content, turning the glass in his hand, smiling. I was so anxious. Not about Raphael— about Daniel. I worried about Raphael's safety, but that was a future problem; Daniel's distress was more immediate.

It was obvious in the morning when they returned from running . . . obvious they'd discussed Nigeria. Raphael had borrowed sweats from Daniel, which hung loose even though they were the same height. You could see the family resemblance, something about the shape of their foreheads, the eyes, despite Raphael's darker coloring and curly hair. Daniel's cheeks were redder, but they always are after running. I doubt Raphael was pushed to the limit.

They didn't speak to me or each other while unlacing their shoes and going to the kitchen for Gatorade, and I kept on watering the ferns as if nothing was unusual. Then they brought their bottles back into the living room. Maybe to have more physical distance from each other than you can get in the kitchen.

Everyone was silent for a bit. Daniel eventually said, "Don't do something stupid just to prove a point."

"What point am I trying to prove?" Raphael asked. "And what part is stupid?"

This isn't verbatim, Bernice, but Daniel's answer was, basically, "You have a keen intellect, an intuition about the larger picture, an ability to convey empathy." He brought up Raphael's article that Amnesty had reprinted almost in its entirety. Raphael should work at the administrative level, in other words, not do fieldwork. Fieldwork would waste his talents.

Raphael responded along the lines of "Those so-called talents would be put to use in the church program."

Daniel brought up that Raphael had no military training, and I guessed from Raphael's exasperated tone that he was repeating something said earlier. "We won't be in, or even near, an active war zone."

"That entire region is an active war zone," Daniel sort of snapped.

I might have arguments from later mixed in here. Like Raphael pointing out that Nigeria has over 180 million people going about their daily lives just as we do, and Daniel countering that Raphael wanted to go where people were *not* going about their daily lives, where lives were disrupted by violent "thugs." Daniel used that word more than "militants" or "terrorists."

Raphael never shouted but did get a little excited. "Those are the people who *need* our help!" They went back and forth: Iskoki and the other villages with Christian populations were more of a target; no, they weren't, because of their unique location. That kind of thing.

More of this is coming back while talking to you. Raphael said how Daniel was proud of his grandfather fighting in the Third Army during World War II, and Daniel said his grandfather had been defending his own country, that the US was at war with Germany.

The second those words came out of his mouth, Daniel regretted them. He anticipated Raphael's response. Actually, Raphael didn't *have* to respond—they both knew what the other was thinking. They've always agreed that national borders are an arbitrary demarcation. Why should a suffering family two hundred miles to the north, in Canada, be less of our concern than a family two hundred miles to the south, in Oregon? Or two hundred miles to the east, in Eastern Washington? Why do we erect this arbitrary geopolitical wall to limit our aid?

Have you heard about Raphael's "backyard" argument? I assumed it came up in your other interviews.

There are *practical* reasons for keeping our focus local: it's easier to travel, send supplies. Distance is always a factor, and crossing national borders, you can run into customs problems. Raphael could hop on his bike and be at our local food bank in ten minutes. And we have more information about local needs and how to go about satisfying them. Which officials to contact. So, yes, there are reasons to pay more attention to people closer to home.

On the other side of the scale is history important to both Daniel and Raphael. Many younger people don't realize this, but before Pearl Harbor was attacked, most Americans were against European Jews emigrating here. The general feeling was that helping people beyond our borders wasn't our responsibility. Empathy stopped at the coastline.

I wonder if *this* is how Daniel is Jewish. He never disagreed with Raphael's backyard argument. He strongly believes that a person's nationality, like their race or religion, shouldn't disqualify them from deserving help. Though obviously a single country can't solve all the world's problems. They both understood the reality of limited resources. And limited generosity by the public.

Back to that morning, after their run. I left the living room momentarily to refill the watering can in the kitchen and was on the verge of returning when

I heard Daniel say, "You know you're doing this as part of some unconscious calculus to get Aleecia back."

From where I stood, I could see Raphael, and he could see me, but Daniel was closer to the sofa and didn't know I was just inside the kitchen doorway. Raphael looked surprised at Daniel's comment and answered something like "Wow, that's the most desperate rationale yet."

"I *am* desperate," Daniel said.

"We broke up a year and a half ago," Raphael said. "It's ancient history. I've dated girls since."

Daniel responded, "Heartbreak doesn't disappear just because you date someone new."

Raphael shot a glance my direction, and I quickly withdrew further. I went out the other door into the hallway and upstairs to water the bedroom ferns. I hoped Raphael didn't read too much into Daniel's remark.

When Daniel came up to shower, he looked miserable. I repeated all the reassuring things Raphael had told me: Boko Haram was concentrating its activities elsewhere; its bases were in the forests and mountains to the east, even in Cameroon; Joseph and others in his church had visited the village where they'd be; and they'd have "leverage" if something happened.

Daniel often uses the term "leverage" when talking politics. Raphael was referring to the fact that someone in Joseph's church had a sister high up in the administration—maybe even in the White House—and the German fellow with them, Werner: his father knew Merkel.

I didn't tell Daniel that Raphael had added, "If someone needs to ransom me, there'll be back channels." He'd said that last part with a smile. Not to poke fun, just reassure. I did repeat his saying, "We're not trying to get ourselves killed—it's not a suicide mission." None of this alleviated Daniel's distress.

We, Daniel and I, talked about it many times afterward, until it became clear all we could do was hope for the best. Only once did Daniel get annoyed with *me*. A few days before Raphael and Joseph were due to fly to Nigeria that first time, I had been fretting about Mrs. Stein, who was scheduled to give a survivor talk the following week at one of the middle schools. I had been going back and forth with her daughter about carpool arrangements and let out how frustrating it was, and Daniel snapped that the only reason I could immerse myself in gruesome tragedies was that I believed in an afterlife and divine judgment. "The villains will get theirs," he said, "and the innocent will receive eternal balm."

I don't know if that's true, Bernice, that I believe in an afterlife and divine judgment. But it was beside the point. He was hurting. And he apologized. Said he wished *he* believed in some religion and a benevolent God.

Yet it may surprise you to know that we adjusted more than either of us thought possible, during the year Raphael spent in Borno. I guess I should save that for next time.

CHAPTER 35

Mia and Clara

MIA: YOU DON'T MIND INTERVIEWING us together? Because there's a sale up in Alderwood, our big mall, and I need to hit a few stores. Clar, she wants to know if we remember the discussion at dinner when Raphael announced he was going to Nigeria. I sure do. Not the specifics, just the mood. Sit down here, so we can both speak into the mic.

Clara: Scoot over more. You mean Dad's memorial dinner? He picked a silly time to announce it.

Mia: He didn't pick it—I asked him his plans. He said he was going to Nigeria for a year. Not in the Peace Corps, but something like that. We could have let it drop.

Clara: *I* would have. Ryan didn't. *That* I remember. He's not back yet, is he? Ryan, are you eavesdropping in the kitchen?

Mia: His rental car isn't out there. Didn't he go for groceries?

Clara: Well, let me know if he pulls up and comes in the kitchen door. You can hear absolutely *everything* between these two rooms. What was I saying about him?

Mia: I remember you accusing him of not believing in God.

Clara: She means Ryan, Dr. Williams, not Raphael. Ryan *doesn't* believe in God. *I* don't believe in God. I'm sure this makes no sense to you, out of context, but I can explain. Raphael said the region in Nigeria he was going to had taken their children out of school because Boko Haram was raiding schools and killing the students. Killing children! Did you know the name Boko Haram means "Western education is bad"?

Mia: Of course she knows—she's written a book—

Clara: That's right. So Raphael says he and a friend, under the auspices of the friend's church, were going to smuggle in Western education materials and school supplies.

Mia: Don't picture cargo containers—

Clara: Not large quantities—they needed to be discreet.

Mia: Their village wasn't near the ones Boko Haram was targeting, but the villagers pulled their kids out anyway, in an abundance of caution.

Clara: It was a Christian village—why *wouldn't* it be a target?

Mia: It was *mixed*, Christian *and* Muslim. It wouldn't be a target because it was tucked in a little out-of-the-way spot. Which might have been when Ryan came up with his brilliant idea that it "would make a lot more sense if the villages just converted to Islam." That's how we got onto religion.

Clara: Obviously our brother's not the Spartacus type. Anyway, all *I* said was that you can't expect people to abandon their faith like switching mouthwash brands. He shrugged it off with something like "If it means keeping your kids safe, you do what you've got to do." Which shows a complete lack of understanding of the role of religion in people's lives. I'm an atheist, yet I still am able to understand what religion means to other people.

Mia: Beth—Ryan's wife—she's Jewish, and her grandparents barely got out of Germany, and it bothered him that if they hadn't escaped, there was nothing they could have done to save their own and their children's lives. Converting to Christianity wouldn't have helped or joining the Nazi Party and shouting "Heil Hitler" all day long. Mao and Stalin and what's-his-name, the Cambodian, sent people to reeducation camps, but with the Nazis, there wasn't any escape hatch. All Jews were going to be killed.

Clara: So Ryan thinks if the villagers refuse to convert to Islam, they have only themselves to blame if Boko Haram kills them? Where would civilization be if no one ever fought back against oppression?

Mia: I'm not saying Ryan's right. Or wrong. He does think the villagers have an escape hatch that Jews didn't. Don't you remember Gillian's story about the trains to the concentration camps? When the trains slowed at stations, mothers handed their babies out the windows into the arms of total strangers. All they could do was hope for the best. I still shudder . . . I guess those are the most extreme examples, far beyond our own experience. But all parents make choices we wished we didn't have to make.

Clara: The only point Ryan made that I agreed with—and thank God he saved it for when we were alone—is that anyone who witnesses the aftermath of an explosion can't help but think of leaving the region. The amount of *blood* that gets splattered everywhere. I'm not even talking about body parts but just blood: blood on bodies, on the street, on walls and cars and bicycles—

Mia: I still don't think you can condemn the families who stay or convert.

Clara: Now I remember Raphael saying something like "You can't live life always calculating the risk of death." That's a young man, for you!

Mia: No, Clara, think of Gary Cooper in *High Noon*. Refusing to run away from the men coming to kill him? He didn't want to spend the rest of his life looking over his shoulder. It's adaptive behavior. Dr. Williams, Gary Cooper was one of our mother's heartthrobs. *Many* heartthrobs.

Clara: Honestly, I never understood how Dad put up with her endless list of actor crushes. Imagine if he went on and on about Marilyn Monroe.

Mia: Oh, please—if anybody so much as *winked* at Mom, she'd run away in a panic. I tell my guilt-ridden clients: letting the *eyes* roam doesn't cause trouble in a marriage. It's the hands you have to control.

Clara: Flirtation is a slippery slope. A *very* slippery slope. Not a triviality *at all*. Anyway, Mom could have kept it to herself while he was alive.

Mia: Dad got a *kick* out it! He liked her not being prim and proper. If this conversation makes it into your book, Dr. Williams, I don't know what your readers will think. I apologize for putting you through so much editing.

Clara: All right, back to Raphael. Didn't he bring up Syria or somewhere else in the Middle East? And Mom said she was glad he wasn't going there?

Mia: What I remember most about that evening is how *mature* he looked. He had none of that "I'm off to save the world!" He spoke about it as matter-of-factly as getting a sales job at REI.

Clara: I agree with you.

Mia: Make sure *that* sentence makes it into your book! Otherwise she'll never admit she said it.

Clara: I admit he didn't act like he was delivering earth-shattering news or that we should besiege him with questions.

Mia: Which people did anyway.

Clara: And he wasn't a Pollyanna either. Which is why those newspaper articles calling the group of them "foolhardy" were so offensive.

Mia: Mom said she hoped Daniel didn't read the articles, but I think he did. Otherwise why would he have told her he was avoiding talking to the media? Back to Clara's point about Raphael seeming adult. Adulthood isn't a single phase, and right then he was in the phase of "concern for the welfare of strangers." That's very different from the phase of "building a family."

Clara: Yes, a time comes when you *should* focus on your family . . . if you decide to have a family. Even if you don't—and *many* of my friends have decided not to—a time comes to construct a foundation for whatever lifestyle you choose. If it's just for yourself, then to establish a career or pursue art or education. And I don't mean formal education necessarily. My best friend from college defines herself as a lifelong student of the world. She means she never stops studying and learning about people, experiences, different cultures. I tell her she's a true philosopher. Insatiable curiosity.

Mia: She's fabulously wealthy, by the way.

Clara: The point I was trying to make is: unless you're the rare individual who devotes your entire life to strangers, there comes a time when it's appropriate to concentrate on those close to you and even yourself.

Mia: Therapists have a term for people who try to be saints— never mind, it's getting late. We should head out. Mom wants us to stop at Bed, Bath & Beyond for those freezer containers.

Clara: Let me finish, because I remember a conversation, and Raphael could've been there. Again, my point is that the instinct to care for family, especially children, is deep, what I would call "transcendent." I know, Mia, that's not a psychology term.

The conversation I'm remembering, which is sadly ironic, was actually with Daniel and Gillian. Derek and I had seen a production of *Macbeth* that was coming to Seattle, and they wanted to know what we thought of it, and for some reason we were discussing the scene near the end when the good Scots, including Macduff, are getting ready for battle against Macbeth. Macduff has just learned that Macbeth has slaughtered his entire family—Macduff's family. He's of course crushed, and a comrade in arms tells him to channel his grief and fury into revenge. I think the advice was meant partly as a pep talk, to get Macduff psyched for battle.

But Macduff answers that his thirst for revenge could never be slaked, because he couldn't inflict comparable pain on Macbeth since Macbeth had no children. The feelings of protectiveness toward our children are deeper than anything. We can't *help* but want to protect them . . . Why the discussion went in that direction I have no idea. But you're right; we should get going.

Mia: It probably didn't go that direction. You were just eager to parade your knowledge of Shakespeare.

Clara: Sisters are *so* supportive. Come, let's try to beat rush hour.

CHAPTER 36

Pat

I CAN SEE MY DAUGHTERS DIDN'T GIVE YOU a lot of time. Do you want me to squeeze in a short session before my book club? Usually we stick to the rule: nothing longer than three hundred pages, because, frankly, some of the books are duds. But we like Marge Piercy, and this was one of her better. *Small Changes*? It captures the time *perfectly*, the fastidious fifties reduced to ashes, and the rise of the phoenix, the liberated sixties. Dark Ages to Renaissance, that's how we pictured it. If you ever had to wear a girdle, you'd understand!

Mia and Clara, did they talk about the second world war at my dinner table? I know I gave you a "coming attractions." I can't regurgitate all the arguments—my grandson wasn't here to tape them. It was the one-year anniversary of Arnie being gone, and I wanted it to be nice, a *nice* remembrance. We'd say a few things, make toasts, and eat well. Joke, laugh—what *he* would've liked. I don't know if you've lost someone close, but I like to think he's still with us, looking down from heaven. He can't be part of the scene but can watch and enjoy it just the same. I always put a sliver of pie aside for him. I'll wait three days before eating it myself.

And without all the grandkids, I thought the meal would be civilized. Not that they misbehave, but you know what I mean. We'd have a quiet, genteel dinner.

Ha! Someone asks Raphael his plans, he says he's going to Nigeria to help the poor, and all hell breaks loose. Why, I don't know. One of the girls in my book club trotted off to Ghana a few years ago to work for an NGO, and she's sixty-six! But Mia, Clara, Ryan, they jump down Raphael's throat, Boko Haram this, Boko Haram that. I told you: I thought it was a rock band.

He kept repeating that the church running the show wouldn't send White volunteers just anywhere, so it was safe, the village where they'd live. Off the beaten path and tiny, tiny, tiny. The locals know these things. I have a story to prove it.

A friend of mine moved to Chicago back in the seventies.

"My kind of town, Chicago is . . ."

Her mother, a middle-aged White lady, drove all the way from Little Rock to visit. At the highway exit, she had to go through a tollbooth, and the man inside, who was Black, asked where she was going. When she told him the address, he said, "You can't go there from this exit, not this time of night. You turn right around and go to the next exit and ask directions from the employee there. I'm not allowing a White woman to go this way." He knew what the area was like. Keep in mind this was *long* before GPS.

When I told Ryan that story, he said the guy in the tollbooth was lucky he didn't get sued. Things *are* different now. But my friend's mother was grateful and not interested in suing anybody.

So when Raphael mentioned the church people thought the village was safe for White people, I figured the locals knew what was what, and I wasn't too worried. Or paying much attention, too busy passing out the food. I remember thinking how nice it was to have candles on the table—I wouldn't risk that with the grandkids. As for Raphael's answers to all the questions, I expected I'd get specifics from Daniel another time.

My granddaughter Amy talks about joining the Peace Corps after college. We'll see if it's more than talk—I never see her without her phone. I think it's sewn into her palm.

Arnie used to complain that people are fools about risk. His uncle was in London way, way back in the twenties, the Roarin' Twenties, and somebody asked wasn't he afraid to go home to Chicago, with Al Capone and Dillinger shooting up the place? As if ordinary people were being killed out of the blue. "Poppycock," his uncle told them, using their own language. If you want to talk of being killed out of the blue, *Susan* was, standing on a residential sidewalk in Seattle in broad daylight. By a stupid driver, not a gangster. So what's the risk of this or that?

Yes, I had many other things on my mind, things that didn't seem trivial. And Raphael was in such good physical shape, so full of life, you did believe he could survive anything. And he *did* survive—the whole year. He went, and twelve months later he came home in one piece.

No, the discussion at that dinner did not please me, what my own flesh and blood said. You can print that. If I have learned anything these seventy-three years on the planet, it's that children are not cookie-cutter versions of their parents. Maybe in the villages *you* study, but not any place *I've* lived.

Oh look, Ryan's back from the store. Let him finish up so I can go off to my book group.

CHAPTER 37

Ryan

CLARA PHONED A MINUTE AGO on her cell, said where she and Mia left off, if you want me to pick up there. They're just in for the weekend, so it's their only chance to go shopping. Clara came out for a conference, so Mia and I decided to bop up, it being our mom's birthday in a few days too.

You have an aunt in Seward Park or Rainier Beach, that end of town, she says. We played games around there, soccer, in high school. Man, I'm out of shape now.

Raphael used to kick the ball around—my sisters always freaked he'd break a window. If you've never played, you think it's random where the ball goes, but it's not—not with skilled players.

So this dinner when Raphael said he was going to Nigeria . . . I don't know how people remember these things—it's what, three, four years ago? I can't remember what Beth and I argued about last *week*. And what I do remember from three or four years ago probably doesn't jibe with what they do. You have to wonder if we were all in the same room at the same time. My daughter had us watch this movie *Rashomon*, and can't say it impressed me, but it had to do with people seeing the same events differently. I guess if we didn't, the earth would be one big happy family, right?

By the way, I hope last time I didn't give the impression that only my parents like the Solomons—my sisters and I do too. Clara used to get into these long, drawn-out discussions with Daniel and Gillian about academic stuff—trust me, after a few days of me and Mia, she was happy to have people interested in the Trojan War. Which I'm not knocking, just saying I'd rather watch a good ball game. And Mia and Daniel could get going about camping, like in the Cascades or on the peninsula. Mia isn't into hiking, but she's a good sport hanging around the campsite while Fred and the kids trek off, and if he catches a trout or something, she knows how to cook it. So she and Daniel liked to compare different parks and campgrounds, talk about stuff like that.

Clara also tipped me off that she told you I knocked religion. That's not true. Religion's just not something I'm used to talking about. Or *thinking* about, if you get right down to it. But I was all for instilling it in my kids; I want them to believe we have a purpose on the planet and they should be decent people and all. Beth's the same. She wasn't up for the whole bar mitzvah route with the boys—she can get pretty sarcastic when it comes to the "do this, don't do that" aspects. She thinks like I do: God's got to care about bigger things than whether people rest on the Sabbath or eat bacon. "Just be a mensch" is kind of her philosophy. Like when I tell off the guy who didn't watch where he was going and ran his grocery cart over my foot. Though she had no problem telling off the guy who tried to overcharge her on the muffler.

And like I mentioned before, she goes to temple sometimes. I go to church. Okay, maybe only once in a blue moon—you could accuse me of just keeping my hand in. But I do believe religion's a good thing, a civilizing influence.

Back to the dinner when Raphael said he was headed to Africa. The arguing wasn't as cutthroat as the big Thanksgiving blowup, the one my mom has, I swear, a photographic memory of. The Africa dinner, Raphael didn't have a girlfriend along to stir the pot. I wouldn't even call it a blowup.

You must've heard the basics: he said he was going to Nigeria to help kids who couldn't go to school because terrorists were killing them. If I'd heard of Boko Haram back then, it was just from skimming the paper. Clara probably filled us in. They're like ISIS—think that spouting the Koran excuses them for chopping people's heads off. The Islam bit is bull. They're anti anything White, European, American, Christian, Jewish, democracy, the whole idea of "live and let live." Africans who adopt those values are Uncle Toms in their book. They go after Muslims *too*. If you're a peace-loving Muslim, somebody who's actually into charity and good stuff, you're a target.

I get why some folks there would *resent* White people. Hell, Whites marched in and colonized the place. But you can't hang everything you do now on what people did to your ancestors hundreds of years ago. You know how many people the *Norse* wiped out? Vicious as hell—chopped up their enemies' kids and *fed them to their parents*. You should read the Norse sagas—heads impaled, intestines wrapped 'round swords, blood and gore everywhere. And the guys doing those things were the *heroes*. I'm not kidding you.

Does that justify somebody coming after me just because my dad's family was Scandinavian? No, I don't buy that.

Raphael didn't get on the whole guilt-trip bandwagon, and maybe that's why he never got on my nerves the way my freshman roommate did. He—the roommate—thought you should dedicate your life to helping starving people or whatever. It was wrong to have a Fourth of July barbecue, in his book, because families in Guatemala or somewhere were being gunned down by death squads. I used to tell him, you help those folks escape to America, and guess what? Grateful, happy as all get-out, *they're* throwing a Fourth of July barbecue. It's human nature.

I also think "All work and no play makes Jack a dull boy." And let me tell you, my roommate, he was pretty fricking dull.

Mia was even worse, way back when—tried to make us give up meat, paper towels, something else. Fortunately, Fred's a reasonable guy, knocked some sense into her. Don't go taking that literally. I just mean her crazy theories now are all about psychology.

My sisters were the first to jump all over Raphael for going to Nigeria. I threw in my own two cents, for sure, but it's hard now to separate out what I was thinking and what I actually said. It did sound crazy, an American kid with zero combat experience diving into a terrorist jungle. Wait—let me correct that: he was going to learn to use a rifle. But that was in case they ran into lions or hyenas or something. Guess it makes sense—a rifle won't do you much good against the Boko Harams. When I asked was he getting military training, he said no, but the village they'd be in was secluded, hard to find, barely on a real road. And they were "taking precautions." Like safe sex, right?

I did bring up how anyone could tell he was a westerner, plus he wasn't fluent in the language like someone born there, so how would he know if the people seeming friendly actually meant it or were just putting on an act? Tone's harder to get in a foreign language. And different dialects could do sarcasm differently. I might've asked how much trust he could put in the Nigerian Army—that kind of thing.

Not sure I said it out loud, but I was also thinking that plenty of places in the US could've used his help—why not do that. Join VISTA. I read somewhere that schools in Alabama or Arkansas, maybe both, are in bad shape— kids graduate barely able to read and write. Talk about your tax dollars wasted.

If Raphael was set on a foreign country—heck, I get it. Beth and I talk about a vacation in Australia once Amy's through college. But if going to another country's important, pick someplace where the crazies aren't shooting everybody up.

A woman I work with did some church stint somewhere, Costa Rica maybe. Not missionary, just helping the poor—or that's how they billed it. So she goes on and on how she *loved* the people, just *loved* the people. Felt a special *bond* with the *people*. A special *affinity*. I'm not BS-ing you.

I thought it was BS. She would've loved "the people" *anywhere*: Kenya, Uzbekistan, outer Mongolia. What she loved, in my opinion, was being treated like royalty. Not actual royalty but an American there to hand out favors: medicines, educational stuff, whatever.

Look, I'm not knocking groups like that—I'm sure they do good, and the people are probably genuinely grateful. Those programs spread goodwill a helluva lot more than the asinine Iraq War did. All I'm saying is that American volunteers are treated as special, and that's got to feel good to them. So they turn it into "I love the people."

Amy claims she's going into the Peace Corps someday, but I think that's just a line for her college applications. VISTA isn't as impressive, according to the guidance counselor.

I'll say this for Raphael: at my mom's dinner, he had answers to every objection. I wasn't persuaded, but he *had* thought it through, lots of little details. The location, the folks supervising, connections in the embassy. Not like Clara hitchhiking around Romania with some girlfriend or Mia white-water rafting—she can barely dog-paddle. And he wasn't going solo but as part of a church program that had been up and running a couple of years. It didn't change my mind it was a bad idea, but he wasn't walking into it blind.

Look, a friend of mine rock-climbs—the big cliffs, where you need fancy equipment and practice a gazillion hours. He'll get himself killed someday, for sure. At least Raphael hoped to accomplish something more than bragging rights.

If you're looking for a big mea culpa from me, about what I said then, this is probably it: hitting him on the danger. Plus, it was a mean thing to do to his father. I'm not claiming I'm the greatest son in the world. I've just always tried not to have my folks worry about me once I was out of the house. They worry enough while you're growing up: Are you doing drugs, drinking, flying high as a kite behind the wheel, are you going to knock up some girl? So the least you can do is give them some peace in their golden years. I don't think I actually said *that*, though. Sure hope I didn't.

CHAPTER 38

Daniel

GILLIAN SAID SHE TOLD YOU about after graduation, Raphael staying on at the university for the summer, finishing up a research project in the linguistics department. Not until he came home in September did he spring Nigeria on us.

Neither of us knew that much about the country, and I had never heard of Borno, the state. I knew about Boko Haram's atrocities, generally speaking, but otherwise just some basics: the country is extremely populous, hosted a series of corrupt regimes in the last few decades, and produces a lot of oil. I assumed it was deeply scarred by its colonial past.

I *was* pleased to learn that the official language is English, although Raphael would have been fine with others. I think that was the only fact that struck me as a positive. The climate—the heat and humidity—I can do without. And the sandstorms ... did you experience that? Joseph described them as tornados of swirling, sandy dust. But harsh weather didn't seem to matter much to Raphael. Some people wonder how we can live *here*, in an earthquake zone with forecasts of a "big one."

I have to say, he was very upfront about the reason schooling had gone underground. He told us that Boko Haram meant "Western education is forbidden," like you say in your book. *Western education is forbidden.* How was I supposed to argue that that isn't a battle cry worth opposing? How could I argue against helping young people who *want* a Western education, who will risk death for it? In his own way, Raphael, too, could go for the jugular.

Still, he tried to minimize the risks. I think he minimized them in his *own* mind. If there was any misleading, it was Raphael misleading himself. You can't, in this day and age, fool other people anyway, with Google at our fingertips.

He used air travel as a comparison. A jet goes down, and many lives are lost—it's an unspeakable tragedy, especially for those directly affected. But how often does that occur? Another example was the PLO or IRA setting off bombs in stores, restaurants, buses. It didn't deter all tourism or public activities—security was beefed up, people took protective measures, learned to manage. He pulled out statistics—deaths from car accidents, industrial accidents, accidents at home—which were meaningful to him but not to me. His point was that Boko Haram violence was sporadic. That's how he portrayed the situation. And to a certain extent that was true. In the years *before* he went.

The thrust of my argument against his going wasn't the danger. It was always: Weren't there better uses he could make of his abilities, better ways he could further the very same causes? He wanted to dedicate himself to "humanitarian crises," fine, great. Plenty of groups both in and out of government did that. He could work in DC in the administrative offices of an NGO that had programs in Nigeria, or even the embassy. And if he was determined to live there, what about positions in Abuja? Why go out to Borno for hands-on assistance that can be done by local people?

I never claimed the people in Nigeria are undeserving of help—you can't read about the wars and violence without feeling sick. Our arguments were more theoretical: long-term fixes versus short, like I've mentioned before. Raphael said the church program was a medium-term fix, a holding pattern.

I'll be all right—just give me a minute.

What else did he argue? He knew I opposed student deferments, opposed them on principle—I was too young to be drafted during Vietnam so never was actually put to the test. Still, my position has always been that nonstudents shouldn't bear a greater risk of losing life and limb. So Raphael said: Why should *he* be privileged to stay above the danger? My own arguments coming back to bite me. He *knew* he was pulling out all the stops.

After weeks of this, it became clear he had firmly decided to go. And Gillian convinced me I'd feel bad if he left knowing... how did she phrase it? Knowing I withheld my blessing. He was trying to make a positive difference in the world. She was right, obviously, so I shut up. Did I give him my blessing? Those weren't words he or I ever used, not really part of our vocabulary.

Among my many regrets—*many* regrets, Bernice—is that I never actually articulated how proud I was of him. It would've been a lie at first—I was just worried sick. But when he returned the following year, I could've put into words all I felt. Which definitely included pride. Plus some awe. Of course respect. Gillian said he could tell anyway, from my behavior. I'd like to think so.

That fall—we're in 2012 still, before he went to Nigeria for the first time—I helped out buying gear, discussing medical insurance, visas, all the rigmarole foreign travel entails. I didn't spend the month before he left sulking—in my own clumsy, conflicted way, I tried to be supportive. We went on a few runs, and I used the opportunity to ask what he knew of the climate and topography and local customs. He'd learned quite a bit—Joseph had been there and filled him in.

I got a library book with photographs taken specifically in Borno. Truly beautiful photographs of panoramic views, mountains in the distance, the plains scattered with long grasses—I could imagine them swaying in a strong breeze. Nothing like our prairies, with crops filling every square inch water can be channeled. Did you like it, the untamed savanna? Happen to see any of the

fauna: wildebeests, elands, giraffes … whatever else thrives on grass and space?
And becomes easy prey. I asked Raphael if he expected to see lions, rhinos,
leopards, that kind of thing, and he said he didn't think the area had rhinos
and wasn't sure about the other animals—they might have been restricted to
preserves. He did assure me the villages themselves weren't in the middle of
open terrain, so I shouldn't worry he'd get stampeded or become a juicy tidbit
for a tiger.

I remember that the presidential race helped a little to distract us from
his impending departure. This was the year of Obama's reelection. Gillian had
a mile-wide grin when she hung up the phone after talking to her father. He
wasn't voting Democratic—hell will freeze over first—but he was full of praise
for Romney. Up to that point, Mormons were no better than heretics. I guess
he concluded a heretical Christian was better than a heathen Democrat. He
knows Gillian voted for Obama and generally supports Democratic candi-
dates, so he must assume I'm a satanic influence. Doesn't realize I have no sway
over her leanings, theological *or* political.

Yes, I tried to give Raphael a cheerful send-off. Gillian assured me I didn't
come across as phony, though, honestly, it *was* an acting job. I remember
when he flew down to Tulsa for language training before leaving for Nigeria,
and we dropped him off at the airport, and Gillian and I walked back to the
parking garage, her chattering away about the month he'd spend at Joseph's,
me scouting out the best place if I had to vomit.

One very astute thing she did was load me up with books about Nigeria.
I don't mean the ones with photographs. Fiction, actually. You must've read
some of the authors who've become world famous, like Soyinka, Achebe,
Adichie? Many others crop up in anthologies. I don't usually read fiction, but
Gillian intuited it would make me feel connected to Raphael.

A few centered on violence—the colonial wars and coups and government
brutality—but most had ordinary settings: family tensions, lovers' quarrels,
frictions between tribal and European cultures. I'm not a literary critic and
can't say how well written they were, but they did make me feel Raphael wasn't

so remote. Gillian's no dummy. Though I have to wonder about her settling on me.

How did *she* cope? I may have mentioned before: She doesn't display her emotions—*publicly* display them. But make no mistake, that quiet exterior conceals the full spectrum of human feeling, from empathy to passion to . . . In some ways she's tougher than I am. You should see the support she provides the Holocaust survivors—it's far more than a chauffeur's job. She'll never get on a soapbox or blow her own horn, but I doubt you can find a single positive trait where she's not the equivalent of forty of me.

Yes, in some sense, she got the short end of the stick. But to get her to say she wants more—the times I've pressed her to divulge any unmet needs, she claims she hasn't any. Brushes away the idea with a line about being a minister's daughter. I'm tempted to retort . . . Never mind.

Again, apologies I don't have as much time today. Next session I can tell you what I remember from that year he was in Nigeria, 2013, and what he told us of his experiences.

CHAPTER 39

Aleecia [telephone interview]

THANKS FOR DOING THIS BY PHONE. I called because I was cleaning out an old email account from college that I used for private stuff and ran across something you might want to include in your book. Usually Raphael and I IM'd, but if his phone or network was acting weird, we switched to this email. I don't want to forward the whole chain, because it contains a bunch of personal stuff about me woven in. I printed it out and highlighted the sentences about him, and if it's okay, I'll just read that part.

He was in Seattle for break and telling me about a conversation with his father. He actually wrote some of it out like dramatic dialogue, not "He said, I said." I'll try to make my voice different so you know whether it's him talking or Mr. Solomon. This is Raphael:

I asked him why I was an only child, why he and mom didn't have more kids. Was I that obstreperous they couldn't handle a second? He said they actually had been trying for another child but had a series of miscarriages.

"Why didn't you adopt?" That's Raphael again.

This is his father: *"We were looking into it, but each time we began the process, which is quite a bit of paperwork, your mother got pregnant again. And miscarried. Always late in the first trimester."*

"Why didn't you stop trying to get her pregnant and just settle on adopting?"

"We gave it one last shot. If that pregnancy didn't come to term, we agreed we would adopt."

"And?"

"She made it to the second trimester—to fifteen weeks, actually. You never realized it because she didn't show much. We planned to break the news shortly, both to you and Grandma and Grandpa."

"But she miscarried again?"

"No."

"What do you mean, no?"

"The accident. The car."

I was silent a bit, Raphael writes. Then asks his dad, *"Why didn't you ever tell me?"*

"What would be the point?"

"I had a right to know."

"I suppose that didn't occur to me. I may have felt I was shielding you—from knowing you lost a sibling too."

That's where the dialogue stops, Bernice. Then Raphael writes: *I'm so pissed at him. I had a brother or sister I never knew about. Don't give me a lecture on fetuses not being people—I'm not saying women shouldn't have the right to choose. But nobody chose for my sibling not to be born.*

That's the only email with stuff that's not super personal—I mean about me.

It's funny, but printing this out had me thinking, wondering again why we broke up, trying to understand it. Why I *wanted* to break up. This doesn't need to go in your book—for all I know, you'll end up leaving out all my stuff, and that's okay. Besides, the reason I give today might not be the reason I'd give tomorrow. But I want to pin it down for myself, to know what I was feeling and thinking. Maybe I'm doing penance—that's what David thinks. Did I tell you he's at Oberlin?

Raphael's resilience got to me, like a sore spot that wouldn't heal. No matter *what* happened, in the news or wherever, and no matter *who* treated him badly—even me—he was never down for long. Bad stuff didn't *stick*. He always rebounded.

I sound awful, don't I? So much in him was good. If I decide someday to have kids, I'll do my best to make *them* resilient. But to be honest, I have to say his happiness got to me and made me stop loving him.

Now I'm thinking Carl might've had a version of that . . . that resentment. Carl's always *proving* himself. Won't let people forget he's smart, educated, cultured. Raphael didn't have to prove a damn thing—people assumed it about him, at least once he started talking. Carl knows *Latin* and wears Italian suits and rakes it in on Wall Street. Raphael could wear jeans and hoodies and get treated better. Carl didn't say much when I called and told him Raphael died. He could've been feeling guilty, you know, for not liking him.

Don't think that Raphael wore jeans and hoodies at my folks' at Christmas—no way! He was eager to please, especially them, and dressed nice. Though if they'd been hostile or rude for no reason, he never would've taken it personally. That's what I mean. Probably would've chalked it up to the natural consequences of people being subjected to White racism. He just couldn't stay mad.

Not that I'm looking to date somebody angry or bitter—I'm so done with that. I don't know *what* I want. I'm a fucking mess. It doesn't really matter, does it, but I hope he got over me quick.

CHAPTER 40

Gillian

PAT SAID SHE AND HER CHILDREN gave you an earful about the remembrance dinner for Arnie? So I won't go into that. And I don't remember much anyway.

Raphael stayed here until after the election, busy with getting his passport, visa, immunizations, other preparations. Already his thoughts were in Nigeria—he wasn't glued to the TV when the returns came in the way he said he'd been in 2008, the way we *all* were. Back then he had phoned us the minute Ohio was called. But of course, that election was more momentous.

The week before Thanksgiving, he went down to Tulsa for language lessons—a few members of Joseph's church know Hausa and Kibaku. Many of the older villagers in Borno speak only one, Raphael said, while younger people may know both and are learning English. Was that your experience too? I was surprised English is the official language—I assumed once people threw off colonial rule, they'd select an African language. Maybe that would've created more disputes, all the different ethnicities competing against one another, a Balkan situation. Daniel said the civil-servant class was already used to English.

We didn't go to Pat's that year, because Daniel wasn't feeling well. A quiet meal at home was fine with me. And Raphael was at Joseph's. We did go to Pat's Thanksgiving the following year, 2013, which was fun, all of us anticipating Raphael's return in January. But this past year, we skipped it. Maybe someday we won't dread being a damper on their family liveliness.

The boys flew to Nigeria in late December 2012, and Raphael called from Abuja and then Maiduguri. He couldn't promise when he'd call again—the cell service in Iskoki was out, they'd heard. And he couldn't be sure there'd be service the next time he was in Maiduguri.

As I mentioned, he blamed the outages on poor maintenance and the harmattan, which I guess you managed to avoid? It was only later that we learned Boko Haram was specifically targeting communications facilities. Such different years, 2012 and 2013. Yet the Nigerian government didn't impose the state of emergency until May of 2013. And Boko Haram wasn't even on our State Department's Foreign Terrorist Organizations list—Daniel checked regularly. It wasn't added until November, shortly before the boys returned home. I guess it takes time for people to distinguish among the different groups—they spin off and splinter from one another. Al-Qaeda, ISIS, al-Shabaab, al-Qaeda in the Maghreb—and I know there are many more. Boko Haram is separate from all of them.

Have you heard it characterized as an umbrella organization? Someone told us that it was, and for *dozens* of West African groups, each having its own leader and ideological twist. We Americans lump them into one: "Muslim extremists." Which quite obviously is unfair to the millions of Muslims who oppose violence.

To be honest, as the terrorist attacks became more frequent, I made a point of avoiding, of not scouring, the news. Daniel subscribed to online editions of the *Guardian* and BBC, and any mention of Nigeria caught his attention.

One positive consequence: He developed an interest in local cultures. Not just Kibaku and Hausa but also Igbo and Yoruba. He read a number of books and was telling me how groups and villages ruled themselves through a council of elders. Or by elected leaders, or a family dynasty. Clergy might be powerful, or else there could be a complete separation of church and state. I teased him he'd become the first to teach West African history in high school. I think he was eager to compare what he'd learned with Raphael's firsthand experiences.

What fascinated *me* was reading about Nigeria's World Heritage cultural landscapes. You too? The photographs are stunning, and to actually *visit* Osun-Osogbo and see the sacred grove: That dense foliage and trees drooping over the river and lagoons, the sense of lushness. And elaborately carved walls and figures and twisted bark arches . . . those massive wooden statues with their enlarged heads and torsos . . . all of it so arresting. What a treat to walk among the shrines. I know many of those sculptures were made recently, but they represent long-standing Yoruba culture, like the worship of fertility goddesses and other spirits. And people today repeat the ancient religious rites and festivals. Were you able to visit Sukur? I've read that their furnaces date all the way back to the Iron Age. The photos of the steep crop-filled terraces . . . so much ancient history right before your eyes.

Okay, as I said, Daniel kept up on the news. I didn't realize how closely until Raphael phoned in the spring and told us about the state of emergency. After they hung up, Daniel filled me in a little more on the terrorist attacks. He said the president's name should have a comma in it: Goodluck, Jonathan.

The church moved Raphael and his group to another village, Lambu, which was even smaller and more isolated. Some residents had never seen a White person except on TV. Which struck me as funny—that people can be isolated enough never to have seen a White person yet still have TVs. No electricity either—I guess they run on batteries? A generator? I don't understand those things. Now that I think of it, Raphael said only a few families could afford a TV. Their homes became the hangout whenever the kids had free time, between school and chores.

We were grateful he was able to call and email sometimes, at least from Maiduguri. If only Joseph was able to make the trip to the city for supplies, his sister Yvonne would be sure to relay a message. Poor thing, she was stuck playing the intermediary; his parents weren't up to it. They were *extremely* upset Joseph had gone, despite it being their church's program. A lot for her to handle—she's only in her early twenties.

In his quick phone call from near Lambu after the state of emergency, Raphael said he only had a few minutes left on his phone card and just wanted to let us know there was a beefed-up military presence and checkpoints everywhere, so we shouldn't worry. Later we learned a military presence isn't always good news.

You of course know about the Baga massacre, but we didn't. The first reports Daniel came across—I think in late April—the attack was blamed on Boko Haram, and he said the only civilians killed were accidentally caught in the firefight when the army arrived. Later, Raphael told us an *army* unit was responsible. I couldn't believe it: an army unit massacring hundreds of villagers, setting fire to homes, shooting children and the elderly. What kind of army is that, in this day and age?

Raphael tried to set our minds at ease by contrasting his own situation. Baga being much farther north and east, around Lake Chad, in "solid Boko Haram territory," it was less surprising the army went berserk there. That doesn't make it any more excusable, and he was as horrified as anyone. But he wanted us to understand it was a little less random so we wouldn't think he was in increased danger.

Yes, he kept repeating they weren't in a large population center—even Iskoki wasn't a hub or regional marketplace, somewhere that would attract outsiders. And both towns were in savanna or hard scrub, with few trees, plus some distance from the forests and mountains where Boko Haram liked to take cover. I called the Iskoki-Lambu area their "pouch" because it was nestled away from all the main roads. You yourself said you'd heard nothing about them until after your research on your book was done. You were very brave, going there.

What else? The boys rarely left the village. Joseph always drove the van with everyone who was White huddled in the back behind tinted windows. I remember Yvonne trying to allay our fears by saying the villagers in Iskoki and Lambu felt safe enough to not bother enlisting in the Joint Task Force. Daniel and I didn't know what that was until googling. We were *not* reassured. If local civilians need to band together to augment the police force, how safe can it be?

Still, it was sweet the way Raphael made me promise I wouldn't let Daniel get "gloomy." Daniel doesn't get gloomy—if something upsets him, he does yard work or goes for a run. I'm the moody person here.

When violence *was* in the news, even in other parts of Nigeria, Raphael usually managed to get us word he was safe. The first few times he phoned, it threw us into a small panic—seeing the international number pop up—but it turned into a good thing. "It's Raphael," we'd shout if the other one was in a different room.

Let me leave the subject of danger and tell you some of the interesting things from their year there. I assume it doesn't matter if I mix up what we knew at the time and what Raphael and Joseph told us after they returned?

There were two others in their group: a German fellow, Werner, and a Dutch, Ismail. I think Ismail's family originally was from Morocco. In Iskoki, the first village where they stayed, all four housed with a farmer's family. He grew locust beans, nuts, and some form of rice. Raphael said that every winter, the farmer had to worry the rains would be late, which could spell disaster.

All the houses in Iskoki are single-story, and dirt floors and thatched roofs aren't unusual, but the four of them "lucked out," Raphael said, because the farmer had a tar roof. Daniel and I didn't learn until much, *much* later the reason the farmer was so prosperous, relatively speaking: because many families farther to the northeast had to flee their farms to escape Boko Haram attacks. Not just in Borno but Chad and elsewhere. Which created a serious food shortage in the region. So the Iskoki farmers never lacked for buyers if they were willing to take their goods to other villages.

Initially Raphael and the other boys worked on procurement, going into Maiduguri for educational materials. Abuja or Lagos were too far away. By mid-February, many of the experienced teachers in Iskoki had left, whether because of violence or opportunities for better pay, I'm not sure. But Raphael and Joseph and the others suddenly were in demand for hands-on instruction. As you might imagine, for Raphael at least, it was like offering candy to a baby.

He was assigned to teach teenagers English, maybe some French and even a little Arabic, which he'd begun to learn in college. They did a form of team-teaching, Raphael integrating words from the history and science lessons into vocabulary lists.

I don't know what it was like in the villages you were in, but some of the children Raphael taught were already trilingual, speaking Kibaku at home and Hausa with family and friends living elsewhere and meanwhile becoming fluent in English. And there was a *fourth* language—I believe Joseph called it Kanuri. The younger people pick up bits of the ones they're not taught, I guess the way I've picked up some Spanish just from signs. But on top of all that, studying French or Arabic!

Iskoki, though small by our standards, is large enough for several churches, several marketplaces, several wells for drawing water. A number of schools have remained open—only the children attending the sister church to Joseph's were in their program. Like other villages in their area, there was a mix, religion-wise, for generations. Interfaith marriages between Christians and Muslims weren't rarities. I think they were all Kibaku, though, and very proud of their ethnic heritage more than their religious identity. Particularly the Kibakus' reputation for courage, which complicates having to accept powerlessness in the face of Boko Haram's weapons.

Daniel may talk more about this, because it impressed him so much: the mix of modern and primitive. The bathrooms were certainly primitive. Raphael said their water had to be hauled from a sink hole, and in either Iskoki or Lambu, their toilet was a hole in the ground in the backyard. The hole was kept covered with corrugated iron or plastic, I suppose to keep out animals and keep in odors?

He said mud-brick houses were the norm, without plaster or paint. Some families lived in huts. But Iskoki had a few paved streets. Joseph later joked that they lived with paved streets in Iskoki during the dry season and in unpaved Lambu during the rainy, which was like swimming in mud. I'm sure he exaggerated. He had a teasing sense of humor.

Though it's a little funny to me how most people think that dirt floors and dirt roads and going barefoot are always deprivations. One of my fondest childhood memories is a family vacation in Florida when I was eight, leaving behind a Minnesota winter for a bungalow on the Gulf. My brothers and I went barefoot and lived in our swimsuits the entire week. Right after breakfast, we raced out to the beach. I still remember the feel of the waves washing over my knees and then receding. And how after a full day of swimming and digging in the sand and building sand castles, I'd collapse into bed at night. Never wore a pair of shoes or put on real clothes. A true beach urchin.

What we love in childhood doesn't always last, I know. I haven't been anywhere tropical for twenty years, not since visiting a college roommate in San Diego. Sometimes I wonder if I might still like that kind of vacation. Not the digging in the sand—maybe scuba diving? Several colleagues have raved about Kauai as a true getaway.

Daniel isn't averse to roughing it. He and Raphael liked to go camping. I'm sure that experience helped Raphael adjust easily to rural Nigeria.

Actually, I have a photo he printed once he got home, of the students in their uniforms. Let me get it—I left it on the table. Oh, and a few others.

This was actually a photo of a photo; the original was taken when they still attended school. Such nice, crisp, starched white shirts. Yet I can't help but think how uncomfortable they must have been in the heat. And I wonder how they ironed them. This was their old school—Raphael said it was pretty typical of the ones he saw, plain rectangular buildings made of what looks like brick. The roof may be zinc. The houses they picked for home-schooling had high walls. The students and teachers would divide into small groups in the courtyard.

And this photo here—you must have seen similar things, the women at the market carrying food baskets on their heads. The clothing is so colorful, bright reds and yellows and greens, and the bright turbans. I think this is actually a vendor. What did he write on the back? *Shoppers and woman selling dabino.* That's right, those are dates in her basket.

I really do love the tops: bold orange, yellow, lime-green, turquoise—so eye-catching. And the geometric shapes in the skirts, not just stripes but rectangles and diamonds, sharp angles—the busy-ness looks like modern art. It surprised me that even women in Iskoki and Lambu wore bright colors, because the sermons Raphael told me about seemed austere, you might even say puritan. I don't mean the style of dress is risqué, just exuberant. Like the singing and dancing. Although he said men and women didn't dance together. You must know all this, but it was new to us.

Traditional gender roles are still the norm in Raphael's villages. The fathers and sons earn a living farming, hunting, or as merchants, and the mothers and daughters do the shopping, cooking, cleaning, laundry. Is that true in the larger communities you researched? I think how much we complain about traditional women's chores, but we have electricity and appliances. Raphael said the women also had to gather wood every day to heat water for washing and cooking. They never would let him help, and it made him very uncomfortable, the subservience. He kept having to rebuff offers to wait on him and massage his feet—something the women did for their husbands. That would make me uncomfortable too.

But he was amused by other things that fit traditional roles: girls whining to their parents for clothes like their friends had or they saw on TV. Wrestling seems to be big among the boys? I guess it doesn't require much equipment. Raphael was sorry neither Iskoki nor Lambu had soccer teams for the kids, although everyone followed the professional games on the radio. Do they call it football? What surprised me is soccer's *so* popular that even the professional women's team is cheered on. I suppose that happens here too. I think my parents were genuinely proud when I was awarded my PhD, not simply relieved to have something positive to say when the neighbors asked "What's Gillian up to?"

But Raphael thought things were changing, and many of the younger generation, the girls, are very intent on careers. High-level careers too. Esther and Mary, two sisters in Iskoki, typify, to *me* at least, a variation you often see in American families. Esther wants to be a pediatrician, and Mary sets her sights on marrying a handsome "city man," not because she wants to leave her village but to show off to her friends and neighbors a great catch. Isn't that like an American fourteen- or fifteen-year-old? Mary could've been from my hometown in Minnesota. *I* was the one who always felt the oddball.

Unfortunately, as I'm sure you know, families like Esther's have to pay not just for tuition but also for textbooks, notebooks, school fees, uniforms. A small silver lining: while they are being taught "underground" through the church, they don't need to wear uniforms or pay fees.

Other impressions . . . A father constructed a makeshift stage in the courtyard so his daughters could act out plays and skits. The girls were able to fashion costumes and scenery from things at the local market, and Raphael and the other program instructors got to watch one show. But it was in Kibaku when he hadn't been there long, so he couldn't catch a lot of the dialogue. He *was* entertained by the squabbles beforehand over who got to be the heroine and who got the singing part, that sort of thing. I was reminded of *Little Women* and Jo's theatrical productions.

I never had that, growing up with brothers. My siblings were more interested in sports. All our playing was outdoors, games like tag and hide-and-seek and dodgeball. We made snow forts but not for drama, only to defend against snowball assaults by the neighbor kids. It tickled Raphael to think I was a bit of a tomboy. I had to be, if I wanted to play with my brothers and their friends.

I assume the plays the girls put on were Nigerian, but I never asked. He said one of them loved Shakespeare. And many loved makeup and jewelry—whenever Raphael or Joseph drove into Maiduguri, they were saddled with lists of things like lipstick and bracelets and necklaces, inexpensive ones. Plus snacks—the local versions of potato chips and cookies. One girl craved toffee. I was able to find a few tins to include with one of Daniel's packages and got a text message out of the blue, a thank-you-Mrs.-Solomon, from a Nigerian number. The next time we spoke, Raphael said it was for the toffee. I guess he didn't want to mention we're not married.

Bernice, I won't pretend it was an easy year. The main thing helping us through it was knowing how much fun Raphael was having. As he said, violence wasn't the day-to-day reality for the people in Iskoki and Lambu. They were concerned with their jobs and studies and relationships and—in Daniel's words—"what to put on the table for dinner." The atrocities in other parts of Borno may have hovered in their consciousness—I don't know. I guess that's what you wrote about.

Raphael used to say: when people have hope, they can bear more than they imagined possible.

Chapter 41

[Emails from Raphael, in Nigeria, to various recipients]

[January 11, 2013, email to Daniel and Gillian]

Came in to Maiduguri last night for supplies and have few minutes on friend's computer. Ismail at doctors without borders interview—told you he's just biding time with us. Good to have a doc around for no other reason than deal with Jos's panic every fever's lassa. Reality is more deaths due to lead poisoning from the mines. Relax, dad, no lead mines in Borno ;)

I'll be sorry if Ismail leaves for dwb because I've been picking up some Dutch from him and he corrects my Arabic. Werner is keeping my German going while I try to immerse in Kibaku.

Not all supplies we're getting are for school, some are food, things hard to find in Iskoki. Tell Pat to google jollof rice and moin moin to see great stuff we're eating. You can google too, ingredients aren't that exotic but the way they prepare them I'll have to master. Doubt you can get decent pawpaw or baobab in states though. And you might want to use chicken versions unless you find a store selling goat. Jos almost gagged on it, he's a wimp.

Harmattan not bad, though dirt roads dusty enough anyway. Werner said last year dust completely blocked windshields, even with windows up it got in hair, eyes, nose. The plus side is it cools things off, which welcome in our area. We have little overhead cover because not enough rainfall to support tall trees. Some places totally treeless, flat, Jos says reminds him of Okla prairie. Baobab look like gigantic gnarly bones, skeletal, not living vegetation. Haven't tasted fruit yet. According to Ismail farther north even less vegetation.

Nigeria's about five different climates. We are in savanna, quasi tropical, low rocky hills. Shade happens when a hawk flies by with a guinea fowl in its clutches. Another downside of harmattan is you can't bike. Will get one soon—pretty common mode of transport, at least till rainy season turns roads to mud. Will donate most of winter clothes, it's unlikely we'll manage a trip to the Sahara, and here temps don't get lower than 50s. Many villagers go barefoot or slippers, never wear shoes. Got to run, R

[January 24, 2013, email to Daniel and Gillian]

Glad we had a chance to talk because access to phone iffy and I only have a few minutes now. J and W trying to scare me about rainy season, not flooding but humidity. J says it's like wearing a wet balloon clinging to your skin in a sauna. W says like wearing a turtleneck, wool hat and gloves in a warm bath filled to your chin. I won't repeat their other metaphors. Like I said on the phone, the nonstop sun doesn't bother me, it's novelty if nothing else.

[February 2, 2013, email to Daniel and Gillian]

Killing time in Maiduguri waiting for the guy with supplies to show up. Last few weeks studied bunch of curricula and syllabi. Super frustrating that things we need like textbooks and histories could be at the touch of their fingertips if students had computers. But pretty hard to have computers with no wifi not to mention electricity. And the towns that have libraries stink both in number of books and literally, sometimes treated as garbage dumps.

One of the apt guys here is part of a group trying to train teachers in computers so they can go to villages if and when they get on some kind of grid. Like J was telling you at Thanksgiving (2011?) part of the problem is all the palms that need greasing to get anything done.

Still haven't figured out nuances to clothing/class differences, just within Hausa/Kibaku. Igbo and Yoruba have their own distinctions. Here some villagers wear plain caftans and some wear designs. Ditto the dashiki. I don't know if it's a money signal or maybe family. Same with folks who go barefoot versus sandals. Certain local teachers dress very western (not cowboy western) like white buttoned shirts and long black pants and polished shoes. J says guest pastor used to dress that way in Okla, no matter how hot, wore a suit under his robe. That's what clinched it for J not going into the seminary.

Main animals in Iskoki are horses, donkeys, cows, goats, chickens but actually saw a couple of camels. One family has oxen. No pigs that I'm aware. I'm leaving out the unwelcome animals.

[February 2, 2013, email to Sarah J.]

Great meeting you. The minute Ismail walked in the door this morning I pumped him for the local diseases so you can compare. I don't know why he wants to join msf, given Nigeria's cornucopia: TB, hiv, malaria, dysentery, and the "easily preventable if vaccines were supplied" chicken pox, measles, whooping cough, tetanus, polio (I thought we'd eradicated it, shows what I know). And, sorry to say, a few others that I'd never heard of and didn't manage to ask him to spell. I think one sounded like miasma.

He loaded up on wound stuff like bandages and antibiotics. Accidents aren't the only problem. Rat bites pretty common. Kids are taught to wash hands really carefully before going to bed so rats aren't attracted by the smell of dinner. You probably don't want to hear some of the injuries doled out by parents as punishment, stuff that would get child protective services at your door in no time back home. Let's just say harsh spices placed on sensitive membranes. One girl got it from her father because he caught her squeezing a boy's hand.

Anyway, we really appreciated the yams, they're actually hard to come by in our area, maybe lack of water. And sorry I probably won't be able to get down to Benin before you split. If you think you can make it back to Maiduguri again, try to get us word.

Raphael

CHAPTER 42

Daniel

ARE YOU SURE YOU DON'T WANT some water, soda, coffee?

Gillian said she started to mention details about his year in Nigeria. You're familiar with the area, but when my students asked, I used to tell them that Borno State is our Maine, tucked in the northeast corner of the country and viewed as a hinterland by the rest of the population. Though the temperatures in Borno rarely dip into the forties.

I taped a large map on the back wall of the classroom because a few students expressed interest. Maiduguri was near the top, and about thirty or forty miles south, I drew an imaginary line, a narrow ellipse running east–west. The area within the ellipse wasn't seeing any Boko Haram activity either in 2012, before Raphael went, or in 2013. Iskoki and Lambu were located well within the "imaginary line."

One of my students, a World War II buff, quipped that Raphael was within the "Imaginot Line." Pretty clever. I couldn't bring myself to remind him the Nazis *circumvented* the Maginot Line. I suppose I was in as much denial as prewar France.

Gillian said she liked to picture them concealed within a pouch, I guess like a kangaroo pouch.

The only place Raphael and his colleagues—his White colleagues—ventured was to Maiduguri, which was where we sent supplies. They wanted graph paper, language workbooks, maps, the periodic table—I forget what else. Frequent travel wasn't an option, not just because of safety concerns but because the church van was shared among several villages. I have since wondered whether the van was tempting booty for terrorists. Boko Haram, I know, prefers motorbikes, which allow a brief stop to shoot or toss grenades and make a quick getaway. Still, a van could come in handy, and groups in other villages might have found uses for it. Raphael did mention people in the cities had small cars or pickup trucks, but where he was, most used bicycles. Was that true in your area? And he said the streets were narrow and unpaved, so cars weren't necessarily practical even if you could afford one.

The van trips pretty much stopped by spring, when Boko Haram attacks increased, and in May, when the state of emergency was declared, Maiduguri went under curfew. Raphael's little group had already relocated to Lambu and rarely ventured out. Even with increased surveillance and army presence, the terrorists struck again in June. Killed nine students taking exams. There are no words for such vileness.

I suppose you had to deal with army checkpoints? Joseph likened them to highway robbery. The police did only a cursory search for weapons, and if you forked over some money, it was even more cursory.

Let's move on to less depressing things . . . like Raphael's impressions of the country. The first photos he texted when they arrived in Maiduguri were too blurry to make out much. Nondescript three- and four-story buildings scattered here and there, Quonset huts, residential streets that could've been in Houston. One university's walls were painted bright yellow, orange, turquoise—colors like that—which Gillian said reminded her of Florida motels. A far cry from the stone and brick and ivy we tend to associate with universities.

The phone service pretty much stopped once they left Maiduguri, and to be honest, we got better pictures off the internet and library books. Some beautiful mosques—did you see any? Of course, the books go for the picturesque. We saw many photos of women carrying water on their heads in attractive containers, glass jugs encircled with twine or colorful pottery. Joseph told us later that most water is carried in those gaudy-yellow plastic jerry cans. Not the ideal image if you want to promote tourism.

Quite a rocky, low-brush terrain in Borno. The internet photos of baobabs make them look shadeless, although Raphael said a large one in Iskoki near the marketplace provided enough shelter from the sun that men gathered under it listening to the radio. Their transistors picked up a BBC station broadcasting in Hausa.

I assume you were struck by the astonishing juxtapositions, like in Maiduguri. Raphael's photos were surreal: Mud huts with thatched roofs sitting right alongside modern glass office buildings. Open sewers beside debit card kiosks. Cars on paved streets dodging cows and goats. He said the women carrying jugs on their heads have cell phones in their pockets. Traditional ways going back centuries if not millennia and technology less than ten years old, compressed together in a single city block.

Were the villages you were in as remote as Iskoki? He said the women still cook over open pits, fanning the flames with leaves or blowing on them. The men still farm with hoes and machetes. And to bathe, they draw well water and heat it over a fire. Yet they watch TV, listen to radios, and text to another village the price of groundnuts. The teachers use slate boards with chalk and leaves for erasers while explaining modern physics. It's hard for me to imagine.

And the *speed* of change is breathtaking. Cultural shifts are hard even when spread out over generations. The loss of the "old ways" ... Not that I subscribe to the view that all cultural shifts are bad. My students bandy about the phrase "cultural imperialism" whenever Western ideas are introduced to a new region, and I give them a hard time about it. Colonial powers do terrible things, but like in everything else, change can be a mixed bag.

For instance, I've read that some African groups held to a superstition that twins were demonic—did you encounter that? The groups practiced infanticide. And even today some believe that albino body parts have magic powers, so they murder in cold blood to harvest organs.

Obviously these barbarities aren't unique to Africa. *Many* cultures have practiced human sacrifice. My point is only that you don't have to glorify colonialism to be thankful for the ways in which certain European ideas changed certain cultures for the better. In one of those ironies that historians love, it was the *British* who banned the slave trade in Nigeria, not the groups the British colonized. I'm not saying the British or the other European colonial powers weren't barbaric on a grand scale—they were. Hundreds of thousands of Africans were tortured and killed—the inhumanity was, as my students say, "epic." Yet European society also had its better angels.

I'm reminded of an argument Pat's daughter Clara had with her own daughter. An argument that typifies a phase many teenagers and young adults go through—a rite of passage, practically. This was at one of Pat's large Thanksgiving dinners, which you've heard about.

Jody—she must've been thirteen or fourteen at the time—was criticizing American society for being selfish and self-centered compared to . . . I forget whom exactly—I think it was farmers and fishermen in one of the Central American nations. She delivered quite a speech, kind of a noble-savage take and the virtues of a simpler existence compared to our highly technological society. After a two- or three-minute harangue, she took a breath and awaited her mother's response. And Clara said, sort of matter-of-factly, "These noble farmers and fishermen consider it their God-given right to beat their wives." Jody was left speechless.

Sorry for the digression. Again, my only point is we're not doing truth any favors by pretending that simpler societies are all goodness and light.

Nigeria . . . what else . . . Gillian said she told you about Raphael and his colleagues switching from procurement to teaching. The impression I had was that the church group had a rigorous curriculum for subjects the students were tested on to get into the university and not much of a curriculum for other subjects. Except for English, the language instruction was loosey-goosey.

Raphael was asked to teach English and also Arabic and, later, a little French. The Dutch fellow was a doctor and taught biology; Joseph did math and physics and maybe some chemistry; and Werner's bailiwick was Western history and literature. It seems funny that the curriculum included the classic European civilizations, early Greece and Rome. Perhaps a vestige of British influence. Certain aspects of British culture are still openly admired, despite the history of colonial rule.

The fellow who'd taught Arabic left behind detailed lesson plans—basic grammar and vocabulary—as did the French instructor. I'm not sure about lesson plans for English, but Raphael could easily have punted. He did have us send him certain middle school ESL workbooks.

Speaking of digressions, if you've taught at all, Bernice, you know some of the most rewarding lessons occur when you deviate from your teaching plan. Raphael joked he could always justify going off on a tangent if he did it in the language the students were studying. The math and science instructors had considerably less freedom, since the state-administered exams were too important, the students' only ticket out of the village.

Raphael loved the teaching, but he also liked getting to know his students' families. As one example: he had extended discussions with an older sister of one of his students—I might have mentioned her, Esther? She was already fluent in English and at sixteen could engage him in debate at his level about current events. She had formulated cogent opinions about the US presence in Afghanistan, a young person in a remote African village with only occasional access to Google and online news! It's ironic: I assumed a certain provincialism in people in remote villages, and I'm the one guilty of provincial ignorance. She knew more than many of my own students, and her own country wasn't even directly involved.

Her position, by the way, was that the American military presence in Afghanistan is a *good* thing. For girls and women, life under the Taliban would be harsh. Raphael argued in favor of the US disengaging, bringing the troops home. Which wasn't unusual—he often criticized US foreign policy for over-using the military and underusing diplomacy.

"Hard power versus soft power" is a debate you can't have in the abstract. Each region and time period has its own peculiarities. And, to his credit, Raphael was not dogmatic about one approach over another. If I had *any* effect on his thinking, Bernice—which I have often wondered—it was probably in the parsing of situations, avoiding the broad brush. Still, as I say, he tended to favor soft power over military intervention. The fiasco in Iraq had that effect on a lot of people. And, in an earlier generation, Vietnam. You could say that Kuwait and Kosovo stand out as exceptions, situations where hard power accomplished good. And World War II, but that's ancient history to his generation.

Despite their disagreement, something Esther said resonated strongly with him. I wish I could recall her exact words. The gist was this: the pluses and minuses of *any* given policy depend on whose ox is being gored.

Her idea might strike us as obvious, but keep in mind, sixteen is young for grasping this unhappy truth. Human beings at *any* age want to anoint one answer as right and another as wrong—we don't like a mishmash of pros and cons. My students hate studying conflicts with no perfect answer. Just as Jody didn't want to have to reconcile the simplicity of some less-technological societies with a common practice of wife-beating.

What I don't know, and I probably have no business postulating, is that Raphael's tutoring may have been the reason she arrived at a sophisticated perspective for her age. I'm probably falling into the doting-parent trap again.

We better stop now so I make it to pickleball on time. We have to reserve the court for a single hour.

CHAPTER 43

[Emails from Raphael, in Nigeria, to Daniel and Gillian]

[March 5, 2013]

Sorry phone call cut out, par for the course. We're in Maiduguri for supplies.

You'd get a big kick out of my students, dad. Two have a running debate right up your alley, Hobbes versus Locke. They've read more than I ever did. Before he left for msf, Ismail said their bio education is pathetic, not even at Gregor Mendel's peas, and Mendel was 150 years ago. Jos is trying to pick up Ismail's load, on top of math, physics, chem. But two students know enough to be like TAs, one knows calculus and his cousin is a math whiz. At least most kids are super motivated. Girls especially because if they don't get university education, stuck under father's thumb or husband's. Not like in US where a hs grad can get a job, own apartment, live independently.

And not just motivated but incredibly well behaved. I thought it was because they didn't know what to expect from a white person, but Werner said it was because they can't believe we won't use a switch like the regular teachers. I'm waiting for novelty of a white teacher and fear of corporal punishment to wear off and get the full range of sass and acting out.

Oops, gotta run, van's leaving. Love, R

[April 27, 2013]

To elaborate on phone call and dont know if you'll get this, cant go into details of transmission, all 3 of us moved to Lambu, which isnt that different from Iskoki, just smaller. Families welcoming. Like I said, nothing to freak out about, just someone in Iskoki getting paranoid we made them more of a target. Btw, no signs of bh anywhere near. Most wanted us to stay and Jos got pretty vocal arguing with the ones who didnt but Werner and I said whats the point—our goals not adding dissension to the community. Consulate knows we moved. If worried about me, think about Ismails parents—msf may send him to Congo instead of Burkina.

Iskoki families threw nice going away party with singing and dancing. Esther, the history sage who wants to be pediatrician, gave me a great poster she drew herself as a goodbye gift. Her sister Mary sorry only about Werner leaving because he knows who famous movie stars are and has been to California—and hes German! I wish she knew as much about African independence movements as about Nollywood. Will try to call or email again soon but no guarantees given electric service. [238]

Gotta run, love to everybody, R

CHAPTER 44

Clara [telephone interview]

I HOPE THIS WON'T OFFEND YOU, Dr. Williams, but the reason for this call is to find out how many more times you'll interview my mother. Because it always upsets her. I know you don't mean to, and it's not that you're pushy or ask prying questions. But Raphael's death coming just a few years after my father's, she's very vulnerable. She might try to hide it, but trust me, people can act hard as nails on the outside and be quivering Jell-O on the inside.

And they were only neighbors. She has her own children and grandchildren, and he had *his* own family. Gillian was like a mother, and if anyone tells you different, it shows how unsuccessful second- and third-wave feminism have been. We're *still* expected to be nurturing in all the traditional ways: staying home, baking cookies, et cetera, et cetera. Gillian didn't do a lot of that, but she was a reliable presence in Raphael's daily life, reliable and sympathetic.

I'm lucky—I like to cook. My mother taught me and Mia when we were kids; she put us at ease in the kitchen before we knew what we were doing.

I'm sure there were flops galore, but she never scolded, so throwing together a dinner is second nature. The other domestic arts *completely* escape me. My daughters couldn't show off fancy art projects in school like their friends did; they had to fend for themselves in that arena. Who had time to mix up papier-mâché and glue macaroni noodles and stock the house with yarn and glitter and whatever else I was supposed to manage? Academia is a demanding profession, as you well know.

Thank God I got tenure relatively quickly. It allowed me to anchor the girls while Derek flew here, there, and everywhere. Granted, an international practice is lucrative and gave Brooke and Jody certain advantages, but one week he was in Japan, another, London or Tel Aviv or Berlin. He tried to block out a few times for staying put so I could visit *my* family for more than a day or two, but except on those rare occasions, *I* was the one getting the girls off to school in the morning and putting dinner on the table at night. And if anyone tries to tell you that commuting every day into Boston from Newton is some kind of a *picnic* . . .

Then, before you know it, all that hectic rushing around to school and playdates and piano lessons and clothes-shopping—bam!—they're grown and gone. You tell yourself that the reason they're happy far away is that you raised them well, you prepared them, it's right that they venture off to do their own thing. I wasn't any different, *very* eager to travel. And they keep in touch—my God, where would I be without email, texts, Skype? I shake my head thinking how my mother had to manage on just a phone call a week, if she was *lucky*.

Maybe Ryan's right: that's why she latched on to Raphael when the three of us left home. She doesn't like email and texting. I don't know. I am very fond of my students; they're good kids; and I like my role as teacher and mentor. Very much. Still, it's not the same. If Derek weren't gone so much, if I weren't always returning to an empty house . . .

I really hate my house. A friend is after me to contact *Better Homes and Gardens*, to encourage them to take a tour and photographs. She says my house is "beautiful, pristine, and tasteful." It is, but . . .

In seventh grade I brought a new classmate home. She seemed so cool, and I wanted to be friends really badly, and I thought if she saw the amazing loft bed my dad had built for me, she'd be impressed. We walked in the front door, and I was *completely* mortified. Ryan's ratty sweatshirt hung off the closet doorknob, and you could smell his soccer stuff bunched in a heap. Mia's art pencils were scattered on the sofa. The dining room table was a mess of newspapers and mail. I vowed then and there that when I became an adult, I would *never* let my own home be untidy. But, honestly, now I would love to see my daughters' clothes and shoes and makeup scattered everywhere. It would be a welcome sight to come home to.

The two of them would die laughing to hear me say that, but it's true. Of course, to Derek's family our house is a hovel. What, no tennis court? No heated pool? How can we survive?

Look, Daniel's pain and Gillian's are a living hell. Like the parents of the girls in Nigeria—the girls who weren't found—or whose children were killed. But I don't *know* them. I *do* know Daniel and Gillian, and it breaks my heart.

And to see what my mother is going through . . . It's selfish, I admit, my wanting this unspeakable tragedy behind her. For Daniel and Gillian, it will never go away, so they may find your project palliative. My mother has the opportunity to eventually move past it.

People used to criticize Americans for being phobic about death. The classical period, the early Greek and Roman cultures, didn't brush it under the rug. Now I see obituaries inviting people to *celebrate* the deceased. My sister is big on "facing death directly," says we should accept that death is a part of life.

Death is *not* a part of life—it's when life ends. My daughters would paraphrase: death sucks. Grief is the natural response, not all this emphasis on celebrating. To me, that's even *more* death-phobic. It's certainly grief-phobic. Hate the bastard—don't pretend death's welcome.

At least my mother doesn't pretend it hasn't been hell. But she claims she's coping fine by keeping busy with friends and book club and pottery. If I thought that, I wouldn't fly cross-country every other month. Not that she'll ever acknowledge my visits help. Still, we don't do these things to be thanked, do we?

I'm not putting down her book club and friends and other keep-busy activities. I encourage my daughters to do the same when "shit happens." A boyfriend dumps you, you didn't get chosen for this team or that award: turn to a favorite hobby or take up a new one. Join a club. And they handled things well. Even in high school they adhered to our rules and curfew, kept up their grades. Okay, Brooke *might* have stretched curfew once in a while. They didn't do drugs—the bad ones, at least. Played in the school orchestra—Brooke, flute, and Jody, clarinet. Jody was on the school newspaper.

I tried to balance opportunities and choices. I do the same with my graduate students, and my relationships with them have been good—most of them. There was one—oh, never mind him. He left the field altogether.

And they're still doing fine, my daughters. I don't meet the boys they date, but how can I? Brooke's in Barcelona for her junior year, and Jody hasn't brought anyone up this way, not yet. Derek met one young man, took them to dinner in Manhattan a few months ago. A musician. I thought maybe Juilliard, but apparently some emo band, and don't assume I know what that is. I dated many types before Derek—it doesn't mean anything.

You know, on paper, Dr. Williams, I have everything: career, marriage, two daughters in good schools. Years ago I gave an interview for the alumni magazine for a column they ran on "success stories." I *felt* like a success story. That's not a boast—I've had lucky breaks galore. I'm *well* aware of my privileges. I just want to explain how that feeling of success that I had was feeling *in control* of my life.

I have less on my plate now and more actual control, but I don't feel it. I just don't. Is it because in a few years I'll turn fifty? You think how you rushed around, worked crazy hours, juggled a million things, all to make the people you care most about happy, and then learn you were making them miserable.

Why am I talking about all this?

Listen, I believe in scholarship; you know that. I would be a hypocrite to tell you to curtail your research. I'm just looking out for my mother. So the sooner you wrap up her role, the better. And I know she likes you, so please don't take my request personally.

CHAPTER 45

Gillian

WHERE DID WE LEAVE OFF? I know I mentioned Boko Haram's attacks escalating in 2013, especially in rural areas, something we didn't truly appreciate until Raphael's return. Since he couldn't claim the violence was still sporadic, he defended not having come home earlier by arguing we have drive-by shootings and murders every day here.

Daniel said there was no comparison, that ideological motivations make all the difference. They turn violence into terrorism, *parlay* it into terrorism. The example he gives his students is: a Black family buys a home in a previously all-White neighborhood, and a cross is set aflame on their lawn. They are the victims not only of that single act of violence but of the threat it will happen again if they don't move. Assuming they do move, no other Black family will dare buy their house or any other house in the area. So ideologically motivated violence isn't an isolated incident affecting one person one time; it terrorizes a large population.

I don't mean to be explaining that to you; I'm just relaying what Daniel used to say.

Let me go back to the positive things from Raphael's year in Nigeria, the ones *he* found interesting, so I don't bore you with what *we* found interesting. It's hard because we asked so many questions after he returned in early 2014. About different cultures and oral traditions, customs at weddings and funerals, values instilled in the children. He loved talking about his students. Do you want to hear some of those stories?

There were twins in Lambu, Paul and Jenny, fourteen or fifteen, I think. Paul was always arguing with his father, who wanted him to become a pilot instead of an actor. Jenny wanted to become a physicist or opera singer—such different pulls!

What fascinated Raphael was the private language the two had begun developing as babies. They wouldn't teach it to him or anyone, so he kept trying to decode it.

One day, he quizzed Paul about Plato's *Republic*—whether as part of an English lesson or helping another instructor, I don't know. We had to study *The Republic* in college, and I'd forgotten everything until his story brought it back. The shadows on the cave wall? Honestly, all I remember is that Plato believed human beings live in a metaphorical cave, and we see shadows moving along a cave wall and mistake them for reality. When we become enlightened about truth, it's as if we emerge from the cave into daylight and realize we had only been seeing shadows, and now we do see reality.

For me, well, I had been marinated for so long in Thomas Aquinas that these ideas were jarring. Plato's distrust of the senses runs counter to my understanding of the senses as avenues for acquiring knowledge. But philosophy and religious doctrine have always been a little outside my grasp—I didn't last two semesters as a theology major. Still, Raphael's story brought back memories.

Apparently Paul was very intrigued by the shadow metaphor, and as he and Raphael discussed it, Jenny had a running commentary in their private language, and it was making Paul laugh. Raphael tried even harder to decipher the words, and finally, after Jenny completely dissolved in giggles, Paul explained that she was describing friends of theirs and how they would look as shadows in silhouette moving along a cave wall. One walked like a cow; another, a giraffe—that kind of thing—and in between answering Raphael's questions about Plato, Paul would try to guess from Jenny's descriptions the friend she was describing. You can imagine fourteen-year-olds giggling about that, especially when their teacher isn't in the know.

There were other student stories . . . let me think . . . This isn't about students, but Raphael phoned once all excited to say he'd seen a stampede—giraffes, gazelles, wildebeests—I forget which. No, it was gazelles. He was too far away to make out the predators chasing them. When we hung up, Daniel said he was relieved the stampede was far away because otherwise Raphael might have tried to save the doomed ones. He was joking, of course.

Something Raphael knew I would find particularly interesting is Borno having many different Christian denominations. A few are pacifist, which surprised him because the Kibaku boast of being the last to succumb to British rule, among Nigerians. And were only defeated because they had bows and poisoned arrows against British guns. I wasn't surprised about the pacifism. Christ exhorts those in the midst of violence to turn the other cheek. Not that other groups haven't preached the same thing.

My thesis advisor—gosh, this is almost twenty years ago—he said that when a person is trapped in an environment of continual violence, his or her *only* escape is through moral exaltation. I didn't agree; I felt he was reducing an important spiritual insight into a coping mechanism. And, in fact, many of those who survived the Nazi concentration camps did *not* become stoics or ascetics or live lives of deep meditation—if anything, they thirsted for the pleasures of human interaction and joys of music and art and recreation. Are these ideas you discuss in *Communities under Siege*? Daniel and I can't bring ourselves to read it—I'm sure you understand.

I do find it interesting so many Christian denominations exist in Borno. We have many different churches here, all worshipping the same Trinity, reading the same texts, adhering to the same essential tenets, yet insisting on separateness. Denominations and *sub*-denominations. But in Borno I would have expected more banding together because they're not the majority religion, plus they're persecuted by zealots.

The persistence of animism is interesting too. Is that also true for Muslims—do they blend traditional beliefs with Islam? Raphael said a former pastor had tolerated students using leaves to ward off evil, but the new pastor said leaves are the equivalent of false idols.

Which reminds me, I have a photo Yvonne sent—here it is. It's from early 2013, before Ismail left for Doctors Without Borders . . . as you can see, wearing the traditional *dashiki*. So beautiful—deep, rich maroon against the gold. The way Raphael explained it, the garments and colors are symbols of defiance against White colonialism. The White volunteers weren't comfortable wearing them, would have felt like—you know—cultural appropriation? The heavyset fellow is Werner.

Joseph and Ismail were the only ones to venture into Muslim villages. The elders they met were very observant yet *very* anti–Boko Haram. They see Sharia as less puritanical, so giving up singing and dancing and holiday festivals was sad for them. But it was safer. Still, they continued to watch TV and DVDs with Western content. The better-off, that is—most people only had transistor radios. Raphael said it was a running joke in one Iskoki family that to get their parents to learn English, the children watched English-language movies, not Hausa. I had the impression they were soap operas and had the parents entranced.

One thing I'm curious about and never got around to asking Raphael: Is extramarital or premarital sex considered a terrible sin? I forgot—you're the interviewer. Maybe when we're done, you can tell me.

I know that among very religious Nigerians, both Christian and Muslim, sex outside of marriage, and even public displays of affection, are serious sins. But what's considered unacceptable publicly is often indulged privately. The reason I'm curious about Borno is that often in areas of high childhood mortality, pregnancy is a blessing because so few infants survive, and Raphael did say infant mortality is high. So perhaps out-of-wedlock births are not frowned upon? Though the mortality in Borno isn't simply infants: Boko Haram is killing children at eight, ten years old and teens. That has to be more heartbreaking.

I don't know, I'm not one to say. A year or two after I moved in here, Daniel asked if I wanted children of my own. I said I didn't feel the distinct tug many women feel. I couldn't rule out changing, and I wasn't *against* having children. If anything, Raphael made me see all the pleasures they afford. But I wasn't thinking about it, and becoming a mother had never been part of some great life plan. To my parents' chagrin, I'm sure.

Did *he* want children, more children, I asked. He said he didn't "need" more—he felt life was full as it was—but he didn't want to deprive me of something I was secretly pining for. If I did want children, he said, he'd be happy to be a father again. I believed him. He loved doing things with Raphael and watching him grow intellectually, emotionally, morally—all the different ways we mature.

I guess we let the subject drop. My life felt full too, with my research, efforts to publish, running the survivors talks, cranking out grant proposals—which seem never-ending. And, looking back, I can see that even after Raphael went off to college, we stayed busy. Daniel started the school's civics club. He'd hoped it wouldn't become a racket where the kids attended just so they could write something impressive on their college applications. It didn't—he was very pleased. The students were learning how democracy works "despite their best intentions to goof off." And he and some other teachers began a standing pickleball game twice a week. The four of them are still going strong.

I wonder if I should have raised the subject again. Was he leaning toward having another child but leaving it to me to initiate the conversation? That's like him: reluctant to apply pressure. Sometimes we communicate so well, but . . . I guess all couples have their blind spots.

Raphael would have made a great father. He loved children. As I mentioned, telling us about them took up most of the phone calls—the things they said, theories they spun about politics, history, philosophy. I'm sorry I'm blanking on them.

Oh, this was funny: In Lambu they had rap battles. His students made him and the others be judges. You were in Borno, so nothing I say will surprise you, but it certainly surprised *us* to hear that American-style rap had found its way into tiny villages. The children goaded *them* to try rapping, and Raphael said he was pathetic. But Joseph and Werner both drew applause.

On the subject of music: That January when he came back, in 2014, Raphael taught me several Nigerian hymns. Two may be Anglican in origin, but others had a rhythm I would guess is traditional Kibaku. Arnie would've enjoyed them. "Lord, hear our prayer . . ." A very joyful one begins "Raise voices all."

Daniel found the tensions between generations amusing because it's the same here. Older people want to pass on their traditions, and the younger want to break with them. One father in Iskoki was afraid if his son moved to the city, he'd abandon the church—a quarrel played out in this country every day. It's an overgeneralization, though. Some younger people are eager to maintain traditions, follow in the family footsteps.

I almost forgot! I came across another email from Raphael. I must've left it in the printer. Let me get it.

Shall I just read it? He sent the email November 20, 2013, to both of us.

I'm fine so don't get upset I'm in an infirmary in Maiduguri. Broke my leg falling out of a tree—yes, really stupid, not a tall tree, and I'll save the embarrassing story for in person. It's a simple fracture and I'm healing fine and just waiting for the crutches to show up. Jos postponed his flight to hang out with me "till I'm on my feet again." His sense of humor is god-awful but he puts up with my pestering about how to say this and that. Maybe I didn't tell you, he's returning stateside to apply to grad school in civil engineering.

My return date is set: flying out of Maiduguri Jan 2, will send connecting flight info later. I'm planning to check out grad programs too, in international studies. Not frustrated here, just can be more useful doing other things. (If you send me a single "I told you so" the deal's off). We've made a positive impact not only in curricular stuff and supplies but in giving these kids hope. They take our presence as a sign the larger world cares and the crap raining down on them will end. Not one night have I gone to sleep wondering if I've made a difference.

Werner quotes some German proverb that a good conscience is a soft pillow. You can tell we all have our quirks. He wants to visit Seattle, in theory to see me and the scenery, but it's really the microbreweries. Can I reclaim my room till I get a stipend or find a job? Btw tell Pat I learned some great uses for sorghum. Here they call it guinea corn, but US types should work fine.

Love, R

I don't need to tell you, Bernice, how thrilled we were to read this. "Ecstatic" might be more accurate. Daniel ran across to Pat's, and the two of them came back laughing.

He bought new brake pads for Raphael's bike, began removing his own papers and books out of Raphael's room, asked if I thought we should paint it. I said to wait until the warmer weather so we could open windows to disperse the smell, and besides, the paint would dry faster.

CHAPTER 46

Pat

SO NOW YOU'VE SEEN THE STUDIO. A nice setup, isn't it: daylight on the one side? Thank goodness my grandchildren outgrew the foosball table. I was afraid if I got rid of it, they'd never visit. The pottery wheel fits easily. If anything will get me to stick to my diet, it's a fear the stool will crumple.

And like I said, don't worry, I'll let you know loud and clear when I've had enough. Come back as often as you like. You figured out I can talk till the cows come home—*you'll* be the one begging to leave.

But I'm not sure what else to tell you. Raphael only texted me a few times when he was in Nigeria—he hardly got the chance to call or text or email *Daniel*. Though I'll say this: Gillian was very good about filling me in when he did get to a phone or computer. He told her to describe certain foods I would like and said we'd cook them when he returned. *Kosai*—fried bean cakes? And goat, which I tried once, and it didn't agree with me or the other way around. Stay away from baobab powders, he warned, the kind you get on

Amazon, because they're nothing like the fruits. Gillian showed me a picture on her phone, still on the tree, hanging like piñatas.

His texts to me were for care packages—could I send certain things, and he would pay me back when he returned. I didn't mind—they weren't expensive. I don't know why he asked me and not Gillian. Maybe he already was asking her for a lot. What he wanted—get ready for this, Bernice—was tampons and sanitary napkins. *Lots* of them. And cosmetics, women's cosmetics.

I know Gillian and Daniel were sending school things and double- and triple-A batteries and large plastic tubes of skin cream. I was over there once when she was taping up the carton, and she said the skin cream was because Raphael kept scraping his face shaving. Vaseline was too greasy, which is what the villagers used. I would've thought they wouldn't bother shaving, until I remembered the heat. Now *that* would get me to cut my hair!

I didn't tell them he asked me for the female stuff; he must have had a reason. I'm sure the *sales clerk* wondered why I was filling up the cart with those things. Thank goodness he didn't ask for condoms! That would *really* have got them talking: Was I some kind of cougar? I *should* have bought some, you know, the kind with . . . what do they call it . . . ribbing!

I always included a treat in the packages just for him, snacks he liked, since I knew everything else was going to his students. Once I sent a T-shirt with the Mariners logo—he and Arnie used to talk baseball.

We never did manage to find time to cook together, the few months he was home—he was always running hither and yon. So much energy. Not nervous energy, like one of my daughters. Happy energy.

The year he was gone, 2013, I must admit, had me plenty distracted—no time to worry about the situation there. The biggest to-do here was Kirsten, Mia's daughter. She came to live with me temporarily, before checking herself into rehab. More like checked in kicking and screaming. Not literally, thank the Lord.

She'd pleaded for a gap year after high school, and Mia and Fred said fine, as long as she was productive. She moved in with her boyfriend, a sophomore in Eugene, and found a job waiting tables. A *nice* restaurant that gave her experience in the real world. Plus auditing art classes. Wasn't that hunky-dory? I'm thinking: finally one of my grandchildren is taking after me, with the art.

Oh, Kirsten was taking after me all right, getting high with her boyfriend while she was supposed to be auditing. Didn't tell anyone *el* boyfriend had dropped out and was dealing. Using *her* wages to buy from the dealers up the chain! Money laundering is what it was. At eighteen! We Eriksens are a precocious clan.

And that wasn't the worst of it. Mia and Fred get a two a.m. phone call from the ER. The good news: their daughter's alive. The rest of it: she'd OD'd on—wait, I better not say anything to get her in trouble, you know, with the law. This isn't under oath, is it? I'll just deny it, the ancient brain in dementia. If any officers are reading this, it's all hypothetical.

It turns out the child wasn't a novice with the needle. And she'd lost a great deal of weight. For rehab she pleaded to go to some place in Eugene, but Fred wanted her near me, a facility his friend recommended. Which is why she stayed here first—they had a waiting list. I said I was fine with it, but honestly, I had visions of her trying to wheedle every last cent out of me to buy drugs. She's a good kid, but headstrong like her mother. In their own quiet way. You never know you've been butting heads until the discussion is over and your brain feels sore.

I thought of finding a lawyer to figure out how to hide my money, I really did. But we got through it all okay—if she hocked anything, I haven't noticed it yet, and she might've been doing me a favor, helping me declutter. Mia won the big battle, and Kirsten moved back down to a place near them. After her rehab stint, she was able to start at Oregon State, which is in Corvallis, not Eugene near "Mr. P-O-S," Mia calls him. You don't need me to translate?

And now, two years later, the girl's pulling solid Bs and dating an applied physics major. She *is* like her grandmother! There you go, Pat, off on a tangent.

Raphael. I can't imagine he ever used drugs. But that's not realistic—he must have, like everyone else. *I* certainly did my fair share. Arnie wouldn't put up with it—said if I wanted to get stoned or drop acid, give him a call when I was ready to stop, and maybe we could date again. I quit on the spot. They say ultimatums never work. Ha!

Yes, 2013 was a difficult year for everybody. The wildfires near Ryan got so bad they were ordered to prepare to evacuate. Beth, who I always complained—not to her face, of course—I complained to Arnie she was too materialistic . . . well, at the mere mention of the word "evacuate," she throws the kids in the car without packing a single extra piece of clothing or jewelry and drives all night to a friend's in Mill Valley. She didn't waste a second.

Ryan stayed put because it never became an order to evacuate, just an order to *prepare* to evacuate. He wanted to stick around to ward off looters. When he told me that, I let him have it. Mr. Wyatt Earp! If the smoke and fires didn't get him, the looters would've. But they were spared—the flames *and* looters.

Even Clara hit a rough patch. She never said so directly but gave the distinct impression *someone* was stepping out, and it wasn't her. At Thanksgiving, she let slip that Derek wasn't actually on a business trip—they were in couples counseling, and a big family to-do wasn't something he was "up for."

You know what else she said? That she wished some of my go-with-the-flow had rubbed off on her. Not those exact words—I told you, neither of my daughters would be caught *dead* using sixties slang. It was more: "Unlike you, I want people to be perfect, and when they're not, I have a hard time forgiving." I had to hand it to her: she looked in the mirror. That's not easy for *anyone*.

You must know I'm not superstitious, Bernice, though we had fun with tarot cards in the commune. But I do remember thinking at the time that 2013 was destined to be an unlucky year. Still, Clara and Derek ended up going to the Bahamas for Christmas, without the girls. In the photos they look genuinely happy. Who wouldn't look happy on a tropical beach in the middle of December? Yours truly, for one. I can't stand the heat. And the whale-watchers would descend if I showed up in a swimsuit.

Maybe I shouldn't have spilled the beans to you about Clara and Kirsten. Oh, I can't be bothered with that now. Truth is truth. Besides, and no unkindness intended, I just don't see your "supplemental volume" becoming a bestseller. So the family secrets won't travel farther than the family. And the way we jabber, they're probably not even secrets.

CHAPTER 47

Aleecia [telephone interview]

IT WAS SPUR OF THE MOMENT, like I emailed: a bunch of friends came into town and wanted to go for drinks. I didn't know them all—some were a year or two behind me—but three were classmates I hadn't seen for a long time. I think I mentioned I did my last semester in Paris and didn't get back till after graduation?

The bar they picked had a big table where all ten or eleven of us could fit, and we traded seats a lot to talk to everybody. This guy Perry ended up next to me and mentioned knowing Joseph Tanner. I said I just knew Joseph on sight, but I used to date the guy he got killed with. Perry said he'd gotten a phone call out of the blue from Joseph when Joseph was in Nigeria, some question about antihistamines. He knew Perry works for a pharmaceutical.

I asked all sorts of stuff about Joseph and his group over there, thinking you'd be interested, but Perry didn't know much. He said Joseph had a great time teaching, meeting all sorts of people. They mostly lived off-grid, roughing it, but if they got into a city, Joseph beelined for a place with air-conditioning.

And he, Joseph, was frustrated he couldn't figure out the dating rules. He expected Nigeria to be looser than Oklahoma but wasn't sure. He knew not to flirt with the students—it was more the single women his own age. And the problem wasn't just: Was he breaking the rules? It was what the punishment might be. Which made me laugh. You know the story of Abelard and Heloise? It doesn't matter.

Perry didn't know anything specific about Raphael, didn't even recognize the name, just knew there were a couple of White boys there. They almost got into trouble a few times, once when they stole pallets of stuff off a truck belonging to the Nigerian mafia. I have to doubt that story—Raphael wouldn't do something so stupid and pointless, like a frat-boy prank.

The other thing—that *did* get them into trouble, I could believe, because you wouldn't think it was wrong. One of them put up a poster in their bedroom, not near a window or door—nobody outside could see it. It wasn't pro or anti anything, and the picture was a drawing of a deer or eland or whatever, and they were still told to take it down. All it said was "Pardon me, but your 'political' happens to be my 'personal.'" I thought it sounded cool and actually wondered if it's a thing over there, a slogan—if you ever heard of it?

Since I'm calling anyway, there's another thing I'd like to bring up. Remember I talked about trying to figure out the best way to contribute to society? And the felons' rights organization wasn't a good fit? And I thought about doing something like you are, focusing on people in postcolonial Africa?

What actually helped me was rereading *Mandela*. He talks about passion— not the sexual—and says our best contributions to society come from work we're passionate about. Which makes so much sense. And it made me realize that those of us privileged enough to pick and choose among different careers have an *obligation* to find the work we can do with passion. We have to give our all, is what I'm saying.

Think about our enslaved ancestors. Did our great-great-grandparents living in forced labor want their descendants to force themselves to take on work they disliked? That's the *last* thing they wanted. Their dreams were of us doing what we love.

So after a *ton* of back-and-forth, I ended up realizing that where I can find fulfillment *and* give the most is as a teacher. Which includes being a mentor and role model. A university position would be ideal, but I'd do a two-year college without batting an eyelash. Yes, teaching at the university level is something I could do with passion.

I'm a little ashamed at how long it took me to get it. In high school I had the Frederick Douglass quote on my wall "Some know the value of education by having it. I knew its value by not having it." Duh! But my mind blocked that out completely, not sure why. I got all caught up in the incarceration problem. David helped me, said, "What if the guy who gets out of prison wants to study French literature?" I'd never looked at it from that perspective.

Yes, I've thought long and hard about many things. Insight didn't come easy for me. Or too *many* insights came, and I couldn't distinguish the things I wanted to do from the things I could do *well*. Accepting my limitations, that was the hard part. Too fixated on not letting the outside world limit me, I didn't pay attention to my own limitations.

I respect self-care now too, the idea of it. You need to keep yourself fit mentally and physically if you want to give your all. I'm eating a lot healthier and do the elliptical four days a week.

And, to be honest, another thing I've realized is I'm not a little-kid person. My sister must've gotten my dose of mother genes. I used to figure I'd change as I got older, but it's the opposite. And it's not like the planet *needs* more people. But I should volunteer again at the soup kitchen. A lot of families show up, so I could help that way. Yes, I will.

Sorry, you didn't want to hear all this; I should let you go. But something's nagging in the back of my head, something else I wanted to say.

I remember! Those emails I read you, the back-and-forth about Raphael's mother being pregnant when she was killed? I forgot to tell you the conversation we had back at school afterwards.

I asked Raphael if he thought the reason he was so pissed at his father wasn't for keeping *any* secret but for keeping one so important. That was a significant event for his family. But he just shrugged. Just shrugged. Said his anger wasn't really at his father—he was doubly pissed at the driver and *took it out* on his father.

You see what I mean about things never really sticking, about him always bouncing back? I'll let you go, didn't mean to take up so much of your time.

Chapter 48

Daniel

I'M SORRY I PUT THIS OFF, the interview. I do recognize that you try to schedule as many of us as you can before making a trip. Gillian suggests to get started, I should talk about lighter stuff, even if it doesn't seem relevant to the development of Raphael's thinking on moral issues. The story of the Chinese magnate might be an example, though more an example of his *not* thinking. I'll rely on the low likelihood that these interviews get much exposure. You said you were changing the names of the towns?

This incident happened early on after they arrived in Nigeria, while Raphael's main responsibility was procurement. Short version: he and the Dutch fellow, Ismail, commandeered a pickup belonging to a wealthy Chinese national and stole all its contents. I'm not joking. Though "commandeer" might be too strong a word, because the truck driver was in on the scheme. We were as shocked as you must be. That they would do something so foolhardy and, on the surface, wrong.

Here's the longer version: The driver was a member of their church group who'd moved to Maiduguri and gotten a job transporting school supplies—notebooks, paper, that kind of thing. He'd pick up a shipment from a warehouse in the city and deliver it to the magnate's compound in the outskirts. One time as he was leaving the compound, he happened to observe people setting fire to the supplies. Apparently they were just dumped in a ditch and doused with gasoline.

He'd already suspected the magnate of shady dealings, so he thought the supplies were being diverted from a school that had paid for them. Some web of graft, in other words. Which isn't uncommon. I was surprised to learn, after Raphael returned, that kidnappings for ransom aren't uncommon either. A lot of things I didn't know, a lot of lawlessness. In any case, the driver hid nearby after subsequent deliveries and saw the same thing.

I don't know if Raphael was in on the planning or just the execution, but a plot was hatched, and on a day the driver was scheduled to work, Raphael and Ismail drove the church van into Maiduguri. The driver waited until late in the day to do his pickup at the warehouse, and Raphael and Ismail followed him toward the compound. On a poorly lit road after dark, both vehicles pulled over, and the three of them quickly transferred all the cartons from the truck to the church van. They were labeled things like "notebooks," "paper," et cetera. One set said "Trigonometry tables."

They rammed a nail into a truck tire and watched it deflate, then gave the driver a lift to a gas station. His story was going to be that the truck must have been broken into and robbed while he'd gone to get assistance for the flat.

Whether the police were called or what happened with the magnate, I don't know. Raphael and Ismail drove the church van back to Iskoki, patting themselves on the back for a Robin Hood escapade. All I could think of when he told me this was his landing in a Nigerian prison—or worse, a Chinese.

Here's the kicker: After unloading their booty, they discovered that the cartons supposedly containing trig books in fact contained child porn magazines. I assume the school supplies were used as camouflage at the border. One horror after another visited on those poor people.

Raphael and Ismail faced a dilemma: If they turned the magazines over to the police, they risked prosecution for theft and would get the driver in trouble. Plus the church might be blamed, dooming the entire program. So they ended up just burning the magazines.

I think that was for the best. They could've come from anywhere—the Congo, Liberia, Sudan—and the odds of their little group disrupting the pipeline, even if you assumed no corruption by the Nigerian authorities, was nil.

Raphael wisely held back on this story until he returned—I can't imagine what I would've done if he'd told me on the phone while he was still there. Flown over and, what's that phrase, "staged an intervention"? If he tried other pranks, he never let on.

What else. Did Gillian mention Thaddeus and Dorcas, an older couple in Lambu? That was a funny situation. Dorcas tried to corral Raphael onto her side in a domestic quarrel with her husband.

Let me see if I can get the background straight. The two were well-off by Lambu standards, owned quite a few dairy cows. Their children were grown, and one son had landed a decent-paying job in Abuja, something with computers. He wanted to start his own business, but saving enough to get it off the ground was hard because his siblings were always asking for financial help. Not for trivial things but genuine expenses like food, clothing, that sort of thing.

Dorcas believed the siblings should stop petitioning their brother for money. If he could save enough to open his own business, there would be more to go around in the long run. But you know how these things are: even assuming his business did well, he might not see much disposable income for several years. Presumably he'd first have to pay off the loans that got him started.

To make matters worse, a sister's child developed serious health issues requiring surgery in Maiduguri. Thaddeus and Dorcas couldn't pay the full cost, so the son in Abuja sent what he could. Another grandchild developed dental problems, and a third, recurring fevers or something. You get the picture: for all practical purposes, the son would have to abandon his plans if he kept sending earnings home.

As I say, Dorcas felt that enough was enough. She'd learned from this son about investments and other financial transactions necessary to get a business on its feet, and she wanted him to have the chance. He'd already done so much for the family.

Thaddeus felt differently, saw the family obligations as paramount. Complicating matters further, *cousins* had begun asking for help. Some years before, one cousin who had "made good" had provided money for Thaddeus to purchase additional cows, which turned out to be pivotal to Thaddeus and Dorcas's wealth—I'm speaking relative to others in the village. Dorcas argued that the sums had been repaid, but Thaddeus said the Abuja son would be repaid too someday.

Apparently, it was at that point Dorcas shouted, "With what—pawpaw?" Raphael had to work not to laugh—he liked her spirit. Yet he wisely refused to take sides. He did ask them each questions to get them to think about other possibilities and repercussions. And that kicked off a friendship.

An interesting fellow, Thaddeus. On the one hand, as a devout Christian, he hates Boko Haram. At the same time, he's sympathetic to their belief that the British desecrated Nigeria. Whether he was translating Thaddeus's statement into English or Thaddeus spoke English, Raphael used the actual word "desecrate."

And has a beef with modern technology as well, Thaddeus does. Guns, grenades, firearms in general, are bad weapons not only because they're of Western origin but because they're indicia of cowardice. *Anyone* can hurl a grenade or shoot from a distance—where's the courage in that? His ancestors had confronted their enemies man-to-man. So Boko Haram are not brave fighters in his book.

I guess that qualifies as an understatement. Bernice, I still can't comprehend their morality. Strapping explosives to a goat or camel and sending it meandering into a marketplace? Forcing children into vests wired with explosives? And you can't call the teenagers who supposedly agree to be suicide bombers "volunteers." They are impressionable, malleable, like the Hitler

Youth. The desire to be part of a movement, peer pressure, can wreak havoc on an emotionally vulnerable *older* person—a young one is pure putty.

Maybe that's why I prefer teaching high school over middle school. I know I'll get pushback.

It said in the article about you that Boko Haram gets children to provide information by promising their family will be left alone. Who wouldn't agree to that? Though you can't help but wonder if all they have to promise is free cell-phone minutes. Gillian says even teenagers can be enticed with significantly less than thirty pieces of silver.

Where was I? Thaddeus, his resentment of modern inventions. Not all of them—how could he be, with the Abuja son sending home money from his job with computers? Raphael said there was a cousin in Maiduguri that Thaddeus is *extremely* proud of, a man who periodically drives to various villages to let people recharge their cell phones on his generator. For a fee, it goes without saying. Gillian calls it a love-hate relationship with modernity.

Raphael happened to meet this cousin and didn't like him one bit. The cousin was furious with Boko Haram for blowing up cell-phone towers, because then his customers didn't bother with recharging their phones, but he was happy when they just blew up parts of the electric grid, because the phones sometimes still worked and people were forced to turn to him and his generator. Yes, greed transcends all cultural taboos.

Look, how about we call it a day?

CHAPTER 49

[Emails to and from Raphael, in Nigeria]

[June 28, 2013, email from Raphael to Daniel and Gillian]

Hope you get this and got emails I sent April and May, just lucked out with access, hope phones usable soon. Things going well, digs pretty fancy, relatively speaking. House is walled around and nice courtyard in middle, unpaved but use boards in rainy season. Three of us sharing room so have to put up with J's awful jokes first thing in am and W knocking stuff over because he's damn clumsy. Can you tell life's pretty normal when I complain about roommates?

State of emergency keeping us from getting supplies in M. Kids not as prepared and we're starting simpler. They're needed for farming, so parents not that enthusiastic for education. Students eager though.

Mixed feelings leaving Iskoki. The people there won't leave because it's their home and they don't have a livelihood elsewhere. So you'd think they resent us because we can just pick up and move wherever and whenever. But they don't resent, even students who wish they could leave too. I ask myself what right have I to go, to use my privilege?

[June 28, 2013, email from Daniel to Raphael]

I won't know if you still have email access unless you reply to this. It makes no sense to feel guilty about your ability to leave dangerous areas. The Jews able to get out of Germany I'm sure felt terrible for friends and family left behind but still knew that getting themselves out was smart and the right thing and had no qualms about escaping. I'm sure you wouldn't fault them.

Your alumni magazine came and I scanned it for tidbits about professors and classmates you know and saw mention of Aleecia. She's studying for her PhD in French literature at the University of Maryland. I didn't recognize any other names.

Not much news here. Pat has been out front gardening every day, weather permitting. I asked if she was starting a new career as a horticulturist given all her new plants and she said her family is driving her crazy. Until a new part comes in for her potter's wheel, she digs up earth for sanity. In other words, she's her usual self.

Gillian may get a second paper published, two in one year, yet I can't convince her to opt for tenure track. She said to mention that Mrs. Kern passed away, the first woman you met with a number on her arm. She was 95 and asked about you when Gillian saw her in March.

[July 11, 2013, email from Raphael to Daniel]

Appreciate your scanning alumni news—here are some other folks I'd be curious about *[names redacted, BXW]*. Glad Aleecia's going for PhD. Everybody expected her to go into poli sci because she's got strong views but they never had their ears talked off about "the pauses between lines" and "the words not said."

Btw you misunderstood me about feeling privileged. The Jews who managed to get out of Germany had no reason to feel privileged because they didn't actually have the power to leave, it was luck (and incredible courage) if they escaped. I can leave tomorrow if I want, I have a choice, am in control. And a better comparison is someone thrown in prison for a month sharing a cell with a lifer. You can't ignore that temporary hardships are easier to bear. Plus we have no deep ties, but for Kibaku moving to Igbo or Yoruba areas is leaving behind homeland. Just don't get the idea I'm on some empathy or masochism safari, I'm here to help any way I can. Like Pat said (and you can tell her I remember!) "Nobody wants their surgeon weeping into the wound" or something like that. Anyway, J is here and we have to split now. I'll try to get in touch again soon.

[July 19, 2013, email from Raphael to Daniel and Gillian]

Tried to phone, you must be at school/work. How's the community college class going? Are your students more motivated than folks like me, who went to college to party hard?

I'm tutoring these great twins. Paul wanted to be a pilot but now wants to be an actor. Think I fantasized about sailing around the world at same age. Jenny wants to be a nuclear physicist, laughed ten minutes when I asked if that meant how to make nuclear weapons or nuclear power plants. She should be a teacher, managed to get through my thick skull stuff about gamma rays and proton decay my profs never could. Level of instruction bizarrely inconsistent—she knows all this physics and math and zilch about European colonization of Africa, Americas, Berlin conf, Industrial Revolution, Marxism versus capitalism, etc. Except for subjects included on exams to get into university, seems hit and miss with curriculum and even more with teachers, doesn't help the better teachers go looking for jobs in Abuja and Lagos.

[September 24, 2013, email from Raphael to Sarah J.]

Great seeing you again and for longer than Jan, April. Probably just as well next time will be stateside, given weirdness in Borno now. Assume your program lets its residents have a day off once in a while? I've never been to Nebraska. Joseph says it's Oklahoma with more corn. Btw he paid you a huge compliment (as huge as they get coming from him). Said you weren't one of those white women who cry and gnash their teeth (figuratively speaking) over the suffering of black people. He calls it "white center stage syndrome" because they want their sympathy applauded. I know it sounds like a weird thing to be praised for, that you're not obnoxious, but he did mean it as a compliment.

Hope I didn't seem indifferent to boy with albinism, kind of the opposite, and I wasn't in the mood to go there. Why is it so damn hard for children to open up? I'm probably not one to talk, looking back I can see I was a fucking clam. And my dad and Gillian were supportive, never got pissed about anything, not seriously pissed, so what was my excuse? If you ever meet Gillian, ask her about different ways people cope with imprisonment, torture, persecution. She's an encyclopedia on the subject. Some people claw and scrape to get out of their prisons, mental or physical. Others retreat into a mindset or else just give up. He was only nine, so I get the giving up, but it fucking pisses me off.

Not entirely true about my dad never getting pissed. I got ticketed for running a stop sign at 2 am on a completely empty road, barely doing 25, no car in sight. Too bad the cop car wasn't in sight. Was lucky I hadn't been drinking.

Keep in touch,

R

CHAPTER 50

Mia [telephone interview]

THANKS FOR RETURNING MY CALL. You wanted us to contact you if we remembered anything more about Raphael, Raphael Solomon. Yesterday, talking with my mother, she suggested I call to clarify something I told you last time. How he'd discussed the movie *Casablanca* with my niece Brooke? And declared in no uncertain terms that the moral of the film was "Saving the world is more important than love." My mother's afraid you might read too much into that. Besides, those were *my* words, "saving the world." I can't remember how Raphael phrased it.

The point she thinks I should clarify is that his comment wasn't a signal he planned someday to rush off to dangerous places and perform dramatic feats as some kind of knight in shining armor. Remember, he was only maybe seventeen or eighteen when talking to Brooke. A fascination with heroism is *very* typical of males at that age. Joining a revolution, fighting oppressors— they love to boast about changing things in an epic way. *Especially* in front of adolescent females. The boys strut like roosters. A phase I don't take too seriously, having treated *many* late adolescents. And men who never outgrew adolescence. But that's another story.

Besides, any heroic fantasies Raphael had then were over by the time he graduated. Even Clara said he seemed so mature when he told us his plan to go to Nigeria. And look at the spot he chose: an inconspicuous corner in an inconspicuous region. Nigeria wasn't on the media radar then. He could've gone to Cairo or Syria or joined Tibetan protesters or—I don't know—signed on with Greenpeace.

And what did he go to Nigeria *for*? To distribute *teaching* materials. Not guns, not food or medicine. Hardly the stuff of movies.

Please don't think I'm criticizing him. Or those brave people who do risk their lives, the ones joining humanitarian organizations. I would never suggest that, as a group, they suffer from personality disorders. Although my friend's daughter, three years into a job as a Botox nurse, got dumped by her fiancé and *immediately* joined Doctors Without Borders. *That* was impulsive behavior. Less heroics and more "I'll show him."

No, Raphael didn't behave like someone out for glory, not at the time he first went to Nigeria. I saw several cases of histrionic personality disorder during my graduate school rotations. And recently had a client who decided to hike up Mount Whitney *alone*, and the only climbing he'd done before was out of bed. Raphael's goals were practical, *un*ambitious—his original goals. Joining a church teachers group?

People are too quick to apply motives and intentions without evidence. Like Ryan and his silly comment about the razor blades. My mother didn't tell you? She was mailing Raphael a package with skin cream he wanted because he was nicking himself. He was using whatever the villagers used—could've been a crude knife or something—and didn't yet have the hang of it. Ryan wanted to know why she didn't just send him some decent razors, and she said he wanted to get better at the kind there, so my genius brother made some comment about Raphael trying to act tough and not like some namby-pamby westerner. Clara chewed him out. A person can want to follow local customs from simple *courtesy*, not to prove anything. I was on her side in that argument, though it was totally unnecessary telling Ryan he has a chip on his shoulder. He's heard it before.

But I just called to give my opinion on histrionic personality disorder, or lack of it, in Raphael's case. I can't completely rule out *some* leanings toward narcissism—I wasn't his therapist. Only that around us he never acted grandiose or looking for attention. His friend Joseph I met only once, and I wouldn't say he acted grandiose or attention-seeking either, but he certainly didn't mind some of the attention he got from one of my nieces.

Ego boosting isn't always bad. My clients who suffer from depression *need* their egos boosted, the men as well as the women. Clara doesn't agree, says in our culture, men could use a little ego dampening and women the boosting. But appearances are deceiving. Men who swagger in public often are hiding many insecurities. Raphael didn't swagger; my mother's right about that.

His *second* trip to Nigeria, *after* the kidnappings—I can't give an opinion there. A strong impulsive component may have been present.

Such a tragedy. I hope Daniel and Gillian aren't blaming themselves. Parents have little influence over their child by mid-adolescence and virtually none afterward. I'm not saying you just toss your hands up in despair. Or only dish out encouragement. Tough love has its time and place—no question. But if you're holding off on the tough love, at least temporarily, and trying to find the middle ground between providing a soft landing spot and enabling, I wish you the best of luck.

Anyway, Daniel and Gillian's influence after high school was limited. Obviously our parents don't vanish from our minds once we're grown—they remain strong influences our entire lives. But the strong influences are our *remembered* parents, what psychologists call "internalized" parents: the authority figures from childhood. *They're* the ones keeping the grip on us. The parents we interact with once we're adults are like anyone else: bosses, colleagues, friends, et cetera. Their opinions hold *some* sway but nothing on the scale of our childhood parents. Clara wept like a *baby* at our father's funeral—I'm not exaggerating. But right then she wasn't an adult daughter grieving the father she'd visited in hospice a few days before. Those sobs came from the little girl who'd loved her daddy forty years ago.

I hope this isn't confusing for you. You must've taken psychology courses to get your degree. I only bring it up to emphasize that Daniel couldn't have said or done *anything* to change Raphael's mind about going to Nigeria. He was twenty-something, a young man.

That's all I have to add.

CHAPTER 51

Daniel

LAST TIME I TOLD YOU ABOUT THE PRANK with the Chinese magnate. The only other incident that could be called a prank wasn't as foolish. Gillian said she mentioned Paul, the boy with the twin sister? In October or early November, Paul begged Raphael to find some way he and his friends could watch the U-17 World Cup. Nigeria was in the quarterfinals or semis, an important game. In fact, that year they ended up winning the entire tournament.

There was no electricity in Lambu, so Raphael and Joseph borrowed the church van and drove Paul and a few other students to Maiduguri to watch on a friend's TV. When Nigeria won, gunfire went off, and for a split second everyone looked around in panic but decided the gunfire was celebratory. To hear Raphael tell it, the evening was like an ordinary tailgate party here at the university.

What else? I should've written down my memories when they occurred, because I can't seem to conjure them up now. One phone call I asked if he was sorry he couldn't explore much, especially parts of the savanna where herds passed through. He brushed it off with a "I didn't come here to go on a safari." Like it's a crime to take a vacation? I guess I'm not one to talk.

The poetry discussion! Yes, poetry. Not a subject I know well, as you might have guessed. Raphael was excited to tell me about a short poem a student had written. He read it over the phone, knowing I wouldn't understand a word—it was in Kibaku—but he read it twice and asked if I could pick up anything at all: mood, tone, what it might be about.

I said, honestly, all I got was, at most, a light musicality, and it was *exactly* the response he'd been hoping for! He said the poem was about waking up on a lovely morning and hearing the breeze in the leaves and birds chirping, that kind of thing. The student had tied the subject matter to the sounds.

However, the conversation sticks in my mind for another reason altogether, which might be relevant to your book. After he was done raving about the student, I said that his mother's great-grandfather had been a poet of some stature in Poland. Morris somebody. Whether he wrote in Polish or Yiddish, I didn't know.

I felt funny mentioning this Morris fellow even while doing it because, you see, Raphael and I always shied away from delving into our ancestry. Which you might find odd, given I teach history. But we shared a distrust of genealogy. As I'm sure you know, it's often weaponized by bigots. Gillian is pretty much the same way. Pat once asked where her forbears emigrated from, and Gillian wasn't absolutely sure, possibly Scotland or somewhere in Northern Ireland. But no real curiosity.

Living in Africa may have softened Raphael on the subject because he didn't react negatively and, in fact, asked all sorts of questions. What was Morris's last name? Why didn't he emigrate to the US to join whatever children did emigrate? Did he perish in the Holocaust? Did Susan's parents keep copies of the poems? Did she ever read them? I'm ashamed to say I had few answers. Susan didn't speak Yiddish or Polish, so I doubt she read them—she never indicated they'd been translated.

From our conversation, though, I couldn't help but infer that Kibaku culture was teaching Raphael positive aspects of intergenerational threads. Why *I* mentioned Susan's great-grandfather was, to me, the bigger puzzle. As I say, I've always been wary of how genealogy is weaponized.

It was Gillian who offered a plausible explanation. She said I was trying to bring Raphael closer. She used the analogy of a person in a lifeboat trying to rescue someone in the water and throwing whatever ropes or floatable objects are at hand, to make a connection, *any* connection. She might be right. It at least allowed me to save face after all my criticism of genealogy. *She* has a poetic side. I've always been the dry, unimaginative one.

By the way, she said she talked your ear off about the Enlightenment and how my views of it may have made their way into Raphael's thinking. I know she's not as sanguine about progress, moral progress, as I am. As a Holocaust scholar, she has studied in horrific detail how a people steeped in a culture that produced Beethoven, Goethe, Immanuel Kant, regressed into unimaginable barbarities. Perhaps her religious upbringing is a factor, the battle between good and evil a constant.

I still believe in progress. Two thousand years ago, every organized society on Earth accepted and engaged in slavery. The Incas and Mayans, the Chinese, Tatars, Portuguese, Arabs, Africans, the democracies in Greece, the Roman Republic—for all of them, slavery was as common as the wheel. But nowadays no society condones it. Which doesn't mean it isn't practiced out of sight. My point is simply that the *number* of people and societies who condemn slavery has grown steadily over the centuries. There are fewer barbarians at the gate, relatively speaking, and more of us. That is progress. You can't expect it to be unfaltering.

Other things about his time in Nigeria . . . The biking wasn't working out; either the roads were too rutted or muddy or he broke something and couldn't get a replacement part. Only much later did Gillian and I put two and two together and realize he would've been pretty visible on a bike, too visible to people passing through the village, and word might get around about "the westerners."

One thing Raphael didn't share with us until his return was the continuing escalation of attacks. They were in the news—the British news, at least—but you've heard the cliché about the fog of war? Figuring out who did what isn't always clear, at least initially. Gillian said you know about the Baga massacre—that it was probably perpetrated by the army, not Boko Haram. Which of course made it a great recruitment tool for the thugs.

"War is hell," to quote Sherman. He may have been thinking primarily of soldiers but wasn't oblivious to civilian casualties. Atrocities are certain to be committed by all sides, even those we'd call the good guys—I mean those defending democracy, resisting aggression. I had friends shocked by the My Lai massacre. If anything surprised me, it was that the military initiated a court-martial. But that's also a good thing, the idea that atrocities should be punished, that there are codes of conduct for soldiers, for the prosecution of war.

I'm not sure there's anything else to tell you about that year. We didn't want to burden him with demands he keep in touch regularly. After all, he was a college graduate. I remember thinking, when I first finished college, that because I had begun supporting myself, even if only with a graduate school stipend, I was a full-fledged adult. That meant I was entitled to all the perks that go with adulthood, and I intended to indulge in them. Responsibilities, more than perks, they turned out to be.

Gillian can tell you about the months in early 2014, between his return from Nigeria and leaving again. She remembers it as an especially happy time, and I suppose it was. We certainly got along much better, he and I, than during his college years. Our arguments were less fraught with emotion—on either side—and more like the academic debates of old. I should say "discussions," because what characterized them was not so much one of us arguing a side as both of us tossing ideas around from multiple viewpoints. Those are the best kind, really—the ones you learn the most from.

We did revisit the question Aleecia had raised: How would I feel if while he was busy drafting the Constitution, Jefferson was running a Nazi concentration camp on the side? I had to admit I was unfairly dismissive when she posed it—Raphael used the word "defensive." Because I'd asserted there was no evidence Jefferson inflicted beatings and the kinds of cruelties which he and many Virginians looked down upon. They were not Simon Legrees.

That *was* my viewpoint, and again, you're taking a history here. I have become enlightened, or at least *more* enlightened. And I thank Aleecia for that, for forcing me through the humbling experience of realizing my own obtuseness. And teaching me, ultimately, that we should pivot from judging the person to just judging the deed. We need to depersonalize the great accomplishments in history.

I can't believe I'm saying this.

I'll have to call it quits. Gillian and Pat can fill in any gaps. I'm sure they've given you a more objective portrait anyway. I suspect I haven't scrimped on setting out Raphael's strengths, and I mean it when I say I always marveled at the sheer *number* of talents and good qualities united in a single individual. So despite being publicity shy, part of me wants the whole world to know who he was.

This is all nonsense, you realize? I worshipped him because he was my son.

CHAPTER 52

Gillian

AS THE DATE FOR RAPHAEL'S RETURN grew closer, we got more and more excited. Then, in early December, Boko Haram attacked Maiduguri, and panic set in again. We didn't discuss it, Daniel and I, but were worried. I think my first huge sigh of relief came the next month, when Yvonne texted that their flight had landed in Amsterdam. Joseph was with Raphael, was coming to Seattle for a few days before returning to Tulsa—I believe his parents were visiting an elderly distant relative in Little Rock. I think he was happy to wait here a few days before hopping back on a plane.

It was very early January 2014, and it *felt* like a new year, a new time. The sun had already set when we left for the airport, and I remember the air being very cold. And very clear. The lights along the bridges and in downtown buildings shone so bright, some blue and green—the Seahawks colors—and so many holiday lights still up, red and green and gold and silver. All that twinkling against the dark sky just added to the excitement.

I remember the boys coming through the secured area, happy young men carrying backpacks as if they held feathers. Raphael looked fit and healthy and tanned, not like he'd lain in an infirmary for weeks and just spent a day and a half in airports and planes. Joseph looked good too. They joked about being eager for showers, "real mattresses," and favorite foods. They wouldn't let us carry their bags—so lively, they were.

I insisted on sitting in the back seat with Joseph so that Daniel and Raphael could catch up. Raphael did 90 percent of the talking. Not about Nigeria, not then. He gave details about the graduate programs he would apply to, in international relations. He wanted to specialize in West Africa, which was experiencing, in his or Joseph's words, "a resurgence of colonialism," this time with China as the colonial power.

He knew so much about "extractive economies," he called them, and the relationships between dictators and foreign entities, the swap of rights in oil and minerals in return for weapons, things like that. And ways in which the government—*our* government—could help people, how it could structure aid packages and channel the right kind of assistance to the right organizations or agencies. He just knew so much.

Some of what he learned came from firsthand experience, but I think he learned a lot from mingling in Maiduguri with both Nigerians and other foreigners—volunteers from Doctors Without Borders, the Peace Corps, various and sundry NGOs. I gave you the name of the physician in Nebraska, didn't I? He spoke to her several times on the phone, I know, once he got back. She'd been in the Peace Corps in Benin, I think.

Anyway, sitting right behind the driver's seat, I couldn't see Daniel's face but knew he was smiling as Raphael talked. Have you ever wished you could freeze a moment in time and never go forward? I think of that ride home from the airport. Daniel's and Raphael's wishes were in synchrony again. There wasn't just an armistice but an alliance. What schools was he considering, what were the different programs like, how many years to get a degree—such happy questions!

After the boys went to bed, Daniel opened a bottle of wine, and we sat over there, facing the mantel. You saw the pictures of Raphael as a child? Daniel once asked if I wanted him to take down the ones with Susan, but I said no—why would I?

We didn't say much, didn't need to, sipping our wine in the gentle lamplight. It felt good to have Raphael back, asleep in his old room. And a guest in the guest room, giving a sense of *company*. Everything was falling into place. I could tell Daniel was too restless to go to bed, so we sat there quite a while, feeling peaceful and contented.

The next morning, Joseph slept in, and Daniel and Raphael went for a run. It was hard not to compare it to their morning run when Raphael told Daniel he planned to go to Nigeria. This time when they got back, Raphael teased Daniel how he—Raphael—hadn't gone running in over a year and recently broke his leg yet still got less winded. "Youth always trumps age," Daniel joked. Even panting and tired, he couldn't stop grinning. The contrast brought home to me how life changes, how around the bend there *is* a light at the end of the tunnel. It doesn't make sense to abandon hope, no matter the circumstances.

I'm not feeling that way now. But I have known many survivors, Bernice, Holocaust survivors who lost *parents, children, siblings*. And homes, friends, communities—every part of their daily existence. They land in a new place among strangers and have to learn a new language. Yet eventually some manage to embrace life again. Not without emotional scars—I'm not saying that. But still.

I hope Daniel gets there someday. Whether *I* find peace doesn't matter. To many people that sounds anti-feminist. But self-love has never been an ideal to me; love should emanate outward, not inward. I guess I'm still a minister's daughter.

The few days before Joseph went back to Oklahoma were great fun. We did typical tourist things. Showed him Pike Place Market: the array of vegetable and fruit stalls, the famous fish tossers, the arts and crafts. We took him to Seattle Center and parks with nice views of the mountains and water. We stopped at a clam bar for lunch. But he seemed to enjoy nothing more than stretching out on the sofa and reading—he said it was nice to not be bothered by insects.

Raphael went over to Pat's the first day, and she invited us to dinner the following night, and that was fun too. Raphael and Joseph told stories about Nigeria, fascinating ones, though all I seem to remember right now are silly little things, like children squabbling over candy or arguing about which toothpaste tastes best. Fortunately, they spared us stories of the horrors they must have known about.

I remember Pat asking the name of a local church where she could ship care packages, because you can't help wanting to do something. She belongs to an arts-and-crafts swap and, for her pottery, gets knitted sweaters and blankets, but she could swap for other things, since no one over there wants wool. Daniel and I decided to make a regular monetary contribution to Joseph's church's program.

I have to say, over the next few months, Daniel and I stopped reading news about Nigeria. Raphael made no mention of it, though I'm sure he was learning about the escalating attacks. Christian men gunned down, boys murdered in their dormitories, villages burned; *you've* kept track, I'm sure. But we weren't aware of them, not then. We just assumed Raphael was focused on his future, his academic future.

I did know he was making phone calls to DC that February and March—getting in touch with congressional staff and potential administration connections. I assumed it was either networking having to do with his graduate school applications or part of an overall effort to help in the fight against Boko Haram. Fighting insurgencies is a long-term project. And getting our government to focus on *any* foreign crisis is hard, especially one in the developing world. Daniel says our options are fewer—we have fewer ties. The British have a long-standing relationship with Nigeria, it being part of the Commonwealth.

In fact, it wasn't until a brief phone call from Yvonne in late April, after the two of them had already returned to Borno, that Daniel and I learned of the February and March violence. I don't want to repeat the conversation—Yvonne's asked for privacy—so I'll just say this: *her* impression was that up until the April 14 abductions in Chibok, the only role Raphael and Joseph were playing was hounding members of the administration and Congress to help Nigeria rein in the militants. Joseph had never mentioned plans to go back to Borno. I don't think they had any, not then.

Yes, in our ignorance, the period from January to mid-April was *smooth*. When he wasn't busy researching graduate programs and filling out applications, Raphael volunteered at an immigration group, which allowed him to put his languages to good use. Sometimes he came home after we'd gone to bed, so we assumed he was finding time for a social life too.

But of course the 276 high school girls kidnapped made the news. And hit us like a ton of bricks.

CHAPTER 53

Pat

RAPHAEL HAD CHANGED after his year in Nigeria, no doubt about that. Still slender but starting to fill out, the way their bones widen. I remember thinking he couldn't keep that boyishness forever, but some was still there.

He gave me a big hug the second I opened the door. I told you I'm not a hedge person—well, I *am* a hug person. I don't expect everyone's arms to reach all the way around—ha ha ha!

Daniel, those next few months, he looked ten years younger! It was no winter of discontent, I'll tell you. Raphael home, Kirsten pulling herself together to start classes at OSU, and Brooke—my goodness, that girl, piggy-backing a second fellowship in Spain! Which was icing on the cake for Clara and Derek after patching things up. Ryan's children weren't any trouble—yet. You never know what age it will start.

We like to believe we can rest on a plateau of contentment or go from one peak to another without a big slide in between. The valleys aren't steep, we pretend, even if you can't completely avoid them. I'm sure you've had yours. Raphael's little sine-waves theory. Listen to me with my "pearls of wisdom." Mia would have my head on a platter. You're better off trusting tea leaves.

I made a big dinner one night while his friend Joseph was here; it was just the four of them, not the Thanksgiving horde. While Raphael helped with the last-minute details—warming the bread, finishing the salad—Joseph and Daniel took Arnie's old checkers set off the shelf. Beginners, they were—Arnie would've tied them in knots before you could say Bobby Fischer. Joseph was quite the goader. While setting the table, I watched Daniel about to make a move, and Joseph would whisper, "Are you *sure* you want to do that? *Absolutely* sure?" Daniel couldn't tell if Joseph wanted him to make the move or not. Just like Jake, Ryan's younger son— quiet as a mouse half the day, and a game comes along, and he's Mr. Competition.

What did Raphael tell me when we had a few minutes alone here and there . . . let me think. He said he learned what life was like without privacy, where everyone knows what everyone else ate for breakfast. I told him you don't need to go to Africa for that. "Welcome to small-town USA." Or go live on a commune.

We talked about foods, how they prepared vegetables and sauces. A baobab pie sounded worth trying, tangy mixed with sweet. I found out what the tampons and pads were for. He said the girls skip school when they have their periods because all they have are rags that need constant washing. I almost *died* in fifth grade—got my period during PE. On the balance beam! Congratulations, Pat, the first in your class to enjoy the pleasures of menstruating! I told you we Eriksens are a precocious bunch in all the wrong ways.

And Raphael was eager for updates on my grandkids. He laughed at hearing Braden was studying Japanese—the same Braden who used to complain his high school *had* a foreign language requirement. Raphael had taught him to curse in, I don't know, six languages? And Nick—Ryan's oldest—was being scouted by the San Jose Quakes. That's professional soccer. Ryan pretended to be annoyed at Nick for not focusing on a steadier way to earn a living, but secretly he was prouder than a peacock.

About himself, Raphael just said he was applying to graduate schools, didn't mention where. I was hoping it wouldn't be too far away. But after Africa, Miami seemed around the corner.

Bernice, I'd like to say I didn't take him for granted those few months before he left again. The ugly truth is that us older folks resume our routines. *You* might get excited discovering a new restaurant; *I'm* excited when the delivery boy doesn't throw the newspaper in the hydrangea. A book-club friend pesters me to move into a retirement place—what do they call them, "independent living"? She says I'll make "new" routines and be less lonely. How could it be less lonely? All my memories are right here.

Anyhoo, seeing Raphael coming and going was like the sun peeking out from behind the clouds, a little reminder of joy. What we used to call a "refresher toke." Though those always refreshed the mind, and these were the heart.

CHAPTER 54

Aleecia [telephone interview]

I DON'T KNOW IF YOU'RE DONE with your book, but I've been thinking a lot about Raphael and what I've said, and there's one thing I'd like to change. If you're including any of my stuff.

Every time you interviewed me, I thought I was telling the truth, *wanted* to tell the truth. But I wasn't, not really. Denial is a failing of mine. I can't be honest with other people if I'm not honest with myself.

What I'm talking about specifically is why Raphael and I broke up. I said his being able to shrug things off, bounce back from shit—optimism or resilience or whatever you want to call it—got on my nerves. That it's a sign of White privilege.

Now I think I broke up with him for a different reason. And one that doesn't put me in a good light. Whether I'll change my mind later or not, this is *closer* to the truth—I'm sure of that.

The real reason I broke up with him was I fell out of love. I don't know why, or why I fell out of love with guys before him, or why one fell out of love with me. I really have no idea and could come up with a different excuse every day of the week. Maybe he—Raphael—stopped making me laugh as often. Or the sex didn't stay as exciting. Maybe the things you find charming or new or different stop being charming or new or different. We were together almost two years.

What I'm getting at is: I'm starting to realize love sometimes ends without anybody's fault. That's why they have no-fault divorce, right? Instead of blaming Raphael, I have to own that. He didn't do anything wrong. I'm not saying he was perfect, because no one is. But you can't use imperfection as an excuse for something you would've done anyway. I'm a little ashamed to say that.

I'm also ashamed of something else. This is going to sound roundabout, but anyway . . . You know the difference between mortal and venial sins? I wasn't raised Catholic, but my friend explains it as venial sins aren't as bad as mortal. Kind of like misdemeanors and felonies, littering and murder. But the difference isn't just the act itself, what she called the "gravity" of the sin, but how aware you are that it's a sin. If you know what you're doing is very wrong but say "Who cares?" that makes it worse, makes it more a mortal sin than a venial. If you're not sure it's wrong, or maybe you think it's wrong but are doing it half-heartedly, it could be considered just a venial.

To me, Washington and Jefferson committed mortal sins by owning human beings. They knew better, living in the eighteenth century, hearing all the abolitionist opinions, seeing enslaved people in the flesh. To top it all off, they understood *freedom*. That was their highest ideal—they were ready to *die* for it. Still, on a daily basis, they kept men, women, and children, young and old, enslaved. As *their* enslaved, as their *property*.

Raphael's father wanted me to agree they were good people anyway—I told you about that. Well, I won't agree, I don't agree, and you'll never get me to agree.

But the thing is: *He*, Raphael's father, didn't enslave people. *Or* think it was okay. He probably would've been an abolitionist if he'd lived back then. All he was doing was praising the great things the enslavers did, like the Declaration of Independence and Constitution. And though he was overlooking evil or pushing it aside as not that important, the evil he was pushing aside wasn't happening *today*. He was downplaying evil that happened over a hundred years ago.

I understand people come out differently on this issue, and you might think like I do—that his attitude is wrong—but here's my point: Whether right or wrong, Mr. Solomon's *attitude* about Washington and Jefferson isn't a mortal sin. If it's a sin, it's just a venial. He's not praising them for being slave owners. He's not condoning slavery. He's just not giving it a lot of attention. You see what I'm saying? I had no business being unkind.

Sorry, I had to reach for my coffee.

He sent me a card, Mr. Solomon. Said some nice things that couldn't have been easy to write. I don't want to hurt him, to *add* to his hurt. But I'm not asking you not to print what I've said. It's the truth as I see it.

I doubt it will matter much. I'm remembering a story my grandfather told, handed down from a man who'd been enslaved. During Reconstruction, the man went around the North giving speeches to drum up support for the amendments. At one speech someone in the audience asked how he endured the whippings and beatings—had he made himself go numb or turned to God or whatever. The man answered, "When your children are sold and put in a wagon, and you watch the wagon become smaller and smaller and your children turn into dots heading toward Louisiana, children you'll never see again, after that, a whipping's nothing at all."

I should write Mr. Solomon back, describe some of the good times Raphael and I had. Not sure what else I can do.

Guess I've got no more to add. Could you shoot me an email when you publish this, even if you don't include my stuff?

[interview ended]

Then you rose into my life
Like a promised sunrise.

CHAPTER 55

Gillian

RAPHAEL KNEW ABOUT the kidnappings before Daniel and I heard it on the news. He was on the phone pretty much nonstop, and we guessed it was to government officials or people in Maiduguri or even in Lambu and Iskoki. I overheard him talking German, possibly to Werner. But we had no idea he and Joseph were planning to go there. He waited until the day before his flight to spring it on us. Probably to avoid long arguments. He'd already bought his ticket to Tulsa.

Daniel was horrified. "Terrified" is a better word. He actually shouted. "What can you possibly do there to help?"

"Just be a comfort for the families," Raphael said. The army was sending troops, and Boko Haram was retreating to their hideouts in the forest, or so he claimed and possibly believed. As you know, there have been a flurry of accusations that the president delayed sending troops, but we haven't followed the story.

Daniel tried to throw roadblocks up, like: Were their visas still valid? Did they need new immunizations? Raphael insisted everything was being taken care of. To tell you the truth, to this day I don't know if they flew into Nigeria or one of the neighboring countries. I mean: Did they arrive legally or get smuggled in? Many nations share a border: Benin, Niger, Chad, Cameroon.

I kept telling myself that their staying in Lambu wouldn't be as bad—not in the thick of it. We never learned many details—just a little from Yvonne, Joseph's sister. In her first call she said they might be part of a rescue party, kind of an underground-railroad relay type of setup. I prayed Raphael wouldn't join the JTF or try following Boko Haram into their hideouts. She assured us they weren't expecting to confront any militants, much less save all the girls. Like I said before, they weren't naïve. Harriet Tubman wasn't naïve—she knew the risks.

Was it a good thing or bad thing Daniel had to say goodbye at home, that he had school that day? Who knows? He hugged Raphael a little impatiently, I thought—it surprised me. Yet I *was* relieved he wouldn't accompany us to the airport. He would've made the mood . . . I don't know . . . icy? The way it was, Raphael gave a few more specifics, mostly how the local church people were making arrangements for where they could stay. Their main goal, he repeated, was simply to lend moral support to the distraught families.

I remember thinking—and you may find this funny, even daft—that with the time changes, they'd arrive in Nigeria on Good Friday. It's easy to get superstitious in that kind of situation. When he called Monday, after Easter, it made me optimistic.

That was the last we spoke. Daniel was the one to answer and quickly motioned for me to pick up the extension. Raphael only had a minute and was just reassuring us they'd arrived okay.

You know, it still grates, how media accounts painted him and Joseph as meddling do-gooders. They weren't. Daniel tells me don't bother with what the public thinks—it will believe what it wants to believe. But you have to understand, Bernice: they *knew* these girls.

CHAPTER 56

Pat

HYACINTHS HAVE THE MOST BEAUTIFUL fragrance of all, even more than lilacs, which were Arnie's favorite. I always cut a few from the flower box and bring them inside. My bulbs come in order: first the crocuses, then the hyacinths, daffodils, and tulips. The hyacinths are pastels, pink and white and soft purple, cute little petals forming a row of sleepyheads along the flower box. Then come those bolder yellow daffodils and then tulips as brash red as a harlot's lipstick. Having a southern exposure is a blessing in Seattle.

I was busy at the flower box when Gillian pulled up. She tells me she just took Raphael to the airport, he was meeting Joseph in Oklahoma, and they were going to Nigeria. You could've knocked me over with a feather. I knew about the kidnappings—even our local news carried it.

Those days were distressing, very distressing. Yes, I was glad many people were speaking out and wanting to help, the Obamas and celebrities. But I couldn't bear having the TV on. I brought a few casseroles and stews over but wouldn't stay. Here one of my grandsons had gone to all the trouble of installing some super-duper program so I could read newspapers and this and that on my computer, but I stuck to email, mostly with my book club. Was too afraid of the news. So many emotions at once. You feel for the girls and their families. Imagine having a sibling snapped away, snap, like that.

Do you want tea? I don't want any either.

We carried on our routines, Daniel and Gillian and I—what choice do you have, unless you want to drink yourself into uselessness? I only saw them going in and out. Daniel looked stern. It was worry.

Early one evening, Gillian called to me, saw me outside—maybe bringing the recycling to the curb. Said she was about to come over and return my casserole dish, so I followed her in to save her the trouble. She had baked lasagna in it, probably vegetarian, and was returning it full. What would I do with all that, I asked. Wasn't she going to keep some for her and Daniel? She said she already had—she'd made two. Daniel came into the kitchen, and they asked me to stay and eat with them, out of politeness, I'm sure. Daniel looked tired. Then the phone rang.

We get so many commercial calls, I don't even bother answering anymore. They can leave a message. Daniel glanced over at the receiver—he has caller ID—and picked it up. I assumed it was some student confused about the homework assignment. But he didn't move, just said yes and yes and yes and stared at the floor. I couldn't describe his expression if I wanted to.

I knew it was about Raphael. I told myself he was in an infirmary again with a broken leg. Gillian read Daniel's expression enough that when he hung up, she coaxed him into the hall. I stood gazing at the stupid lasagna. Daniel didn't come back in. Gillian did, white as a ghost.

But she looked me in the eye; I'll never forget that. Like she was trying to warn me or protect me or herself. She said, "Raphael has died." Nothing more, no explanation. Not that I wanted one. The two of us stood like statues. Then she went to find Daniel, I'm sure. I took the lasagna and went home. I think I forgot to refrigerate it. Oh boy, I better use the bathroom before there's an accident.

I called Ryan. I don't know why I picked him. Clara was probably asleep, on the East Coast, and Mia—Mia's the therapist—but for some reason I called Ryan. You never know why you do things.

He didn't know what to say—what's there to say? Asked a few questions I didn't know the answers to. Did I want him to come to Seattle? I said no—he had his job and Amy still in school and Beth returned to working thirty hours. After we hung up, my mind must have gone blank. I wandered around the living room. Went to bed eventually, still in a daze.

Ryan came the next morning. Called from SeaTac so I wouldn't think he was a burglar. Until he walked through that door, I was granite, a block of granite. The second my arms were around him, the tears flowed like Niagara, flowed and flowed. He's like his father, Ryan is—sturdy.

Preface to Additional Materials

THE PREFACE TO THE PRECEDING MATERIALS was written in April 2015, about a year after the abduction of the Chibok girls and while the interview transcripts were in the hands of a proofreader. In May 2015, I received an email from Gillian Burke that prompted me to conduct two more interviews. Additional materials, including the transcripts of the two interviews, are set forth in the following pages.

Bernice Xenia Williams, PhD, June 2015, Chicago, IL, USA

CHAPTER 57

[May 16, 2015, email from Gillian to BXW]

Dear Bernice,

I know you had to drop the project but thought I would let you know that Werner Ulrich, the German fellow who was with Raphael and Joseph in Borno, is coming to visit us on May 27. He will stop in Oklahoma to see Joseph's family and then fly up to Seattle. We are eager for it. It will feel a little bit like reconnecting with Raphael.

My work with Holocaust survivors has taught me about some of the changes grief causes, but I had never experienced them firsthand before or seen them up close in another person. And now, a year later, I can't tell which changes will be permanent and which will lessen. I struggle to extract meaning from Raphael's death. Daniel doesn't. In fact, whenever some wide-eyed student argues in class that mutual understanding could eliminate the need for war, Daniel repeats his stock answer: "Aggression and senseless brutality will always exist, so societies will always need to defend against them."

Yet he's an optimist. A belief in Enlightenment values is a belief in progress, in the future improving on the past and the eventual triumph of liberty and justice for all. Even if the arc is long.

Daniel wouldn't say "triumph," he'd say "predominance." The amount of aggression and senseless brutality in the world may wax and wane, he says—it waxed during Nazism—but over time he thinks it will wane.

Excuse the philosophical tangent. I just wanted to let you know about Werner's visit and one other thing, which we haven't told anyone except our immediate families. The seed of the idea was planted after the funeral service last year, when Pat had us all at her house, which was very thoughtful of her. I was in no shape to organize anything except getting the rabbi from Raphael's bar mitzvah to give a small remembrance. It wasn't religious; Daniel wouldn't have wanted that. A short summary of Raphael's strengths and virtues and compassion, that was what the rabbi mentioned.

Back at Pat's after the service, people were milling about in different rooms talking quietly. I stood near the dining room table and, without intending to, couldn't help but overhear a conversation in the kitchen. All right, I confess, I eavesdropped. It was on Pat and Mia, Clara, and Ryan, exchanging ideas of things to do in Raphael's memory. Making donations to the program at Joseph's church was one. Having a memorial stone placed somewhere in Lambu or Iskoki was another. That idea was shot down by Pat, who said Raphael would think it smacked of vanity. She was probably right. The people of Borno have suffered in larger numbers than we have.

Mia mentioned it would be good for Daniel to contact the girls' families to see if he could help from afar. Parents whose grief fuels a cause come to feel their child's death served a purpose. And someone suggested Daniel sponsor a child from Borno. That might have been what started me thinking. I didn't mention it to Daniel, as he was dealing with enough. We both were. But the thought nestled in the back of my mind.

The school gave him time off, though he didn't take much; he wanted to get back in the classroom. And he immersed himself in other activities, like the civics club and pickleball. I knew the grief still engulfed him, but he found a life buoy in keeping busy.

Then came January and February and all your interviews, and after, your email about having to halt the project. I wondered if he'd be disappointed or relieved, but he surprised me by saying he wasn't going to wallow anymore. I wasn't aware he *had* been wallowing, since he'd kept so busy. He said Raphael would have wanted him to carry on his work in Borno, and he—Daniel—was trying to figure out the best way. Did I have any ideas?

So I brought up the possibility of sponsoring a child, and we had a long, long talk, and one idea leading to another, before you knew it, we were considering a child coming to live with us. At first Daniel was partial to helping a child from somewhere *other* than Nigeria, somewhere the child could safely return if he or she wanted. How could he cope with raising a child from Borno who would then take on the same risks as Raphael by going back? But he ended up thinking you can't set a goal of controlling a child's future. That would be, in his words, "hubris of the first order."

We slept on it but the very next day contacted Yvonne, who put us in touch with their church, which led to communications with their sister churches in Borno. Raphael and Joseph left behind an awful lot of goodwill. And so in late summer, Daniel and I will become "foreign exchange" parents. It was simpler than we expected because a number of the church families in Tulsa had already begun the process, doing the same thing, and had established channels and helped us with the paperwork.

Both a brother and sister from Lambu will live with us for a year. Peter is twelve and Martha, eleven. They are *very* eager to come, and their parents are pleased too. I attached a picture. Peter and Martha are standing. The three in front are younger siblings.

Daniel said the funniest thing, and I don't think he'd mind my repeating it. He said he mentioned to you regretting that he never explicitly told Raphael how proud he was of him. When we walked back from the post office after mailing off the foreign exchange paperwork, he wore an odd expression, and I asked if he was having buyer's remorse. I meant feeling ambivalent about hosting the students. He said not at all and the opposite, in fact. He was happy with our plan and was pretending in his mind that Raphael somehow knew about it and was proud of *him*, Daniel.

The year ahead won't be problem free. We do expect Peter and Martha to experience frustrations and bouts of homesickness. And worry about their families. We're trying to make connections with Nigerians in the Seattle area, find ways to smooth the transition. I will ask Pat if she would want to learn a few recipes to remind the children of home. I haven't told her any of this yet; I'm waiting for the right moment. Anyway, if it should go well and Peter and Martha want to stay through high school, Daniel and I aren't averse to considering that. We'll have to see. It will be a different experience, for all of us. But even just looking forward to it has felt healing in a small way.

I suppose I should add we took another step. To make the churches in Tulsa and Lambu more comfortable with our hosting, Daniel and I got married. Neither of us wanted a big to-do, so it was performed by a local judge at the courthouse with several of Daniel's colleagues as witnesses. That's another thing we haven't told Pat yet. I'm not sure why we keep putting it off. Maybe because it feels like asking for congratulations? We certainly don't want wedding presents. We let close family know beforehand but made clear that a small simple ceremony was our preference. My brothers all chipped in to give us theater subscriptions. They know I don't want more possessions. Daniel's sisters sent us a luggage set and gift card to some electronic gadgets store, which we decided may come in handy when Peter and Martha arrive. My parents sent a lovely crystal bowl that I'm not sure when to use.

GPB

[May 27, 2015, email from Gillian to BXW]

Dear Bernice,

I'm sorry to report that Werner doesn't want to be interviewed. He did say that Daniel and I are free to repeat everything he's told us. He brought a letter Raphael wrote right before they were abducted. I can explain the circumstances when you get here.

GPB

CHAPTER 58

SO YOU'RE BACK AGAIN, your trusty little recorder working away. Gillian said she was guessing this trip is on your own dime because your funding dried up. I'm sure the money you *should* have gotten went to some muckety-muck's nephew studying very important things, like how the British royals spend their clothing allowance.

I didn't meet the German, Werner somebody. Clara saw him through the window, a tall, gangly blond. I thought of Peter O'Toole when she said that, but I was cleaning out the kitty litter, not the best time to drop everything and run-peek.

She's visiting for a few days—gave a lecture in Phoenix and says Seattle's on the way back. Not on any map *I've* seen. Ryan once tried explaining how airlines make money flying people places they don't need to go, but I couldn't repeat it if I tried. Anyhoo, if you hear me talking in the kitchen while I'm fetching the tea, it's to Clara—I'm not going wacko, not *completely* wacko.

What can I add? Gillian will give you the details of the German's visit. All she told me was that four of them—Raphael, Joseph, the German, and another fellow—helped some girls get home, back to their families. The media's full of poop, saying the boys died in vain. Daniel can have *that* at least—Raphael was a hero. Though he'd cut my tongue out for saying it, Raphael would.

Your email also said time passing can jostle memories. Or did I change my view of anything I've already told you. No, all the changes were when he died.

Daniel and I, we don't greet each other anymore. In the yard, we just go about our business. He still mows my lawn and does the edging. We know the other one's there, but making eye contact would be like looking in a mirror. I don't do that either.

Gillian and I do say hello or at least nod, and she thanks me when I drop off my cooking. Who wants to cook for one? She said she emailed you about the German coming to visit, but I haven't seen her the last few days. She must've put the recycling out in the middle of the night.

If anyone's changed, it's her. Yes, Gillian's become a tad friendlier. Not that she's getting much in return. Oh, I'm sure she understands, doesn't take it personally.

Sometimes I see them both in the backyard. She points to the upper branches, a Steller's jay or pileated woodpecker—we get lovely birds, bright-blue and bright-red flashes in the trees. Daniel seems to take an interest. Or pretends to. They want to be kind to each other. No one wants to cause pain. Maybe she just looks sprightly in comparison . . . or is the energy in her step an act to keep Daniel from sinking too low? Not as bad as that false gaiety we used to get from the hospital nurses. Not the *hospice* nurses—they were different. God bless every last one.

The tea should be done steeping, let me fetch it, I won't be but a second.

Are you heading to the gym already?

Yes. You said you'd come too.

I can't—Bernice is here—you can hear us. Go ahead without me.

What's *that*?

I made us tea.

I mean the cookies.

I'm offering her cookies. Is that a crime?

You have enough for six people. *You* plan to eat some. You promised to follow the diet.

I didn't promise, and you need to MYOB.

You'll get diabetes and heart disease.

And you're my doctor?

You used to walk everywhere—now you drive even the three blocks to the grocery store.

I can't carry those cans all the way home.

Why are you drinking soda? You used to drink water if you wanted something cold.

Diet soda. Can't a soul have a little pleasure now and then?

Mia and Ryan and I want you around for a *long time*. Your *grandchildren* want you around. You're only seventy-three, but at this rate—

I'm sure Bernice is enjoying this immensely. It's probably going into her little machine.

Good. I want to shame you into taking care of yourself. I'll put off the gym until later, and you'll come with me. At least lay off the cookies.

I'll only have one.

Bernice, if your machine caught all that, go ahead and print it. Let us be reminded of our trivial lives. Mother-daughter quarrels, probably older than Adam and Eve. I guess nothing's older than those two.

"We were put here to suffer," the nuns liked to tell us. They got that right. Did you ever notice the women in the Bible only do two things: have babies and sin? Eve gets saddled with the fall, of course. Madonnas and whores—that sums us up from a man's point of view, and it *is* still a man's world.

Here, have some cookies. Better you than me. Maybe your aunt likes chocolate.

Thank God there are decent men. Obama's everybody's dream son-in-law. And Ryan and my daughters' husbands: they're no more imperfect than yours truly here. And Genial Daniel. I hope Gillian gives him a baby—I know women who've had children in their forties. I'm going to whisper here—I'll try to do it in the mic. Mia suggested they adopt from Chibok—*not* in front of them—and Clara bit her head off. "The Chibok parents have *lost* children—why would they want to part from the ones they have left?"

"So they'll be safe," Mia said. No, that was Ryan. He started to explain about the Kindertransport, and Clara said she knew quite a bit about it and the situations were different. And all I can think is: In this time of sorrow, isn't there *anything* we can agree on?

Speaking of Clara: *Clara*, what on *earth* are you cooking? Smells like skunk cabbage.

I don't know what else to tell you, Bernice. Here, take the cookies—I'll get you a bag.

CHAPTER 59

Gillian

I DIDN'T REALLY EXPECT YOU'D COME all this distance just to hear what Werner said. Visiting Seattle must please your aunt, though.

The one-year anniversary of Raphael's death passed, and it was almost a relief because it had loomed for so long. Dates stay with you. We didn't go to the cemetery—Daniel had school—but we go every Sunday.

He didn't want a second memorial service—we couldn't imagine who would attend. Many people came last year: some of Raphael's former classmates who live in town, food-bank staff, and a surprising number of Daniel's students and former students. And colleagues. Pat's children too, Clara all the way from Boston. Even some of Pat's grandchildren, those on the West Coast. Brooke, I think, was still in Spain and Jody, in New York. To be honest, I was surprised at how many. And one of Daniel's sisters came, with her husband. I think they stayed with friends on Mercer Island. I talked to them only briefly.

Afterward, whenever I mentioned people who'd attended, Daniel seemed surprised. They all expressed their condolences in person, but he didn't remember. Still, I think it was good for him to sense a crowd.

But a year later? It would be us and Pat. My parents are planning to visit in the fall—they couldn't come last year, because my mother was still shaky from knee surgery. I haven't been back to Minnesota since 2013; it hasn't worked out.

Okay, Werner's visit. He apologized for waiting so long, which he didn't need to apologize for—he's had multiple skin grafts. But he felt he should deliver a letter in person. Raphael had written it to Daniel. Werner didn't know what the letter said, although Raphael had given him permission to read it—in fact, Werner was supposed to have opened and read it and typed the contents into an email to us last year. But the envelope was accidentally sealed, and Werner felt funny—I'll explain in a minute. He'd been planning to come to the States anyway and decided just to bring it. He went to Tulsa first. I don't know if Joseph had written a letter home too.

It was difficult, the visit. I'll try to be methodical. Let me know if I lose my train of thought.

For starters, the reports about their car hitting an explosive device were false. Werner was debriefed by the German government sometime later back in Hamburg and told them the true story. For whatever reason—maybe it was a diplomatic hot potato—our State Department was kept in the dark. So was the German media and the Dutch and everyone else.

Which may have contributed to Werner's determination to come here and tell us in person. We don't know if the State Department has the full account even now or still thinks it was an IED. Maybe you can contact them. It doesn't matter to us.

As I said, there was no explosion; they weren't in a car. The four of them—Raphael, Joseph, Werner, and their old colleague Ismail—were abducted by militants their second week in Borno.

He didn't need to tell us more, Werner said, and the only reason he was offering the whole story was because of something Raphael had said back during their year teaching. They were lounging outdoors one night, talking and stargazing. You could see so many more constellations, Werner explained, without light pollution from cities, the stars and planets were vivid against the darkness, it being after the harmattan and before the rainy season.

They talked about home, about family and friends and memories from childhood. Raphael described Daniel as someone who always wanted to face up to the truth, face facts, even when they were unpleasant or overturned cherished assumptions. Daniel was, quote, "willing to look ugly realities in the eye." So Werner was giving him a chance to hear some ugly realities.

Daniel didn't glance my way. We sat at opposite ends of the sofa. He nodded for Werner to continue.

After the Chibok kidnappings, the four of them were in touch and met up in Maiduguri; Ismail might've still been in Africa. They got a ride to Iskoki and learned that several girls from the village and from Lambu were among those kidnapped. The fathers, brothers, neighbors, and a number of their friends from Muslim villages joined together to go into the wooded areas to the east, splitting into smaller groups along the way. They weren't expecting to fight the militants, just hoping to find the girls or at least get information to relay to the Nigerian Army. As you know, some girls managed to escape.

After some unsuccessful nights, Raphael's group found a few girls hiding. Two were from a village near Lambu, and Raphael, Joseph, Ismail, and Werner agreed to lead them home. Which they were able to do. Then word came the army was on its way and humanitarian organizations were sending people too. Werner now thinks that wasn't entirely accurate, but they had no reason to doubt it at the time. So they planned to leave the next day for Maiduguri, and Raphael and Joseph would fly back to the States.

A village elder put them up for the night. Before going to sleep, Raphael wrote Daniel a letter, which, as I said, Werner was supposed to type into an email in Maiduguri and send to us while Raphael and Joseph scrambled to find flights. Werner watched him writing it and thought it was long for just alerting us to his flight plans. Raphael put it in an envelope and tucked it in the money belt they shared, which contained their passports and cash and whatever other papers they needed. The four of them took turns wearing the belt, and that night was Werner's turn. He wore it to bed. The moisture from his body and being pressed against the passports was probably what made the envelope seal. Which he didn't realize until much later, and by then, like I said, he felt funny opening it.

They were fast asleep when militants raided the house. It was chaotic, being woken in the dark and flashlights in their eyes and being handcuffed and muzzled and bound. The money belt slipped below Werner's waistband and, with the paunch he said he'd had at the time, apparently wasn't noticeable. He's not at all stocky now—the opposite.

He doesn't know who or what tipped off the militants they were in that village or house. They hadn't hooked up with the JTF, but it wouldn't have mattered, Werner said. "We were westerners, end of story." All he found out later was that the four of them weren't part of a general roundup or massacre. He hasn't tried to learn more—I got the sense his family is urging him to focus on his health. And after the IED story, he's skeptical of all official reports.

Once bound and blindfolded, they were put on what he guesses was a flatbed truck. It felt like his face was resting on metal. It remained dark for most of the ride, which might've been an hour. The captors didn't speak to them or say much to each other. Werner caught a few words in what he guessed was Kanuri, which he doesn't know well. He had no idea at the time whether Raphael or Joseph or Ismail were with him or on another truck or what.

Eventually they stopped and he was dragged off and shoved into a room. He lay on the floor a few minutes until someone removed his blindfold—it was Raphael. He'd gotten his own hands free.

They were in a windowless shed. It must have been dawn, because light filtered in the holes between the boards. Joseph and Ismail were also lying there blindfolded, and Raphael and Werner helped them—for some reason, they'd been tied up worse. Ismail was unconscious and bleeding badly from his arm. They used his shirt to make a tourniquet but couldn't do anything else.

Whispering amongst themselves, they decided not to hand over their papers, which Werner still had in the belt. Years ago, being connected to America and European powers might have given them leverage, but their feeling was that it would only enhance the militants' delight in their capture.

And they weren't positive it was Boko Haram—it could've been one of the loosely affiliated groups. Raphael had heard someone on the truck say, "Allah be praised" in Arabic, but Joseph had the impression the abductors were young and probably wannabes. Especially because no one searched them for weapons—they only took their phones. Werner mentioned—something Raphael had never shared with us—that mixed among the splinter groups were teens and young men perpetrating violence for *no* rhyme or reason, targeting anyone. Such a contrast, Bernice: teens eager to learn and teens eager to kill. Teens so eager to learn they'll do it at risk of being killed.

All right, the shed. They decided they were being used for ransom or a prisoner swap. Werner said being held captive with no links to the outside world makes you develop theories that have a happy ending. It was the happiest they could come up with.

He tried to remember their conversation—he knew we were hungry for details even while dreading them. Raphael had said he preferred a prisoner swap to ransom because he didn't know how much money we could raise. That sounds ridiculous, doesn't it? We would have gone to everyone we knew, taken out loans, remortgaged the house, *sold* the house. Joseph said he hoped his parents wouldn't borrow from his grandmother, because she'd charge exorbitant interest, sticking him with working off the debt until he was fifty. Werner kept recalculating the euro exchange rate for naira. They were just using humor to keep each other's spirits up, I think.

They heard a steady hum of voices nearby, but no one came to check on them. Werner guesses they were in the shed two hours, maybe longer. They were thirsty. Raphael joked that fear either emptied your intestines right away or froze them solid, so you didn't have to worry about defecating. Joseph said they were probably east and either in or close to the Sambisa, and the army was likely to come from southwest. They tried to tell directions from the differences in the daylight seeping through the cracks.

At some point talking to us, Werner paused and asked Daniel if he wanted him to continue, because it would be about how Raphael and Joseph died. Daniel said yes and looked at me, to see if I wanted to leave the room. I wasn't going to desert him.

It was still light when we'd first sat down. Dusk came soon after, but neither of us rose to turn on lamps. The darkening room gave us privacy.

Amazingly, we both held it together. Maybe because Werner was so scarred. The burns were mostly on his body, he said, but you could see scarring on the right side of his face. I think that made us steel ourselves.

The shed door was opened suddenly, before they had a chance to put their blindfolds and wrist ties back on. It was broad daylight. About ten or twelve men stood in a semicircle a short distance away. They looked young—teens, twenties—and pretty ragtag, not like the Boko Haram militants you see on the news with machine guns and ammunition belts. These young men had only rifles and machetes, and Werner thought Joseph was right about them being wannabes or else recent recruits.

Two came in the shed and grabbed Joseph. It happened so quick, Werner and Raphael didn't have time to react. Joseph didn't resist—no one knew what was going to happen. The men dragged him to the center of the semicircle, to the center if it had been a complete circle, but they left a segment open so Werner and Raphael could watch—the shed door was left ajar. But guarded by men with machetes.

A young man wearing a keffiyeh recited something. Werner didn't recognize the language and couldn't tell if it was a passage from the Koran or a prayer or what. The moment he stopped speaking, the men with machetes stepped forward and struck Joseph. One at a time. Werner didn't say how many blows until he went unconscious or if he cried out in pain. Just that they took turns.

While this was happening, almost reflexively, Werner said, he and Raphael tried to go through the door. The guards stabbed them, and Werner fell back.

He saw them dragging Raphael to where Joseph was. Raphael put up a fight but eventually couldn't anymore, he was losing blood. The one with the keffiyeh again recited something, and the men in the semicircle again moved forward.

They started striking Raphael but halted suddenly. Jeeps had burst through the brush. Guns were fired, and the militants ran into the woods. Werner thought it was the army, the Nigerian Army, but now he thinks it was local police.

Before running away, one of the militants threw a lit stick or explosive at the shed, possibly to keep the soldiers distracted with rescuing any hostages. Raphael may have heard the jeeps, because he twisted his neck to look up.

The last thing Werner remembers before waking in the hospital is some uniformed man asking him if there were "others kidnapped besides the three dead."

Werner's passport and papers were returned to him in the Maiduguri hospital, along with the envelope containing the letter, which the soldiers may have assumed was his. Raphael's and Joseph's passports were sent to the American Consulate. I assume Ismail's went to the Dutch.

So that's what happened.

Give me a moment.

Would we have been better off learning all this last year? I don't know, I really don't. The initial pain came back sharply while Werner was talking, so maybe it was good we didn't hear everything at once.

My father gives a sermon that grief is the measurement of love. Are grief and love quantifiable?

And how much grief must we endure to fulfill our duty as our brother's keeper? Why must the injunction to love our neighbor lead us down into a bottomless pit? And even if the arc of history bends toward justice, unless there's salvation, where is justice for the *individual*?

That's not something ethnographers ask, do they? You're concerned with communities. Here on Earth, there's little justice—there wasn't any for the Christian martyrs or millions who perished on the Middle Passage or enslaved or murdered in the Holocaust or Khmer Rouge camps or Nigeria.

I'm sorry to ramble, Bernice, I'm sorry. And I *am* glad you'll be putting the interviews into a printed compilation, even if it doesn't end up in bookstores. Daniel will draw comfort from it. I'm not sure how much he'll read right away, but just holding something *solid* in his hands—something to honor Raphael … We never got his body back.

Anyway, here's a copy of the letter Raphael wrote his last night. You might as well read it now, in case you have last-minute questions.

Dad,

Headed home & have story to make your hair stand on end. Short version: we helped 3 girls. One, Naomi, is cousins with Esther & Mary, remember in Iskoki I tutored Mary in history? Army finally coming plus other help, so leave Nigeria tomorrow. Werner will type/email this while J & I at the airport. If I can, in Abuja or Lagos or wherever, will give heads up, flight nos, times.

You don't have to worry about me dropping everything & rushing across the globe again. I had what Gillian calls an epiphany. Remember I told you back in Oct Thaddeus & I had long discussion about family obliga-tions? I left out the part where he said a child owes a duty to care for his parents. I didn't argue, understood where he was coming from, culture, traditions (spared him my whole backyard bit). I just said you didn't need me to take care of you yet.

I spent past days with families strategizing, sharing info, doing night searches, returning empty-handed. Pretty rough on everybody. Last night found the 3 girls huddled in bushes. J, Werner, Ismail & I chosen to bring Naomi and Grace to their village. They'd barely eaten for days but were real troupers. At least we'd brought pawpaw & oranges.

Arrived right before sunrise. Everyone asleep. Air unbelievably fresh, soft. Streets were empty, thatched roofs looked like a row of nests, but only fowl around were some chickens scratching the dirt. Serene & quiet & I prayed sense of peace wouldn't end. It did when someone spotted us and shrieked Naomi & Grace's names. Within seconds, I swear, people poured in the street, parents, brothers, sisters, grandparents, friends. Happiness on their faces beyond everything, beyond ecstasy, joy, elation. Yet something grounded & deep too. We couldn't help smiling idiotically.

After a minute, though, it hurt. Their happiness hurt. Because it reflected what they'd been through. They were in heaven because they'd been in hell. And what that did, what it told me, was what you've been through. What I've put you through.

I don't regret guiding the girls to safety. How can I? Not sure what I'm saying. Spin it another way. I'm ridiculously egocentric & want to plaster that smile on your face.

So I'm coming home for at least a few years. Don't get delusional I'll be your devoted vassal & serve your every need. You'll get some runs & bike rides & maybe a camping trip. Love to Gillian, see you soon,

R

You can keep that copy, Bernice. Daniel will be here soon—I need to start dinner. Good luck on your projects.

Acknowledgments

I AM GRATEFUL TO Kaveri Hurwitz, Merri M. Monks, and Bobbie Simone for reviewing and critiquing the entire manuscript. I thank Robin McQuinn and Ruth Pettis for providing special knowledge about certain customs and practices. Finally, a thank-you to Erin Cusick and Troy E. Wilderson for excellent professional assistance.